To Lorra
love

x xx

THE
MOTHERS *of*
MERSEY SQUARE

Pam Howes

BOOKS BY PAM HOWES

A Child For Sale

Fast Movin' Train
Hungry Eyes
It's Only Words

THE
MOTHERS *of*
MERSEY SQUARE

PAM HOWES

bookouture

Published by Bookouture in 2023

An imprint of Storyfire Ltd.
Carmelite House
50 Victoria Embankment
London EC4Y 0DZ

www.bookouture.com

ISBN: 978-1-83790-994-0
eBook ISBN: 978-1-83790-993-3

Dedicated to the memory of Eddie Cochran, 1938–1960. 'Twas but a short time, but you left us with a legacy of songs we will never forget.

1

AMBLESIDE, THE LAKE DISTRICT, FEBRUARY 1964

Jane gazed out of the hotel window. Lake Windermere sparkled in the mid-afternoon sun and the far-reaching views of snow-capped hills took her breath away. She gave an involuntary shiver that had nothing to do with the cold, crisp weather, nor was it one of joyful anticipation of the night ahead.

Mark had his back to her and was busy unpacking his case. He'd barely spoken all morning.

'Beautiful scenery,' she ventured.

He turned to stare at her, lips curling in a smile that didn't quite reach his cool grey eyes. 'That all you can say?'

'Err, well, the room is nice, too.' She walked across to the four-poster bed. The room was actually *very* nice, with thick pile carpet, antique furniture, pink and cream satin drapes and a matching bedspread. It was very grand and they had their own bathroom; not what she was used to at all. 'I wasn't expecting this.' She tried what she hoped was an enthusiastic smile and felt her stomach do a loop. 'When you said to take Friday off work and pack a small case, I thought we were just having a day out in The Lakes and then staying at your mum's house tonight, or... well, I don't know what I thought.'

'It's Valentine's Day. I wanted us to do something special.' He sat down on the bed and took her hand. 'I thought a night away somewhere nice might help. I know we haven't been getting on well lately. We never seem to have any fun these days.'

Not getting on well lately was an understatement, Jane thought. She and Mark were engaged, reluctantly now on her part. She didn't want to be, not any more, and agreeing to marry him was the most stupid thing she'd ever done. Mark had picked up the pieces after Eddie. It was a rebound thing and now she wanted out. Since he'd slipped the ring on her finger he'd changed, become possessive, and she feared his reaction to her dumping him. Valentine's Day and her heart was elsewhere. She'd rather be home alone, staring at a photo of Eddie.

But it was too late. Eddie was married to Angie Turner and they had a two-year-old son. Things had been okay with Mark at first. They started dating a few weeks after she split up with Eddie. He was the bass player in The Scorpions, a rival band to The Raiders. He also had a respectable day job at Lloyds Bank. Her mother thought the sun shone out of his backside because he wore smart suits and shirts and ties. She was forever going on about how lucky Jane was to have found such a nice boy after that Mellor lad and all his black leather.

There was a knock at the door. Mark got to his feet. 'Another little surprise for you.' He crossed the room and let in Jane's best friend, Sammy, and Sammy's boyfriend, Roy, both wearing anxious expressions.

Jane could see the pair looked uncomfortable and had no doubt they'd been coerced into joining them, probably against their better judgement.

'Hi, you two.' She rushed across the room and hugged them. 'What are you doing here?'

'Mark invited us,' Roy said. 'He thought it would be nice for us all to spend some time together. Sammy had college this morning, so we got the train to Kendal and a bus up here. But we'll have a lift home on Sunday.'

'Sunday?' Jane echoed. 'I thought we were only here for the night?'

'I booked the whole weekend,' Mark said. 'We'll see how it goes, we can always go back early.'

'Right, we'll leave you to it and go and unpack,' Roy said. 'What time's dinner?'

'Eight,' Mark replied.

'Great, we'll give you a knock.' Roy pushed Sammy towards the door.

'Why didn't you tell me they were coming?' Jane asked as her friends left the room.

'Didn't want to spoil the surprise.' Mark shrugged. 'Roy told me The Raiders weren't playing this weekend so I thought a foursome might be good, seeing as it seems you can't stand being alone with me at the moment.'

Jane ignored the jibe. 'I've only brought enough clothes for one day. You should have said something before we left.'

Mark dug in his case and handed her a large, flat box. 'Happy Valentine's Day. You can wear this when we go down to dinner.'

She stared at the box with dismay. Across the front was the legend, Estelle Modes – Fashions of Distinction. Estelle Modes was the most old-fashioned dress shop in Stockport. Even her mum wouldn't be seen dead wearing anything from there and that was saying something. Last month Mark had bought her a black wool skirt that hung below her knee, knowing full well she favoured the new-style mini. The skirt now resided at the back of her wardrobe. She was forever making excuses as to why she didn't wear it.

She placed the box on the bed, gingerly lifted the lid, removed several layers of white tissue paper and lifted out a high-necked, long-sleeved, shapeless dress in thick blue Crimplene. Her heart sank. It wasn't even a colour that suited her. Mark was watching her, smiling, head on one side. She forced a smile back.

'What do you think?' he said. 'Mum helped me choose it.'

Jane swallowed hard. Now why didn't that surprise her? 'Erm, it looks a bit big,' she mumbled. 'I'm only a size ten.'

'It *is* a size ten.' The smile left his face.

'I'll try it on later.' She pecked him on the cheek. 'Thanks. It's very kind of you.' She put the dress on a hanger, hung it in the wardrobe and began to unpack her case.

* * *

In the bathroom, Jane pushed her fingernail through the flimsy nylon and stared at the ladder running up her slender leg. 'Whoops!' She smiled as it ran over her knee. She'd have to wear her black velvet flares and red silk shirt now instead of the new dress. Mark wouldn't be very pleased. He'd say she should have brought an extra pair of stockings. Well, it was too bad – he was lucky she was here at all.

She knew exactly why he'd chosen the dress. It covered almost every inch of her. For crying out loud, he was trying to turn her into his bloody mother. Well enough was enough. She picked up her lipstick, slicked her lips and smiled. He'd be pacing the room now, looking at his watch every few seconds, getting more agitated as time ticked by. She slipped on her silk robe and walked back into the bedroom. There he was, pacing the floor, doing his watch-checking thing. He stopped pacing and his jaw tightened.

'Why aren't you dressed?'

'Laddered my stockings,' she said, looking away from his gaze. 'Only pair I brought with me, too. I won't be able to wear the dress now. Don't want bare legs this time of year. I'll put my other outfit on.'

'For God's sake, Jane, you're so clumsy. We're due down-stairs in ten minutes.'

'Sorry. Won't be long,' she said, reaching into the wardrobe. 'I've done my make-up and nails. I've only got to brush my hair and get dressed. If you're that bothered, go down and tell the restaurant staff we'll be a bit late.'

'Well, hurry up. Sammy and Roy will be knocking any minute.'

Jane stomped back into the bathroom. She stared at her reflection in the mirrored walls and wished she were anywhere but here. She pulled on her trousers and buttoned her shirt, leaving the top three buttons open. That would annoy him. Mark hated her showing flesh when other men were around. But it was only Roy, for goodness' sake, and she'd known him since she was fourteen. Anyway, Roy never looked at other girls. He was devoted to Sammy and the pair were engaged.

She couldn't understand why Sammy hadn't said anything to her about this trip. She saw her every day and they usually told each other everything. She must have been sworn to secrecy and she'd looked *very* worried when Mark let her and Roy in. Sammy knew she wanted to leave Mark and had urged her to tell him it was over.

Mark had no idea that she'd lost her virginity to Eddie Mellor. Although they'd been going steady for two years, Jane told him she wanted to wait until their wedding night. It hadn't been easy, but so far, he'd grudgingly respected her wishes.

But there was no doubt in her mind that tonight he was hoping to make love to her. Why else book a room as Mr and Mrs Fisher? She dragged the brush through her hair and sprayed herself with In Love perfume. The very thought of going all the way with him made her stomach turn.

She heard a knock at the door, and Mark letting in Roy and Sammy. She gritted her teeth, walked into the bedroom and caught Sammy's raised eyebrow.

By the look of mild amusement on her face, Jane guessed that her friend had also been in on the dress surprise. She gave a wry smile.

'Right, I'm ready,' she said and picked up her handbag.

'About bloody time,' Mark grunted. 'Fasten your shirt properly.'

Jane looked down and smiled sweetly. 'It *is* fastened.'

'You look lovely, Jane,' Sammy said as they left the room. 'That red really suits your colouring.'

'Thanks. I got it in the sale at C&A last month. It's nice to get a compliment from someone.'

Sammy grabbed Jane's arm and let Roy and Mark walk on in front.

'I've forgotten my lippy,' she called. 'You two go ahead and we'll nip back to get it.'

Mark turned and frowned. 'Don't be long, we're already late.'

Sammy hurried Jane back up the corridor and into her and Roy's room that was a twin of hers and Mark's. 'Jane, I'm so sorry,' Sammy began as she shut the door. 'We didn't want to come. When Mark called Roy and invited us, we were going to refuse, but then I realised you'd be all alone with him up here and you'd hate it.'

'Thank God you changed your mind.' Jane hugged her. 'I guess you knew about the dress he bought me to wear tonight?'

'Yeah! It's hideous. How did you get out of wearing it?'

'Laddered my only pair of stockings, accidentally-on-purpose.'

'What are you going to do about later? Mark's pinning everything on tonight to bring you closer.'

'I can't sleep with him, I just want to go home. Why has he done this, Sam? We've hardly been speaking, never mind anything else. And how the heck did he clear it with Mum? I told her I'd be home tomorrow.'

'He told Roy he's done it to try and save your relationship. And he hasn't cleared it with your mum. She thinks you're staying the weekend at his place with his mother. He says you've been acting weird since New Year and he doesn't know what he's done wrong. He's trying to put things right.'

'Shit!' Jane sighed. 'He hasn't done anything wrong, well... except for being a possessive so-and-so, telling me what to wear, and his mother being a pain in the arse.'

'Bloody hell, Jane, that's enough to put any girl off.'

'I know. But it's not just that – getting the lovely card from Ed at Christmas really unsettled me.' Jane sniffed, tears springing to her eyes. 'Now I can't stop thinking about him.'

'I'm not surprised,' Sammy said softly. 'Ed shouldn't have sent it. He's so fed up with Angie, he's not thinking straight.'

'He's as unhappy as me.' Jane ran her hand across her face. 'We're both trapped, but it's worse for Ed because of little Jonny.' She thought back to the morning, just before Christmas, when Eddie's card was delivered to the record shop where she worked. Satin-covered, with a picture of a robin, the words, To Someone Special, printed across the front. Inside, he'd written that he missed her, still loved her and would never forget their last night together. She didn't respond to the card, but from that day her feelings for Mark changed. Now she was desperate to speak to Eddie, to tell him that she still loved him, too.

'Come on,' Sammy said. 'Let's go downstairs. Throw a couple of glasses of wine down your neck and you might relax a bit. Roy will moan if I leave him alone with Mark for too long.'

Jane nodded, crossed to the mirror and dabbed at her mascara smudges. She linked arms with Sammy as they strolled back down the thickly carpeted corridor.

'It's a beautiful hotel,' Sammy said. 'Very generous of Mark to treat us.'

'It *is* lovely,' Jane agreed. 'If you're with the right man, that is.'

* * *

'Ah, at last,' Mark said as they took their seats at the table. 'You've been ages. How long does it take to find a bloody lipstick?'

'We were having a chat,' Jane said. 'You're always clock-watching. Why can't you just relax? What's the hurry anyway? The waiters look rushed off their feet.' She glanced around the busy dining room that was decorated with Valentine's hearts and balloons; each table lit with red candles in silver holders, encircled with red roses.

'Choose something to eat.' Roy passed around the menus. 'I'm starving.' He caught the eye of a waiter, who hurried over. 'Another bottle of house red, please.'

'Another?' Jane said as the man dashed away.

'There's not much left.' Roy split the remains of the bottle between Sammy and Jane. 'We had to do something to pass the time while we waited for you.'

The waiter brought more wine and took their food orders. Roy topped up his and Mark's glasses and smiled.

'Happy Valentine's Day,' Mark said. He clinked glasses with Jane.

'Same to you.'

'You okay?'

She nodded. 'Bit tired.'

'Maybe we should have an early night.' He leered at her cleavage.

She realised he was drunk and looked at Roy. 'Have you two had something to drink as well as the wine?'

'A whisky, while we waited to be seated,' Roy said.

'A double,' Mark slurred as the waiter brought the food to the table.

Jane frowned and toyed with her meal. Mark was always argumentative when he'd been drinking. Great. That was all

she needed. She stared at him, as he tucked into his prawn cock-
tail, and wanted to cry.

* * *

They said goodnight to Roy and Sammy outside their room and
carried on down the corridor. Jane unlocked the door and Mark
pulled her inside. She shook his arm off, made for the bathroom
and sat on the side of the bath, tears running down her cheeks,
wondering what sort of a Valentine's Day Eddie and Angie
were having. She thought back to the night Angie had
presented them with her news and replayed the scene in her
head, as she'd done so many times. She'd leapt out of bed,
pushed Eddie out of the way and ran into the bathroom, retch-
ing. He'd knocked on the door with her clothes in his hand,
white-faced, telling her it couldn't be his kid. He told her he
loved her, would sort it out and not to worry, they would soon
be married. But it was Angie he was forced to marry a month
later.

Mark knocked on the door, startling her from her thoughts.
'Be out in a minute,' she called. She slipped out of her clothes
and into her silk robe, tying it tightly round her middle. He was
sitting on the bed, naked to his waist and held out his hand. He
ran his finger over the Woolies fake wedding ring he'd made her
wear. She stared into his eyes, her stomach flipping at the
unfathomable look he was giving her. He pulled her into his
arms and kissed her long and hard. She wriggled away but his
grip tightened and he pushed her backwards and lay on top of
her. He tried to force her legs apart as she struggled against his
weight.

'Stop it, Mark. Get off me.' She pushed against his chest
with all her might. He flopped onto his back and she leapt off
the bed.

'What's wrong with you?' he shouted. 'For God's sake,

you're supposed to love me. Why else did you agree to marry me? Come on, stop playing hard to get.' He jumped up and glared at her. 'This should be a special night for us, first time and all that.'

She backed up to the door as he came towards her. She should tell him now, get it over with. 'It's not,' she said, 'my first time, I mean.'

He stared at her, his eyes cold. 'What are you saying?'

She swallowed hard. 'I slept with Ed.'

He grabbed her shoulders. 'You've been shagging Mellor behind my back?'

'Of course not. It was before we got together.'

He shook her roughly. 'So why have you been acting the innocent with *me*? Saving it for our wedding day? You're a bloody joke!'

'I'm sorry,' she cried. 'I just can't. I loved Ed. I don't love *you*. I should have told you before, but I didn't know how.' She pulled off her rings and threw them at him. 'It's over.' She shot out of the room, down the corridor and hammered on Roy and Sammy's door.

Roy, a towel wrapped around his middle, opened the door and Jane ran in, startling him.

'Shut the door, Roy, quick.'

Sammy came out of the bathroom, also wrapped in a towel. 'What's going on?' she said as Jane collapsed on the bed, sobbing. There was a loud hammering at the door and Roy let in Mark.

'Jane, get back to our room at once,' Mark demanded, face like thunder as he went to grab her arm.

'Hang on a minute, mate.' Roy pulled him back. 'What the hell's going on? Why's Jane in this state?'

'I told him I don't love him,' Jane cried. 'And I've told him about Ed. I've given him back his ring. It's over, Mark. Go away.'

'P-p-please come and talk to me,' Mark stuttered, his face twisted with anger. 'You owe me that at least. You've led me on all this time and lied to me. You little slut.' He lunged for her again and Roy thumped him squarely on the jaw.

'Leave it,' he said as Mark reeled backwards. 'Get back to your own room. I'll be with you when I've put some clothes on. Jane, stay here with Sam. I'll stay with him.'

'You sure?' Jane sniffed. 'I've spoiled your night.'

'Don't worry, Jane.' Sammy put her arms around her. 'I'd rather you were safe in here with me.' She glared at Mark. 'I knew this would happen. You shouldn't have booked this weekend. If you'd any sense you'd have seen signs that it was over weeks ago.'

Mark frowned and rubbed his chin. 'I was trying to put things right. How was I to know she'd slept with Mellor?' He turned to Jane. 'I might be able to forgive you for that in time. Have your ring back. Come and talk to me.'

'No!' she shook her head. 'It's finished. Just go, Mark. Leave me alone.'

Mark clenched his fists. 'Well, if I can't have you, I'll make sure nobody else does!'

'Right, that's enough.' Roy pushed Mark towards the door. 'Get out. I'll be with you in a minute.'

Mark left, after giving Jane a final cold stare.

She shook her head. 'I honestly thought he was going to rape me. He had such a weird look in his eyes.'

Roy poured the girls a brandy from the drinks tray. 'Get that down you and try to sleep. We'll take a train home first thing tomorrow. I don't fancy travelling back in the car with him. Not after that bloody threat. I wouldn't trust him not to wrap it round a tree and kill us all.'

* * *

Left alone with Sammy, Jane stretched out on the bed.

'I'm really sorry, I spoiled your night,' she said again.

'It's okay. We had a good time before we went down to dinner. It'll keep us going for a while.'

'You *are* lucky, Sam, being with the boy you love. I so wish I was with Ed. If only we could turn the clock back.'

'Ed feels the same,' Sammy said. 'Roy will tell him what's happened this weekend. I'm sure he'll want to get in touch. He asks us every week if you're still with Mark and he always looks sad when we say you are.'

'Does he?' Jane's face lit up, followed by a frown. 'What about Angie?'

'Ed's ready to walk. He only stays with her for Jonny.'

'So you think there's a chance he might leave her?'

'I think there's every chance, Jane. Especially when he knows you're free.'

2

STOCKPORT, CHESHIRE

'For Christ's sake, not again!' Eddie leapt backwards as the tin of paint hit the factory floor with a resounding thud. The lid flew off, spun like a two-bob bit and ended paint-side down by his feet.

He slammed a fist on the packing bench, face and overalls spattered in sticky red gloss. 'That does it, Jack,' he bellowed to his workmate above the noise of the six o'clock hooters. 'I've had enough of this bloody place to last me a lifetime.'

As Eddie's co-workers downed cans and gathered round the viscous pool on the workshop floor, he continued, 'If that arsehole of a foreman thinks I'm staying behind to clean up this mess, he can think again.'

'That "arsehole of a foreman" says clean it up now, Mellor, or collect your cards!' said the man himself. 'And you lot can keep your beaks out,' he added as two men moved forward to help. 'Or you can *all* collect your cards.'

Eddie spun round as the group quickly dispersed. So much for support, he thought as George Hill towered over him. Bunch of arse lickers. Didn't they realise they were worth more than this?

'Clean it up yourself,' Eddie said, squaring up to the foreman. 'If the bloody handles were fixed on properly in the first place it wouldn't have happened.'

George bristled and leant in close. Eddie could smell his sour breath and took a step backwards. 'Either clean it up, or sod off and don't come back!' George said.

'Fuck you and fuck your job!' Eddie yelled. 'When I leave here tonight, I won't *be* coming back.'

George snorted and stormed off.

'You shouldn't argue with Hill like that,' Jack said. 'You do yourself no favours.' He threw a turpentine-soaked rag in Eddie's direction. 'Get yourself cleaned up in the bogs then we can go.'

* * *

Jenkins Paint Factory was housed on the ground floor of a redundant cotton mill and the gents' toilet block stank of decades of stale piss. Eddie stared at his face in the cracked mirror. The dim light and peeling yellow paint did nothing to enhance his pale complexion. He looked weary and older than his twenty years.

Hardly surprising, the lifestyle he'd been forced into. His carefree Jack-the-Lad days were long gone. His blue eyes had lost their sparkle, his brown hair was in need of a good wash and the frown lines and two-day stubble made him look like his dad. He sighed. Some days he felt life wasn't worth living. He'd let everybody he cared about down; his mates in the band, his parents, but most of all, Jane.

He swallowed hard and rubbed at the paint splashes, bringing a glow to his cheeks. He wiped his boots, chucked the rag on the floor and turned to the chipped and stained urinal. 'I could murder a pint,' he muttered, as he unzipped and peed.

'Them paint-can handles are useless,' Jack began when

Eddie rejoined him in the packing department. 'They couldn't hold water, never mind five gallons of gloss. And now look, you've gone and lost your bloody job.'

'Never mind that, look at the state of my new boots!' Eddie stripped off his overalls and tossed them onto the bench. 'They're ruined.'

'Shouldn't wear decent boots to work,' Jack said.

'I've nothing else. My other pair's full of holes. But that's it, I'm not staying here to be treated like shit by George Hill. He's had it in for me since the day I started. I hate the job anyway, I'll find something else.'

'There's not many jobs out there that don't need qualifications,' Jack said, dragging an almost toothless comb through his greasy quiff. 'Angie'll go bloody mad when you tell her what's happened. How will you pay your way with no wages coming in?'

'She'll have to keep me for a week or two while I find another job. But I don't fancy telling her that.'

'God help you.' Jack smirked and shrugged into a threadbare donkey jacket. 'And you don't half stink of turps. Angie'll be welcoming you home with open arms, I don't think.'

'I'd rather she welcomed me with open legs,' Eddie muttered. 'No chance of that. The only thing I'll get my leg over tonight is my motorbike. I fancy a pint before I go home. The smell should have faded by then. Fancy a quick one in the Black Lion?'

'Dutch courage, eh?' Jack said. 'Not like you to go boozing on a Monday. What about the book-keeping class?'

'Can't be bothered tonight.' Eddie pulled on his leather biking jacket. 'I'd rather go out with my mates, but Angie's got big ideas. Wants a new house with all the trimmings. Reckons the book-keeping course will get me a better job.'

Being stuck in an office all day would be as soul-destroying as the factory though. He wanted to join a band again, make some serious money; see a bit of the world. But every time he brought the subject up, it caused a row.

'Should've kept it zipped up, Ed. Then you wouldn't be in this mess. Don't end up like me, with a grasping missus, a houseful of kids and more regrets than I've had hot dinners.'

Eddie raised his eyebrows. 'Should have told me that three years ago.' The way things were with him and Angie, there'd be no more kids, unless it was an immaculate conception.

Jack smiled and slung his bag over his shoulder. George Hill appeared in front of them. He glared at Eddie and pointed at the paint-stained floor.

'Thought you might have seen sense, Mellor, and cleaned that mess up. You can collect your cards and any wages owing tomorrow at four.' He swaggered away. Eddie stuck two fingers up behind his back and he and Jack clocked out.

'Well, that's that.' Eddie puffed out his cheeks. 'As if my life's not bad enough. Mind you, he's done me a favour. I'll have to find a job I really like now.'

'Want a fag?' Jack pulled a crumpled packet of Woodbines from his pocket.

Eddie flicked up his collar, shivering. 'Ta!' He lit up and blew a smoke ring as they walked into the pub. The smell of tobacco and beer perked him up.

Jack headed for a space at the bar and waved to catch the barmaid's attention. 'Let's have that pint then before I have to get back to the ball and chain, or she'll be thinking I've left home. How's your boy doing, by the way?'

Eddie smiled proudly at the mention of his son. 'He's a little devil, but Jonny's the best thing to come out of the last three years.'

'Two pints of mild, Mary, and have one for yourself.' Jack turned back to Eddie after staring at Mary's cleavage. 'Put your cash away, lad, it's my treat tonight.'

Eddie led the way to a vacant table at the back of the

crowded pub. He and Jack sat in companionable silence, supping their beer. They looked up as a bunch of morose-looking men strolled in and stood by the bar.

'See that lot.' Jack pointed with his glass. 'They're from Jackson's Brickworks down the road. Married fellows for the most, and I bet you a penny to a pound that none of 'em wants to go home before downing a pint of Dutch courage. I don't know what the hell happens to some women after you marry 'em, but they all turn into their mothers eventually.'

'Angie couldn't be more like her mother if she tried.' Eddie knocked back his drink. 'The interfering old bat does my head in.' He belched loudly and banged his empty pot down on the table. 'Fancy another?'

'No ta, mate, this is enough for me.' Jack swallowed the remainder of his pint.

'I'll get off home then.' Eddie stood up, stretched his arms above his head and yawned. 'I'll call at my mum's first, see if there's any messages from my friends. Want a lift?'

'It's out of your way, Ed. I'll get the bus. Good luck telling Angie your news.'

'Thanks, I'll need it. See you tomorrow when I collect my cards.'

'Not if I see you first, sunshine!'

* * *

Eddie strolled back across the square to the factory car park. He nodded to two men who were erecting stalls for Tuesday's market and looked up at the clear, starlit sky, his breath making clouds in the freezing night air. Too cold for snow, as his mum would say. He could smell the hops from Robinsons Brewery and wondered how something that stank so foul could taste so wonderful when finished. He climbed aboard his old Triumph motorbike and shot off in the direction of his parents' home, loving the way the wind whipped his hair around his face. He pulled up outside the neat semi-detached house that had been his childhood home and switched off the engine.

'Hi, Mum,' he called out as Lillian Mellor opened the front door, a welcoming smile lighting up her lined face.

'I thought I heard the bike. Come on in and get warm, love. You look perished. I was hoping you'd call in tonight. Roy rang earlier and said if I saw you, I was to tell you he's got some news for you. He's helping his dad in the fruit shop, so you can phone him there.'

Eddie kissed his mother's cheek and followed her down the hallway into the warm parlour. The house smelled clean and fresh, of Dettol, bleach and lavender furniture polish. It felt homely and familiar and he swallowed the lump that rose in his throat, wishing he still lived there. His mum was wearing her old checked cleaning skirt, her feet encased in blue fluffy slippers and her grey curls tucked inside a neatly tied turban.

'Did Roy say it was good news or bad?' Eddie smoothed down his windswept hair and removed his jacket. He dropped it on the floor and held out his cold hands in front of the blazing fire.

'He didn't say one way or the other. Go and call him while I pour you a mug of tea. You should wear your gloves on that bike, it's bitter out there.'

Eddie grabbed the phone from the hallstand, sat down on the bottom stair, and dialled Cantello's Fruit Shop.

Roy's Italian father answered: 'Eddie! How's the bambino?'

'Jonny's fine, thanks. How's things with you, Bob? Any more thoughts on going back to Italy?'

'When Roy's famous and earning a packet I might retire to Italy,' Bob replied, his tone wistful. He lowered his voice. 'Between me, you and the gatepost, if Irene refuses to come with me, I'll find myself a nice little signorina to serve my needs.'

Eddie smiled into the receiver. 'While you're about it, find one for me, too.'

He heard Bob chuckle and then reply, 'You've only been married five minutes. Wait until you've done twenty-five years, *then* you'll know what I mean. Right, I'd better get back to the counter before Irene comes cracking the whip. Roy's here now, so I'll say *arrivederci*.'

'*Arrivederci* to you too, Bob, and thanks.'

'Hi, mate. How you doin'?' Roy said.

'Could be better, Roy. And you?'

'Pretty good, thanks.'

'Mum said you had news for me?'

'I do, and boy, will it put a smile on your face.'

'Great! I could do with some good news for a change. Well, come on then, what is it?'

'Meet me at seven thirty tonight in the Royal Oak and all will be revealed.'

'Sounds mysterious. Can't you tell me now?'

'No, Ed. This news is far too important to tell you in a hurry. Anyway, I want to see your face when you hear what I have to say. So does Sammy and she'll lynch me if I tell you when she's not there.'

Eddie laughed.

'A word of warning,' Roy continued. 'Don't bring Angie. This news is not for her ears.'

'I won't. She'll think I'm going to night school anyway.'

'Right then. See you later.'

'Bye.' Eddie hung up and rejoined his mother in the parlour.

'Well?' She handed him a mug of tea as he sank down into the comfort of his dad's fireside chair. She adjusted the anti-macassar behind his head and smoothed his fringe from his eyes.

He smiled. She still treated him like a little boy sometimes, but he didn't mind.

'Roy wouldn't say. I've got to meet him and Sammy later in the pub.'

'Thought you had night school on Mondays?'

'I'm giving it a miss tonight. Roy's news is more important, apparently.'

'Well, have your cuppa and then you can get off home. You look tired. Are you sleeping properly?'

'So, so.' He took a sip of tea and stared thoughtfully into the fire, wondering if he should tell his mother about losing his job. He decided against it – Angie should be told first.

'Are things no better between you and Angie?' Lillian interrupted his thoughts.

He shrugged. 'Much the same. I'm still sleeping on the sofa.'

'If only things could have been different,' she said wistfully. 'You might have been wed to young Jane Wilson now. That girl thought the world of you.' She took a sip of tea and continued. 'It's a shame you didn't take the engineering apprenticeship your dad had lined up for you at Bennett's. You'd have had a good job for the future there. You'll never make anything of yourself at that paint factory.'

He raised an ironical eyebrow and nodded. 'You're right. But there you go, I didn't and I'm too old to start an apprenticeship at nearly twenty-one. Anyway, if I had my time again I'd still be with The Raiders. They're making decent money now. But what choice was *I* given? You got the girl into trouble; do the right thing and marry her. Give up the group. Get yourself a proper job. Does it all sound familiar, Mum?'

'Ed, there's no need to take it out on me. Your dad and I helped you as much as we could. We thought you'd be better off working properly, not swanning around the country with the group. It seemed the best thing all round at the time. Angie's parents thought so, too. You can't just blame us.'

'I've never blamed you and Dad. Old Mother Turner would have had me hung, drawn and quartered if I hadn't done the right thing by her bloody daughter.' He grinned wickedly, adding, 'It was my fault. Like Roy says, I should have worn wellies when I took a bath.'

'Eddie!'

'Sorry, Mum.' He finished his tea and placed his mug on the coffee table. 'Right, I'm going.' He leapt to his feet. 'Angie should be home from work by now and her mother will have dropped Jonny off. I like to get back after the old witch has gone. She can't stand to be in the same room as me and the feel- ing's mutual.'

'Well, you can't avoid the woman forever. She's Jonny's granny at the end of the day.'

'She's also my worst nightmare.' He shrugged into his jacket. 'With a bit of luck, I might get a decent meal tonight. Last night it was beans on toast, again! I get better fed here and at Roy's place than I do at home. Still, like you're always telling me, you make your bed, etcetera, etcetera.'

'Get off with you.' She handed him a small paper bag. 'Take these jelly babies for Jonny and don't you be stealing all the black ones.'

'Thanks, Mum. Might see you tomorrow.'

* * *

Eddie climbed the stairs two at a time to his second-floor flat. He put his foot up the backside of his neighbour's mangy ginger tom cat, who hissed at him as he walked past, and wrinkled his nose at the dingy, peeling paintwork and the permanent smell of boiled cabbage and cat pee in the communal hallway.

'Daddy's home,' he called as he let himself in.

Jonny hurtled down the hall into his outstretched arms. Eddie swung him up into the air and twirled him round and round. Jonny shrieked for more, big green eyes sparkling with excitement.

'No more, you'll be dizzy when I put you down. You might fall over and hurt yourself. Let's go and find Mummy.'

'She in da kitchen,' Jonny said, beaming. 'You got sweeties?'

'Yes, jelly babies from Nana, but you have to eat all your tea up first.'

'Had tea at Granny's.'

'Did you now? Well, here you are then.' Eddie handed over the bag. 'Go and sit on your little chair in the living room while you eat them.'

Jonny chuckled and toddled off down the hall, clutching his bag of jelly babies.

Eddie gritted his teeth before popping his head around the kitchen door, wondering what sort of mood Angie would be in tonight. She hadn't called out a greeting as he'd come in, but he'd rather the cold shoulder than have her pick a fight for no good reason. There'd be enough for her to complain about when she found out he'd lost his job.

She was standing at the cooker, frying sausages and onions. In stark contrast to the shabby kitchen with its old-fashioned cupboards hanging off the walls and the cracked tiles and torn lino, Angie was, as always, dressed in the latest style.

Her white sweater clung to her curves and her short black skirt showed off her long legs. She'd tied a frilly apron around her waist and her light-brown hair tumbled in a mass of soft curls onto her shoulders.

'Sausage and mash?' he ventured, his mouth watering at the aroma. He strolled across the kitchen, put his arms around her waist and pecked her on the cheek. 'Smells really good.'

She turned to him with a half-smile that failed to reach her green eyes. But in spite of her indifference he leant in to kiss her. She pushed him away and his heart sank.

'Well, it's more than I can say for you.' She screwed up her face. 'You stink of paint and booze *and* you're late.'

'I had a quick pint with Jack and then called in to see my mum. Can't help the paint smell, I'll get a bath in a minute.'

'Right!' She turned back to the sausages.

'Any objections?'

'No, but you've got night school. You're usually in a rush to have your tea and go. Not only that, you shouldn't be spending money on drinking. We're supposed to be saving up to get out of this shithole!'

'Jack treated me. He's a good mate.' Eddie folded his arms across his chest. 'Anyway, one pint's hardly going to break the bank compared to what *you* spend on clothes and make-up.' He should do it now. Tell her she had to quit spending because he'd been sacked. He opened his mouth to continue as she muttered something under her breath. 'What was that?'

'I said Jack's common, the way he speaks. He drops his h's and wears scruffy clothes. Hanging around with him is not going to help your image when you finish your course and start looking for a new job.'

'He's not common. And you've only seen him in his work clothes. The trouble with you is your head's so far up your own arse, you think anyone with a local accent's common. Jack's a proud man and a bloody hard worker. I won't be taking him with me when I go for interviews. So what's your problem?'

'Nothing,' she spat, turning back to the cooker. 'You'd better get ready. Tea won't be long.'

'I will in a minute.'

'Can you try and switch the sitting-room fire on, please. The knob's sticking again and I couldn't turn it. It's freezing in there and Jonny's starting with a cold. You'll need to put the heater on in the bathroom, too. There was ice on the window when I came in from work.'

'Is there money in the meters?'

'Of course there is. I wouldn't be able to cook if there wasn't.'

'Just asking. No need to snap.' He reached under the sink for his pliers and shook his head at the chaos in the cupboard. For a girl so fussy in her appearance, she was such an untidy mare around the house. Soap powder spilled out as he rooted. He scooped it up, spotted mouse droppings, sat back on his heels and scratched his chin. Blow it, he wasn't mentioning mice now or she'd be up on a chair shrieking and he'd get no tea, again.

In the sitting room, where Jonny was playing with his cars on the faded, threadbare carpet, Eddie removed the fireguard and turned the knob of the old gas fire with the pliers. He lit a match, the fire spluttered to life and he put the fireguard back, smiling at Jonny, who wiped his little red nose on his sleeve, leaving snail trails on his blue sweater.

He flopped onto the shabby sofa, pulled Jonny onto his knee and rubbed his cold hands. In spite of his best efforts in painting the mouldy walls magnolia and buying a new red hearth rug, the place still looked squalid. Angie's sister Sally had given them her old curtains and cushions, but he hated the gaudy red and orange pattern and it did nothing to set off the room.

'One day, son, I promise I'll get us out of this dump. We'll have somewhere with your own bedroom and a nice garden for you to play in.' He tickled Jonny, who giggled and rolled off his knee. 'I'd better go and see if Mummy needs any help.' Remembering, as he passed, he switched on the bathroom heater and went back into the kitchen.

'Cathy's coming round later and Alison and Carol from the salon said they might pop in, too,' Angie said.

Eddie couldn't hide his smirk. 'Shall I get the cauldron out?'

'Don't be so nasty about my friends.'

'Why not? You're always nasty about mine.' He lounged against the kitchen door, grinning.

'Only because they make it so obvious they don't like me.'

'That's rubbish.'

'No, it's not. When we went to Talk of the North club last month, they all ignored me.'

He rolled his eyes. 'Roy and Tim tried their best to include you in the conversation, and Sammy and Pat asked you to dance. But you sat there all night wearing your *I'm sucking a lemon* face! Roy said later that you take after your mother in more ways than one.'

'There's nothing wrong with my mother.' Angie drained boiled potatoes over the sink, steam engulfing her face. She slammed the pan down on the draining board and reached for the masher.

'Nothing that a personality transplant wouldn't cure.' Eddie ducked as she grabbed a plate from the rack and hurled it across the kitchen in his direction. It smashed off the door and broke into jagged pieces.

'You nearly hit me, you stupid cow!'

'God, I hate you, Eddie Mellor.' She burst into tears. 'I don't know why I married you.'

'You were pregnant,' he reminded her. 'Or has that fact conveniently slipped your mind?'

'I could have managed well enough on my own,' she cried. 'Other women do.'

'Oh, is that right? Well, that's great! Now she tells me. Do you think *I* want this crap every night when I come home from work? I didn't want to marry you, I gave up The Raiders and Jane for you. It sickened me when I had to sell my drum kit so you could buy the most *expensive* cot and pram.'

'You'll never let that one go, and how dare you mention *her* in my home,' Angie sobbed. 'I don't know why you don't just leave us. Go back to your bloody mother, if she'll have you.'

'Here we go again,' he said. 'Tell you what, I might just do that this time.'

'Well, you won't see Jonny again. I'll make sure of it.'

'You can't stop me seeing him, he's my son.'

'Huh, is he though?' she muttered, turning her back on him.

He grabbed her by the wrist and pulled her round to face him. 'What the fuck do you mean by that?'

'I didn't mean anything. Of course he's yours. I was just getting at you. You only stay because of Jonny.'

He let her go and turned at the sound of whimpering by the kitchen door. Jonny was standing on pieces of broken china. His face crumpled as he burst into tears and ran to his mother, clutching her legs.

'No shout,' he sobbed.

'Get your sticky hands off my new stockings,' she shrieked, frightening the little boy further. 'You'll ruin them.'

Jonny bawled as she pushed him away.

'Come here, son.' Eddie swept him up. 'It's nearly bedtime. Mummy says I stink. You can share a bath with me and we'll sail your boat.' He turned to Angie, who was wiping her eyes on the tea towel. 'This has to stop happening in front of Jonny. He's shaking, poor kid.'

'Well, you started it by implying my friends are witches.'

'For God's sake, Angie, it was a bloody joke. Can I help it that you don't have a sense of humour?' Sighing, he carried Jonny off to the bathroom and yelled over his shoulder, 'Stick my tea in the oven, please.'

The mood *she* was in tonight there was no way he was telling her he'd lost his job until he'd thrown a few more pints down his neck. She'd be chucking more than plates at him later.

* * *

Eddie walked into the kitchen, a towel wrapped around his middle, carrying a freshly-bathed and pyjama-clad Jonny. He watched as Angie tipped the sausages into the bin. 'Why have you chucked them away?'

'They were burnt. I went into the bedroom and forgot all about them.'

'So, no tea again?' He shook his head and put Jonny down. 'It would be nice to come home to a hot meal occasionally. I suppose it'll have to be fish and chips on my way home from night school.'

'I can do you beans and there are still the potatoes,' she offered.

'Forget it. They'll be cold by now.' He looked closely at her tear-stained face. 'This can't go on. We need to talk. I mean seriously, without the bawling and shouting.'

'I know we do. Maybe later? I'll warm Jonny's milk and then sort my face out before Cathy arrives.'

'Shall I expect some pain around my nether regions tonight?' he teased as she poured milk into a saucepan.

'What do you mean?'

'I mean, when Cathy gets out the effigy of me that she's made. She'll probably stick a big pin right where it'll hurt most.'

'Don't start about witches again.'

'I'm trying to lighten the bloody mood here, that's all!' He stomped off in the direction of the bedroom.

'Oh, Jonny, what will we do with your daddy?' Angie picked him up and cuddled him. 'Let's make your milk and get you to bed.'

'No cry, Mamma.' Jonny stroked her wet cheeks as she ran her hands through his dark curls. 'Dadda sorry.'

'Is he? I don't think so somehow. But that's not your problem, little man.'

3

Eddie drummed his fingers on the table as The Rolling Stones' 'I Wanna Be Your Man' blasted from the jukebox. He felt relaxed and almost sleepy, sitting by the roaring log fire in the Royal Oak's smoky lounge. He swallowed the last of his pint and waved at Sammy and Roy, who had just strolled in. 'Over here!' he shouted, above the noise of the music.

Eddie thought the tall, slender pair made a great-looking couple with their matching black leather coats, red and white striped scarves flung casually around their necks. His mate bore more than a passing resemblance to Elvis, with thick black hair and smouldering eyes while Sammy could pass for a brunette Bardot any day.

'Your usual, Ed?' Roy called from the bar as Sammy made her way over.

'Please, Roy.' He stood up to greet Sammy and kissed her on the cheek. She sat down opposite, flicked her long hair over her shoulders, and removed her scarf and gloves.

'It's bloody freezing out there, but that's a nice cosy fire.' She rubbed her hands together. 'It's busy in here tonight.'

Eddie nodded, looking round. 'Most of them will be off to the flicks shortly,' Eddie said. '*Dr. Strangelove*'s on at the Plaza.'

'We're going to see it on Friday,' Sammy said. 'You look a bit brassed off, Ed. Another row with the lovely Angie, perhaps?'

Eddie sighed. 'Is it that obvious?'

'Why do you put up with her moods? Leave her. It's not working. Don't you think you've given it long enough?'

He shrugged. 'I stay because of Jonny. She won't let me see him if I walk out.'

'She can't stop you – you're Jonny's father.'

Roy made his way over with a tray of drinks.

'Here you go, get that down you.' He slapped Eddie on the back. 'You look like you need it.'

'He's had another row with Angie,' Sammy said. 'She won't let him see Jonny if he leaves her.'

'She can't stop you seeing him,' Roy said and sat down.

'That's what I told him.' Sammy picked up her drink and took a sip.

'See a solicitor,' Roy advised. 'Find out how you'd be fixed if you did a bunk. You were bloody daft to marry her, other blokes clear off. Phil Jackson's put two birds in the club since he joined The Raiders. He denies responsibility. Tells them he's sterile due to mumps as a kid.'

'And the crafty sod backs it up with a forged doctor's letter,' Sammy chipped in.

'If he can get away with it, good luck to him,' Eddie said. 'Anyway, what's this news guaranteed to put a smile on my face? Because believe me, I could do with something good happening in my life.'

'All in good time.' Roy offered Eddie a cigarette. He lit up himself, took a long drag and blew a circle of smoke. 'My halo! Remember the last year at school when we failed our O levels? We learnt to blow perfect smoke rings, formed The Raiders and knew all the words to "Johnny B. Goode". Now that's what *I* call education.' He took a swig of beer and smiled. 'There's a couple of things I want to talk about, but first things first. Me and Sam went to The Lakes last weekend. Posh hotel, four-poster, the works. We planned a perfect night of pure lust but spent it in separate rooms.'

'Why would you do that?' Eddie frowned.

'Because a certain young lady of our mutual acquaintance dumped her fiancé on Saturday night. I ended up looking after her ex to make sure he didn't top himself and my lovely, sexy Sammy here spent the night looking after Jane.'

'Jane? *My* Jane!' Eddie exclaimed. 'She's finished with Fisher? I don't understand. I thought she was dead happy with him.'

'Well...' Roy took another drag. 'The reason she dumped him is because she's still in love with you, Ed.'

'No! She hates me for putting Angie in the club.'

Roy related the happenings of the weekend and finished, 'Jane asked if you'd call her tomorrow. Get together and talk. You could meet up occasionally for a bit on the side.'

Eddie shook his head slowly. 'Jane's worth more than that. Leave it with me, I'll work something out. I can't believe she's got rid of Fisher – he was never right for her.'

'She's been fed up for a while,' Sammy said. 'But *you* sending her that card at Christmas started the real rot setting in.'

Eddie felt his cheeks warm and he grinned. 'I had to let her know I still cared.'

'Well, it worked. Here's Tim and Pat.' Sammy waved to a tall, blonde-haired, leather-clad couple who had strolled in and were standing by the bar. 'They look a bit windswept.'

'They'll have come on the bike.' Roy held up his glass. 'Two pints of mild and a 'Cardi and Coke, please, Tim.' He tossed a coin in Pat's direction. 'Stick some Cochran on the jukebox, it's too quiet in here.'

'Yes, your Lordship!' Pat's blue eyes twinkled as she caught the shilling piece, dropped a mock curtsey and chose a selection. She bent to kiss Eddie and Roy as the jukebox burst back into life and Eddie Cochran belted out 'Summertime Blues'. 'It's really nice to see you again, Ed. We miss you.'

'Not half as much as I miss you lot.'

It was good to be surrounded by his mates. It didn't happen often enough. Angie preferred the company of her own friends. She expected him to spend time with them. Not that he had much in common with a bunch of posey hairdressers, but it kept the peace.

Tim carried the tray of drinks over. 'Good to see you, Ed.'

'And you, mate.'

Tim turned to Roy. 'You told him the good news?'

'Yeah! He's gonna give Jane a call. I wanted to wait until you got here before I dropped the next bit on his toes.'

'Great,' Tim and Pat chorused and flopped down next to Eddie.

'Right,' Tim said. 'We're here now, so get on with it. He's looking puzzled.'

'We've got a proposition for you, Ed,' Roy began. 'We're not happy with Kris on drums. I know you can't afford another kit at the moment, but we wondered if you'd consider rejoining The Raiders as a singer alongside me. Our duets always went down a bomb. We miss having you on stage with us.'

'We've a gig at Mario's this Saturday,' Tim said. 'He's extended into the premises next door. It's the re-opening night.'

'It's called The Roulette Club now,' Roy added, as Eddie's face lit up. 'It's really smart with proper dressing rooms for the artistes. Much better than that stinky old room we used to get changed in. So, what do you think? I'll pay you a fair share of our wages of course. Perhaps you could save up for another kit or get one on the drip and pay for it with your gig money. Tim's just got a new bass and it's only a couple of quid a month.'

'Fuck! Shit!' Eddie almost dropped his pint. 'Are you taking the piss? Of course I want to get back with the group. To be honest, I could use the money – I got sacked today.'

'Bet that went down well,' Sammy said. 'What did Angie say about you losing your job?'

'Haven't told her yet. I'm feeling overwhelmed with all this news, not to mention pissed. I'm drinking on an empty stomach. I'll get something to eat on the way home.'

'Finish your drink. We'll take you for a curry, our treat,' Roy offered. 'You need feeding up a bit. You're far too skinny these days.'

'You *have* lost loads of weight,' Sammy said. She leant across and pushed his floppy fringe off his face. 'Mind you, the lean look suits you. You've still got that lovely dimple in your chin and your eyes look bluer than Paul Newman's.'

'So, Sam, you reckon Jane will fancy this leaner me?' Eddie teased. 'I mean, I'm half the man she used to love.'

'Most definitely,' she replied. 'Give her a call tomorrow and arrange to meet her.'

Eddie sighed and then smiled. 'Oh, to hell with the consequences! I'll do it.'

Roy raised his glass in a toast. 'Here's to the future! Come on, sup up. Let's go and get that curry. Leave your bikes in the car park. You can collect them tomorrow and we'll take a taxi home.'

'Thanks for a great evening.' Eddie swayed as he stood up.

Tim caught his arm. 'It's not over yet, mate.'

* * *

'You been crying?' Cathy peered closely at Angie, who dropped an armful of ironing on the kitchen table.

'Yes.' She sniffed and ran a hand over her eyes. 'I had a row with Ed.'

'Another?' Cathy said, helping her sort the clothes into a tidy pile. 'You shouldn't have married him. You can't go on like this.'

'I know. But what can I do? He just blames *me* all the time for the mess we're in. He knows I have to look nice for work, yet he begrudges every penny I spend on clothes.'

'He does have a point – you spend a fortune. Look at this lot. I've never seen you wear half of these.' Cathy shook her head. 'If you spent less on clothes and shoved some money in the bank, you and Ed could soon be moving from this awful flat and things might improve between you. He shouldn't blame you though,' she added, in a kinder tone as Angie's eyes filled with tears again. 'If he'd taken precautions, you wouldn't be in this mess.'

'Yeah, then I'd have been free to see Richard again,' Angie said quietly, chewing her lip.

'Richard? Richard Price?' Cathy's eyebrows shot up. 'Is *he* back on the scene? I thought he was living in Wales?'

'He was, but his marriage didn't work out. He's back at the salon as our head stylist.' Angie wound a curl around a finger and lowered her eyes. 'I had lunch with him today.'

'Hope lunch was all you had?'

'Cathy!' Angie blushed. 'I'm a married woman.'

'You had a fling with Richard before you married Eddie. You weren't even sure that Jonny was Ed's.'

'Of course he's Ed's. It was only the once with Richard. Ed doesn't know and he mustn't find out. He'd go bloody mad.'

'Well, he's had *his* share of flings.'

'No, he hasn't. There was only Jane and me.'

'Huh, and the rest,' Cathy snorted.

'That's just not true,' Angie said. 'He wouldn't.'

'He would, but let's not argue about him. He's not worth it. Dry your eyes while I stick these clothes in the airing cupboard and we'll open that bottle of Blue Nun I brought and you can tell me all about your lunch date with the handsome Richard before the others arrive.'

* * *

Eddie clambered out of the taxi and shouted goodbye as it sped off into the night. He looked up and waved at Angie and Cathy, who were glaring at him from the kitchen window. 'Bloody hell,' he muttered. 'What's up with her face now?' He fumbled in his jeans pocket for his key and climbed the stairs to the flat. He dropped the key and was on his knees, scrabbling around, when the door opened and Angie appeared, arms folded, a peeved expression on her face. He could see Cathy hovering behind as he struggled to his feet, swaying slightly. 'Evening, ladies.' He pushed his way past them into the hall, kicked off his shoes and flung his jacket on the floor.

'You're pissed,' Angie snapped. 'Why were you in a taxi? Where's your bike and where have you been?'

'I'm not pissed and which bloody question would you like me to answer first?' he slurred, wobbling into the kitchen. 'Coffee?' He waved the kettle in their direction. 'Bike's in the pub car park and I've been for a curry with Roy, Sammy, Tim and Pat.'

'What about night school?' Angie shouted.

'Yeah!' Cathy folded her arms, glaring at him.

'Christ, have I got two fucking wives now?' He placed the kettle on the stove and belched loudly. 'Couldn't be bothered going to night school. And don't shriek like a banshee, you'll wake Jonny.' He turned his back on them.

'Well, I'm waiting,' Angie said. '*Why* didn't you go to night school?'

'Had something more important to do.' He lurched towards a chair. 'Make me a black coffee, Cath, I need to sit down.'

'Before you fall down, you mean,' Angie said. 'You'll never

get a decent job if you fail your exams. How can getting drunk be more important than that?'

'I'm rejoining The Raiders,' he announced. 'Singing for now until I can afford a new drum kit. That's more important to me than a so-called decent job. Fag, Cath?' He waved the packet in her direction.

'I don't smoke,' she replied, banging a mug down on the table and slopping coffee over the sides. 'Make your own bloody coffee next time.'

'Whoops, temper, temper! I forgot you don't smoke, Little Miss I've No Vices!' He tried to light his cigarette but dropped the lighter.

'Don't you be so rude to Cathy.' Angie picked up the lighter and threw it at him. It hit the side of his head and bounced onto his knee. He tried again to light up and succeeded while she ranted on. 'And you can forget about rejoining The Raiders, or buying another drum kit.'

He slammed his fist on the table. 'Don't you tell me what I can and cannot do! Who the hell do you think you are?'

'Your wife, in case you'd forgotten.'

'Wife! Wife? Where did you get that notion? You can't cook, the flat's a pigsty, and when was the last time you let me into our bed?' He turned to Cathy with a smirk. 'We haven't had a shag for months. But I expect you know that, seeing as she tells you everything.' He ignored her blushes and Angie's embarrassed gasp and continued. 'She couldn't get enough of me in the early days. Wasn't fussy where I screwed her. But now, well, she's just a frigid cow who makes me sleep on the sofa!' He stood up, grabbed Angie by the shoulders and backed her against the wall. He tried to kiss her and forced his leg between her thighs. She screamed and pushed him away. 'See what I mean? Frigid!'

'Leave her alone, you animal.' Cathy shoved him back onto the chair. 'You're disgusting, Eddie Mellor. I don't know how Angie puts up with you. I would divorce you if I was her.'

'Well, thank Christ you're not!' He turned on Cathy with a growl. 'I wouldn't touch *you* with somebody else's never mind my own. Ever wondered why it was always Angie got the lads when you were out together? Why no one looked twice at you? Shall I tell you why? You're chalk and cheese. She's a moody madam, but she's got style. But *you*, well, you're hardly the belle of the ball!'

Angie raised her hand and smacked him soundly across the face. 'How dare you speak to Cathy like that? You're a complete bastard.'

Without stopping to think he slapped her back, knocking her into the door. 'At least I'm fucking honest!'

'Right, that does it, I'm leaving you,' she yelled as Cathy stepped between the pair, tears streaming down her face.

'Good! I was gonna tell you I want a divorce anyway. Oh, and by the way, I got the sack today, *and* we've got mice!'

* * *

Angie stared open-mouthed as the reality of Eddie's announcement sank in. Cathy shot him a venomous look, put her arms around her friend's shoulders and led her away to the bedroom, where, in spite of all the noise, Jonny still slept soundly.

'What will we do?' Angie choked on a sob. 'We won't have the money to pay the rent or put food on the table. And mice! Oh God, I hate this dump.'

'Calm down and get ready for bed,' Cathy said. 'I'll stay with you tonight. Tomorrow, you can pack some things and I'll drive you and Jonny to your mother's. I can't leave you here with Eddie after all that.'

'I don't want to go back to my mother's. It's worse than

prison. I want a new house. Jonny deserves somewhere nicer than this bloody dump to grow up in.'

'Of course he does, but for crying out loud, Angie, Eddie just told you he's lost his job. *You* announced you're leaving him. A new house is out of the question. Anyway, how can you stay with a bloke who slaps you?'

'He's never ever raised a finger to me before. I'm sorry for what he said to you. I feel so embarrassed. Wedge a chair behind the door in case he tries to come in.'

* * *

Eddie sat down on a kitchen chair and put his head in his hands. What the hell had he been thinking? He'd hit a woman, his wife. No matter how much she'd provoked him, he shouldn't have done that. How the hell had she managed to turn him into a wife beater? And he'd insulted Cathy, which was unfair. Then to announce his job loss like that had been uncalled for, too. He should have told Angie in private. He walked to the bedroom door and tapped lightly: 'Angie, I'm sorry. Can we talk on our own?'

'Get lost, Eddie! I'll talk to you tomorrow.'

'No, we need to sort this out now.'

'I've nothing to say to you. Leave it until the morning when you're sober.'

'I'm sober now. I didn't mean to hurt you. I'm sorry I insulted Cathy.'

'Go away, Ed, please.'

He stumbled into the sitting room and flopped down on the shabby sofa. Choking back tears of anger and frustration mixed with sorrow, he wondered how the hell he'd managed to make such a mess of his life. He curled himself into a tight ball and slipped into a restless sleep.

4

Jane picked her way carefully across the icy cobbles of Stockport High Street, shivering against the biting wind. Flanagan and Grey's Record Emporium came into view and her junior assistant, Carl, was already there, sheltering in the doorway. If she looked as miserable as she felt, there would be a million questions from him. She broke a big smile.

'Morning, Carl.' She fished in her handbag for the keys.

'Hurry up and open the door, I'm frozen.' Carl stamped his feet as she fumbled with the lock.

'Put the kettle on for coffee while I get the shop warmed up,' she said and switched on the lights.

'I'll pop across the road and get some milk while the kettle boils. Fancy a Mars bar, my treat?'

'I'd love one. It might buck me up a bit.'

'John Grey said you weren't too well yesterday when you didn't come in to work. You've got dark circles under your eyes.'

Here come the questions, she thought. Smile mustn't have been big enough. 'I didn't sleep much last night.'

'How did the weekend in The Lakes go?'

'Get the Mars bars, make the coffee and I'll tell you later.'

* * *

Jane went downstairs into the cellar-like record department. The cream-painted walls, plastered with music posters and album sleeves, the subdued lighting and the permanently smoky atmosphere implied the feeling of being in a small club. She sat on a stool behind the counter, took off her boots, placed her feet on top of the nearest fan heater, flicked the switch and wriggled her frozen toes, sighing blissfully.

A record sat on the nearby turntable and she placed the needle on it. The harmonious voices of The Ronettes spilled from one of the wall-mounted listening booths. She smiled as they serenaded her with 'Baby, I Love You'. A quick root in her handbag for her compact and a cursory glance in the mirror told her Carl was right, she had eyes like a panda. 'Nothing that a good night's sleep won't put right,' she muttered and touched up her lipstick.

She dragged a brush through her hair, flinching as it caught in the tangles. The bell rang out and someone entered the shop. She threw everything back in her bag and looked up to see the deliveryman from EMI struggling down the stairs with a large carton.

'Morning, Jane.' He placed the carton on the floor and handed her an invoice. 'Sign that, my love. It's brass monkeys out there today. *You* look as beautiful as ever though, even with your little red nose.'

'Flattery will get you everywhere, Paddy.' She signed the invoice. 'Fancy a coffee?'

'Thanks all the same, but I'll be on my way. Everyone's sold out of *With the Beatles* album. The van's full, they'll all be waiting for me.'

Jane glanced behind her at the nearly-empty shelf. 'We're almost out, too. Hardly surprising, it's a brilliant LP.'

'You've fifty in that carton. Should keep you going until Friday.'

'No doubt. Bye, Paddy,' she called as he left.

Carl carried two mugs of steaming coffee downstairs and placed them on the counter with the Mars bars. 'So come on, tell me about your weekend then.'

Jane sipped at the coffee and sighed. 'Not much to tell really.' She explained what had happened. 'Mark's devastated. Keeps phoning to try and persuade me to change my mind.'

'Blimey! I wasn't expecting that. I thought you and him were dead happy?'

She nibbled the corner off her Mars bar. 'So did I, once. Let's just say he's the wrong man. I'm still in love with my ex, Eddie Mellor.'

'But Eddie's married.'

'I know.' She wrapped her hands around her mug.

'What you gonna do then?'

'Not much I can do where Eddie's concerned. I intend to enjoy my freedom and have some fun. That'll do for starters.'

'If you fancy going to the flicks or dancing, erm, I'd be happy to take you,' Carl stammered.

'Carl, you're a sweetie. I don't think your mum would approve of you asking me out. I'm older than you.'

'Only three years.' He blushed and changed the subject. 'John Grey told me yesterday that his dad's opening another shop in Wilmslow. He said he'd transfer me, make me up to junior manager.'

'Blimey! Well, I'm pleased you'll be getting a well-earned promotion. On the other hand, you make the best coffee in the world. I'll really miss you.'

'I'll miss you too.'

'By the way, if Mark phones, tell him I'm busy. I don't want to talk to him.' She drained her mug and shrugged out of her coat. 'Right, when you've finished, take the mugs and my coat up to the staffroom while I make a start on unpacking this order before the Decca and Philips deliveries arrive.'

* * *

Jane knelt on the floor and tore the sticky tape from the carton. As she sorted the stock, her mind went back to the weekend. She felt a huge sense of relief that the relationship was over. Mark was a control freak, she'd definitely done the right thing. The ringing phone disturbed her thoughts and she went to answer it, hoping it wasn't him. It was John Grey, area manager, and only son of one of Flanagan and Grey's founders. He was calling to say he would be at the shop later and to send Carl out for chocolate éclairs to have with their coffees. She smiled as she hung up. It was a wonder she wasn't the size of an elephant, the amount of cakes and chocolate she consumed in this job.

* * *

When John Grey ran down the stairs mid-afternoon he found the shop quiet and his staff singing along to *With the Beatles*.

'Hi, kids, how's it going?' He rubbed his hands together and manoeuvred Jane off the stool closest to the heater. 'Bit too cold for customers today. Come on, shove over and make room. You're warm as toast. I'm freezing!'

His Buddy Holly-style glasses misted over and he wiped them on a hanky as Jane stood up and stretched her arms above her head, yawning loudly. 'You look knackered, Jane. Try getting some sleep when you go to bed.'

She blushed at the implication and sent Carl off to brew up while John chattered excitedly about his plans to employ more staff for the proposed new store.

'I need a junior to replace Carl here and a manager and junior for the new place. I'll advertise this week. Anybody suitable can train here until the new shop opens. I want a manager who knows his stuff. Roy and Tim might know if any of their musical mates are looking for work. Unless...' He paused. 'I don't suppose Mark would be interested, would he?'

Jane held up her ring-less left hand. 'We've split up. I couldn't work alongside him. Anyway, he'll never leave the bank in a month of Sundays – he's too fond of his security.'

'Just a thought. I had a feeling there was something more when you called in sick yesterday. What happened?'

'Poor lad,' John said as she told him the events of the weekend. 'But you know your own mind. Would you give it another try with Ed if he were free?'

'Maybe. I'll see how things go.'

'Play the field a bit,' he advised. 'You were far too young to be settling down.'

'I was,' she agreed as Carl came downstairs with a tray of coffee and cakes.

John picked up an éclair and sank his teeth into it, a look of bliss on his face as the cream oozed out. 'Oh, yum! By the way, talking of settling down, Margaret and I are getting engaged in April. We're throwing a party to celebrate.' He sucked the sticky chocolate icing from his fingers.

'John, that's wonderful.' Jane hugged him.

'We've been together since college, so it's high time I made an honest woman of her. I suppose I'd better be on my way,' he said as the doorbell rang. 'I want to catch the barber before he closes – I've had some stick from Dad about the length of my hair.'

'I'm not surprised,' Sammy said, strolling down the stairs, portfolio tucked under her arm. 'Roy and I were saying we'll have to start calling you Shirley Temple with those curls.'

'That's what Margaret said. How's the course going, Sam?'

'Great. I love it. They say I've got a natural flair for dress design.'

'Mary Quant, eat your heart out,' John said. 'Thanks for the coffee and cake and I'll see you all later in the week. Good luck, Jane, if and when you meet up with Ed.'

'Thanks.' She smiled as he shot off up the stairs.

* * *

'Wash the mugs please, Carl,' Jane said as Sammy took a pew on the coveted stool by the heater. 'Fancy a coffee, Sam?'

'No, thanks. It's just a flying visit to see how you're feeling today.'

'I'm okay. I felt really churned up yesterday, I couldn't think straight. I'd have been better off in work, mind – Mum bent my ear about Mark all day.'

'She liked him a lot,' Sammy said. 'But then again, surely she wouldn't expect you to spend the rest of your life with someone you didn't love? Not to mention his mother.'

'Please, don't.' Jane rolled her eyes. 'Argumentative old so-and-so! Anyway, there's plenty going on here to take my mind off things. John was in to discuss the new store they're opening in Wilmslow. Don't suppose you know of anyone who might be interested in the job of manager?'

'Not off hand, but Roy might. I'll ask him later. The Raiders don't have a gig tonight. He and Tim are coming over to our place. Join us if you want. By the way, has Eddie phoned you?'

'No. Did you get a chance to speak to him?'

'We did. We told him about the weekend. He said he'd be in touch with you today. Ah, I've just had a thought...' Sammy continued as Jane's face lit up. 'Ed got the sack from the paint factory yesterday. He's collecting his cards at four. Maybe he'll call in to see you after that. *He'll* be looking for work. You could tell him about the job.'

'I will. It'll be right up his street.'

'Roy's asked him to rejoin The Raiders. He's singing with the group on Saturday at The Roulette Club's opening night.'

'Really? Oh, that's brilliant. I bet he's dead pleased.'

'He's over the moon. But you be careful, Jane. Angie will be gunning for the pair of you if she finds out he's in touch with you again.'

Jane nodded and chewed her lip. 'I will.'

'I'd better go,' Sammy said. 'Mum asked me to pick up some baking stuff from Redman's. I'll see you at the bus stop in Mersey Square at six.'

* * *

Mark sighed as he looked at his watch for the umpteenth time in as many minutes. It had been a long day. He'd been unable to concentrate on his job. He couldn't get Jane out of his mind. If she would give him the chance to apologise face to face, he was sure they'd be able to sort things out.

He shouldn't have called her a slut. She'd only slept with that bastard once, or so she said. He'd do anything to get her back, promise her anything at all. He said goodnight to his colleagues, turned up his collar and stepped out onto the icy street.

'Hey, Mark, fancy a pint later?' His colleague and fellow band member, Tony Collins, followed him out.

'Not tonight, Tony, thanks all the same.'

'Still thinking about Jane?' Tony patted his shoulder.

The gesture brought a lump to Mark's throat and he swallowed hard. 'Can't think about anything else.'

'What was the falling-out over? Thought you two had it made. How long was it, three years?'

'Near enough. Turns out I didn't know her at all. She lied to me.'

'What about?' Tony offered him an Embassy cigarette and lit one himself.

'Thanks.' Mark took a long drag, his hand shaking. 'She slept with someone, but cracked on she was a virgin.'

'You mean you never had a shag?' Tony exclaimed. 'Christ, Mark! She's very tasty, is your Jane. I'm surprised you could keep your hands off her.'

'Wasn't easy. Said she was waiting for the right time. I booked the bloody trip to get us back on track. We had a fight, then she drops it on my toes that she'd slept with Eddie Mellor.'

'Oh, mate, I'm really sorry. I remember her dating Mellor. But he's married now anyway. Knocked up that hairdresser bird ages ago.'

'Exactly. So what the hell she thinks is gonna happen there, I don't know.'

'Listen, I'm gonna have to go,' Tony said, looking at his watch. 'I'm meeting Sarah. Why don't you wait for Jane finishing work? See if she'll talk to you. I mean, three years, it's a lot to give up on.'

'Suppose so, but I don't think Jane would see it that way.'

Tony said goodbye. Mark watched him stride off down the road and considered his suggestion. Jane would be cashing up about now, then she would be coming up the steps that led onto Broadgate to deposit in the bank's night safe. He decided to hang around, see if she'd allow him to walk her to the bus stop. His mind made up, he stepped into the darkened doorway of Estelle Modes dress shop and waited.

* * *

Jane cashed up as Carl swept the shop floor. Eddie hadn't phoned and she felt disappointed. Maybe he'd changed his mind; after all, it was a big risk to take.

There were plenty of decent lads who constantly asked her

out. She wouldn't be short of a date or a dancing partner. The Raiders' Phil Jackson had made it clear that he fancied her, but she'd always turned him down. Any other girl would give her right arm for a date with a sexy, blond guitarist.

She smiled at Carl as he emptied the dustpan into the bin. 'Lock the front door and turn off the main lights when you take the dustpan and brush back upstairs.'

Someone hammered loudly on the door as Carl sauntered back to the record department. He peered up the stairs and tutted. 'It's a man. Shall I tell him we're closed?'

'Please,' Jane said absent-mindedly. She filled in the bank slip and popped the cash into the leather pouch. 'Tell him to come back tomorrow.'

'Jane, he won't go away. Says he wants to speak to *you*.'

She frowned and looked up at the young man, who was smiling and waving at her through the glass door. Her stomach lurched.

'It's Eddie. Let him in, please.'

Carl unlocked the door and Eddie stepped into the darkened shop.

'Hello,' he greeted Carl, who was eyeing him curiously.

'Hi. Jane's downstairs.'

'Thanks, mate.' Eddie squeezed past Carl and ran down the stairs.

Sensing that Eddie wanted to be alone with her, Jane told Carl to go home.

'I'll finish off here, go and find Sammy. Tell her to go home without me. She'll be at my bus stop in Mersey Square.'

'Will you be okay?' Carl asked.

'I'll be fine. Off you go and I'll see you tomorrow.' She handed him his jacket and bundled him up the stairs. She turned to Eddie, who smiled and held out his hands. Aware of enough electricity in the air to light up Blackpool Illuminations, Jane shivered.

'Hi, you,' he said, melting her with his blue-eyed gaze.

'Hi, yourself.' She moved towards him.

They fell on one another, kissing slowly and passionately, Eddie's wandering hands moving over her body.

'Jane, I love you.' He pushed her back against the counter, kissing her again.

'I love you too, Ed. I've missed you so much,' she whispered as feelings overwhelmed her and tears ran unchecked down her cheeks.

'Don't cry.' He kissed her once more and wiped her eyes with his fingertips. 'I've missed you more than you'll ever know. Roy and Sammy told me about the weekend. I'm so sorry, it's my fault. I ruined it for you and Mark.'

'You didn't ruin anything. I couldn't give him what he wanted. It wasn't fair to make him wait any longer, he deserves better than that.'

'You deserve better than me, Jane.' He ran his hands through her long, silky hair and kissed the top of her head. 'I'm married, got a kid, no job now, no money either. Nothing at all to offer you except my love.'

'Your love will do just fine,' she said, looking into his eyes.

'Good!' He crushed her to him. 'Can't keep my hands off you. If we stay here much longer, I won't be responsible for my actions! Will you meet me tonight so we can talk properly?'

She nodded. 'Where would we go?'

'My parents' place. They'll be at the pictures. If we leave now you can still catch the six o'clock bus. I'll meet you in Mersey Square at seven thirty on my bike. Is that okay?'

'Perfect. I've got to drop the takings off at the bank first. Are you on the bike tonight?'

'Yeah, it's parked down the road. I'll walk you to the bus stop and collect it later. Shame I can't give you a lift home, but I don't think your mother would be too happy to see me.'

'She'd have a hairy fit. Hey, by the way, Sammy told me you're rejoining the group. I'm so happy for you.'

'Yeah, so am I,' he said, beaming.

He grabbed her hand as they slipped and slithered down the icy street and up the steep stone steps to the bank on Broadgate. Jane dropped the pouch into the night safe. Eddie pulled her close and kissed her again, holding her like he'd never let her go. They drew breathlessly apart, and with their arms around one another, walked towards Mersey Square, stopping every few minutes to steal further kisses.

So absorbed in their delight at being together, neither saw the shadowy figure standing in Estelle Modes' doorway.

Sammy watched in amusement as Eddie swept Jane into his arms and gave her another lingering kiss, this time in full view of the bus queue.

'See you later,' he called as he walked away.

'Well!' Sammy raised an eyebrow. 'Didn't take you two long!'

'We're meeting later to talk, his parents are going out.'

'Last time you were on your own at Eddie's mum's house, Angie copped the pair of you in bed!' Sammy reminded her.

Jane blushed at the memory. 'Hopefully she won't turn up this time and we're only going to talk, like I said.'

Sammy raised an amused eyebrow. 'It *is* the same Eddie Mellor we all know and love that you're meeting?'

'Of course, but he's changed,' Jane said lamely, remembering Eddie's hands all over her in the shop and no doubt they would be later too.

As they sat on the bus going home, Sammy squeezed her arm. 'Joking aside, you look happier than I've seen you look for ages. But in view of Eddie's track record, just remember two little words when you're alone with him.'

'What?'

'Take precautions!' she teased.

Jane felt her cheeks warming, sure that the whole bus had heard.

* * *

Mark struggled to accept what he'd just witnessed. Eddie Mellor kissing Jane. *His* Jane. And she'd been laughing as he'd put his arms around her. Mark stood for a while longer in the shop doorway as jealousy raged through him. How dare they make him feel a fool? His hands shook as he lit another cigarette.

He wished now that he'd taken up Tony's offer of a pint. He didn't feel like going home. His mother would only bend his ear about his broken engagement, yet again. Unable to admit the truth about the weekend, he'd lied that Jane had had a change of heart about getting married.

His mother's unsympathetic reply had been that it was for the best as she was a flighty piece, what with her short skirts and make-up. Mark clenched his fists as he remembered she'd followed with, 'Never mind, Marky, she was only after your savings. Now you can stay here with me instead of buying your own house. We were happy together until you took up with that girl.'

'No, Mother, we weren't,' he muttered. 'Because *you're* never happy unless you're getting your own bloody way.' He finished his cigarette, made his way to the Black Lion and ordered a pint of cider and a double whisky. Choosing a secluded table tucked in a corner at the back of the crowded room, he knocked back the whisky and downed the cider in record time. He ordered another pint and this time drank it at a more leisurely pace. The alcohol blurred the edges of his pain. For the first time in three days he felt able to relax. He lit another cigarette, picked up a copy of the *Manchester Evening*

Chronicle that someone had left on the table and turned to the back sports page.

'So, you decided to venture out after all?'

Mark looked up into Tony's smiling face. He was with his girlfriend Sarah, who sat down opposite.

'I'm really sorry, Mark, about you and Jane, I mean...' she began, patting his hand.

'S'okay, Sarah,' he slurred. 'It's over and I couldn't give a flying fuck about her.'

Tony frowned. 'Didn't you get to see her after work then?'

'Oh, I saw her all right. She was with Mellor. They passed right by me and didn't even know it. They were all over one another. He's probably got her in bed by now, screwing the arse off her!'

'Mark!' Sarah exclaimed.

'That's a bit strong, Mark,' Tony said.

'Is it? Couldn't give a damn, to be honest. I was right to call her a slut, because that's exactly what she is. Do you know what really pisses me off though? I ordered roses to be delivered to her house. More fool me. She'll probably chuck 'em in the bin. Anyway, I don't wanna talk about her any more. Let's have another drink.'

'Are you sure you should, mate?' Tony said. 'What about having something to eat first?'

'I'm not hungry, and I'm dead sure.'

5

As Eddie entered his flat, the silence overwhelmed him. Before he left for work that morning the conversation between him and Angie had been stilted. He'd been both horrified and ashamed to see the bruising on her cheek.

Cathy had avoided even looking at him. She'd dressed Jonny and announced that she would drop him off at Angie's mother's house.

'So, what do you want to do?' Eddie asked when he and Angie were left alone. He lit a cigarette and drew deeply.

'I'm going to stay with my mum for a few nights,' she said, shaking cornflakes into a bowl.

'What about Jonny?'

'He'll be with me of course.'

'I won't see him for a while then.' He flicked ash onto a saucer. 'I'm not coming to your mother's house.'

'Tough! You should have thought about that before you insulted Cathy and slapped me.'

'You hit me first.' He held up his hands as she opened her mouth to retaliate. 'Okay, before you start giving me earache,

I'm sorry. I shouldn't have hit you back and I apologise for insulting Cathy.'

Angie stared at him for a long moment then lowered her gaze. 'Did you mean it when you asked for a divorce?'

'I never said that.' He frowned and shook his fringe from his eyes.

'You were so drunk, you probably won't remember half of what you *did* say. It's probably as well, seeing as you were ranting on to Cathy about our lack of a sex life!'

'Was I?' He groaned and put his head in his hands.

'You did, and you definitely said you want a divorce.'

'We need some time apart,' he said. 'A bit of breathing space. Instead of you going to your mother's, I'll stay at *my* mum's and you can stay here. Then we don't have to mess Jonny's routine up. I'll collect my stuff later and disappear.'

'Okay, Ed,' she agreed. 'The less my mother knows about our problems, the better. I'll bring Jonny home about eight and then he won't cry after you.' She pushed her uneaten breakfast away. 'So, you're definitely going ahead and rejoining The Raiders?'

He nodded and stood up. 'I am, I miss performing. We need the money, so it's not up for negotiation. Right, I'm off to look for work. I need something to keep us afloat until the gig money starts coming in. I'll see you in a few days.' He patted her shoulder and left.

Only the thought of contacting Jane had kept him going all day on his fruitless search for work and then joy of joys, she'd agreed to meet him tonight.

He sat in the quiet kitchen and ate the fish and chips he'd brought home, then washed, changed and threw a few clothes and toiletries into a holdall. It was too early to meet Jane so he decided to drop the bag at his parents' home first. Make sure they were definitely going out.

* * *

Enid Wilson dropped the last peeled potato into a pan of water as her daughter shot past her like a four-minute miler.

'For heaven's sake, Jane, what's the rush?' She lifted the pan onto the stove, wiped her hands on her floral apron and anchored a straying blonde curl behind her ear. 'There's a fresh brew in the pot.'

'I'll have a quick one.' Jane plonked herself down at the kitchen table. 'I'm in a hurry tonight. Gotta get ready to go out.'

'Anywhere nice?' Enid passed a mug of tea over.

'Err, John Grey's house,' Jane fibbed, hoping her cheeks weren't going red. 'He's invited me and Carl over for a drink. His dad's opening a new store in Wilmslow. We've been asked to help with some promotional ideas.'

'I see.' Enid smiled proudly. 'Well, it's very nice of them to get you both so involved. It might lead to something good for the future.'

'Mum, I already manage the Stockport branch. I think I'm doing quite well for a nineteen-year-old.'

'You are, but Wilmslow's such a nice area. You never know who you might meet. By the way,' she continued as Jane rolled her eyes, 'did you see the red roses in that bucket in the porch as you came in? They're from Mark. Well, it looks like his writing on the envelope.'

She frowned as her daughter got up from her chair and stomped into the porch. She came back carrying the roses and tossed them onto the draining board.

'What's wrong? They're beautiful. It'll be Mark's way of saying he's sorry for falling out with you. He's probably ready to make up.'

'Mum, we're finished. There's nothing *to* make up. I don't love him, I told you that on Saturday.'

'All couples have tiffs. The trouble with you, young lady, is that you don't know when you're well off! You'd never want for a thing married to Mark. Not like that Mellor boy you went out with, always in bother.'

Hands on hips, Jane faced her mother. 'Here we go again. You won't let it drop about Eddie, will you? You were never even prepared to give him a chance.'

'He was nothing but trouble.' Enid folded her arms. 'All that black leather and no proper job. Just be thankful it wasn't you that he got into a mess. He's a bad lot and he'll never have two ha'pennies to rub together.'

'Oh, and what would *you* know?' Jane retorted. 'At least he wasn't a jealous, controlling creep. Anyway, I'm not making up with Mark and that's that.'

Enid watched closely as Jane removed the envelope from the bouquet, glanced at the card and pushed it into her skirt pocket.

'See, you're blushing. I bet he's written something nice. At least give him a call and thank him.'

'No! And I'm not blushing. *You* have the roses if you're that bothered about them. Stick 'em in the dustbin for all I care.'

'Well, you callous little madam! That lad's probably heart-broken and you want to put his peace offering in the bin.'

'How many more times? I don't want them. I'm going to my room to get ready. I don't want any tea either, I'll get something at John's.'

Enid sighed and picked up the bouquet. 'I'll find a vase for these then.'

'You do that, Mum,' Jane said as she left the kitchen.

* * *

Upstairs on the landing, Jane pulled the little card from her skirt pocket and re-read it.

Dearest Jane, I love you more than life itself. I'm prepared to forgive you for sleeping with Eddie Mellor if you'll have me back. I promise it will never be mentioned again. Yours forever, Mark.

'Oh yeah,' she muttered, shoving the card back into her pocket. 'Never, except every time we have a disagreement, which would probably be most days.'

She popped her head around her brother's bedroom door. He was standing in front of the dressing table mirror, brushing his hair. His eyes lit up when he spotted her.

'Hiya!'

'Hi, Pete. Look at the state of this room. Do you ever pick anything up?'

She trod gingerly across a carpet strewn with *Dandy* and *Beano* comics, records and cast-off clothes. Propped in the corner was the old stand-up bass her father had bought for Pete from The Raiders bass player, Tim Davis. Not that her brother had learnt to play and it was currently doing duty as a hanger for his school blazer.

'I'm only thinking of Mum when I make a mess,' he said, eyes twinkling. 'She's home all day. Picking up after me gives her something to do.'

Jane laughed at his reasoning. 'Are you trying to do your hair in a Beatles style?'

'Yeah!' He turned back to the mirror. 'But it's a bit too short. Mum made me have it cut after school today.'

'Never mind, it'll soon grow. Brush it into a full fringe like Paul McCartney's. With your big brown eyes, you'll be a dead ringer. All the girls at the youth club fancy you,' she teased.

'Which girls?'

'Oh, come on. Don't pretend you don't know. Sammy's sister Susan and her friend Anna are both crazy for you.'

'Huh, they're only kids.' Peter smiled at his mirrored reflection. He picked up a hairbrush, held it like a microphone, and sang the chorus of 'Please, Please Me'. He turned around with a swagger. 'I like my women older!'

'Well, Susan's only two months younger than you.'

'Yeah, but I'm fifteen now. Give her a bit of time to mature.'

'See, you are interested, little brother.' Jane laughed as he strutted around the room, strumming an imaginary guitar.

'Stop calling me little brother. I'm taller than you.'

'True, but you're nearly four years younger. Anyway, I'm off to get ready to go out. See you later.'

'See you, Jane. By the way, did you like the flowers lover boy sent?'

'They were very nice, but I gave them to Mum.'

'Why?'

'Because Mark sent them to try and win me back.'

'And you don't want that?'

'No, I don't.' She fished in her skirt pocket and handed him the card: 'Read that.'

Peter's eyes widened as he glanced at the neatly written card. 'Jesus, Jane, Mum'll go spare if she sees this.'

'Don't you dare say a word.' She shut the bedroom door and lowered her voice. 'I'll chuck the card away when I go out. I'm seeing Ed tonight, but I told Mum I'm going to John Grey's.'

'But Eddie's married now. He's got a kid. She'll go bloody nuts.' Peter's voice shot up an octave as Jane put a warning finger to her lips.

'He's not happy in his marriage. We still love one another.'

Peter sucked in his breath. '*I* won't say anything, but you're taking a hell of a risk. Make sure you're not seen together by anyone who might snitch on you to Mum.'

'Don't worry, I'll be fine. Have a good time at the youth club. Is Harry from next-door going with you?'

'Yeah, his sister's trying to flatten his hair with water and lacquer but it sticks out all over the show 'cos it's so curly.'

'You pair of posers!' Jane said, grinning as she left his room.

* * *

Over black lacy underwear, Jane donned a denim mini skirt and a red angora sweater. She did her make-up, pulled on long black boots, brushed her hair and checked her appearance in the mirror. The hot bath had brought a flush to her cheeks and her eyes sparkled. A quick spray of In Love perfume and she was ready.

As she collected her handbag and jacket from the kitchen, her mother pursed her lips: 'That skirt's far too short for this time of year. I can almost see your knickers when you bend over!'

'God!' Jane tugged ineffectively at her hemline. 'Can't stop to argue, I'm running late as it is.' She dashed out of the kitchen before her mother could read her mind and try to stop her.

Her stomach looped and her legs felt so wobbly she could hardly run to the bus stop. The thought of being alone with Eddie was overwhelming. She'd never had such wonderful feelings of anticipation prior to dates with Mark.

* * *

'Only me,' Eddie called as he let himself into his parents' house.

His mum greeted him with a welcoming smile as he plonked his bag on the hall floor. 'Is that more dirty washing, love?'

'Err, no, it's clean stuff. I'm home for a few nights. Angie and I need to put a bit of space between us.'

'Had another falling-out, lad?' His dad offered him a cigarette and lit one for himself.

'I'm afraid so. It was bad this time. She pushed me to the point where I slapped her last night.'

'Oh, Eddie, no!' His mum's hand flew to her mouth and she sank down on the sofa.

'Angie hit me first,' he told them. 'I know that's no excuse but it was a natural reaction. Before I knew it, I'd lashed out and caught her on the cheek. Her face was a right mess this morning. God knows what her mother will say. More ammunition against me, I suppose.'

'The whole situation's a bloody mess.' His dad shook his head. 'What are you going to do? You've that little lad to think about. No matter what you and her ladyship decide, Jonny must come first.'

'I know that and he does. But I can't get along with Angie, no matter how hard I try.'

'You're welcome to stay here as long as you like,' his mum said. 'Your bedroom's always ready. We're off to the pictures now. Will you be all right on your own for a while or do you want to come with us?'

'I'm going to Roy's actually,' Eddie fibbed. 'He and Tim have asked me to rejoin The Raiders. Singing for now, then drumming again when I can afford a new kit.'

'I thought all that bloody group nonsense was over and done with!' his dad snapped. 'You've got a proper job now.'

'It's not nonsense, Dad. And I got sacked yesterday. I hated the job anyway. I enjoy singing, I know it's something I'm really good at. I need a bit of freedom and pleasure in my life. For fuck's sake, I feel like I'm continuously being punished for having a bit of the other with Angie!'

'If you hadn't filled her belly with arms and legs, you'd have had your freedom and all that goes with it. You've only yourself to blame, Ed. And don't use that language in front of your mother. Show her some respect.'

'Don't you two start arguing again,' Mum bellowed above their raised voices. 'I had enough of that when Eddie lived with us. I'll chuck the pair of you on the street in a minute. Give the lad a break, Fred. He's only doing a bit of singing with his mates, where's the harm in that?'

'You've always been too bloody soft with him, woman. He brought the trouble on himself, mucking about with that young lass.'

'Eddie's no different than you and your mates were when you were a lad, so you just think on!'

Dad coughed and patted Eddie's shoulder. 'I'm sorry, son. I reckon you've enough problems without me adding to them. No doubt the money from singing will come in handy.'

'Well, thank the lord for that.' Mum pulled on her hat. 'Get yourself to the toilet, Fred, otherwise, we'll have just got nicely settled in our seats and you'll need to go.' As he left the room, she pushed a hatpin into the front brim of her hat. 'One of these days I'll ram this ruddy hatpin where it'll most hurt you both.'

'I reckon you would too, Mum,' Eddie said and hugged her.

'Why didn't you tell me you'd lost your job when you came round last night?'

'Because I wanted to tell Angie first.'

'Is that the reason you had another argument?'

'That and a million other things. I'm sure I'll find something else soon enough. Anyway, what time will you be back tonight?'

'About quarter past eleven. We always collect fish and chips on the way home and take them to your Auntie Minnie's. We like to have a fish supper and a cup of tea with her on a Tuesday night, she looks forward to it.'

His father strolled back into the parlour and announced he was ready.

'Have a good time then.' Eddie saw them out and rubbed his hands together. Hallelujah! Over three hours to spend with Jane.

* * *

Jane spotted Eddie waiting for her by the fire station. She jumped off the bus and ran across Mersey Square, planted a kiss on his lips, hitched up her skirt and climbed onto the back of the bike. 'You sure your mum and dad are out?' She wrapped her arms around his waist.

'Positive. I've just come from their place, we should be okay for a few hours. Hold on tight.'

'Why are you parking here?' Jane asked when he pulled into the back garden.

'So the bike's out of sight. If I park on the street and they come home early and spot it, they'll expect me to join them for a fish supper at Auntie Minnie's.' He rolled his eyes and grinned. Jane giggled and followed him indoors.

In the kitchen he pulled her into his arms and kissed her. 'We can either go into the parlour or up to my old room, whichever you prefer.'

'Your room.'

'You sure?'

'I've never been so sure of anything in my life.'

He took her hand and led her up the stairs. The room was exactly as she remembered: white walls and a blue and black swirly patterned carpet. She drew the blue stripy curtains. Eddie switched on the lamp and pulled off his boots and jacket. Jane slipped off her boots and jacket and turned to face him. He grabbed hold of her and they tumbled onto the bed, tearing off one another's clothes, lips frantically possessing.

She gazed at him as he took in her naked body with hungry eyes.

'I didn't think you could be any more beautiful than you were the last time we made love,' he whispered. 'But you look... well... good enough to eat!'

She smiled and ran her hands over his flat stomach. He moaned softly as she reached to caress him. Time stood still as he kissed and stroked every inch of her. She gasped and arched her back as his fingers explored.

She was close to orgasm as he entered her. Sammy's earlier warnings about taking precautions were forgotten as he slid his hands under her and pulled her closer. He thrust deeply as she writhed beneath him. She called his name as she came and as he exploded to his own shuddering climax, she heard him cry, 'I love you, Jane!'

'Love you too, Ed.' Tears of happiness spilled down her cheeks. They lay silently together, cherishing the moment. Jane buried her face in the sprinkling of dark hairs on his chest, breathing in the sensual scent of the two of them. Their love-making had left her with a feeling of such utter completeness that she knew with certainty she would never have found with Mark Fisher.

Eddie stroked her hair tenderly. 'That was the most amazing shag I've ever had!'

She leant up on one elbow and looked into his eyes. 'Was it? We're supposed to be talking tonight, not making love.'

'How the hell could we stop? I was desperate for you.' His eyes clouded with uncertainty as he gazed into hers. 'Please don't tell me it was a mistake, Jane.'

'Ed, I'm teasing you. Of course it wasn't a mistake, I was as desperate as you. I would have made the first move if you hadn't, believe me.'

'Well, you almost did, you little hussy!' He grinned, relaxing again. 'When Roy and Sammy told me you'd dumped Mark and that you still loved me, I couldn't believe it. I was a bit nervous about calling you at work in case John Grey didn't approve so I decided to catch you tonight before you left to go home. I didn't realise Carl would be there, too. He's a funny little fellow, isn't he?'

'He is,' Jane said, laughing. 'But he's very sweet and caring. John wouldn't have minded you ringing. He knows how bad things are for you and he asked me today if I would consider going out with you again if you were free.'

'And what did you tell him?' He tickled her ribs until she squealed.

'What do you think?' She squirmed away from him. 'Stop it or I'll scream!'

'So, you still fancy me then? Even though Sammy says I'm skinny these days.' He pinned her arms above her head and rained kisses down her front.

'You know I do. Couldn't you feel the electricity between us when we were in the shop?'

He smiled. 'It's a wonder we didn't set the place on fire.'

'And this bed. By the way, talking of Carl and the shop, we're opening a new branch in Wilmslow and he's being transferred. Promoted to junior manager, in fact.'

'Lucky devil,' Eddie said. 'I need a new job, I got sacked yesterday. I'm pretty desperate.'

'I know you did.' Jane gazed at him thoughtfully. 'John Grey's looking for a manager for the new place.'

'Do you think I'd be in with a chance?'

She smiled at his eager expression. 'That's why I mentioned it. You'd be perfect. We'll be selling musical instruments as well as records. But what will Angie say if you're working for the same firm as me?'

'Who knows?' He shrugged. 'But after that soul-destroying factory, managing a music store would be fantastic. I wouldn't even mind wearing a poncey suit and tie for a job like that.'

'I'll let John know you're interested, then. He'll probably arrange to interview you on Saturday.'

'Sounds great. Enough about all that for now though, we need to talk about us.'

'We do,' she agreed.

'I think we're meant to be, Jane. Third time lucky eh, kid?' He reached for his jeans. 'I need a ciggie.' He rooted in the pockets, lit up, took a lengthy drag and blew a wobbly smoke ring.

Jane reclined on the pillow. 'So, Ed, what next?'

He smiled reassuringly. 'I'm not sure, but somehow or other we're going to be together. I'll have to sort things out with Angie, make sure she and Jonny are provided for. I'll tell her I'm leaving because I've had enough. Neither of us is happy as you know and we can't go on like that. But if she finds out I've slept with you, she'll go fucking loopy. Your mum and dad would soon get to know. She'd make damn sure of that and they'll go berserk. They hated me dating you before. I can't imagine for one minute they'll welcome me with open arms now.'

Jane sighed. 'I dread telling them. Mum will go mad. She was having a go at me before I came out, making comparisons between you and Mark.'

'It's not going to be easy,' he said. 'But as far as I'm concerned, my marriage is over.' He took another lengthy drag and looked at her through narrowed eyes.

'What is it?'

'I slapped Angie across the face last night. We had a terrible argument. It was retaliation because she slapped me. I'm staying here for a few days to give us some space.'

'That's not the Eddie Mellor I remember,' Jane said.

'It's not the Eddie anybody remembers,' he said quietly. 'Angie brings out the worst in me. I've never done it before and I never will again. I hope she won't use it against me to stop me seeing Jonny. I think the world of my son.' He stubbed out the remains of his cigarette in an old tobacco tin on the bedside table.

Jane rolled onto her front and looked into his eyes. 'She won't be able to stop you seeing Jonny. I'll support you all the way and wait for as long as it takes while you sort everything out, because you're the only one for me.'

He smiled, tipped her onto her back and kissed her tenderly. 'And you for me,' he whispered.

* * *

Eddie took Jane home on his motorbike and dropped her on the corner of Primrose Avenue. He kissed her goodnight and promised to call her at work the next day.

As he rode away she waved goodbye and strolled up the path to Sammy's house. She raised her hand to knock and the door flew open.

'Saw you from the window. C'mon, we're all dying to know what happened.' Sammy bundled her inside and propelled her upstairs to the bedroom, where Roy and Tim were singing along to Chuck Berry's 'Sweet Little Sixteen' playing on the Dansette.

'What do you reckon, Jane?' Roy asked as the song came to an end. 'We're thinking of doing it at Saturday's gig.'

'Sounds pretty good to me,' she replied. 'Will you duck walk, like Chuck?'

'I may do.' He winked. 'You'll have to wait and see.'

'Want a drink, Jane?' Pat sloshed cider into glasses from a stone flagon.

'Please, I could murder one!'

'Sit down,' Sammy ordered, dragging the bedroom chair towards Jane. She tossed her design portfolio and a mountain of half-completed garments onto the floor. 'Check there's no pins on it first.'

Roy put down his guitar and stretched out his denim-clad legs on Sammy's bed. He looked at Jane through narrowed eyes and smiled. 'Well?'

'Well what, Roy?' she teased.

'Oh, come on, Jane, don't keep us in suspense.' Sammy

handed her a glass of cider. 'What's happening? Is he leaving her? Did you, erm, sleep together?'

'Sammy, you don't half ask some personal questions!' Pat exclaimed.

'Pat, shut up,' Sammy tutted. 'We're her best friends. Jane doesn't mind telling us, do you?'

'Jane doesn't need to tell us anything,' Roy said. 'Look at her face, Sam. That wide-eyed sparkle says it all.'

6

Mark stopped beside the trunk of a giant oak and pulled Jane into his arms.

'I love you,' he whispered, lips on hers, fingers running through her long silky hair. 'Don't leave me again, please.'

As Jane responded to his kisses, a shrill voice rent the air.

'Marky, are you awake, love? Don't forget you promised to take me shopping this morning.'

He opened his eyes a fraction and squinted at the clock on the bedside table: eight o'clock! *Eight o' bleeding clock on a Saturday morning and she's mithering already.*

'For God's sake, Mother, I'm having a lie-in,' he yelled. 'Wake me at ten if you want a lift with your shopping and not before.' He pulled the pillow around his head, trying to recapture the dream. He'd dreamt about Jane most nights this week – when he'd managed to sleep, that was.

A sharp pain shot through his head and his guts rolled uncomfortably. Too much whisky. But he couldn't do without it. It helped blot out the memory of seeing Jane in Mellor's arms the other night. He'd woken with a hangover every morning this week. He was in trouble at work. His manager had told him to take stock of himself and warned that unshaven, slovenly appearances were unacceptable in Lloyds Bank.

Mark's thoughts turned to yesterday afternoon, when he'd been summoned to a meeting with the personnel officer. He'd declined Miss Robbins' suggestion of a holiday, but told her he would consider a transfer to the Chester branch. A vacancy for a senior clerk had been advertised recently. The possibility of a change of scene appealed to him. She told him she would look into it and get back to him next week.

'Marky, I've done you some toast and a mug of tea.' His mother appeared beside his bed and placed a tray on the bedside table.

He sighed and sat up. 'Didn't you hear me say to wake me at ten?'

'Well, you know I'm a bit deaf.'

'You're not. You're just a stubborn old so-and-so! Always wanting your own way.'

'That's not fair, Mark. I'm only trying to do my best for you.'

She handed him the mug. He sipped his tea, wishing she'd leave him alone to wallow in his pit of misery.

She smoothed out the rumpled eiderdown and parked herself on the end of his bed.

'You look dreadful, son. Your hair needs a damn good cut and you're too pale by half. Pull yourself together. It's not worth going to pieces over a girl like Jane.'

Mark winced at the mention of her name and flicked his unruly hair from his face.

'I'm growing my hair, it just needs a wash. And what's that supposed to mean? A girl like Jane!'

'Well, she was out to trap a decent man. You happened to fall for her charms, for what they're worth.' She pursed her lips and carried on. 'I grant you she's pretty, but that girl gave you the run around. She's had a change of heart because she's set her sights on someone else. Who is he, a wealthy sugar daddy or something?'

'You're way off beam, Mother. Jane's still in love with her ex. He's as far removed from a sugar daddy as possible. He's also married with a kid.'

His mother caught her breath and clutched her chest. 'Well, fancy that! I knew she was a right one as soon as I clapped eyes on her. Out with all and sundry.'

He shook his head wearily. 'Leave it. You don't know what you're talking about.'

She folded her arms under her ample bosom. 'Some girls have no principles.' She stood up, wincing. 'That bed's too low for me, it's set my hip off again. Finish your breakfast and I'll wash the dishes.'

'Can you manage the stairs?'

'I'll be fine,' she said, limping out of the room.

'I'll take you shopping when I'm dressed,' he called after her. How the hell would she manage if he *did* move to Chester? Mind you, she'd have had to manage if he'd married Jane. There was not a cat in hell's chance of the pair living in harmony under the same roof.

His bass guitar, propped against the wardrobe, reminded him that The Scorpions had a gig tonight in Macclesfield. He'd broken a string last week, so a visit to the music store in Stockport was a must. Pity Flanagan and Grey's didn't sell guitar strings and then he would have a valid reason to call in and see Jane. He could tell her he was going to be working in Chester soon. See what her reaction might be. Sod it, he'd call in and see her anyway. Mind made up, he climbed out of bed and padded to the bathroom.

* * *

Eddie knotted his tie in front of the parlour mirror and slipped on his jacket. He pulled at the waistband of his trousers and grimaced. 'Just look how loose my old wedding suit is now.'

'It's because you hardly eat a decent meal,' his mum said. 'Your dad has a belt you can borrow, I'll nip up and get it from his wardrobe. You'll walk that interview, son. You've sales experience from your old job at Jerome's and you've got your musical skills. You can't fail.'

'Well, let's hope not, eh, Mum? I need to start working again as soon as possible and this job would be perfect. When I spoke to John Grey, he told me I was the only one being interviewed for the position.'

'Does young Jane still work at the Stockport branch?'

He averted his gaze and smiled. 'She does.'

'Hmm, I thought there was more to it than meets the eye. Coupled with the fact that you haven't mentioned a word to Angie about the interview.'

'Well, I haven't seen her all week.' He ran a comb through his hair.

'True. But she called last night over the rent money. You could have told her then.'

'No point causing arguments, Mum. Let's wait and see if I get the job first. I'll tell her when I'm good and ready.'

'Well, *you* know best. I'll get that belt then you can be on your way.'

Eddie lit a cigarette and thought back over the last few days. He'd managed to see Jane after rehearsals every night and tonight was the gig at The Roulette Club, so he would be seeing her again. He smiled, thinking back to how thrilled she'd been when she told him that John Grey said he was more than willing to interview him for the manager's position.

His mum returned with the belt and interrupted his thoughts. 'Here you go. You might as well keep it. He hasn't worn it for ages, his fat belly keeps his trousers in place.'

'Thanks.' He pulled the belt through his waistband loops and did up the buckle. 'That feels better. Wouldn't want them falling down when I jump off the bus.'

She smiled and gave him a hug. 'Good luck, love. Are we having Jonny this afternoon?'

'Yeah. I'll pick him up about one and bring him back here. Then Angie will collect him and the rent money I owe her on her way home from work. But don't forget to keep quiet about the job.'

'My lips are sealed. Me and Dad will take Jonny out for a couple of hours before tea. He'll enjoy that and so will we. Go on now, or you'll miss the bus.'

* * *

Jane smiled at Eddie as he ran down the stairs to the record department.

'You look nice,' she mouthed as John Grey's friend, Stuart Green, who helped out on Saturdays, finished serving a customer.

He said goodbye to the young girl and grinned in Eddie's direction.

'Who are *you* out to impress with your fancy suit and tie, then?'

'It was either this outfit, or my Levi's and biking jacket,' Eddie said, laughing.

'Ah well, fair enough. John said to go straight up to the stockroom.'

'Okay, but don't I get a good luck kiss first?'

'Not from me, mate!' Stuart quipped. 'I'm sure Jane will oblige though.'

Jane put her arms around Eddie and wished him luck. 'You'll be fine, Ed. You look very businesslike. That suit alone will impress John.'

'I feel a bit nervous. So much hangs on me getting this job. Not least *our* future. Your mother might eventually accept me if I can stay on the rails and do something decent for a living.'

'Well, the job's as good as yours anyway. Only don't let on to John that I told you. Let him tell you himself.'

* * *

Eddie knocked on the stockroom door and entered at John's request.

'Come in, Ed. Have a seat.' John peered over the top of his glasses, shuffled the sheaf of papers on his knee and smiled reassuringly. 'You're looking very dapper. I was expecting you to be wearing jeans and a leather jacket for some reason.'

Eddie smiled and sat down on the chair John pushed towards him. He took off his jacket and felt instantly at ease.

'Right, well this is just a formality. The job's yours anyway. I know you well enough, I couldn't wish for anyone better. I think Jane's already told you that as well as records and sheet music, we'll be stocking musical instruments?'

'She has.'

'As manager, you'll be responsible for both departments, with the help of Carl as your assistant manager. I've interviewed a young lass called Tina Pickles, who'll be your junior sales assistant. She's a school leaver. We'll see how the three of you manage for the time being. Stuart will help you Saturdays and college holidays. If you feel you need extra staff, just let me know.

'I've lined up a young lad for Jane's new assistant, name of Sean Grogan. He's the grandson of my dad's golfing partner. Seventeen, good-looking; full of dubious Irish charm. Has a look of The Beatles about him, so he'll go down a bomb with the young girls who gather in here after school.'

'Sounds good.'

'The only problem I foresee is Angie,' John continued. 'How will you manage to keep her and Jane apart? The last thing you need is fur and feathers flying between them in your workplace.'

'Leave it with me, John. I'll sort it. Jane and I are keeping our relationship low-key. Sammy and Pat's parents saw me kissing her the other night outside their place and asked what's going on. But they've agreed to say nothing to Jane's mum and dad until we're ready to break the news ourselves.'

'That's good,' John said. 'I remember there was no love lost between you and Jane's mum.'

'Don't know why my girls' mothers don't like me. They must see me as a threat or something.'

'Lock up your daughters and throw away the key!' John laughed.

'Something like that. Anyway, my marriage is more or less over. Just as long as Angie lets me see my little lad, that's all I'm bothered about.'

'Who'd ever have thought a rebel like you could turn into such a doting parent? Have you seen Jonny this week?'

'No. I'm having him this afternoon. Only problem is, I've got to collect him from Old Mother Turner's place and the woman hates my guts.'

'What time's she expecting you?'

'One o'clock.'

'Well, let's go and tell the others you've got the job, then I'll run you to your dreaded ma-in-law's. I doubt she'll say anything out of place with me there. By the way, your wages will be eight pounds a week while you're training and ten when you're managing the store. You'll get twice-yearly raises, two weeks paid holiday, bank holidays and ten per cent commission on any instrument sales you make. How does that sound?'

'Fantastic.' Eddie shook John by the hand. 'When would you like me to start?'

'A week on Monday suit you?'

'Perfect.'

* * *

Mark left Stockport Music Exchange with a packet of bass strings stashed in his jacket pocket. He popped into the Black Lion for a quick pint and then made his way towards Flanagan and Grey's. As he rounded the corner, he stopped at the sight of John Grey and Eddie Mellor leaving the shop. The pair hadn't seen him; they were walking in the opposite direction and appeared to be deep in conversation.

Mellor was smartly dressed in a suit and looked happy and confident. A far cry from the down-at-heel young man in the paint-stained jeans and biking jacket who had held and kissed Jane the other night. Mark shrugged and continued on his way into the shop.

Stuart looked up from the newspaper he was reading. He greeted Mark with a friendly smile. 'Hi there, Mark. How you doing?'

'So, so,' he replied. 'Is Jane in today?'

'She's upstairs, having lunch. Would you like one of us to call her?'

'Please. I'd like a quick word.'

'I'll go and tell her,' Carl volunteered.

'Be quick,' Stuart said. 'Take a seat while you're waiting, Mark.'

* * *

Perched upon a stack of LP boxes like Miss Muffet on her tuffet, Jane finished her sandwich. She looked up from reading the problem page in *Honey* magazine as Carl popped his head around the door. 'What's up? You look a bit frazzled.'

'Mark's downstairs. Wants to see you.'

'What?'

'He says he wants to see you,' Carl repeated.

'I heard you! I don't want to see *him*.'

'What shall I tell him?'

'Oh, I don't know. Tell him to go away.'

'What if he won't go away?'

'Tell him to come up here then. I don't want a scene in the shop. Thank God Eddie's gone home, or else!'

'Or else what?'

'They might have had a punch-up!'

'Two men fighting for your love. Just like the films at The Plaza.'

Jane stood up and brushed the crumbs off her skirt. 'No, Carl, not a bit like the films at all.'

'I'll tell him to come up, then.'

Carl disappeared. Jane brushed her hair and touched up her lips though why she was bothering when it was only for Mark she couldn't imagine. 'Come in,' she called at the gentle tap on the door. 'Hi, Mark. What are *you* doing here?'

'I don't know,' he faltered. 'Old habits die hard. I always used to come and have lunch with you on Saturdays. All I *do* know is that I just had to see you.'

'Why? There's nothing more to say, except... thank you for the roses. It's a bloody good job Mum didn't have a nosy at what you'd written on the card!'

'Sorry. Wasn't thinking. I've come to tell you that I'm moving to Chester, getting a transfer with the bank very soon.'

'Oh, right. Well, that will be nice for you,' she said, thinking, thank God for that. 'What about your mother?'

'She'll have to manage without me. If you and I had married, she'd have lost me anyway.'

'I think not. She'd never have let you go. Maude rules your

life. All I could see ahead was years and years of her living with us.'

'Is that why you dumped me?'

'No, I told you the reason that night.'

'Ah yes, so you did. You shagged Mellor. I just saw him leaving here with John Grey.'

Jane ignored his sarcasm. 'Eddie had an interview for a job at the new store.'

'Did he get it?'

'Yes. Though what it's got to do with you, I don't know.'

'So, you're seeing him again?'

Jane looked down at the floor and chewed her lip. 'No, but we're friends. Soon we'll be colleagues.'

'Why not give *me* another chance then?'

'Because I don't want to be tied down. I'm seeing Phil Jackson now,' she fibbed. Mark moved towards her. She wished he'd go away. He was giving her the creeps. Staring at her with cold grey eyes, like that night in The Lakes.

'Couldn't we just date one another without the engagement ring? I won't pressure you or anything. I'm sure Phil won't mind. He has enough birds in tow to spare *you* occasionally.'

'No, Mark.' She turned her back on him. 'It's over, leave me alone.'

He caught her arm and pulled her round. 'You're lying, about Phil Jackson, I mean. I saw you with Mellor on Tuesday night. You were all over one another. Why lie about dating Phil?'

Jane groaned and tried to pull away from him. 'Okay, so I'm back with Eddie. He's splitting up from Angie. Don't you dare go causing trouble for us. Things are difficult enough as it is. Eddie, Roy and Tim would soon sort you out if you interfere. Now let go of my arm before I call for help.'

'And don't *you* dare threaten *me* with the Stockport Mafia!' He pushed her away in disgust. Then lunging towards her again, he gripped her shoulders. 'If he ever lets you down or lays a finger on you, he'll have me to answer to. I'll wait for you. One day you'll need me so badly, you'll be *begging* me to take you back.'

She shivered at his words and pulled away from his grasp. 'Don't bet on it. I wouldn't want *you* if you were the last man on earth. Now get lost, or I really will call for help.'

Mark stared at her then looked at his watch. 'I've an hour to kill. I'll go and see your mum, have a cup of tea with her. She told me I'd make the perfect son-in-law. She was so glad Mellor was out of your life. I wonder what she'll say when I tell her he's screwing her daughter.' He left the stockroom without a backward glance. Jane slumped down onto the LP boxes, tears streaming down her cheeks.

* * *

On his way back into the shop from buying lunch, Carl sidestepped as Mark brushed roughly past him. He frowned and continued downstairs. 'What's got into him?'

Stuart looked up. 'You okay? Thought you were going for lunch. I suppose you want the *NME*?'

Carl nodded and picked up the *New Musical Express*. 'Mark's just stormed out with a very angry look on his face. Go and see if Jane's all right while I hold the fort.'

* * *

Stuart ran quickly upstairs. He could hear Jane sobbing as he opened the stockroom door. 'Hey, come on.' He took her in his arms. 'What's wrong? You were happy as Larry earlier.'

'Mark's gone to tell my mum I'm seeing Eddie,' she cried and took the handkerchief Stuart offered. 'I've got mascara all down your shirt, Stu.'

'Never mind, it'll wash.'

'He was scary and threatening. I don't want Mum to know yet, it's too soon. The time needs to be right or she'll hit the roof. Should I call Eddie, tell him what Mark's up to, or just leave it?'

'If you want my opinion I think Mark's bluffing about going to see your mum. He hasn't the guts for one thing. He's trying to make you suffer because he's hurt and feeling rejected. On the other hand, if you were *my* bird and someone was upsetting you, I'd want to punch his bloody lights out. So yeah, call Ed.'

Jane nodded. 'Thanks, Stu, for listening and for the advice.'

'Hey, what are friends for? After all, it was John and me who introduced you to Eddie in the first place. I'd love to see the pair of you together, I think you're soul mates.'

'Really?' she smiled through her tears.

'Really,' Stuart said. 'Take a few minutes to compose yourself and then come on down. I'll keep Carl out of the way for a while.'

'Thanks again, Stu. Eddie should be home by now, I'll try calling him there.'

'Use the phone up here then. It's a bit more private than the shop phone.'

* * *

'Can you get that, Mum? It might be Roy for me,' Eddie yelled from upstairs. 'I'm just getting changed.'

His mother shouted that the call was for him. Eddie ran down the stairs and took the phone. 'Who is it?' he asked but she walked away with a shrug of her shoulders. 'Hello. Oh, hi, Jane. What's up?' He detected a voice wobble. 'Has something upset you?'

He listened, anger rising as Jane related what had happened between her and Mark. 'Right, leave it to me.'

'What will you do?'

'I'll sort it. Nobody threatens *my* girl and gets away with it.'

'Eddie, don't do anything silly, please.'

'I won't. But there's no way he'll be telling tales to your mother when I've had my say. Where does he live?'

'Don't hurt him,' she pleaded and gave him Mark's address.

'I won't. A verbal warning should do it. I'll see you tonight. I love you.'

'Love you too,' she said.

Eddie replaced the receiver. He turned to find his mother standing behind him, buttoning up her coat.

'That was young Jane on the phone.'

'Well, of course it was. *You* answered the call. She's got a problem. I promised I'd help her.'

His mum wagged a finger at him. 'I want no lies from you, Eddie Mellor. I just heard you call Jane your girl. Then you told her you loved her. What's going on, son?'

'If you heard me say that, then isn't it obvious? I'm seeing her. I love her. I'm going to marry her as soon as I can divorce Angie.'

'I see. Oh, Ed, you do make problems for yourself. Does Angie know you want a divorce?'

'I've hinted at it. I was thinking how to go about things while I was upstairs. I'll move back to the flat, just temporary, to see a bit more of Jonny. I'll ask her for a divorce then. But I'm definitely not telling her I've got the job. She'll want to know the details. I'm not having her threatening Jane.'

'Okay. But I think we should keep things from your dad for now until you know exactly what you're doing. Meantime, I'll keep your bed aired.'

Eddie put his arms around her and hugged her. 'Thanks, Mum! I'm sorry for all the trouble I've caused you and Dad over the last few years. I'll make it up to you, I promise.'

'I want to see you happy and settled, Ed. Whatever it takes is all I ask.'

'I *do* love Jane, Mum. I've always loved her. I only started seeing her again on Tuesday. Roy told me she'd broken off her engagement so I got in touch.'

'I'll help you all I can, love, but be careful how you go about things. You'll have Angie threatening all sorts and we don't want to lose contact with our Jonny. Anyway, you think on what I've said and I'll go and round up your father and the little fellow while you get yourself off to Roy's.'

* * *

Roy was playing his guitar, posing in front of the dressing table mirror. He smiled as Eddie walked into the room and sat down on the bed.

'Gotta get the look just right, Ed. Girls love it when I lower my eyelids and look sexy!' Laughing, he placed his Fender Stratocaster on its stand. 'Fancy sharing a joint before we go through the playlist for tonight?'

'We need to go somewhere first.'

'Sure. Where?'

'I'll tell you when we're on the way. Can we take the group's van to save time?'

Roy pulled on his leather jacket and picked up the van keys. 'Lead the way.'

They drove across town to leafy Maple Avenue. At Eddie's brief, Roy pulled up a couple of doors down from number 22.

'Right, Ed. Let's go and sort the bastard out!'

By mutual consent the pair decided they weren't spoiling for a fight, but that Mark should be left in no doubt he must leave Jane well alone. They swaggered along the gravel drive, glancing up at the smart semi with its neat and tidy front garden.

Roy lit a cigarette and tossed the spent match into the bed

of colourful crocuses beside the front door. Eddie rang the door-bell and stepped back, rocking on his heels.

'You sure you don't want a fag, Ed?'

'I'll have one on the way back.'

The door opened and a plump, grey-haired woman peered shortsightedly through her spectacles at them.

'Is Mark in?' Roy asked.

'He's in his bedroom playing his guitar. Are you from the group?'

'Yeah, that's right,' Roy spoke up quickly.

'Well, you'd better go up then. Mark told me he was expecting Tony. He didn't say anything about the others coming too.'

'Last-minute change of plan,' Roy said before Eddie could open his mouth.

'Well, put that cigarette out before you come in here. I don't allow Marky's friends to smoke in my house, it's a filthy habit.' She turned and went back inside, muttering, 'Just follow the noise, you'll find him.'

'That was easy,' Roy hissed as he and Eddie crept quietly up the stairs. 'Christ though, I'm glad she's not *my* mother with rules like no smoking in the bloody house!'

They stopped outside one of the doors on the landing and Eddie nodded. 'Bit of an old bag, isn't she?' he whispered. 'This is the one. Do we knock, or just go in?'

'The element of surprise is the best approach,' Roy said and opened the door.

Mark had his back to them. He was seated on his bed, playing his bass, oblivious to the interlopers in his room. Roy coughed and Mark turned, his eyes widening in disbelief.

'What the hell are you two doing here? Who let you in?'

'Your mum, of course,' Eddie replied. 'She's thinks we're your mates, M-a-r-k-y!'

Mark stood up and placed his guitar down on the bed. 'Say

what you've come to say, Mellor, and then piss off! You're trespassing in my home.'

'Actually,' Roy said with a smirk, 'we're not trespassing
because your old mum kindly let us in. As far as the law stands,
we're visitors.'

'And you can piss off too, Cantello!'

'Just shut your gob and let Eddie get on with telling you
why he's here. Then we *will* leave you in peace,' Roy said, the
friendly smile leaving his face. 'You've no argument with *me*,
Mark. Who was it picked up the pieces for you last weekend
after Jane gave you the elbow? Who stayed with you all night to
stop you topping yourself, instead of lying in the arms of my
lovely Sammy?'

'I wouldn't have topped myself over that little slut. You
needn't have wasted your night with me. You could have had
the pair of them, Roy, a threesome. They're both tarts!'

'Right, that does it.' Although two inches shorter than
Mark's six-foot frame, Eddie sprang into action and thumped
him on the jaw, knocking him against the wall. 'Don't you *ever*
call my girl a slut or a tart again. You stay away from her, Fisher.
Don't even *think* about blabbing to her mother, or I'll fucking
swing for you!'

As Mark regained his footing, Roy knocked him back down
with a swift right and blood spurted from his nose. 'That's for
calling my Sammy a tart!' Roy rubbed his knuckles as Mark
staggered to his feet. '*Nobody* calls my Sammy a tart and stays
upright. You'll do well to remember that.'

'Get the fuck out of my house or I'll call the police,' Mark
yelled, hands covering his nose, blood seeping through his
fingers.

'Just going,' Eddie said calmly, though he was seething
inside. 'Keep away from Jane,' he warned again and left the
room followed by Roy.

Mark's mother was standing in the hall as the pair walked down the stairs.

'What was all that shouting about?' she asked. 'Is Marky all right?'

'Nothing that a damp flannel and a bottle of TCP won't put right, Mrs F,' Roy said with a wry smile as they left the house, leaving her with a bewildered expression on her face.

'Want a fag now?' Roy threw Eddie the cigarette packet after they'd driven several miles in silence. 'Light one for me too.'

'Fucking hell, Jane will go mad! She told me not to hurt him.' Eddie lit two cigarettes and passed one to Roy.

'He asked for it though, Ed. He can't go around calling our girls tarts and get away with it.'

'Yeah, you're right, he did ask for it,' Eddie agreed, 'But Jane will still go mad. What if he presses charges?'

'He won't if he's got any sense.' Roy drew up outside his home. 'Fancy that joint now? Then we can get down to practising some songs for tonight.'

'Please, but don't let me overdo it. Angie's collecting Jonny later from my folks and she'll kick up a fuss if she suspects I'm even *slightly* stoned.' Eddie ran his hands through his hair. 'What a bloody day!'

'You need a bit of a lifter, Ed. You deserve it with all the crap you've had to put up with. I won't let you overdo it, I promise. You can catch up tonight at the gig. I'm really glad you got the job, by the way.' Roy patted his shoulder as they made their way indoors.

* * *

'Mark, who were those lads?' his mother called, struggling upstairs.

'Nobody, Mum.' He held a handkerchief to his nose.

'They said they were from your group. Oh, Marky, what have they done to you? I thought they were your friends, love.'

'Well, now you know different. Call Tony for me before he comes to pick me up. I can't play tonight looking like this, I'll probably have two black eyes later.'

'Young thugs! All that black leather and the way they swaggered upstairs as though they owned the place. I'm calling the police.'

'No, you're not. Do that, and I'll walk out and I won't come back.'

'Don't be such a silly boy, Mark. They attacked you in your own home. I don't care what you say, I'm calling the police.'

Mark stood in front of the door, barring her way. 'You're doing no such thing. And for fuck's sake, I am *not* a silly boy. I'm a bloody grown man. Jane was right about you today when she said you ruled my life.'

'Jane? When did *you* see Jane today?'

'I saw her at lunchtime. I asked her to give me another chance but she doesn't want to know.'

'I'm beginning to see things a bit more clearly now.' She narrowed her eyes. 'One of those thugs was the married man she dumped you for. She sent them round here to sort you out, didn't she?' She clutched at her chest. 'I feel quite ill when I think of how close you came to marrying that little trollop. Your father was a wonderful man. He would turn in his grave if he knew how you'd been carrying on with her.'

'Oh, don't start the theatrics again. I didn't have a father. Why do you go on and on about him as though he was some bloody saint? Okay, so you had a roll in the hay with some bloke who cleared off when he knew you were in the club!'

She caught her breath as Mark yanked open the top drawer of his dressing table and threw an envelope at her.

'I found this last year in one of the boxes you keep your private papers in. It's my birth certificate. It states quite clearly

Father Unknown. Don't look so bloody surprised, you old fool,' he spluttered as she collapsed on his bed. 'How long did you intend keeping the truth from me? Telling me he passed away before I was old enough to have known him properly. Knowing all the time I was a bastard! Well, you've dragged it out for a little too long, Mother. All that bloody virtue and piety. You called Jane names, never gave her a chance, when all the time *you* were no better. Talk about pot and kettle.'

She watched him throw the bloodied handkerchief to the floor and pick up his jacket from the bed.

'Forget calling Tony for me. I'll get cleaned up at his place.' He stormed out of the room and slammed the door.

Maude sat for a moment, breathing deeply. She could hear Mark rummaging around downstairs, probably looking for his car keys. She wiped her eyes and heaved herself off the bed. She made her way onto the landing and could hear her heart thudding in her ears. It drowned out the sound of her voice as she tried to speak. The front door slammed shut. She lost her footing on the top stair and yelled his name, but Mark was out of earshot as she tumbled head-first to the hallway below.

7

Eddie strolled into The Roulette Club, shook hands with Mario, his son Vincento, and gave Mario's daughter Rosa a kiss on the cheek. He waved at Roy and Phil, who were standing beside the stage where Kris was setting up his drums.

'This place looks fantastic.' Eddie looked around at the cream-painted walls hung with gold-framed publicity photos of stars and wondered how long it would be before The Raiders were up there with them. The seductive lighting cast shadows in the corners, where chrome chairs and tables decorated with vases of colourful freesias stood. His feet sank into the plush black and cream carpet. The place smelt of fresh paint and he breathed in the heady scent of the freesias, reminding him of his mum's perfume. 'Looks like the lounge of a posh hotel. It's a vast improvement on the old coffee bar, Mario.'

Mario smiled proudly. 'Thank you, Eddie. The flowers are Rosa's touch. It will be good to see you back with the boys, it's been a long time.'

'Too long,' Roy said as Kris dropped a cymbal and stamped about the stage.

Eddie turned and stared at the young man, whose skinny

profile seemed to bristle with suppressed rage. He was distracted by the opening of the entrance door as Stuart arrived with Sammy and Pat.

'Where's Jane and Tim?' Roy asked, planting a kiss on Sammy's lips.

'Tim's unloading his gear. Jane's on her way with John Grey and Margaret,' Sammy said, slipping off her coat and scarf. 'Is the cloakroom open yet, Rosa?'

'Follow me,' Rosa said. 'I like your outfit, Sam. Is it one of your own creations?'

'It is, and thanks,' Sammy said, of the blue silk halter-neck top and short black velvet skirt. 'Can we reserve that large table at the edge of the dance floor, please?' she asked as she and Pat followed Rosa to the cloakroom.

'I'll get you a card from Dad's office.' Rosa took their coats. She handed over numbered tickets and smiled as Sammy slipped hers into her shoe.

'Safest place. I can never find a cloakroom ticket if I put it in my bag,' Sammy said.

Rosa got the reserved card and gave it to Sammy. 'The tables to the left are reserved for family members. Though why all my aunts and uncles want to come, God only knows. They'll only complain about the noise. But it's a special night for Dad, so I suppose their presence is to be expected.'

'Mac and Jackie are coming later. We'll need quite a few chairs,' Sammy said as she popped the card on the table.

Roy's face lit up as he overheard the girls' conversation. 'Mac's coming? Brilliant, I'm almost out of supplies.'

'Shhhh!' Vincento looked to where his father was standing by the bar, his back to them. 'If Dad thinks Mac's dealing in the club, he'll ban him forever.'

'It's okay,' Roy said. 'I've enough to be going on with. My folks have gone to the caravan for the weekend so we're back at my place after the gig. You and Rosa are very welcome to join us.'

Vincento's face broke into a broad smile. 'Okay if I bring a bird?'

'Bring as many as you like, Vinnie. The more the merrier, although *I* of course only have eyes for my lovely Sammy,' he added, as Sammy shot daggers at him.

'Watch your step, Cantello,' she warned him.

'Of course, my petal. Is that bar up and running yet? A man could die of thirst in this place.'

'I'll go and see,' Sammy said. 'Come and help me carry the drinks, Pat.'

'A quiet word, Roy.' Eddie pulled him to one side.

'What's on your mind?' Roy offered him a cigarette and a light.

'It's Kris.' Eddie took a lengthy drag and exhaled slowly. 'Don't think he's very happy that I'm singing with the band tonight. Hasn't even let on to me yet.'

'He's a miserable fucker at the best of times,' Roy said. 'Probably sulking because I told him you'll be drumming with us again in a few weeks.'

'Thought so. Look, I don't want to upset the applecart with the group.'

'This band was ours, Ed. Me you and Tim, *we* founded The Raiders. Kris was only brought in on a temporary basis and he's always known that.'

'Yeah, but he's been with you three years now. He probably looks on it as a permanent job. I can't afford to buy another kit at the moment, you need to keep him sweet.'

Roy patted his shoulder. 'Buy a set when you start your new job. Get them on the never-never. You'll get a good staff discount, too.'

'I will. But let's get tonight out of the way first. I feel a bit nervous. It's a long time since I was on stage.'

'Well, look.' Roy pointed to the door, where Jane was entering with John Grey and Margaret. 'Here's the love of your life, looking incredibly sexy in that little black dress.' He handed Eddie a set of keys. 'Go and relax with her in the back of the van for a while. We'll do the soundcheck without you this one time.'

'You sure?'

'Positive. We sounded pretty good together earlier. But then, we always did,' he added modestly.

Eddie burst out laughing and went to greet Jane. He kissed her and took her hand. 'I love you,' he said.

'Love you, too.' She wound her arms around his neck and kissed him back.

'You look lovely in that little black number.' He squeezed her affectionately.

'Thanks, Ed. Mum said it was too short, as usual.'

'It's just right. But don't bend over in front of Phil and Roy. I take it you didn't get any aggro from your mum about me when you got home?'

'Nothing was said. Mark must have been bluffing about going to see her. Did you have a word with him?'

'Err, yeah. We need to talk about that but not right now.' He dangled the van keys in front of her. 'Fancy half an hour on our own?'

Her eyes lit up and she smiled.

He slung his arm around her shoulders and led her outside. 'Love your perfume. What is it?'

'Chanel No5. I treated myself. Needed cheering up after the row with Mark.'

'He won't be bothering you again.' He unlocked the van door and helped her inside.

'It's a bit dark,' she muttered, stumbling over something.

He flicked his lighter on and looked around. 'There's some blankets and cushions on that little bunk.' He grabbed an armful, spread them out on the floor, pulled her down beside him and kissed her. 'I can't get enough of you.'

'Nor I you.' She sighed blissfully as his lips lingered on hers and his hand stroked her thighs.

'We haven't got long. Take your dress off, it'll get really creased.' He undid the back zip, helped her out of it and placed it on the bunk.

'Ed, did you remember to get anything? We can't leave it to chance again.'

'Course I did.' He fished a Durex from his jeans pocket, wriggled out of his clothes and flung them on top of hers. He pulled her back into his arms, dropping kisses down her front. Then he kissed her, sighing into her hair. 'Oh, babe, I need you so much.' He quickly rolled the Durex onto his erection. 'I've dreamt about moments like this so often.'

She arched her back as he entered her, and wrapped her legs around him, running her fingers down his spine, pulled him ever closer as he thrust into her, lips searching frantically. Her orgasm was intense and she shuddered and cried out his name. With every nerve in his body on fire he felt relief almost simultaneously and collapsed on top, his face buried in her shoulder.

'Christ, Jane, that was good!' he gasped. 'Sorry it was short, but it was most definitely sweet. We'll have more time later when we go to Roy's.'

They lay a while longer, locked together, murmuring endearments when someone knocked on the door.

'Only me,' Sammy called and pushed the door open slightly. 'You decent? Can I come in?'

'Hang on, Sam.' Jane pulled the blankets around her and Eddie. 'Okay, come in and shut the door before anyone sees us.'

'Sorry to intrude. Roy sent me to say the group's on in ten. Also, Cathy's just walked into the club with a few girls. I didn't see Angie, but I thought you should know.'

'Fuck! The bloody coven's the last thing I need in there

tonight.' Eddie sat up and lit a cigarette. 'You sure she wasn't with them?'

'Positive. Rosa hasn't seen her on coat check. Neither has Vinnie on the door.'

'She told me she was going into Manchester tonight with Cathy and the girls from work.' He frowned. 'So where the hell is she?'

'Maybe they changed their minds. Perhaps Angie's gone home already,' Sammy said.

'Doubt it. She's never home before two when she's out with that lot.'

'Well, she's definitely not in the club, so don't worry about it. But I thought I'd better come and warn you about the others. It's getting quite crowded in there now. They're sitting right at the back. You can probably sneak in without them seeing you.'

'Thanks for that, Sam,' he said. 'We'll get dressed and come back in separately. Tell Roy I'm on my way.'

'Okay. See you soon.' She closed the door behind her.

'I *hope* Angie doesn't turn up,' Jane said, reaching for her clothes.

Eddie took a final drag on his cigarette and stubbed out the end on the van floor.

'So do I. Bet she's sent Cathy to spy on me.' He jumped to his feet, pulled on his pants and jeans, and Jane handed him his T-shirt. 'I'm sorry to drag you into this bloody mess, Jane.'

'Hey, don't be sorry,' she said. 'I wouldn't be here if I didn't love you.' She put her clothes back on, brushed her hair and touched up her lipstick. 'You ready?'

He nodded. 'Fancy a ride on the bike tomorrow?' he said as he helped her down the van steps. 'We could go out to Wilmslow, have a look at the new shop then take a stroll in Norman's Woods. We need time to talk about Mark, I don't want to spoil tonight by talking about him now.'

'What's so bad that you can't tell me later?' she said as he locked the van.

'Because we'll be at Roy's house and everyone will be there. Much better if I tell you tomorrow.'

At the club entrance he pulled her into his arms. 'You go in first. Tell Roy I'm coming. He'll no doubt have spotted Cathy and the coven. He'll understand the delay. I love you, Jane. Thanks for a wonderful time.'

'Thank *you*. I love you too.'

He watched her walk away, shapely hips swaying, and glossy brown hair swinging on her shoulders. In spite of the problems he knew lay ahead for them, he was proud as Punch that she was his girl.

* * *

Jane found Roy at the reserved table chatting with Phil, John Grey and Margaret. They were joined by Roy's dealer friend Alan Mackenzie and his girlfriend, Jackie.

'Jane, long time no see.' Mac greeted her with a friendly grin. 'Roy tells me things are back on with you and Ed.'

'They are,' she said, smiling at the handsome young man who had the mysterious dark looks of a Romany Gypsy. 'But it's kind of top secret.'

'My lips are sealed,' he said, as Eddie sauntered into the club and waved in their direction. 'He's looking a bit worse for wear. What have you done to the poor lad?'

She giggled and handed the van keys to Roy. 'Thanks, Roy. Much appreciated.'

'Better than The Lakes last weekend, eh?' Phil winked knowingly.

'No comparison.'

'Well, that's it now. You've blown your chance, Jane. You'll never forgive yourself for not taking me up on my offer of a date.'

'What I've never had I'll never miss, Phil,' she quipped back.

'Sammy's trying to catch your attention, Jane,' Roy said. 'Looks like she's bursting with gossip. Go and see what she wants while we get Ed ready to go on stage.'

Jane joined Sammy by the coat check with Rosa. 'What's up?'

'I asked Cathy where she'd been earlier. She said the Royal Oak. I asked where Angie was, and she said she's probably with Eddie. I told her Eddie was here tonight to sing with The Raiders and her face went really red. She said she'd forgotten about that. But Eddie definitely said Angie was going out with Cathy tonight, didn't he?'

'He did,' Jane confirmed.

'Well, she's obviously lying to him about where she's going and who she's with,' Sammy finished on a triumphant note.

'I don't know what to think,' Jane said, frowning. 'Unless she's gone into town with some of the girls she works with.'

'Two of the girls with Cathy are from the salon. They looked sheepish as well,' Sammy said.

'Oh well, as long as she doesn't turn up here I don't care. I'm going out with Ed tomorrow. He'll probably have an idea what she's been up to by then. Anyway, look, they're going.'

They watched as Cathy and the coven rose as one and made for the door.

* * *

Eddie took another drag on the joint he was sharing with Roy and handed it back. 'I feel better for that.' He changed into stage clothes of red satin shirt, black leather trousers and matching waistcoat, identical to the other Raiders.

'Ready, mate?' Roy ground the joint end out on the dressing room floor. 'You do a solo first, then we'll go straight into our Everly Brothers duets. You still feeling nervous?'

'I'm okay. The joint helped.'

'You'll be fine,' Tim said and Phil patted his arm, while Kris nodded in his direction.

'It's like riding a bike, Ed,' Roy said. 'You need to get back in the saddle. You've a fantastic voice, not to mention your bloody good looks. The birds will go crazy when they see you again. Right, come on, the jukebox has just gone off. Stand behind the curtain and I'll give you a big intro.'

* * *

'This is it,' Jane whispered to John Grey. The jukebox fell silent. The house lights dimmed. 'I feel sick with nerves, so God knows how Eddie must be feeling right now.'

'He'll be fine, Jane. He's like Roy, born to be a performer,' John said. 'Frank James is here tonight, but he's keeping a low profile. Roy called him to let him know Ed's back. He hasn't told the group in case they panic and do a poor show.'

'Wow! Roy's been going on about a contract with Frank for ages. Since the time he turned them down because Eddie left.'

'Best agent in town. Fingers crossed, eh?' John smiled as Roy appeared from behind the black velvet curtains and people on the dance floor surged towards the stage.

Roy cleared his throat, one, two-ed into the mic and grinned broadly at the ripple of applause.

'ARE YOU READY TO ROCK?' he yelled.

'YESSSSSS!' the audience roared back.

He cupped a hand to his ear. 'I didn't hear you! I said, ARE YOU READY TO ROCK?' A wild cheer rose and Roy nodded. 'That's better. So you're all awake then? Now, the moment you've all been waiting for... I'd like to introduce you to our new band member. You'll remember him as our original drummer, but tonight we're lucky to have him sing again with The Raiders. Ladies and gentlemen, put your hands together for MR EDDIE MELLOR!'

The curtains swung back, the band struck up with the opening chords of Sam Cooke's 'Another Saturday Night', and Eddie leapt forward, grabbed a microphone and began to sing.

Girls at the front of the stage stared up with adoring eyes as Jane watched her boyfriend singing in front of a captive audience for the first time in over three years. Tears tumbled down her cheeks. Jackie passed her a handful of tissues.

'Thanks, Jackie. He loves it – he should never have left.'

The song came to an end, the applause subsided and Eddie leapt wildly around the stage. 'Thank you,' he shouted. 'THANK YOU. I'm thrilled to be back. The next three songs will be Everly Brothers duets with Roy.' The pair launched into 'All I Have to Do Is Dream', their voices harmonising perfectly. Eddie looked across, caught Jane's eye and smiled.

She felt a shiver down her spine and smiled back: their song.

The audience went wild as Eddie and Roy followed with 'Wake up Little Susie' and 'Cathy's Clown'. The girls at the front reached out to shake their hands.

'Thank you, thank you so much,' Eddie called out. 'What a great audience you are. Our next number is a song Roy likes to think was written especially for him!' He grinned as Roy rolled his eyes, played the opening chords, and the group launched into 'Great Balls of Fire'.

The audience jived and Jane pulled Sammy to her feet. 'Come on, I haven't done this for ages.'

Sammy was laughing fit to burst. 'Trust Ed to say that about Roy,' she howled. 'Many a true word's spoken in jest!'

The song ended and Sammy whistled through her fingers. Tim strolled to the front of the stage and took a bow. 'It's the quiet one's turn now,' he announced, laughing as the audience cheered. 'This is for all you Chuck Berry fans.'

Tim's rendition of 'Sweet Little Sixteen' brought cheers and stamping. Roy did the duck walk up and down the stage while playing his guitar.

The deafening applause and whistling died away. Roy wiped his hand across his sweaty forehead and announced, 'To give the rest of us a well-earned break, I'll hand you over to our resident Love God, MR PHIL JACKSON! Be careful, girls, light the blue touchpaper if you must, but stand well back.'

Phil stepped forward, to the delight of the fans reaching out to him. 'One at a time, girls, please! Thanks for the intro, Roy. I'm gonna dedicate a little ditty tonight to two very special people. One of them's our own Eddie Mellor.' Jane's hand flew to her mouth as he continued, 'The other is a lovely lady who's turned me down so many times. Jane, darling, this one's for you and Ed.' Phil began to sing Eddie Cochran's 'Three Steps to Heaven'. As he reached the chorus, Eddie joined him.

Jane leant towards Sammy, a tear in her eye. 'Fancy Phil being so romantic.'

'Yeah, who'd have thought? Look at Ed's face, Jane. He can't take his eyes off you. It's the best thing that's happened to him in a long time. That and getting back with you.'

Jane smiled through her tears. 'I can't stop crying tonight, but they're happy tears.'

'You big softie,' Sammy said, handing her a tissue.

* * *

Roy watched Eddie enjoying himself. He'd been right to encourage him to sing tonight. Frank James had shown his face at the beginning of the show and smiled in Roy's direction. He nodded discreetly towards Kris, slid his hand across his throat then looked pointedly at Eddie. Roy got the message. With Ed onboard drumming again, Roy knew the group would stand a much better chance of that coveted contract with Frank's organisation. Not only could Ed sing well, he'd always had a reputation for being the best drummer in the area.

* * *

The audience went wild, shouting for more. Phil and Eddie grinned with delight and Eddie blew a kiss in Jane's direction.

Roy slowed down the tempo next. Eddie excused himself and leapt from the stage, fighting his way through the tightly packed crowd to claim his girl. He pulled her into his arms and kissed her while Roy warbled 'Love Me Tender'.

'What did you think?' he whispered, nuzzling her ear.

'You were wonderful, Ed. The whole show, it was brilliant. When you sang with Phil, I had the biggest lump in my throat.'

'Trust him to do that dedication. No doubt it'll get back to Angie, but I don't give a toss. I suppose Phil thinks we're a real couple now.'

Jane grinned. 'Well... if that earlier performance in the van was anything to go by...'

He laughed and hugged her. 'Quite! Better get back on stage for the last song,' he said as Roy took his applause and strutted up and down. 'Just look at him go; he bloody loves it. He's desperate for fame. Mind you, aren't we all?'

'You'll be famous one day, Ed. I feel it in my bones,' she said.

He kissed her and ran back into the crowds, a huge grin on his face.

* * *

Eddie picked up Jane on Sunday afternoon and they rode to the small but rapidly expanding town of Wilmslow. He pulled up in front of the new shopping development.

'They're very tall.' Jane clambered off the bike and gazed at the smart façade of the three-storey, red-brick buildings. A patrolling security watchman caught her eye and smiled.

'Afternoon. Anything I can do to help you, miss?'

'Do you have any idea which one will be the music shop?'

The man pushed his cap to the back of his head. 'Well now, music shop's second from the left, with a ladies' dress shop right next door.'

'Thank you. Why are the buildings so tall?'

'Two floors for shops and top level's luxury flats. The access to them's round the back with their own car park. We're having paving and landscaping at the front here and there'll be fancy cast-iron benches to sit on.'

They said goodbye to the watchman.

'Blimey, it's a bit posher than Stockport High Street,' Jane said enviously. 'No grotty old cobbles for you *and* you've got fancy benches. You won't know you're born!'

'Bit of jealousy?' Eddie teased as she pulled a sulky face. 'Get on the bike, Norman's Woods the next stop. We might bump into Roy and Sammy.'

'They'll be at his house making the most of their time alone,' she said, with a knowing grin. 'Sam told me his mum and dad aren't back until tonight.'

'"Great Balls of Fire", eh?' He laughed and revved up the engine. 'Hang on tight.'

In a small clearing, Eddie took off his jacket and laid it on the floor. Jane sat down and patted the space beside her, slipping off her own jacket. She placed it around both their shoulders and snuggled close, shivering.

'You're a bit edgy today, Ed. What's bugging you?'

'Don't go mad with me.' He lit a cigarette and took a drag. 'I thumped Mark on the chin yesterday. I shouldn't have, but he was calling you names. Roy thumped him too, made his nose bleed.'

'Oh, you didn't! Was he badly hurt?'

'Not really, just his nose.'

'Why did Roy thump him?'

'I warned Mark to stay away from you. A verbal warning, that's all it was supposed to be. Then he starts mouthing off, calling you and Sammy names. Roy saw red and lamped him one.'

'Sammy's never done Mark any harm,' Jane said, frowning.

'Well, it serves him right then. Now tell me what else is on your mind.'

'It's her, Angie. I took my stuff to the flat earlier. I told you I'm moving back in for a week or two to sort things out and see a bit more of Jonny. I tried calling her at work, but she won't discuss anything with me on the phone. She can't ignore me if I'm under the same roof. She was looking rough as a bear's arse when I walked in. I asked her where she went last night and she nearly bit my bloody head off. Said she'd been to a club in Manchester with Cathy and the girls from work. I called her bluff. Told her Cathy was at The Roulette Club. She stared at me for ages, grabbed her bag and stormed off.'

'Do you think she's seeing someone?'

'Yeah, I do. A guy she works with, but I've no proof. I want a divorce, Jane, as soon as possible.'

'Have you mentioned divorce yet?'

'I've tried, but like I said, she won't speak to me. It's pointless staying married to her now I'm back with you. I want to be able to see you without us having to sneak around.'

Jane looked at his unhappy face and her heart went out to him. 'It'll be all right, Ed, you'll see. But promise me one thing when you move back into the flat.'

'What's that?'

'Don't share a bed with her.'

'I'll be on the sofa, as usual,' he assured her. 'I won't be able to stand being there for long, but I miss Jonny so much. I wish I knew for certain whether or not she can stop me seeing him. I'll have to take Roy's advice and talk to a solicitor.'

He rolled onto his stomach and flashed a wicked grin. 'Fancy coming to my folks' place tonight while they're playing whist at Auntie Minnie's? I wanna make love to you again.'

She smiled. 'Yep. That's more like my Ed.'

'Good. I'll get another flat as soon as I'm sorted. We need somewhere private to be together. I could ask about the new flats that bloke just mentioned. Be handy for work, living above the shop.'

'True. But I bet they'll be dead expensive.'

'We'll see. Let's walk before we can run.'

8

Mark rubbed a hand over his bristly chin, fidgeting to get comfortable on a plastic chair in the hospital waiting room. He was tired, hungover, and his mouth felt like the bottom of a budgie's cage. He could murder a fag and wished the nurse would hurry up with the promised tea. He glared at a snotty-nosed kid, peeping out from behind his mother's skirt. She had her nose stuck in a magazine, oblivious to the brat, who was now sticking his tongue out.

Mark glared and the kid glared back. Mark clenched his fists and shut his eyes. His head was pounding and the brat was squealing now. The noise was piercing his brain and he felt ready to strangle the little sod. He could still smell the perfume of the girl he'd picked up last night. Cheap shit. Not like the stuff Jane wore. He couldn't even remember the girl's name now. Vicky, Nicky, something like that. She'd been a good shag though. He wished he'd got her phone number now.

Perhaps Tony's bird would know it. Anyway, that was the least of his worries. He glanced at his watch: 9:00 a.m. He'd been here over an hour. What a fucking joke. The milkman had found his mother at the bottom of the stairs. Stupid old bat. That was a fucking joke, too. What the hell happens now? They told him she'd broken her hip. Well, *he* couldn't look after her. She'd have to go in a home. He could kill Eddie Mellor, this was all his fault.

The door swung open and the nurse waddled towards him with a steaming mug, followed by an equally large bearded doctor, who frowned at the noisy brat. Mark took the mug and had a good drink of tea. The brat's name was called and the mother grabbed his hand and led him away.

'Thank Christ for that!' Mark grunted.

The nurse smiled and left him alone with the doctor.

'Is Mother okay?' he asked as the doctor looked at his notes.

'She's in surgery, Mr Fisher. She's broken her right wrist as well as her hip and right ankle. We'll be keeping her in hospital for some time.'

'And then what?'

'We'll have to see how she goes on. Stairs will be out of the question. She has arthritis, her joints won't heal quickly.'

'Okay.' Mark nodded slowly as he took in the news.

'I suggest you go home and come back this afternoon with some nightwear and toiletries. We'll have another chat then.'

'Right,' Mark said. 'I'll do that.'

* * *

Mark wandered around his mother's bedroom. He took a small suitcase from the wardrobe and threw in a couple of flannel nighties, her quilted housecoat and the pink pom-pom slippers he'd given her last Christmas. Her floral toiletry bag contained talc, scented soap and a new white facecloth; it was almost as if she was expecting to be going somewhere at short notice.

He packed her reading glasses and the book that lay open

on her bed. If he walked past the allotments on his way to
Tony's place, he could get a bunch of daffodils. Tony was going
to run him back to Stockport General when he was ready. He'd
enjoyed a long soak, shaved, washed his hair and donned clean
jeans and a T-shirt.

On a stupid impulse, prior to packing the case, he'd called
Jane's home. Her mother answered. She said Jane was out, probably with Sammy and Pat.

'Can I pass on a message?'

'Not really,' he replied. 'Mum fell downstairs yesterday and
she's in hospital.'

'I'm sorry to hear that.' Jane's mum sympathised when he
told her his mother was on the floor all night. 'If there's anything
I can do, get in touch. I'll tell Jane to call you when she gets
home.'

He slammed the receiver down. Jane was probably out with
Mellor. When she got his message, she might work out that his
mother's accident happened shortly after Eddie and Roy's visit
to his home. He was in no doubt that Mellor would have
boasted of the punch-up. She might think it was *his* fault that
his mother was injured. She might even be so angry with Mellor
that she'd dump him and come back to where she belonged.

'And pigs might fly,' he grunted. Why on earth would Jane
give a toss about his mother? He made tea and toast, carried
them through to the lounge and sat with his feet up on the
coffee table, something he was normally forbidden from doing.
He lit a cigarette and blew a cloud of smoke above his head. He
smiled. Smoking indoors, something else he was forbidden from
doing. If his mother were kept in hospital for ages, he would
have some freedom. Throw a party or two. Find out who he
shagged last night and get her to stay over the odd time.

Studying the old-fashioned floral wallpaper and drab
brown-velvet curtains that had been around since his childhood,
he decided he'd make some changes. Trendy bright colours

would look good in here and modern pictures and plants. He'd buy a copy of *Ideal Home*, get a few ideas. If his mother ended up in a nursing home, he could live and work in Chester during the week and spend the weekends here. The more he rolled the idea around in his head, the more he liked it.

What if she died? Was the house paid for? She always said, when she was gone, the house would be his. But he'd never seen any proof she owned it. He finished his toast and coffee, lit another cigarette, revelling in the fact that she wasn't there, nagging him to go outside. He took his mug and plate back to the kitchen to wash but dumped them in the sink instead.

In the spacious dining room, he opened the sideboard cupboard and took out two boxes containing his mother's private papers. He picked up a sheaf and sifted through the insurance policies and old bills dating back years. Did she ever chuck anything away? He came across his old school reports and paused for a moment. He'd been privately educated. How had she managed to pay for that? He'd never thought to question it, but the money must have come from somewhere.

He threw the bills and policies back in the box, returned it to the cupboard and took out the smaller box, in which he'd recently discovered his birth certificate. He remembered now the shock of seeing it and how he'd kept removing it from the envelope, re-checking, just in case there had been a mistake. But there was no getting away from the truth: he was a bastard. He'd been dying to confront his mother every time she'd called Jane names, but never meant yesterday's confrontation to happen as it did. He felt sure that after all these years she'd never tell him the truth about his father.

At the bottom of the box, concealed away in a chocolate box with a traditional thatched cottage picture lid, he found a bundle of letters addressed to his mother. Each bore an Isle of Wight postmark. He felt his heart skip a beat. His place of birth had been registered as the Isle of Wight. There were two dozen letters in all and they dated from 1942, which, he reckoned, would tie in with his conception. He opened the first letter. Someone called Amelia Saunders had signed it.

He read the first few lines. Amelia was a married friend of his mother who lived on the island. There were references to escapades that had happened during their twenties. The days referred to were long ago. By his reckoning his mother would have been in her forties when she received this letter.

He skimmed through the rest of the neatly written lines. There were no clues as to his birth. There was an enquiry about his health and a request for an up-to-date photograph, but the contents were mainly about Amelia and the fact that she was undergoing hospital tests.

As he continued to read the rest of the letter, the afternoon stood still. 'What the fuck...?' he muttered and stared at the pages in his hand. He threw them down and snatched up another envelope. Tearing it open, he hurriedly scanned the contents. He ignored the telephone when it rang. It grew dark outside as he ploughed through the rest of the letters. The phone rang again. This time, he answered.

'Mark, it's Tony. I thought you were going back to the hospital to see your mum? I called earlier but nobody answered.'

'Yeah, I'm sorry, mate,' Mark said. 'Can you come over? I've made a discovery and I've no one else to share it with.'

'Sure. I'm on my way.'

Mark was sifting through the letters again, putting them in date order, when Tony knocked on the back door.

'In here,' Mark called as Tony strolled into the dining room, waving a bottle of whisky. 'Ah, brilliant, and bloody hell, am I ready for it! Grab a couple of glasses from the cupboard in the lounge. Get the posh ones.'

Tony hurried back with two cut-glass tumblers and placed

them on the table. 'Old Maude would have your hide if she saw you drinking out of these.'

'Not any more,' Mark said. 'They belong to me. Everything does – the house, the contents and a whole lot more.'

'What do you mean?' Tony frowned and sat down opposite. 'Has your old lady popped her clogs?'

'In a manner of speaking, yeah, she has.'

'I'm really sorry, mate.' Tony patted his arm. 'I know you didn't get on with her, but still, she *was* your old mum. Were you with her at the end when she actually snuffed it?'

Mark shook his head. 'No, unfortunately, I wasn't. She passed away when I was two years old. I never really knew her.' He smiled at Tony's puzzled expression.

'What you on about? You been at the booze before I arrived?'

'It's simple really: Maude's not my mother.'

'What? Don't be so fucking stupid! Of course she's your mum.'

Mark indicated the letters on the table. 'I've been trying to find out if this house is paid for in case she dies. I was concerned about my future and it's something I've never discussed with her so I've looked through her private papers. I told you I was illegitimate that day I found my birth certificate. If only I'd had the guts to look a bit further. Anyway, no matter – I suspect the old cow kept this from me for her own selfish reasons.'

'But you showed me your birth certificate. It says Maude's your mother.'

'That's what really pisses me off, the deception. While I was having a root, I found this box of letters. My past's been hidden away in a cupboard almost all my life.'

'You've lost me.' Tony scratched his head. 'Pour us a drink and explain.'

Mark's hand shook as he poured the whisky and he knocked *his* back in seconds.

'I needed that. It's a long story. I've pieced it together from the letters and made a few notes as I read them. Anyway, the basic facts are these. My real mum was Amelia Saunders, a friend of Maude's. She married a naval officer and they lived on the Isle of Wight. She had an affair with the local doctor, who got her pregnant.'

Mark looked at Tony, who was staring at him. 'Her husband was away because of the war, so apart from my father, Maude was the only other person who knew about the expected baby. My father agreed she should look after Amelia, before and after my birth.'

He poured himself another drink and took a slug while Tony listened intently, nodding now and again.

Mark stood up and paced the room as he continued. 'Amelia and my father couldn't be together because of his wife and kids so they decided when she gave birth that Maude's name would go on the birth certificate as mother. Amelia hid her pregnancy. The plan was to tell her husband that her friend Maude had given birth to a baby she daren't take home and Amelia would bring me up – she and her husband were unable to have kids of their own. You following me so far, Tony?'

'Erm, I think so,' Tony said and knocked back his whisky.

'My father delivered me at Amelia's place with Maude's help. They got away with the plan for a year or so. Maude returned home, Amelia had her own baby to look after, and my father's wife and kids were none the wiser. Then Amelia's husband was injured and sent home. He didn't want her looking after Maude's baby any more, but she refused to give me up. They split up and he went off with another woman.'

Mark paused, offered Tony a cigarette and lit one himself. 'According to the letters, Jack Mainwaring, my father, was a wealthy man. He'd inherited money and property and supported Amelia and me for another year. Then she was taken ill and he asked Maude to come back and look after me while she was having treatment for cancer.'

'Bloody hell!'

Tony refilled the glasses.

'She died a few months later. With my father's permission, Maude brought me to Stockport. This house and my private education came out of his pocket. He paid Maude an allowance to take care of me. There's a couple of letters from him confirming their arrangement. There's a trust fund set up for me, which I'm to receive on my twenty-first birthday. The house is mine; *everything* is in fact.'

'So, Maude's your guardian, not your mother? Maybe she's planning to drop it on your toes on your birthday in July?' Tony said. 'A surprise, like.'

'I doubt it,' Mark sneered. 'All those fucking years she's laid down the law! That bloody woman ruled me with a rod of iron. Well, no more, Tony – the worm's well and truly turned.'

'It's some story. But are you sure you've read everything properly and you're not getting all mixed up?'

'No mix-up. I've read and re-read the letters. There's a solicitor's letter here too. It's from a practice in Portsmouth acting for Jack Mainwaring. I'll ring them tomorrow to verify the details. Here's a photo of me with Amelia and Jack and also one of them together. Just look at my parents. Weren't they a good-looking couple? My mother's so pretty compared to plain old Maude.'

Tony took the black and white photograph. Amelia was slender with long, curly hair. Jack was tall, of slim build, and they were smartly dressed in the fashions of the forties. He smiled and nodded. 'That's where you get your six foot from, mate. They're an attractive pair. Actually, you look just like your father.'

'That's what I thought.'

'Is he still alive?'

'Don't know. He was a lot older than Amelia, about fifty-six when I was born.'

'That'll make him seventy-seven now,' Tony said. 'Is there a contact address?'

'Just a box number. If he didn't want to know me then because of his family, he's hardly likely to want to know me now. I'll ask if he's still alive when I call the solicitor tomorrow, but it may be best to let sleeping dogs lie.'

'Probably wisest,' Tony agreed and sat back in his chair. 'So, this gaff's all yours then?'

'Yeah, and I'm gonna make some changes. I'll re-decorate and get shut of Maude's old junk. You could be my lodger. We can have girls stay over whenever we want. By the way, did that bird from last night leave her phone number for me?'

'Vicky, yeah.' Tony dug in his jeans pocket and handed Mark a page torn from a diary. 'There's a bit of a message with it. She likes you, Mark.'

Mark ran his hands wearily through his hair. 'I'll get in touch with her. Don't want anything serious though. I still love Jane. I know when I'm pissed off I call her names, but I'd have her back now and forgive her everything.'

'You don't seem too upset or bothered by your discovery,' Tony said. 'I'd be freaking out all over the show if it was me.'

'I feel fucking angry more than anything. That woman's deprived me of so much. She'd no right to keep something so important from me. I need to come to terms with it, take stock, make changes. I'll start with this place, make it my own. And I'm determined to get Jane back from Mellor. I'll have that ring on her finger again if it bloody well kills me!'

Tony sighed and swallowed the last of his drink. 'What do you intend to do about Maude? This is her home, you can't just chuck her out on the streets.'

'I'll put her in a nursing home or get her a flat. She was having trouble with the stairs here anyway and it'll be even worse now. I'll have a word at the hospital, see what they suggest. When Jane hears I own this place and we can get married and start a family without having to save up for years, she'll be back like a shot,' he insisted. 'Mellor's got sod-all to offer her in comparison and you can't live on so-called love alone.' He waved the whisky bottle in Tony's direction. 'Let's finish this in the lounge and smoke a joint to celebrate.'

9

MARCH 1964

Eddie switched off the insistent alarm, stretched his cramped limbs and groaned. After a week of sleeping on the sofa again, he'd had enough. He leapt up and folded the blankets, grinning with anticipation. It was the first day of his new job and he was really looking forward to it, not least because he would be in Jane's company all day.

He could hear Angie talking to Jonny as he passed the bedroom door. The one thing he'd really missed while staying with his parents was Jonny's big smile first thing in the morning.

He washed and shaved carefully. His appearance hadn't mattered at the factory, but the last thing he needed on his clean shirt was a dribble of blood. He splashed on Old Spice, fighting the urge to shout 'Ouch!' In the sitting room, his one and only suit, brown pinstriped, hung from the picture rail, alongside a new cream shirt and brown and beige spotted tie. He dressed hurriedly, went through to the kitchen and made a mug of coffee.

Angie appeared behind him, followed closely by Jonny.

'Morning,' she grunted. She lifted Jonny onto a chair at the kitchen table and fastened a bib under his chin.

'Morning, yourself. Err, you look nice.' It was an effort to be civil but it was better than rowing in front of Jonny. She was immaculate as always, but her pretty face was twisted with her usual scowl. He sighed as she stared at him. 'No hidden agenda, I'm just paying you a compliment.'

'Thanks.' Her hand flew to her mouth. 'Give Jonny his breakfast. I think I ate something at my mother's yesterday that didn't agree with me.'

Shoulders heaving, she dashed away. He could hear her throwing up and shook his head. 'Too much Bacardi, that's what's wrong with your mummy.' He tipped cornflakes into a bowl, splashed on milk and sprinkled them with sugar. 'There you go, Jonny, eat up, then you'll grow into a big boy.' He ruffled his dark curls. Jonny beamed at him and tucked in, milk dribbling down his chin.

Angie shuffled back into the kitchen and sat down. He placed a mug of coffee in front of her. She pushed it away, turning up her nose. 'No thanks, Ed. I'll have water, please.'

'Feeling better now?' he asked, handing her a glass of water.

'So-so. I knew I shouldn't have had that sandwich, pork and me have never seen eye to eye.' She stared at him. 'Where are *you* going, dressed up like a tailor's dummy?'

'I wondered if you'd notice.' He sat down next to Jonny, picked up his mug and took a sip. 'I'm starting a new job today.'

'You've got a new job?'

'Yeah! I'm not totally useless, you know.'

'I never said you were. Why didn't you say something? You're supposed to discuss things like that with your wife. That's what marriage is all about.'

'Really?' He raised an eyebrow. 'I always thought marriage was about two people loving and respecting each other. You wouldn't even begin to know the meaning of the words, Angela.'

Jonny looked from one to the other, his lips trembling at their raised voices.

Eddie lifted him down, wiped his chin and removed his bib. 'Go and find your cars, son. Mummy will take you to Granny's soon and Grandpa will play racing with you.'

Jonny toddled off down the hall as Angie stared at Eddie, blinking back tears.

'You *never* loved me, or respected me for that matter. Well, I'll make it easy for you. You've been itching all week to bring up the subject of divorce – well, fine, go! If freedom's what you want, clear off! But you won't see Jonny, and I mean that.'

'You can quit using that threat. It won't wash with me any more. Anyway, I've no time to argue. I'll be late for work, and that's the last thing I need on my first day.'

'You still haven't told me about the job,' she called as he made to leave the kitchen. 'Is it in a nice office or something?'

He turned. 'Nothing so bloody boring.'

'Well, what then?'

'You're looking at the manager of the new Flanagan and Grey's music store in Wilmslow.' He was unable to suppress the hint of pride in his voice as her jaw dropped.

'Oh! But I thought those new shops weren't opening for another month or so?'

'That's right, they're not. I'm training at the Stockport branch for a few weeks, getting to know the ropes.'

'Jane works there.' She spat the words out with venom.

'She does.' He looked her in the eye. 'So?'

She stood up and pushed back her chair. 'I bloody knew it! You're seeing her again. I heard a rumour that she'd dumped Mark Fisher. It all falls into place now, it's because she's seeing you.'

'Don't be ridiculous! Do you honestly think Jane would want to know me after what I put her through?'

'You *are* seeing Jane, you liar! I can tell by your face. You're seeing her again and I bet you're screwing her!'

'Can you blame me?' he yelled, forgetting momentarily that

he was trying to protect Jane. 'You haven't let me near you for months. What more can you expect?'

'So, you don't deny it? You're having an affair with Jane.'

'I'm admitting nothing.'

'You don't need to, you bastard! Well, you can get lost. I don't want you here. Go back to your mother, if she'll have you, and I bet she won't. Not when I tell her what you've been up to.'

'Mum already knows.'

'Your mother knows?' she screeched. 'She approves of you having an affair, knowing you're married to me? Oh, this just gets better.'

'I didn't say she approved but she knows how bad it is between us. I'll move out again but I want to see Jonny. You can't stop me. He's *my* child too, I have rights.'

She stared at him for a long moment then turned away. 'You can see him on Sunday afternoons,' she mumbled over her shoulder.

'Sunday afternoons. Is that all? What about in the week? He'll wonder where I am again. Who'll read him a bedtime story if *I* don't? *You* can never be bothered. You're always too busy doing your bloody nails or something!'

'Just be thankful I've agreed to Sundays for now. You should have thought about Jonny before you started shagging Jane.'

'Well, who's shagging *you*, Angie?' He moved closer towards her and backed her into a corner.

'I don't know what you mean,' she said, fear registering on her face as he leant in until their noses were almost touching.

'Come on, Angela, out with it. You must think I'm stupid. You go out of this flat dolled up to the nines. Fancy knickers, new clothes, and expensive perfumes we can't afford. *I've* heard a rumour too. Richard Price is back at the salon. Tim and Pat saw him when Pat had her hair done. Are you seeing *him* again?'

'What do you mean, again?' She put both hands on his chest and pushed him away. 'We were friends, there was nothing between us.' She turned her back on him and flounced out of the kitchen.

'Don't you walk out on me when I'm talking to you.' He grabbed her arms and pinned her against the wall. 'Are you seeing *him* again?' he repeated, shaking her roughly.

'And what if I am, what do *you* care?' She tried to wriggle free from his grasp, but he dug his fingers into the flesh of her upper arms. She squealed with pain and he loosened his grip slightly.

'So *you're* not denying it either? Richard Price is screwing *you* and probably has been for months and you have the fucking cheek to lay the blame for our marriage not working on me. Well, that's it, lady.' He raised his hand to slap her across the face, but as she flinched, he pushed her away. 'God help me, I'll end up killing you if I stay here. I'll go back to my mum's, I'll look for another flat later in the year when we're sorted.'

'Sorted. What do you mean?' she said, a sob catching her throat.

'I'm divorcing you for adultery with Richard Price. *And* I'm applying for custody of my son.'

'You can't do that, you can't take Jonny away from me.'

'Watch me try.' He pushed past her and walked through to the sitting room, where Jonny was sitting on the carpet, his fists stuffed into his eyes, sobbing loudly.

Eddie picked him up and sat down on the sofa, cuddling him. 'It's okay, Jonny. It's all over. I'm sorry we frightened you.'

'No like shouting,' he sobbed.

Eddie blinked back his own tears, stroking the little boy's curls. 'No more shouting, I promise. Daddy has to go to work now but I'll be home at teatime and I'll read you a story.'

'Okay, Dadda,' Jonny sniffed. 'Bring sweeties from Nana.'

'I will. Go and find Mummy now. You look after her,' he said as Jonny slid from his knee, nodding solemnly.

Eddie slammed the door behind him without a backward glance. He ran downstairs and out onto the street, jumping on the first bus that came along.

In Mersey Square he spotted Jane alighting from *her* bus and called her name. She turned as he ran across the road and caught her in his arms, relaxing as he breathed in the comfortingly familiar scent of her perfume and lemon shampoo.

'Kiss me, Jane. Just kiss me, *please!*'

She kissed him and looked into his eyes. 'Ed, what is it? You're shaking and you look really upset.'

He told her what had happened as they walked hand in hand down Stockport High Street. 'I nearly hit her again, she almost drove me to it.'

'So, your suspicions were right: she *is* having an affair.'

'So are we.'

'Well yes, I know we are. But it doesn't feel like an affair because *we're* in love.'

'No, it doesn't, but we are.' He grinned at her reasoning. She was such a wonderful romantic and he loved her for it. She lifted him so high with her smile that he felt he was walking on clouds.

'So, what now?' she asked. 'You're actually going to divorce her?'

'Yeah. I'll move back to my folks' place and start the ball rolling as soon as I sort out a solicitor.'

'John Grey will know of a good one,' she said. 'But what about Jonny?'

'I'll apply for custody. If I fail then I want reasonable access. Poor little sod was terrified again this morning. We can't put him through that any more.'

'The mother usually gets custody, Ed, unless you can prove she's unfit for the job.'

'Apart from being an adulteress, she's not such a bad mum,' he said. 'She doesn't play with him properly but she keeps him clean and fed, and she loves him.'

'Well, whatever happens, you'll always be Jonny's daddy.' She squeezed his arm. 'No one can ever take that honour away from you, Ed.'

* * *

Angie fastened Jonny into his pushchair and set off on the short walk to her mother's house. If Eddie thought for one minute he was taking her son away, he could bloody well think again. She'd speak with Richard when she got to the salon – she knew he'd support her and help her find a solicitor to fight for custody.

Richard had been her stalwart since the night Eddie slapped her. Appalled by the bruising on her face, he'd urged her to leave him immediately. She told him Eddie had gone to stay with his parents for a few days so she was safe for the time being.

During Eddie's absence Richard had visited the flat, bringing flowers and bottles of wine. Feeling neglected, she'd succumbed to his charms. He'd been so loving and gentle. Now she had another problem to contend with: on top of everything else her period was late. It was very early days, but she was convinced she was pregnant again. When she'd confided in Richard on the Saturday night, he said he'd stand by her.

With Eddie's announcement that he wanted a divorce, there was nothing to stop her and Richard being together but fighting for custody of Jonny *must* come first. She'd read in a magazine that a mother was usually given custody of her child, so she wasn't unduly worried by Eddie's threats. Besides, she had an ace up her sleeve but only if things became desperate would she dare to use it.

* * *

Richard Price was checking the day's appointments with the receptionist when Angie arrived at Crimpers Hair Salon. He took one look at her pale face, ordered the junior stylist to hold the fort and led her upstairs to the staffroom.

'What's wrong?' He put his arms around her and held her while she sobbed on his shoulder. Tilting her chin, he kissed her. 'Take your jacket off and sit down while I make coffee then you can tell me what's upset you.'

She removed her jacket and he frowned, staring at her upper arms, where fingermarks were turning to faint bruises. 'What the hell has he done to you now?'

'He pinned me against the wall while we were arguing. I thought he was going to hit me again. He knows about us, he wants a divorce and custody of Jonny.'

'Right, let him have the bloody divorce! The sooner the better as far as I'm concerned.' Richard handed her a mug and joined her on the sofa. 'We'll go and see my solicitor at lunchtime and fight for custody of Jonny. I'll take you to the flat tonight after work to get your things. We'll tell Eddie together you're expecting my baby and you're moving in with me.'

'No, Richard. I can't tell him I'm pregnant, he'll use it against me to get Jonny. He'll say I'm an unfit mother for having an affair. God, what a bloody mess everything is.'

'It's not a mess.' He put down his mug and tilted her chin again. 'Now listen to me, I love you and I want you and Jonny. I can give you a good life. Much better than you'd ever have living in that shoebox on Eddie's pittance of a wage.'

She looked into his kindly green eyes and smiled through her tears. 'Thanks, Richard – for loving me, I mean.'

'Loving you's the easy part. I'm not allowing you to go back to the flat alone. God knows what Eddie might do if the fancy takes him. If you can't face telling him with me, then we'll go and collect your stuff now and take it to my house. Leave him a note, there's really nothing more for you to say to him.'

'Okay.' She wiped her eyes.

'You can give him my phone number, but not the address,' he continued. 'We don't want him turning up, causing trouble. You'll have to talk to him to arrange access for Jonny, but my solicitor will advise you on that. The bruises on your arms are fresh – you can show the solicitor those today.'

'Ed never used to be violent. It was after Jane Wilson came on the scene that he changed. He dated us both until she dumped him for playing around. She took him back and that's when I told him I was pregnant with Jonny.'

'I remember when he was giving you and Jane the runaround. You came to work and cried on my shoulder.'

'And you took me out and bought me a meal to cheer me up.'

'And we made love on the back seat of my car,' he said. 'From that moment I was smitten but you were determined to get Eddie back from Jane's clutches.'

'Well, *you* were engaged to Louise,' she reminded him. 'You married her three months later.'

'We all make mistakes,' he said with a wry smile.

'I've lost Eddie to Jane for good now.'

'He's having an affair? You never said.' He grinned triumphantly and ran his hands through his hair.

'I didn't know until this morning. He wouldn't admit to it outright. He's got a new job at the shop where she works, that's what sparked off the latest row. He hadn't even bothered to tell me. I only found out when he appeared in his suit.'

'That's brilliant. An affair with Jane is just what we need. You can divorce him on two counts now: violence *and* adultery.

I'll rearrange today's appointments and phone my solicitor. We'll get you settled at my place.' He knelt in front of her and placed his hand over her stomach. 'I don't want anything happening to you or this baby.'

She smiled and stroked his thick, dark curls. 'It's very early days, Richard. What if there isn't a baby?'

'I think there probably is. You said yourself you're never late. We did nothing to prevent it. Meantime, I'll get some practice in with Jonny.'

Angie took a deep breath, still stroking his curls as the tears slid silently down her cheeks.

'Richard, there's something...' She faltered as the door flew back on its hinges and the junior stylist appeared.

'Oooh, sorry,' Carol apologised. 'Am I interrupting something?'

Richard got up from his knees and raised his eyebrows. 'Has anyone ever told you to knock?'

'Well, yeah. But I thought you'd like to know that Mrs Castle can't make her appointment this morning.'

'That's good. I'll let you off the hook then. Ring my clients, reschedule for later in the week. I'm taking Angie home, she's not feeling too well.'

'Sorry to hear that. Nothing serious, I hope?'

'Just the usual, you know, women's problems,' Angie muttered, blushing slightly as Richard squeezed her hand.

Carol nodded in sympathy. 'Tell me about it. Men don't have a bloody clue!'

Richard rolled his eyes as she left the room. 'Right, let's go home. By the way, what were you going to say when she barged in just then?'

'Oh, n-nothing,' Angie faltered. 'It'll keep for another time.'

10

APRIL 1964

Jane said goodbye to the young man she'd finished serving and looked up as Eddie ran down the stairs, his smile a mile wide. 'How did it go?'

'I can have Jonny every weekend. Mr Gregson needs to agree it with Angie's solicitor. If she doesn't raise objections, it should be okay.'

'That's brilliant. Will your mum look after him while you work?'

'I'm sure she will,' he said, lighting a cigarette. 'I'll work through my lunch hour, seeing as John gave me time off this morning. Do you fancy a curry tonight with Roy and Sammy to celebrate?'

'I'd love to, but we don't get paid until Friday. I've hardly any money left and I know *you're* almost skint.'

'I'll borrow a few quid from Mum. Pay her back from Friday's gig money.'

'You've got a date then.'

* * *

Eddie's parents had welcomed him home with open arms. Now that Angie's affair with Richard Price was common knowledge they were being very supportive.

When his dad was told of his relationship with Jane he'd sucked on his teeth and sighed heavily. 'Bet Jane's parents aren't too happy at her getting involved with you again, lad. They used to say you were a right bad lot. What the hell must they be thinking now?'

'Actually, Dad, Jane's not told them yet,' Eddie admitted. 'She says she'll do it when she's good and ready.'

'She'd best shape herself,' his mum said. 'Stockport's a small town. Some nosy devil's bound to see you together and tell tales.'

His dad nodded his agreement. He offered Eddie a cigarette. 'Your mum's right, Ed. Jane should tell them as soon as possible. Another thing, let's have no repeat of the Angie affair.' He pointed his cigarette at Eddie. 'You be careful with Jane, or you'll have her father down on you like a ton of bricks.'

'Dad, I'm nearly twenty-one. I think I know what's what these days.'

'Twenty-one or not, you're still daft as a brush so you think on what your dad's telling you.'

His mum blushed and hurriedly changed the subject. 'Anyway, he's got a proposition to put to you, along with your Aunt Celia's agreement. Haven't you, Fred?'

'What's that then?' Eddie smiled and flicked ash into the fire. Dad's sister Celia lived in Brighton and as her only nephew, Eddie was the apple of her eye.

'You used to dream of having a VW Beetle before you saddled yourself with a wife and kiddie,' his dad began. 'We've an endowment we took out on you as a little lad. It paid out recently. There's a good deposit to put towards a car. If you sell your motorbike, you'll have a bit more cash to pay off the balance. Celia's prepared to pay half the instalments if you can meet the other half.' He sat back, face wreathed in a benevolent smile. 'Look on it as an early twenty-first present from us all.'

Eddie's jaw dropped. 'Dad, are you sure? I don't deserve it, not after all the trouble I've caused you both.'

'Aye, well, it's behind you now. Things will get better. I reckon you deserve a lucky break. We could have a look round the car showroom on your day off. Perhaps arrange a test drive.'

'Brilliant! Thank you. I'll call Aunt Celia now and thank her, too. I'll tell her about my new job and that I'm back with Jane – she liked Jane the one time she met her.'

'She knows you've left Angie, so it won't come as too much of a surprise,' his mum said. 'Celia's off to America next month for six weeks. You'd best call her right away, then she can make arrangements to send some money before she goes.'

* * *

Wednesday was Enid's usual day for cleaning upstairs. As she yanked Jane's bed away from the wall to clean behind it, her daughter's best handbag slipped off the corner of the headboard, spilling its contents onto the carpet.

'Damn and blast it! Why doesn't she fasten the bloody thing?' She got down on her knees to retrieve the errant make-up and loose change and popped them in the bag. Something nestling at the bottom caught her eye. She delved in and pulled out a small flat box, eyes widening as she realised she was holding a Durex packet.

'What's she doing, carrying these things around?' she muttered. More to the point, why was the packet almost empty? To her knowledge, since Mark, Jane didn't have a boyfriend. Anyway, her daughter was a good girl. Certainly not the type who'd give her favours freely to a man before marriage. Wasn't she? Not that she'd ever discussed the subject of sex with Jane. It had never cropped up.

She rose to her feet, heart pounding. The walls of the little room crowded in and she flopped down on the bed. The black and white pin-ups of The Beatles and the scruffy, unwashed Rolling Stones grinned mockingly at her. That Mack Jigger, or whatever the devil he was called, was positively leering, she thought, shuddering. What was the world coming to? All the debauchery you read about in the papers caused by these wild groups of lads. Was her innocent daughter being led into the seamy side of life? 'Who's doing the bloody leading?' she said out loud.

She opened the window to let in some air. The pink and white floral curtains fluttered in the breeze above the dressing table with its clutter of make-up jars and perfume bottles. She picked up Jane's balding, one-eyed teddy bear from the floor and placed him on the pillow, a sob catching her throat.

She ran a duster over the chest of drawers, closed the lid of the record player and straightened a stack of singles that was in danger of toppling off the edge, her mind racing. What should she do? Call Jane and tackle her? Wait and tell husband Ben of her findings? 'No, bad idea,' she mumbled. 'He'll go bloody mad and anyway, I should find out who the packet belongs to.'

Perhaps Jane was looking after them for a friend. Maybe they were Sammy's. That made perfect sense. Sammy's boyfriend was a right cocky devil and they probably got up to all sorts. Then the doubts came rushing back. Why didn't Sammy keep them in *her* handbag? Pushing the Durex box into her apron pocket, she made her way downstairs to the kitchen and brewed a pot of tea.

She clutched her mug, looking at the packet that now lay mocking her on the kitchen table, until she could stand it no longer. Before she changed her mind, she ran out into the hall, stared at the telephone for a few seconds, snatched up the receiver and dialled Flanagan and Grey's number, almost collapsing with shock as a softly spoken male voice answered.

'Good morning, Flanagan and Grey's, Eddie Mellor speaking. How may I help you?'

She slammed down the phone as though it had bitten her ear. Eddie Mellor? What the devil was Eddie Mellor doing answering Flanagan and Grey's phone? Was he working there? If so, why on earth hadn't Jane mentioned it? A feeling of dread crept into her heart. Surely her daughter wasn't carrying on with Eddie Mellor? There had to be a better explanation.

She whipped off her apron and put on her coat. There was one person who might be able to throw some light on this: her friend, Molly Mason. Molly's daughter, Sammy, Jane's best friend, was engaged to Roy Cantello, who, Enid knew, was a close friend of Eddie Mellor's. Pushing the Durex into her pocket with her keys, she left the house.

* * *

Molly answered her front door to the urgent knocking and smiled broadly.

'Enid, come on in. I was about to make coffee. Will you join me?'

'Please, Molly.' Enid stepped into the hallway and took off her coat.

'Come through to the kitchen,' Molly invited. 'I've some nice biscuits, might as well enjoy them while we can. When the hungry hordes are here later, they'll scoff the lot. I've never known anybody eat as much as Roy Cantello and not put an ounce on. Take a pew.'

Enid draped her coat over the back of a kitchen chair and sat down, sighing loudly.

'Oh dear! Why the big sigh?' Molly placed two steaming mugs beside a plate of chocolate digestives.

'I've made a discovery that I'm none too happy about,' Enid

began as Molly sat down opposite. 'I wondered if *you* had any idea what might be going on.'

'Try me,' Molly said and broke a biscuit in half.

'I was cleaning Jane's bedroom and found this.' Enid placed the contraceptive packet on the table. 'When I called her at work to tackle her about it, Eddie Mellor answered the phone.'

'Ah, I see. I knew something like this would happen.'

'What do you mean?' Enid's voice raised an octave. 'Molly, what do *you* know about my girl that *I* don't?'

'I'm sorry, Enid. I warned Jane not to keep things from you as you'd find out sooner or later.'

'Find out what, exactly? What the hell is she up to? Tell me now, or else I'll go down to Flanagan and Grey's and drag it out of her.'

'It's not my place to say,' Molly began, 'but you mustn't go down to the shop and cause a scene. They'd never forgive you. It would be so embarrassing for you.'

'Well, *you* tell me what's going on then and I won't do anything until she comes home.'

'You won't like it,' Molly warned. 'Jane's having an affair with Eddie. He left his wife and he's living with his parents. He's working with Jane, training as manager for the new store.'

Molly took a sip of coffee as Enid stared, her face draining of colour. 'From what Sammy told me, Eddie's ex is having an affair with someone she works with and she's living with him,' Molly continued. 'Eddie's in love with Jane and she with him. That's why she broke off her engagement to Mark Fisher.'

'But Mark's worth ten of Eddie Mellor,' Enid cried. 'I'll never understand that stupid girl. Fancy throwing herself at a ne'er do well when she can have Mark. Eddie's a tearaway, always has been. Wait until she comes home, I'll wipe the bloody floor with her.'

'What's the point, Enid? She's old enough to make her own decisions about who she sees and what she does with them.'

'Not while she's under my roof,' Enid fumed. 'She's not seeing him again, I'll make damn sure of that. I can't believe she's being so sneaky and underhanded. I'm so upset, Molly. I don't know my own daughter any more.' She sobbed into her handkerchief and Molly patted her shoulder. 'My Jane was a good girl. She wouldn't have done anything like that with Mark. He's a decent lad, always showed a lot of respect for her.'

'But she doesn't love him,' Molly pointed out. 'You'll lose her if you treat her like a child. Eddie's made a smashing young man. He's totally besotted with her. If I were you, I'd put that packet back where I found it and say nothing. She'll talk to you when she's good and ready. Banning her from seeing him won't get you anywhere.'

Enid twisted her wet handkerchief between her fingers. 'Err, you said he's training to be a manager?'

'He is – he loves the job. He's trying to get custody of his little boy, too. At least he's acting responsibly towards the child. He's not just upped and abandoned him without a second thought. Roy's got him singing again with the group. It gives him a bit of extra money. He's a sound young man. The wild rebel you hated has long gone.'

Enid drained her mug and put on her coat. 'I'll never approve of what they get up to, but I'm going to take your advice. I couldn't bear to lose my only daughter, never have her speak to me again. So I've made my decision: I'll wait while she tells me about Eddie herself.'

Molly patted her arm. 'Accepting our kids are adults is never easy but it's the best way forward.'

* * *

Enid walked home, still feeling worried. Back in Jane's room, she popped the packet in the handbag and pushed it to the bottom out of sight. She picked up her duster, and ignoring

The Rolling Stones leering grins, leant across the bed to wipe the dust from the skirting board. Her head was still reeling when Peter arrived home early from school, complaining of feeling ill.

He swayed in the doorway of Jane's bedroom, his brown eyes rolling in his head, his green-tinged face doing contortions as he tried to stay upright.

'Out of here, quick!' Enid manhandled him into the bathroom, where he vomited copiously down the toilet. 'Pete, have you been drinking?' The stench of alcohol was overpowering and she backed away.

'Only cider, Mum,' he slurred, before vomiting again.

'Well, *that's* alcohol,' she shouted. 'Oh, for crying out loud, if it's not one of you, it's the other! Where the bloody hell have we gone wrong?'

'Why, what's our Jane been up to?'

'Never you mind!' She gripped the back of his neck and wiped his face with a damp flannel. 'You just wait till your father gets home. You'll be for the high jump, my lad.'

She flushed the toilet and Peter sat back on his heels, grinning. With a wave of his hand, he did the best Rhett Butler impression he could muster and said, 'Frankly, my dear Mother, I don't give a damn!'

* * *

Eddie dropped the telephone receiver onto the cradle as Jane ran down the stairs, clutching a Boots paper bag.

'I got that new Breck shampoo that Brian Jones uses,' she said. 'It's supposed to make your hair really shiny. You can try it tonight. You okay, Ed? Something wrong?'

'You could say that.' He arched an eyebrow and turned to Carl. 'Make us a brew, Carl. Take your time over it, I need to talk to Jane while the shop's quiet.'

'I'll nip out and get cakes,' Carl said. 'That'll take me a few extra minutes.'

Eddie fished in his trouser pocket and handed him a ten-shilling note. 'Buy them with this and get me twenty Benson & Hedges as well, please. Sit down, Jane,' he ordered as Carl left. 'I've just taken a call from Sammy's mum.'

'Oh!' Jane frowned as she plonked herself on the stool behind the counter and flicked her hair over her shoulders. 'What did Molly want then?'

'To warn that your mother knows about us.'

'Shit! Who's told her? Mark Fisher. I bet it was, getting back at you for thumping him. Devious swine! He leaves it all this time so we start to feel safe and then he does that. God, I hate him!'

Eddie shook his head. 'Surprisingly enough, it wasn't Mark. According to Molly, your mum was cleaning your bedroom, knocked your bag onto the floor, and when she was putting stuff back, she saw a Durex packet in there. *You* were supposed to be keeping them out of her sight.'

'I must have forgotten to lock my handbag,' she gasped, staring at him in horror. 'That's it, she'll stop me seeing you. I'm not going home tonight.'

'Calm down. Your mother went to Molly's because she was upset. Molly thought it best to tell her the truth so it's out now, no more lies and sneaking around.'

'She'll never accept us, Ed. She thought the sun shone out of Mark's backside and *you* were the worst rebel on two legs. God knows what she must think of you now.'

'According to Molly, she's *sort* of accepted the situation and she's prepared to wait until *you* decide to tell her about us so you'd better do it soon.'

'I can't. It's one thing telling her we're dating, but now she knows we're sleeping together. What if she tells Dad? He'll kill you and probably pack me off to his brother's in Ireland.'

'Jane, we started this affair with our eyes wide open. There's no going back. I'm getting divorced, then we'll be married. We need to put your parents in the picture. We can do it tonight after work. I'll come with you.'

Jane ran the back of her hand over her eyes, smudging her mascara.

'Okay,' she sniffed. 'But if she starts having a go at us, that's it, I'm off!'

He pulled a handkerchief from his pocket. 'You look like a panda,' he said, wiping her eyes. 'If she *does* start then you can pack your things and come home with me. I'll call Mum now, tell her what's happened, that I'm bringing you home for tea and you might be staying. She'll get the spare room ready. There'll be no chance of her allowing you to share *my* room. We'll have to save our night out with Roy and Sammy for later in the week.'

Jane smiled through her tears as Carl reappeared with a tray of coffee and cakes. 'I'll go and wash my face while you call your mum.'

'Good idea. I've made a worse mess than you, trying to tidy you up. Cheer up, Jane. I love you.'

'I love you too, Ed, but it doesn't stop me being terrified of facing Mum.'

* * *

Sammy and Pat were sitting on the top deck of the bus as Eddie and Jane ran across Mersey Square and leapt on board.

'Phew, that was close,' Jane puffed.

The vehicle pulled out of the bus station and she and Eddie collapsed onto the seats behind their friends.

Sammy turned and frowned. 'Where are *you* going, Ed?'

'Home with Jane,' he replied and lit a cigarette. 'Want one?' He held out the packet.

She shook her head, eyes wide with shock. 'Eddie Mellor, have you got a bloody death wish? You know Jane's mum never approved of you *before* you knocked Angie up! After that, well...'

Eddie took a drag of his cigarette as Jane explained why he was accompanying her home.

'Rather you than me,' Sammy said. 'Batten down the hatches. World War Three's about to kick off!'

* * *

Enid smoothed the creases out of the sheet she was folding. She looked up as Jane walked into the kitchen, closely followed by Eddie Mellor. She was about to order him out of the house when she saw the pleading looks in the young couple's eyes and the way they were holding hands. Molly must have had a word with them, she thought. It had taken some guts for the pair to face her like this. The least she could do was hear them out. She mentally counted to ten and fixed on the brightest smile she could muster: 'Hello, you two. What can I do for you?'

'Mum, we need to talk, you know, about what you found in my room today,' Jane began.

'Yes, you're right, young lady, I think we do. Go and sit in the lounge while I put the ironing away and make a pot of tea.'

'I'll make the tea,' Jane offered.

'I'll do it. Go and keep Eddie company, he looks like he needs it.' She watched them walk into the lounge and sighed. The mundane tasks would give her a few minutes to compose herself.

She placed three mugs on a tray with a sugar basin, then steeling herself, carried the tray into the lounge. Her daughter and Eddie were on the sofa, holding hands and looking deep into one another's eyes. He was stroking her hair with his free hand, telling her not to worry. Enid swallowed the lump that rose in her throat. She recognised the look of love when she saw it and these two were so absorbed in one another, they hadn't even heard her come into the room.

'You can let go of him, Jane. He won't disappear into thin air.' Managing a smile, she placed the tray down on the coffee table and got two wary smiles in return. She sat down on the chair opposite and began: 'Right then, who's going to start, or shall I tell you what *I* know, and you can fill me in on the details?'

'We know what you know, Mum,' Jane said. 'Eddie's spoken to Molly. We love one another. I was too frightened to tell you. You hated me going out with him before. Now it's even worse because he's married and got a child.'

'I'm in the throes of getting divorced, Mrs Wilson,' Eddie said, spooning sugar into his tea. 'I want to marry Jane as soon as possible.'

'Right, enough!' Enid held up her hands. 'It'll take about three years for you to get a divorce. You can't marry until then anyway. It will give you plenty of time to decide if marriage is what you really want. What about your responsibilities to your wife and the little lad?'

'They're living with Angie's boyfriend,' he replied. 'I'm trying to get custody of Jonny but for now, I pay towards his keep.'

'And what if you *do* get custody?' Enid frowned. 'Do you expect Jane to take on a mother role? Because I'll tell you now, seeing to your own kids is bad enough, but looking after someone else's is bloody hard work. You ask Tom and Molly Mason if you want confirmation of that. They've *really* got their hands full with Sammy, Pat and Susan.'

Eddie nodded. 'Tom and Molly are the happiest couple I know. When I got Angie into trouble, I didn't know where to turn. Roy told Molly. She took me to one side and said the same thing had happened to her and Samuel. They married when she was seventeen with Sammy on the way. But she and Samuel were very happy and they'd probably still be married if he hadn't been killed.'

'I didn't realise Molly had told you her life story,' Enid said.

'Molly's not ashamed of her past, Mum,' Jane chipped in. 'She knows all about problems and how to solve them better than you do.'

'Apparently so,' Enid said dryly. She turned to Eddie. 'My daughter means the world to me. I trust you to look after her properly. Otherwise, you'll have me to answer to, not to mention her father.'

Jane stared at her mother in amazement. 'Mum, are you saying it's okay for us to see one another?'

'I am. Just act responsibly, that's all I ask.'

'Oh, Mum!' Jane jumped up and flung her arms around her. 'Thank you. We won't let you down, we promise. Don't we, Ed?'

'Absolutely. Thank you for giving me another chance. I'll make you proud of me one day. You *and* my own mum, you both deserve it.'

'What about Dad?' Jane asked.

'You leave your father to me, I'll tell him what I think he needs to know.'

Eddie stood up and shook Enid by the hand. 'I'm taking Jane to my parents' place for tea, if that's okay? Thanks again, Mrs Wilson, for being so understanding.'

'Enid, please. Mrs Wilson sounds stuffy. I know you use Christian names for Tom and Molly. Ben and me need to move with the times. Though heaven only knows what I'll do with our Pete.'

'Why? Where is he?' Jane asked.

'Upstairs, sleeping off a hangover.'

'Never!'

'Oh yes, he is. He rolled in here drunk as a skunk, threw up and then collapsed on his bed.'

'Oh dear!' Eddie grinned. 'I remember Roy and me getting plastered at that age. I bet Pete's been on the rec behind the school – that's where all the kids hang out with bottles of cider.'

'No doubt,' Enid said. 'Anyway, Ben can take responsibility for sorting him out. I've enough coping with you, Jane. Go and have your tea with Eddie's parents and I'll see you later.'

After seeing the pair out, she watched as they strolled hand in hand down the garden path. She had to admit they made a fine couple. Jane's lovely slender figure, her pretty looks and the glossy mane of dark-brown hair that was her daughter's pride and joy, and Eddie, so strikingly handsome that she found herself wishing she were twenty years younger. She made a mental note there and then: if Mark Fisher phoned this week, as he was wont to do, she'd tell the lad it would be best not to call again.

11

'Come in,' Maude called.

She looked up as Cadet Nurse Cook entered the room, carrying a laden tray.

'Morning, Mrs Fisher. I've brought you some nice scrambled eggs and toast. When you've finished, I'll help you pack, ready for the transfer. I bet you're really looking forward to getting out of hospital.'

Maude blinked back tears that threatened constantly. 'I'd feel better if I knew I was going to my own home.'

'But your son's booked you a place at The Firs. It's a lovely nursing home, the grounds are beautiful and every room has a grand view.'

'I prefer to be in my own bed at night. Now if you don't mind, I'll have my breakfast in peace.'

'Certainly, Mrs Fisher. I'll be back in half an hour. The ambulance is booked for ten thirty – they don't like to be kept waiting.'

'I'll be ready.' Maude dismissed the girl with a wave of her hand and poked the rubbery egg around the plate, pushing it away in disgust. 'What I wouldn't give for a half-decent breakfast,' she muttered. Still, after what Mark had told her about The Firs, they would probably serve up good food.

Leaning back on her pillows, she thought about the time since her accident. The day's in-between had felt like nothing short of a nightmare. Mark avoided visiting at first, sending in a neighbour with toiletries and clothing. The neighbour told her that he had to go to Chester in connection with his job transfer and would visit when he was able. She felt abandoned by him and there had been no explanation, no messages or phone calls. When he eventually turned up, she smelled drink on him and immediately jumped to the conclusion that he was still upset over his broken engagement. But at the mention of Jane he became aggressive, told her to shut her mouth and left as quickly as he'd arrived.

He visited again two days later and announced his plans to put her in a nursing home. When she protested that she required no further nursing and was ready to go back to Maple Avenue, he told her that the house was no longer *hers* to call home. At that point he'd thrown the bundle of letters from the Isle of Wight onto the bed.

Maude went over the ensuing conversation in her head, wondering if she could have handled things better. Mark had taken her completely by surprise and she was unprepared for his verbal assault.

'Where did you find them, Mark?'

'In the sideboard cupboard, waiting to be discovered,' he replied. 'It's easy enough now to understand why we never got on: you're not my flesh and blood.'

'I should have told you,' she said, a sob catching her throat. 'I could never find the right time, I'm so sorry. But please understand that everything we did was in your best interests. Jack was devastated by Amelia's death. *He* couldn't keep you because of his wife and children. I was the only other person who knew the truth. It made perfect sense for me to become your guardian and raise you as though you were my own. After all, I'm the one registered as your mother on the birth certificate.'

'I know all about the deception but you promised Jack that you would tell me about Amelia and you never said a bloody word. I had to find out by piecing everything together from a pile of letters. I was looking for documents relating to the house and whether it would be paid for if you died. Instead, I find that you don't own it. It's actually mine and has been since my father instructed his solicitor to change the deeds a few years ago. You know what sickens me most though?'

'What?' She plucked at a stray thread on the candlewick bedspread.

'You sat at the dining table with me and Jane and watched us poring over the figures we'd worked out to save for a deposit on a house, wondering how we could best juggle the money so that she could give up work to start our family. All the time, not ten feet away, was the bloody proof that I actually owned the house we were living in. You could have made it so easy for us. Would you ever have told me?'

'No, I was frightened of being left on my own,' she admitted. 'I always said you and that girl were welcome to live with me when you married.'

'Oh yeah. The suggestion went down like a lead balloon. Jane hated your guts. Why would she want to live in the same house? No wonder she called off the bloody engagement. All she could see was years ahead of us living with you. That's enough to put any girl off for life.' He clenched his fists before continuing.

'I don't want to be known by your name any more. My surname is now Saunders-Mainwaring, after the two people who brought me into the world. My father's solicitor is changing it by deed poll.'

'Whatever you say, Mark. But please don't turn your back

on me,' she begged. 'You're all I've got, I gave up everything to look after you.'

He ignored her pleas. 'I'll make sure you're taken care of. I've made the nursing home arrangements. The council have reserved you a ground-floor flat in a new block in Stockport. You'll have your pension and I'll arrange a small allowance for the first twelve months. After that, I owe you nothing. You called Jane a gold-digger,' he went on, 'but *you've* been lining your pockets for years from the money Jack gave you to look after me. So why did you always plead poverty? You could have bought me my bass guitar a hundred times over with what *I've* seen stashed away in your bank accounts yet you made me pay for it on the drip. So don't you dare come after me for anything else. All your stuff's in storage. Tony's moved in as my lodger. He'll take care of things during the week while I'm in Chester. We've started to decorate and Sarah and Vicky are helping us choose the new colour schemes.'

Maude clutched her chest. This was it, her one big dread: he'd disowned her because of her deception. If only she'd had the guts to come clean years ago, they could have worked it out together. Now it was too late and he was staring at her with hatred in his eyes.

'Sarah and Vicky. Who the hell are Sarah and Vicky? You've no right to do this to me after everything I've done for you. I brought you up, made sure you had a good education and got a decent job at the end of it.'

'But it wasn't my choice. I wanted to go to art college, not work in a bloody bank! You never once asked me what I wanted to do.'

'Amelia was an artist.' She choked on her words. 'She was good, too. The watercolour in the hall, the one of the harbour where you used to count the boats when you were a little boy, that's one of hers.'

'I saw her signature when I took it down. I've kept it. It's the only thing I've got of my mother's. And Sarah and Vicky are mine and Tony's girlfriends. That's right, Maude, I've got a new girl.'

'Well, let's hope she treats you better than Jane did,' she snapped.

'It's not serious, just a bit of fun till I get Jane back. Because I will, you just watch. She'll be running back to me as soon as she knows you're no longer round my neck and I've got a house, paid for, that we can make our own. We can start our family right away and she'll be mine, lock, stock and barrel.'

'But she doesn't love you,' she yelled, wanting to hurt him for what he'd done to her and lashing out in a way she knew would anger him. 'She doesn't love you or want to marry you. She won't come back now she's taken up with her married bloke. She's nothing but a cheap little trollop!'

At this he'd stormed out of the room without a backward glance and now, here she was, starting out on the first leg of the journey of her miserable new life.

* * *

Mark placed the orange cushions he'd brought home from Chester on the new sofa and stepped back to admire his handiwork. The colour was just right against the chocolate brown velvet and the lounge looked fantastic. All the hard work had paid off and the magnolia-painted walls were a perfect backdrop for the framed prints he'd bought.

There wasn't a trace of Maude in the room now other than Amelia's harbour scene, which hung above the old tiled fireplace. Newly framed in a smart gold leaf finish, he thought it perfect for the chosen site.

Tony sauntered in from the kitchen, carrying two glasses of beer, well topped with froth – 'I can't get the hang of bottled beer, it pours abysmally. Sorry for the big head on your pint, but hey, I'm a bank clerk, not a barman!'

'Looks all right to me,' Mark said. 'What do you think to the finishing touches? You and Sarah did a really good job of getting the painting finished this week. I do appreciate it, Tony. I love Friday nights, coming home, seeing the progress you've made.'

'Think nothing of it, mate. It's great living here. Sarah loves playing house. Stops her nagging me about getting engaged. This is what women like, looking after us men. Making meals, pampering to our every whim. She even did my washing in that new Bendix machine – it's too complicated for me.'

Mark laughed. 'We'll cook tonight for the girls, give them a treat. I got steak, mushrooms and salad and a couple of bottles of red wine. Get 'em in the mood for a bit of loving later.'

'You still okay about seeing Vicky?' Tony said, frowning as Mark shrugged. 'She thinks the world of you. It bothers me when I know you're determined to get Jane back.'

'I called Jane's mother today before I left Chester,' Mark said. 'She asked me not to phone again. She told me Jane's dating Mellor, which of course I already knew. She said they're serious and he's getting divorced.'

'Well, there you go, mate. They'll no doubt get married in time. Sets you free to move on with Vicky now.'

'I don't want to go steady,' Mark said. 'It'll fizzle out between Jane and Mellor when she comes to her senses. I need to be free to pick up the pieces. Anyway, I'm also taking a bird out that I met in a pub in Chester a few weeks ago.'

'Really? You dark horse,' Tony said. 'Is she, you know, as good as Vicky in the sack?'

'She's better.' Mark grinned wickedly. 'Beth could teach us both a thing or two. Right, I'll give old Maude a quick call at the nursing home and then she can't accuse me of *totally* neglecting her. I'll jump in the bath and change my sheets before Vicky arrives. Are she and Sarah staying over tonight?'

'They are,' Tony replied as Mark left the room.

'Great!' he called over his shoulder.

* * *

'Can't wait till it's our turn to do this.' Eddie grabbed two glasses of champagne from a passing tray and handed one to Jane. They were helping John Grey and his fiancée Margaret celebrate their engagement. Eddie had taken a night off from singing with The Raiders and had chauffeured Jane and Stuart in his gleaming black VW Beetle, of which he'd taken delivery the previous day.

'We'll have to wait until your divorce comes through. Anyway,' she teased, 'you haven't actually asked me to marry you this time round. You've just assumed I will.'

'I don't see why we can't get engaged. It's the married bit we can't do just yet.'

'So, that's the proposal, is it?' Jane said, her face expressionless.

'No, but this is.' He got down on one knee and took her hand. 'Jane, will you marry me as soon as I'm free?'

Her eyes filled with tears as everyone in the room cheered loudly. 'Yes, Ed, of course I will.'

He jumped up, hugged her and rained kisses on her face as she grinned with delight.

John and Margaret brought out another bottle of champagne.

'You'll get it right this time, mate.' John laughed as he kissed Jane and shook Eddie's hand.

'I know that,' Eddie said, winking at Jane.

'Congratulations, you two.' Stuart thumped Eddie on the back and kissed Jane. 'Mine and John's act of playing Cupid's finally paid off, five years down the line.'

* * *

'What do you reckon your mum and dad will think of my proposal?' Eddie asked as he drove Jane home.

'I really don't know. Mum's always saying it will be years before we can think of such things.'

'Am I rushing you?'

She reached for his hand and squeezed it reassuringly. 'I want it as much as you do.'

'Will you tell them this weekend? I'll come with you if you like.'

'I'll tell them tomorrow. But I'll do it on my own – I think it would be better that way.'

'Okay, if you're sure. I won't tell my folks until you've told yours. Would you like to come over tomorrow and meet Jonny? We could take him to the park, feed the ducks.'

She nodded as they pulled up outside her home. 'I'd *love* to meet him. I'll see you about two at your mum's place. I love you.'

'I love you too, Jane.' He kissed her goodnight and drove away, singing his heart out, feeling on top of the world.

* * *

'I can't say I'm surprised, I suppose it was only a matter of time,' Enid said. She pulled the belt of her blue quilted dressing gown tightly round her middle as Jane broke her good news. 'But you're jumping the gun a bit, getting engaged when he's only just left his wife. What's the rush?'

'No rush, Mum. We want to make a commitment.'

'Well, you know your own mind, I suppose.'

'I do. I love Ed and I want to marry him as soon as I can.'

Enid smiled. 'Of course you do. You can have our blessing, but be prepared for a long wait. Divorce is a messy business, especially when a child is involved.' She pushed any lingering niggling doubts about Eddie to the back of her mind. So far he was proving that a leopard can change its spots. Anyway, it would be years before they could marry; plenty of time to discover if they were right for one another and not just on the rebound.

'I'm meeting Jonny this afternoon at Eddie's house,' Jane announced. 'But I'm feeling really nervous about it.'

'You'll be fine,' Enid said. 'When the little lad gets used to you, bring him to see us. After all, if, I mean, *when*, you and Eddie marry, I'll be his step-granny.'

'That would be lovely. Eddie will feel like you're accepting his child into the family too.' Jane stood up, stretching her arms above her head. 'I'm off to get ready, then I'm going to tell Sammy and Pat. I wanted you two to be the first to know, apart from those who were at the party last night. You should have heard them all cheer when Eddie went down on one knee to propose – it was very romantic and so unexpected.'

Enid shook her head and watched Jane stroll dreamily out of the kitchen.

Ben folded his *News of the World*, picked up his mug of tea and looked at Enid. 'Well, there's a turn up for the books. How do you really feel, love? I know you have your reservations about Eddie and not without good reason.'

'Actually, Ben, I'm getting more used to the idea as the days go by. She's loved that lad for a long time. If I'm honest, I didn't really give him a chance,' she admitted, taking her husband's mug from his hands. 'But it won't be an easy ride for them.'

'Hey, I've not finished my tea yet!'

'Tough! Go and wake Pete up. The pair of you can tackle that mess of a garden while I get cracking with the dinner.'

* * *

'Angie, are you ready to go, love?' Richard called down the hall.

'I'm coming,' she said, emerging white-faced from the bathroom.

'Still feeling poorly?' He took her in his arms and stroked the straying curls from her face.

'I wasn't as sick as this with Jonny. I thought it would have passed by now, but I feel worse than ever.'

'Perhaps it's a girl this time. My clients tell me that women carrying girls have more morning sickness.'

'You're an old gossip, Richard,' she teased. 'A daughter would be lovely, it would make all this awful sickness worthwhile. I'd better change Jonny before we take him to Eddie's. It's high time he was potty trained. Seems to be taking forever. I'd like him out of nappies before this one arrives.' She patted her rounded stomach.

'Are you telling Eddie about the baby today? It's time you did, before someone else does.'

She pulled a face. 'Do I have to? I don't feel up to a show-down and his mum and dad will be there. I'd rather just drop Jonny off and run if you don't mind. I'll tell him when I'm feeling a bit stronger.'

'It's up to you, but you're showing a lot. Someone at the salon's gonna twig sooner or later and spill the beans. You can't keep wearing baggy clothes without attracting attention. Anyway, go and change Jonny then we can get on our way. I'm looking forward to having you all to myself for a whole afternoon.'

'Me too,' she said. 'Shall we have a walk when we've been to see the new house?'

'Yeah, that sounds like a good idea but only if you're feeling up to it.'

'I'll be okay. Looking around our nice new home will cheer me up. We can measure the windows. I'll buy fabric for curtains next week and ask my mum to make them up.'

'And *there's* another problem,' he said, frowning.

'What?'

'Your mother. You still haven't told *her*.'

'I will, but not until I've told Ed.'

'Okay, but it's going to have to be very soon or I'll begin to think that you don't want anyone to know this baby's mine. They'll all be thinking it's Eddie's.'

'Of course I want them all to know the baby's yours. Okay, if Eddie's alone today, then I'll tell him, I promise.'

'Thank you! That would make me feel more secure with you.'

'Richard, there's no need for you to feel insecure. I love you, you're worth ten of Eddie Mellor,' she reassured him.

* * *

Jane felt sick with nerves as she knocked on Eddie's parents' front door. His mother welcomed her inside with a smile.

'It's nice to see you again, Mrs Mellor.' Jane handed her jacket to Lillian, who gave her a hug.

'And it's grand to see you too, love,' Lillian said. 'Ed's out the back with the little chap. They're kicking a ball about. Go on through and I'll make a pot of tea.'

Jane stood on the back step watching Eddie with the little boy, who was running up and down the lawn, kicking the ball and shouting 'Goal!'. She swallowed the lump in her throat. Eddie looked up and spotted her. He swung Jonny up and walked across the garden to greet her.

'Meet my boy,' he said proudly. 'Jonny, say hello to Jane.'

She smiled at Jonny and her stomach lurched. Jonny grinned shyly back at her. The thought of Eddie having sex with Angie and her carrying his baby made her feel physically sick. She tried to push the vision to the back of her mind, but the nausea was rising.

'I have to go to the bathroom, excuse me.' She fled upstairs and locked the door, leaning over the sink, breathing deeply, remembering the last time she'd stood in the same spot doing exactly the same thing. The awful night when she and Eddie first made love and Angie turned up and announced she was pregnant. It was almost an action replay. Any minute now Eddie would knock on the door with her jacket in his hands, telling her he was sorry but he was staying with Angie.

Seconds later, Eddie *did* knock on the door: 'Jane, are you okay? Let me in, please.'

She unlocked the door and sat on the side of the bath. After glancing at his worried face, she felt foolish for letting her imagination run away with her. He knelt on the floor and took her hands.

'What is it? You're white as a sheet. Is it Jonny, the shock of seeing him?'

She nodded. 'I'm sorry, Ed. It was the thought of you and Angie... you know.'

'But it's over. I love you more than anything in the world. I'll never let anyone come between us again, I promise.' He pushed her hair back from her face and kissed her. 'Come downstairs. Mum's wondering what's going on.' He pulled her to her feet. 'Reassure her that you're okay.'

She composed herself and followed Eddie downstairs, where his mum was standing in the kitchen, wiping Jonny's nose. She looked up with concern as they walked in.

'You all right, lovey? You look a bit off colour. Is it something you've eaten?'

'She's okay, Mum. It's the reality of seeing Jonny in the flesh,' Eddie said.

'We'll have a nice cup of tea and then you can go out and get some fresh air.' Lillian patted Jane's arm and handed her a mug.

Jane smiled, wrapped her hands around the mug and nodded. 'I'm fine, really.'

'Let's walk down to the park. We'll feed the ducks and go on the swings. Jonny, I mean, not us,' Eddie said.

'That'd be nice. Have you got any stale bread?' Jane asked Lillian, who rummaged in her bread bin and produced half a loaf.

'It's not really stale but what the heck? That child needs some spoiling.' She popped the bread in a paper bag and handed it to Jane. 'It's a beautiful day for the time of year. Mind you, you need to be wrapped up. It's chilly when the sun goes in. You watch him near that pond now, Ed.'

'Mum, I'm quite capable of looking after him,' he said as he zipped Jonny into his warm jacket and pulled a woollen bobble hat over his ears. He collected his own and Jane's jackets from the hall. She stifled a giggle when he made a face behind his mother's back.

Lillian fastened a scarf around Jonny's neck and said, 'Well, in that case it's time you took a turn at changing his nappy!'

'That's something I'll pass on if you don't mind. Anyway, Angie said he's almost potty trained now.'

As Eddie fastened Jonny into his pushchair, Jane thought how very different the little boy looked to how she'd pictured him in her mind's eye. His eyes were green, not Eddie's startling blue. His hair, though curly like Angie's, was much darker than she'd expected.

'He doesn't look a bit like you,' she said as they walked down the road. 'I expected him to have your lovely blue eyes.'

'Everybody says he takes after Angie's family with the green eyes and curls. As long as he doesn't have her and her mother's awful moods, he'll be okay.' Eddie looked proudly at Jonny, who chattered incessantly, pointing at things that caught his attention.

'Where's Angie this afternoon?' Jane said as they turned into the park. 'Don't fancy bumping into her.'

'Out with Richard. They dropped Jonny off earlier and they're coming for him at six.'

'Does she ever ask you about us?'

'No. But saying that, she was really odd when she brought Jonny round today. More so than usual, I mean. She stood on the doorstep for a while, almost as though she wanted to say something, then my mum popped her head round the door to say hello and she hurried off.'

'You don't think she wants you back, do you?'

'Course not. I wouldn't go back anyway. She seems happy enough with Richard. Not that I've ever spoken to the guy. I wouldn't recognise him if I fell over him. He always sits in the car with his sunglasses on when they bring Jonny over. He's a bloody poser, if you ask me.'

Jonny's delight with the ducks brought a smile to Jane's face as he threw the bread into the pond. At the children's play area, she lifted him onto a swing and pushed him gently to and fro.

Eddie looked at them, smiling: 'You'll make a great mum, Jane.'

'Give me time. I want us to have some fun as a couple first, don't you?'

'I do. I never thought I'd want more kids but thinking of having them with you is wonderful. I'd like at least two more. Think of the fun we'll have, practising making them!' He grinned lustfully and slipped his arms around her waist.

Jane laughed. 'Do you men ever think of anything else?'

'Now and again,' he teased, running his fingers through her hair.

'I told Mum and Dad this morning. About your proposal, I mean,' she said.

'Honestly? What did they say?'

'We have their blessing. It was as simple as that.'

'Blimey! Really? Right, well in that case, tomorrow lunchtime we'll go to Winters jewellers and choose your ring, make it official. Is that okay?'

'Perfect, Ed. Now let's go home and tell *your* parents our good news.'

12

MAY 1964

Preparations for the new store's opening were in full swing. Over the last few days, Eddie, Carl and John Grey had taken delivery of the stock.

'How's that?' Eddie leapt out of the window and ran outside for a quick look at his handiwork. 'Just the piano to shove in the corner and we're done.'

'Looks great.' Carl joined him on the pavement, looking admiringly at the display of guitars, drums, brass and wind instruments set against a midnight-blue velvet backdrop. A selection of electric organs on stands graced the window's frontage.

They hurried back inside to help John slide the piano into place.

'Thank God it's the display model,' he said, catching his breath. 'We very nearly did ourselves a mischief hauling the bloody thing up!'

Carl ran his hands over the keys. 'It's got a great sound, I can use it to give demos.'

'We'll be calling on your talents soon enough.' Eddie smiled at Carl's enthusiasm. 'That classical training won't go to waste though God knows what your mum would make of you playing like Jerry Lee Lewis and Little Richard. Right, let's see how Jane and Stuart are getting on with the record department.'

* * *

'This looks amazing.' John admired the colourful montage of posters and album sleeves that Stuart had created. 'You can tell he's an art student, can't you?'

Jane popped up from behind the counter, where she was sorting through boxes of records. 'He's been very arty-farty tonight. Wouldn't let me help him at all.'

'You've been filing the records. That's your talent, Jane,' Stuart said, laughing as she poked out her tongue.

'Only because you can't remember the alphabet,' she said. 'He was placing Russ Conway on the shelf before Perry Como.'

'I'd rather shove 'em both in the bin!'

'Now, now, each to his own,' John said. 'Perry Como and Russ Conway fans pay your wages as much as The Beatles and The Rolling Stones' fans do.'

'Everywhere looks fabulous.' Eddie looked proudly around his new store. 'Me and Carl are gonna love working here.'

'I hope my new assistant is as good as the one Ed's pinching from me,' Jane said with a smile.

'I'm sure he will be,' John reassured her. 'Sean Grogan's a nice lad, very into music. Anyway, come next Monday, you'll find out.'

* * *

The Raiders celebrated the official opening day with a live appearance, Eddie taking Kris's place on drums. The shop was packed to the door with fans.

As he sat behind the kit, Eddie realised how much he

missed drumming. A shiver ran through him. His hands shook as he picked up the sticks. Singing with The Raiders was good, and he'd be forever grateful to Roy, but drumming was in his blood, under his skin. It was time to buy another kit. Roy had told him the other night that Kris had boasted of an offer from another group. He was thinking of leaving The Raiders next month anyway, so it was only a matter of time.

* * *

Carl tapped his feet to the music. He caught the eye of Tina Pickles and grinned. The junior sales assistant flashed him a smile, her green eyes sparkling. With her long hair caught up in a swinging ponytail, and her shapely hips swaying in time to the music, Carl thought she was the sexiest redhead he'd ever seen. He moved to stand by her side: 'What do you think of the band?'

'They're brilliant. I've never seen them play before, but my friend saw them at The Roulette Club recently and *she's* a big fan.'

'Err, I'll take you to the club next time they play,' he stammered. 'That's if you want to, of course.'

She smiled. 'I'd like that, Carl.'

'Might as well see them while they're still around. John Grey says they're destined for bigger things.'

'I'm sure he's right.'

* * *

'Are you entitled to a few days off work?' Eddie's mother asked as he and Jane joined his parents for what had become their regular Monday evening meal. 'We promised Aunt Celia we'd go to Brighton to check on her house while she's away but your dad's lumbago's playing up and he can't face the long drive. Do you and Jane fancy a little holiday? Perhaps you could ask Roy and Sammy to go with you.'

'Sounds great, Mum,' Eddie said as she placed heaped plates in front of them. 'I'll ask John if we can have a couple of days off. It's a bank holiday next week so we're closed Monday. What do you reckon, Jane?'

'That'll be lovely. I've never been to Brighton. I'll have to check with Mum and Dad.'

Eddie nodded. 'If they agree, we can set off straight after Saturday night's gig. Just drop our gear at Roy's place and go.'

'Where are you playing Saturday?' his mum asked, sitting down next to him.

'The Manor Lounge Club.'

'Well, at least it's local, so you won't be too late finishing. The group's playing all over the place these days.'

'Well there you go, Mum, fame at last. All we need now is a good agent.'

'Roy said Frank James definitely wants to sign you,' Jane said, helping herself to carrots from the large dish Eddie's mother pushed towards her.

'He does, but he told Roy to get rid of Kris and replace him with me.'

'Well, Kris is leaving The Raiders anyway, so what's the problem?' Jane asked.

'He hasn't actually given Roy a firm date,' Eddie said. 'I won't take his job from under his nose, that wouldn't be fair.'

'The Beatles got rid of Pete Best and brought Ringo Starr in,' Jane pointed out.

'That's what Roy keeps telling me. Anyway, get a move on with your shepherd's pie, or I'll have to finish it for you. What's for pudding, Mum?'

'Apple crumble and custard.'

He licked his lips. 'My favourite. Best cook in the world, my mum. Notice I've put most of the weight back on that I lost during my marriage?' He patted his tummy, grinning at Jane.

'Yes.' She raised an eyebrow. 'Don't get too porky, I like my men nice and slim.'

'Men? You mean man, singular, I hope.'

'Of course.' She twisted her engagement ring around on her finger. 'I've had enough of these, this one's here to stay.'

* * *

Roy slumped forward in the front passenger seat, snoring softly, the map he'd been using on the floor by his feet. Eddie swung into Dorset Gardens and pulled up outside Aunt Celia's Victorian villa. Jane and Sammy were asleep on the back seat, heads touching.

'Good job one of us managed to stay awake,' Eddie muttered and clambered out. 'Or else we'd have been wrapped around a bloody lamp post.'

Once he had opened the front door, he stepped into the hall and flicked on the light. He passed an occasional table at the bottom of the stairs, where family photographs were displayed in silver frames, and picked up a pre-war photo of his parents, smiling as he looked at his father, smartly dressed in military uniform, his mother in a two-piece with a fox fur round her neck, looking up at her soldier boy with adoring eyes.

There was one of himself in school uniform. He remembered that it had been taken almost five years earlier, the last year of school. He looked carefree, with a hint of rebellion in his eyes. He'd had the world at his feet then, but with all that had happened since, it seemed a lifetime ago.

He wandered into the spacious lounge. It felt good to be here again and although Aunt Celia had recently redecorated the room in a fashionable shade of light orange, the brown hide suite, green leafy-patterned carpet and cluttered shelves were familiar to him, evoking memories of childhood holidays spent in Brighton.

The door opened and Roy sauntered in, bleary-eyed and yawning. 'God, I'm absolutely knackered by that long drive!'

Eddie burst out laughing. 'What long drive? You slept most of the way. Anyway, go and wake the girls and bring the bags in while I stick the kettle on.'

* * *

'I can't believe how sunny it is.' Eddie shaded his eyes from the glare of the sun and stared up at the cloudless blue sky.

'I'm roasting in these jeans,' Jane complained. 'I wish I'd brought my shorts with me.'

'Me too,' Sammy said. 'I wasn't expecting the weather to be so nice.'

Following a long lie-in, the friends had strolled through The Lanes and down to the beach. They were sitting close to the sea, watching the waves lapping rhythmically over the pebbles. Gulls swooped and dived, grabbing leftovers from picnickers.

'I'm hungry, I fancy fish and chips on the pier.' Roy smacked his lips.

'It's only a couple of hours since you ate a mountain of bacon butties,' Sammy protested. 'You're always hungry, you gannet!'

Eddie got up and pulled Jane to her feet. They followed Roy and Sammy up to the busy promenade.

'Hang on a minute.' Eddie stared at a crowd of leather-clad youths gathered near the pier head. 'Something's going on. The place is swarming with Rockers.' He placed a protective arm around Jane's shoulders and turned at a roaring noise behind them.

'Fucking hell, look at that lot!' He pointed to a convoy of parka-clad Mods, who were riding their fur- and mirror-bedecked scooters slowly up the promenade towards the Rockers.

'What's happening?' Jane said, as several families made their way along the prom with prams and picnic baskets. Elderly couples, who'd been sitting on deckchairs, began gathering their belongings and hurried to the safety of the beach and esplanade below.

'We should make ourselves scarce,' Roy said. 'Trouble's brewing. Remember the Mods and Rockers riots in Clacton at Easter? Bet this is a repeat of that.'

Eddie grabbed Jane's hand and pulled her across the road. He looked back, gasping as Roy and Sammy disappeared in the sea of scooters and Mods, who advanced with menacing chants of *Down with the Rockers!* And *We want blood!*

Jane waved frantically. Sammy was white-faced as she and Roy reached the safety of the pavement.

Eddie pointed as two Rockers, trying to escape on a Harley-Davidson, were pulled to the ground by the screaming, chanting Mods. 'Jesus, the poor buggers!' he said as the steel petrol tank crunched against the road. 'Let's get back to Celia's, quick.'

Each corner they turned, gangs of Mods and Rockers appeared from nowhere.

'This is gonna be nasty,' Roy said as they hurried into Dorset Gardens. 'Try not to catch anyone's eye, or we'll end up getting caught up in it and it's not even our bloody fight.'

Jane unlocked the front door and they fell inside, slamming it behind them. Eddie shot the bolts in place. 'Thank God my mum and dad stayed home, they'd never have coped with that lot.'

'Go and sit in the lounge, girls, and I'll make us a drink,' Roy said.

Jane and Sammy sank thankfully onto the sofa and five minutes later, Roy carried in a tray of coffee, followed by Eddie with plates of toast and chocolate biscuits.

'Have these for lunch and we'll get fish and chips later. I don't want you girls going anywhere until we're sure it's safe.'

Sammy pulled a disappointed face. 'Me and Jane want to go back to The Lanes. That nice orange and white striped dress I saw earlier will be sold if I don't buy it soon.'

'You're not going out and that's final.' Roy put his arms around her. 'I don't want anything happening to you.'

'I love it when you think you're being masterful, Roy.' She planted a kiss on his cheek.

Roy tucked into the toast and chocolate digestives, then yawned and winked at Sammy. 'That's filled a hole. I'm tired. It must be the sea air. I could do with a kip. What about you, babe?'

'You're so bloody obvious, Cantello!' Eddie said as Sammy smirked.

'Don't know what you mean.' Roy raised an innocent eyebrow. He took Sammy by the hand and led her out of the room, both yawning loudly.

* * *

Eddie turned to Jane. 'I'm glad they've gone off to bed. I want to ask you something.'

'What?'

He knelt on the brown furry hearthrug in front of her. 'The flat above the new shop,' he began, lacing his fingers through hers, 'it's still vacant. I'm thinking seriously about taking on the tenancy.'

'Won't it be really expensive?'

'Maybe, but I've got my wages and the gig money. I'm not paying the rent on my old flat for Angie any more. If you move in with me, we can manage the rent between us. Do you think your parents will have any objections?'

Jane blew out her cheeks. 'They'll have plenty. It took a lot of persuading for them to agree to these few days away.'

'Why? Your mum knows we sleep together.'

'Yeah, but Dad doesn't. He made me promise to share a room with Sammy and no hanky-panky.'

'Hmm,' he said, smiling. 'I can just imagine. But you will ask them? They might just say yes.'

'I'll ask, but don't hold your breath. Anyway, I thought you liked living back at your mum's.'

'I do. But we've nowhere to be alone, except when they're out. There's the group's van, but Phil's usually got some bird in there – we hardly get a chance to use it.'

'Why not ask Roy and Tim to share with you? Split the rent and bills three ways, then we'll all have somewhere.'

'Not a bad idea as a backup plan but I won't mention it until you've talked to your mum and dad.' He pulled her down onto the rug beside him and ran his hands through her hair. 'I'm gonna love you all afternoon.'

'What if Roy and Sammy come down?' she said, yanking his T-shirt over his head.

'They won't, they'll be shagging for England. Would you rather go upstairs?'

'No, we'll stay down here. I like this nice furry rug,' she whispered, losing herself to his kisses.

* * *

'Fuck, look at that lot!' Eddie stared at the seething mass of youths still battling it out on the seafront. There'd been no sign of holidaymakers as he and Roy had walked towards the Palace Pier to buy supper.

They watched as deckchairs were hurled onto the beach and used by the gangs as weapons. Chanting Mods roared past them on scooters. The noise was deafening. The police, trying desperately to control the crowds, appeared to be fighting a losing battle.

'I wonder if anyone's been killed,' Roy said as a bloodied and battered Mod limped by, girlfriend clinging to his arm, her mascara running in black rivulets down her face. 'Look, there are TV cameras by the pier. Let's get out of here.'

'I'm glad we left the girls at the house,' Eddie muttered as they turned back in the direction of The Lanes. 'We'll find somewhere else to buy our fish and chips.'

'We need more dope. There's only enough left for a small joint. I meant to buy some from Mac before we came away. With Sammy hurrying me along, I forgot.'

Eddie nodded. 'I'll go in that chippy and get the supper while you see if you can score anything. Should be easy enough around here.'

Roy went off in search of supplies. He was lucky in the first pub he tried. A smartly-dressed man caught his eye. Roy followed him outside and they struck a deal.

'Thanks, mate.' Roy handed over the money.

Eddie came out of the chip shop, arms laden with newspaper parcels. 'Sorted?'

'Yeah. Nice bloke. Dearer than Mac, mind, but better than nothing. Good grief, Ed, have you got enough bloody food there, or what?! Did you get me some mushy peas?'

'No, Sammy told me not to. Said you'd fart all night. You're bad enough without the peas, apparently. Let's get some cider then we're well stocked.'

* * *

Jane flung open the door. 'Thank God you're back. The riots are on TV. Your mum just phoned, Ed. Call her back and let her know you're safe. I told her you'd gone to get fish and chips and she panicked – she said the news looked like the start of another war.'

Eddie rang his mother and reassured her they were all okay while Jane and Sammy put out the supper. He strolled back into the room, smiling.

'I've asked her to call all your mums in case they've seen the news. I'm starving, let's get that food down us.'

They tucked in at the kitchen table, then took bottles of cider through to the lounge and sat down to watch the riots on TV.

'I've heard enough of this.' Roy leapt up and switched off the set. He fiddled with the dial on Celia's radiogram: 'What frequency's Radio Caroline on, Sam?'

'Car-o-line, one nine, nine,' she chanted as Roy laughed and tuned in.

'That's better,' he said as the powerful voice of Roy Orbison filled the room. He took a matchbox from his pocket and placed it on the coffee table. 'There you go, Ed.'

Eddie pulled a foil-wrapped package from the box and sniffed the contents. 'Bloody hell! Ready wrapped. Decent stuff, too. Shall I do the honours, or will you?'

'I'll do it,' Roy said. 'Yours always fall apart.'

Jane watched as Roy re-wrapped the cannabis, held his lighter underneath, then produced cigarette papers and tobacco. He crumbled a small amount into the tobacco and deftly rolled a large joint.

'Sheer perfection! You joining us tonight, Jane?' He lit up, drew deeply and passed it to Eddie, who took a lengthy toke.

'Oh, nice hit,' he said, an expression of bliss crossing his face. 'Try some, Jane. Go on, take a deep breath and inhale. You'll get the hang.'

She drew on the joint. The smoke hurt the back of her throat and her eyes watered. She spluttered and passed it to Sammy, whose eyes lit up as she took her turn.

'Mm, lovely,' she said, smiling at Roy, who was busy rolling another.

'You and Jane finish that and me and Ed will have this,' he said, taking a quick drag.

Jane took another toke and giggled. 'I feel like I've been drinking loads of cider. I'm so-ooo relaxed, so comfy-womfy!'

'Comfy-womfy! That grammar school education was a complete waste of time,' Eddie teased.

They laughed, relaxing and chatting. Jane switched on the TV for the late news. The riots were ongoing with hundreds of teenagers still arriving in the town.

'Thank God we're safe in here,' she said, snuggling up to Eddie.

'I'm sorry we've had our weekend spoiled,' Eddie said. 'I drag you all the way down here to be stuck indoors.'

'It doesn't matter, Ed.' Roy poured cider into glasses. 'Sam and I are grateful for the time we've spent together.'

'It's been brilliant,' Sammy said, scooping up a handful of peanuts. 'And the best thing of all, Roy hasn't had to get out of bed to go home!'

'Yeah.' Roy grinned. 'I hate doing that.'

'*I've* had a lovely time just being with you so stop worrying,' Jane said.

'Better than the weekend in The Lakes, eh, Jane?' Roy raised an eyebrow.

'Oh God, I'll say! Can't believe that was only three months ago.'

13

Vicky clutched the red velvet box and lifted the lid. She caught her breath and gazed in awe at the beautiful ruby and diamond cluster ring nestling against the black satin lining. Cheeks heating, she replaced the box in Mark's dressing table drawer. He was in the shower. She'd spotted him slipping the box into the drawer on Friday night and presumed it must be for her.

They'd spent the bank holiday together. She'd cooked all their meals. Playing at being Mrs Fisher had been every bit as good as she'd imagined. On tenterhooks all weekend, she'd been waiting for Mark to pop the question. Maybe he was saving it for today, the last before his return to Chester. She plugged in her hairdryer as he appeared behind her, wrapped in a towel.

'I've booked a table at The Black Boy in Prestbury for lunch,' he said, splashing on Brut. 'Put your glad rags on because it's a posh place. I thought we'd have a treat, seeing as it's our last day together.' He bent to kiss her and she smiled.

'Any particular reason for this treat?'

'Not really.' He reached into the wardrobe and took out a white shirt and smart black trousers. 'We've been cooped up most of the weekend, it'll be nice to go out.' He threw on his clothes and brushed his hair. 'I need to make a quick call while you finish getting ready.'

'All right.' Vicky switched on the hairdryer.

He was going to propose today over lunch. Good job she'd remembered to bring her best black dress and shoes.

* * *

Phone in hand, Mark listened to make sure Vicky's hairdryer was turned on then dialled a number. 'Can I speak to Beth Robbins, flat three, please? It's Mark. Thanks, I'll hold.'

Staring at his reflection in the hall mirror, he listened to an exchange of voices in the background, then Beth said, 'Hi, Mark. Why haven't you called all weekend? Is your mum ill?'

'Hi, Beth. Mum's okay, thanks. I've been busy looking after her. I haven't had a minute to ring you,' he lied. 'I'll get her in a home one day then we can spend every weekend together. I'll be back tomorrow.' He took a deep breath. 'Any news? Shit! Don't cry, I'll sort it.' He cocked his ear as the noise from Vicky's hairdryer ceased.

'Mum's calling, have to go. See you tomorrow. Yeah, me too. Bye.' He slammed down the receiver. Fucking hell! He trudged back upstairs. Now what?

He ran his hands through his hair. What should he do? And where was bloody Tony when he needed him? Swanning around Blackpool with Sarah. He'd know what to do. But then, Tony wouldn't get himself into this mess in the first place.

He smiled at Vicky as he walked into the bedroom. 'You're looking very sexy. Shame we've got to rush.'

She sat down on the bed and smiled. 'Did you call Maude?'

'Err, yeah. She was having a moan because I haven't seen her for weeks. She's bloody lucky I bother at all after what she did to me.'

'You could pop in and see her next week.'

'I won't be home, someone at work's having a party. I'll stay over there.'

'Would you like me to come to Chester?'

'No, it's invites only. Mine didn't say to bring a guest.'

There was no party, but if Beth were pregnant, they'd need time together while they decided what to do. He supposed he should offer to marry her. She was a fit bird, they never argued and she was a great shag. But he was enjoying having a girl in each town. Besides, no matter how much he denied it, he still wanted Jane.

'Mark, I asked if you'd be home the following week...' Vicky's voice broke into his thoughts.

'What? God, *I* don't know. Stop being so clingy. This is a no-strings relationship. We agreed at the beginning, right?'

'But I thought... well, with you buying the ring and booking the table...' Vicky faltered, her eyes filling with tears.

'What ring?' He frowned. 'What you on about? Why the hell are you crying?'

'The ring in your drawer,' she sniffed. 'The ruby cluster ring you put there on Friday night. I thought it was for me.'

'You've rooted in my drawer? You've no right to go through my private things.'

'I didn't. I saw you put the box in there. I was curious, that's all. Why have you bought an engagement ring if it's not for me?'

'It's Jane's ring. I take it to Chester and bring it back at the weekend. It's all I have left of her, apart from my memories and photographs.'

'You do *what*?' Vicky stared at him. 'Why? You've got *me* now. Why the hell do you still want Jane? She dumped you. I'm gonna chuck that ring away.' She jumped up and made for the drawer. Mark grabbed her and pushed her back onto the bed.

'Get off me,' she yelled, lashing out at him. 'You're a bloody nutter!'

He pinned her down, hands round her throat. She grabbed

the hairdryer and whacked the side of his head. He let go and she jumped up, holding her neck.

'What the fuck did you do that for?' he said, moving towards her.

'You were trying to strangle me.' She backed towards the door.

'I wasn't,' he protested. 'I didn't want you to touch the ring.'

She stared at him for a long moment. 'There's something you should know about Jane.'

'What?'

'She's engaged to Eddie Mellor. Sarah told me.'

'You're a liar. Tony would have told me.'

'Tony didn't tell you because it would put you in a foul mood. Let her go, Mark. *I* love you, in spite of what you just did to me. I'm sure you could learn to love me too, given time.'

'I couldn't,' he said and sighed. 'Err, there's something I need to tell you.'

'What?' She stared at him.

'I'm seeing someone over in Chester.'

'And is she the reason you're not coming home next weekend?'

'Sort of. I lied. There's no party, I need to spend time with her. We've a problem.'

'What sort of problem?' Vicky's voice wobbled as she looked at him.

'She's pregnant; well, it looks that way.'

'She's what?' Her hand flew to her mouth. 'You bastard! How could you?'

He shrugged. 'Sorry. I'll ring the restaurant, cancel our booking. I'm not in the mood for eating now anyway.'

'Sorry?' she echoed. 'Is that all you've got to say? Why book a table in the first place? You must have known this before you called the restaurant.'

'I didn't, not for sure. I spoke to her while you were drying your hair.'

'So if she'd told you everything was okay, you'd have carried on wining, dining and bedding me?' She picked up a glass ashtray and flung it at him. He ducked as she yelled, 'You're a cheating bastard, Mark Fisher, or whatever fancy name you call yourself these days! Well, that's it, I've had enough. We're through.'

'Okay. Get your stuff, I'll run you home.'

'Get lost, Mark. I'll call a taxi. I can't go home, Mum thinks I'm staying at my friend's until tomorrow. I'll have to go there.'

'Right,' he said, relieved. Vicky going now meant he could go back to Chester straight away and stay with Beth. *A problem shared and all that*, he thought as she flounced out of the room and slammed the door.

* * *

Mark turned over as the alarm shrilled down his ear. He picked up the clock and hurled it across the room, where it hit the wall, shattering into pieces. '*BASTARD!*' he yelled at the white plastic bits lying on the carpet.

Beth sat up, startled, her long blonde hair tangled from sleep and her blue eyes wide. 'Whatcha do that for? I'll have to buy another now.' She got out of bed and clutched her stomach. 'Oh God, I'm gonna chuck up again,' she said, running to the door.

Mark stared after her, hoping the communal bathroom was free. He fell back against the pillows and ran his hands through his hair, glancing around the shabby, cramped flat. He took in the paraphernalia she'd crammed into the twelve-foot square attic room, which included a curtained-off kitchen, and wondered how such a pretty girl could bear to live in this chaotic squalor.

Funny how he'd never noticed the mess at first. Beth always lit candles because the meter was constantly out of money. Bathed in a warm glow after a shared joint and a bottle of wine, the room took on a romantic feel. Besides, she was sexy, dressed up, and even more so naked, and it was as much as they could do to climb the stairs to the flat before ripping off one another's clothes, so the state of the room had usually been the last thing on his mind.

He jumped up, pulled on a T-shirt and jeans and folded up the bed settee. He stowed the blankets and pillows in a chest, drew back the faded blue curtains and grimaced. The gloomy morning did nothing to dispel his black mood and as he filled the kettle and rinsed two chipped mugs in the grimy sink, his thoughts returned to the previous evening.

By the time he'd seen Vicky off and driven to Chester, Beth had gone out. He'd sat in the car outside her flat, waiting. She'd been surprised but pleased to see him.

'I wasn't expecting you until tomorrow,' she said, throwing her arms around him.

'I thought I'd surprise you and come back early so we can talk about our problem,' he said, following her up the communal staircase to the top floor.

'Do we have to? Can't it wait until tomorrow and we can just enjoy our night together?'

'No, we need to make plans. I decided on the drive over that we should get married right away.'

Her jaw dropped and she sat down on the sofa. 'Married? Who said anything about getting married? You said you'd sort it, not marry me. I don't want to get married. I don't want a baby either. I'm only eighteen, I want a life. I've got a job in a Torquay hotel for the summer. Clare from work fixed it up for us. We start next month, or at least we're supposed to.'

'You never said anything to me about going to Torquay,' Mark said.

'I *was* going to tell you. The time never seemed right and with you going back home for weekends, I didn't think you'd be that bothered.'

'Well, you'll have to cancel the whole thing. You can't go off to Torquay if you're pregnant. There's nothing else for it, we'll have to get married.' He paced the room. 'It's the right thing to do.'

'I don't want to get married, Mark,' she repeated. 'I don't love you and you don't love me. It was a bit of fun. Clare knows someone who had an abortion. She gave me the phone number of the man who did it. He lives the other side of Chester. Thing is, I can't afford it.' Tears tumbled down her cheeks and she impatiently brushed them away.

He sat down beside her, taking her hand. He allowed himself a little moment of silent celebration, then immediately felt guilty. 'Are you sure about this? We'll be right in the shit if something goes wrong.'

'The girl Clare knows is fine. She was back at work after a couple of days.'

'What about adoption?'

'No!' She shook her head. 'That's one road I am *not* prepared to go down.'

'Okay, then I guess abortion it is,' he said. 'I'll pay, I've got the money.'

'But it's forty pounds,' she said tearfully. 'Where will you find that sort of money at short notice?'

'I was engaged earlier this year. I saved money for my wedding, it can come out of that.'

'What happened? To your fiancée, I mean?'

'She changed her mind. I'd rather not talk about it tonight.'

'Poor Mark. Do girls *always* let you down?'

'Not all.'

Beth strolled back into the room, disturbing his reverie. She smiled wanly at him and pulled on her dressing gown.

'Feeling better?' He spooned Camp coffee into the mugs and added water.

She accepted the coffee and sat down on the bed settee, shivering

'You cold?' Mark turned on the gas fire, which reluctantly spluttered to life, and sat down beside her.

'Not really, just a bit shaky.' She smiled and patted his knee. 'Thanks for putting the bed away and money in the meters. The bathroom's free if you want to get ready for work.'

'I'm phoning in sick this morning,' he said. 'You should too.'

'But I need to work to pay towards the abortion.'

'I told you last night I've got the money. You're not fit to go anywhere and we need to get in touch with that guy. I think you should see a doctor first though, just to check you really are pregnant.'

'Mark, I *know* I'm pregnant. I don't need to see a doctor. I'm never late, I've been throwing up for England. How much more proof do you need, for God's sake?'

He shrugged in answer and sipped his coffee.

'Why are you so bloody grumpy this morning? Now you're getting off the hook, I thought you'd be jumping for joy.'

'Come on, Beth, I'm hardly off the hook. I offered to marry you, didn't I? I rushed back as quickly as I could so we could talk but you'd already made your decision.'

'Yeah, of course you rushed back,' she sneered. 'As soon as your bloody mother untied her apron strings! It's pathetic the way she rules your life. She won't let you take me home with you at the weekends. I'm not even allowed to phone you. I have to wait until *you* decide to call *me*. If you hadn't been desperate to know how things were yesterday, you wouldn't have bothered calling me until you came back to Chester.'

He sucked in his cheeks to hide his amusement. Beth was saying what Jane had said about Maude ruling his life, except this time it wasn't Maude's fault. He wondered what she would make of his predicament and laughed out loud.

'Why the hell are you laughing?' Beth glared at him. 'There's nothing funny about this. You're a bloody weirdo, Mark Fisher! My sister said you were a sandwich short of a picnic when she met you. I should have listened to her before I got involved.' She took her mug across to the sink. 'I'm going for a shower then if you're not bothered. You can phone work and you'd better call my boss too. Tell him I've got a tummy upset or something and while you're at it, ring that man. The number's on top of the record player. The sooner I get rid of this, this... thing, the better.'

Shoulders heaving, she fled the room, groaning.

Mark shook his head as he heard her chucking up again. Another relationship down the pan, quite literally. Three in as many months. If Vicky hadn't found Jane's ring, he would have had her to go crawling back to. But she wouldn't want him now, she'd made it quite clear. Still, he thought, leave it a couple of days then call her to apologise. He could send her flowers, tell her Beth's little problem was a false alarm. He reckoned Vicky would find it in her heart to forgive him if he told her he'd dumped Beth.

14

Jane dashed into the house to find her mother standing in the kitchen, wearing her coat and headscarf. 'You off out, Mum? Only I need to ask you something.'

'Can't it wait until tomorrow?' Her mother looked at her watch and picked up her handbag. 'I'm going to the pictures with Molly. *West Side Story*'s on again and she missed it first time round. I'm meeting her at the bus stop in a couple of minutes.'

'Well, yeah, I suppose so.' Damn! Eddie had called several times today, reminding her to ask her mother if they could live together. Well, she'd tried; it would just have to wait. She already knew the answer anyway. It would be a resounding NO.

Her father strolled into the kitchen and greeted her with a broad smile and his wife with a peck on the cheek: 'Howdo, girls.'

'Hiya, Dad.' Jane returned his smile.

Enid pecked him back. 'Hiya, love. Hope you've remembered I'm going out. Pete's gone to his mate's, so you don't have to worry about him for an hour or two. Your dinners are in the oven on a low light and there's a rhubarb pie in the larder. Jane will make some custard. Right, I'm off.' She hurried away as Ben swilled his face and hands at the kitchen sink while Jane busied herself dishing up their meal.

'It's not often your mother abandons us,' Ben said. 'This is good,' he added, tucking into his lamb chops hungrily.

'It won't hurt us,' Jane said. 'Mum hardly ever takes a break.'

After dinner she made a jug of custard and dished up the rhubarb pie. Ben smothered his pie with custard and shovelled it down as though he was still starving. He sat back, folding his hands across his stomach.

'Would you like more, Dad?' Jane asked.

'No, thanks, love. I'm stuffed.'

She ran hot water into the sink and dropped the cutlery and plates in to soak. 'I'll wash if you'll dry.'

'I'll do the dishes, Jane,' he said. 'No doubt you've a date with Ed. Go and get yourself ready.'

'I have.' She stretched her arms above her head and smiled. 'He's coming to collect me soon. Ask him to wait in the sitting room, please.'

'Will do,' Ben called over his shoulder as she left the room.

Eddie sat on the sofa, twiddling his thumbs. He wished he had the nerve to ask Ben, who was engrossed in the sports pages of his paper, for permission to go up to Jane's bedroom. He heard the hairdryer switch off and then she was running downstairs and burst into the living room. The wait had been worthwhile. She looked so sexy in her short black skirt, black and white top and knee-length boots that he felt a twitch just by looking and hoped it wasn't obvious to her dad as he leapt up to greet her.

'You look fabulous,' he mouthed, winking as she tossed her hair back with a shake of her head.

'Thanks,' she said, slipping her arms into her suede jacket. 'Dad, we're off out now. See you later.'

'Enjoy yourselves.' He lowered his paper. 'Make sure she's home at a reasonable hour, lad.'

'I will,' Eddie said, taking her arm. He ushered her out towards the car. 'What did your mum say about us living together?' he asked as soon as they were out of Ben's earshot.

'I didn't ask, she was on her way out as I was coming in. I'll ask tomorrow.'

'You promised you'd do it as soon as we got back from Brighton. Shall I come in with you later and we can ask her together?'

'No, Ed, definitely not! Dad will be up and it won't be the right time. She'll say no anyway. I don't know why we're even bothering.'

'She might not,' he said, frowning as he unlocked the passenger door. 'Get in, the others are meeting us at the club.'

'Are you sulking?' she said as he climbed in the driver's seat and slammed the door.

'No!' But he hadn't even kissed her yet when normally he couldn't keep his hands off her.

At The Roulette Club he was silent. He banged their drinks down on the table, lit a cigarette and sat with his back to her.

'Excuse me!' She poked his shoulder. 'What's the matter with you?'

He looked at her for a long moment and sighed. 'You don't want to live with me, that's why you haven't asked your mum.'

'For crying out loud, Ed, that's just not true. Of course I want to live with you.' She pulled him into her arms and kissed him.

'Ahem!' A stern voice spoke behind them. 'Put him down, young lady. You don't know where he's been.'

'Roy, you silly sod!' Jane giggled and looked up to see

Sammy, Pat and Tim laughing behind him. 'We were making up a misunderstanding.'

'So I see. The van's round the back if you want the keys.' Roy dangled them in front of her. 'There's more room in there than the back seat of his car.'

'We'll borrow them later.' She smiled as a look of anticipation crossed Eddie's face.

'Right,' Roy said as Tim came back from the bar with a tray of drinks. 'Shall we tell him now, or later?'

'This is as good a time as any,' Tim said.

'Tell me what?' Eddie said, taking a slurp of cider.

'Kris has finally quit the group. We're offering you the position of drummer – if you want it.'

'Honestly?' Eddie's mouth fell open. 'Oh boy, I definitely do. Where's Kris going?'

'London, to join his brother's band,' Roy said. 'They're a big name in The Smoke and the drummer left recently. It's a chance he can't turn down. It also saves *us* asking him to leave. You know we've loads of gigs lined up anyway, so we'll start rehearsing right away. We've one here this Saturday night. Can you afford to get a set of drums this week?'

'Yeah,' Eddie replied. 'I'll get a discount and pay for it weekly. I took delivery of a Ludwig kit today. It sounded brilliant when I tried it and I've already decided it's mine. The money I earn from the gigs will pay for the drums *and* car, so we could still manage the rent on the flat between us, Jane.'

'What flat?' Roy asked as Jane rolled her eyes.

'The one above the new shop,' Eddie said. 'I've asked Jane to move in with me.'

Sammy looked at Jane, eyebrows raised in amazement. 'And your mum and dad have approved this little plan?'

Jane sighed. 'I haven't mentioned it yet.'

'Well, I wouldn't even *bother* mentioning it if I was you. It'll cause a huge row. I know what Mum and Tom would say and they're a lot more liberal than *your* mum and dad.'

Pat nodded. 'There'd not be a cat in hell's chance.'

'See, it's not just *my* parents,' Jane said. 'Ask Roy and Tim to share with you.'

'Brilliant idea!' Roy exclaimed. 'Both Tim and I have talked about flat sharing, but we haven't done anything about it yet.'

Tim nodded gleefully, rubbing his hands together. 'Freedom, here we come.'

'Wait until Jane's asked her parents. If they say no, we'll make some plans,' Eddie promised.

* * *

Just as she'd predicted, her mum refused to even listen to her pleas when Jane broached the subject of moving in with Eddie.

'Not until you're married.' She carried on folding sheets, ignoring her daughter's pleading expression.

'But, Mum, we would be now if Eddie were free. Please,' Jane begged, close to tears

'It's not right. Eddie's still a married man. If he leaves you for someone else like he left Angie, you'd have no wedding ring on your finger and no security.'

'Eddie would never leave me, he loves me. I'm sick of this. I'm going!'

Jane dragged her holdall from under the wardrobe and began tossing clothes into it.

Her mum appeared at the bedroom door. 'Jane, calm down. You're going nowhere in this state.' She sat on the bed and ordered Jane to join her. 'I'm concerned for you, love. I don't want you to make a mistake. Think about it, only a few months ago you were engaged to Mark and planning to marry *him*. I know you and Eddie love one another, but slow down a bit.' She took a deep breath and gave her girl a hug. 'Listen, I tell you what, a compromise. You can stay with him on Saturday nights.'

'What about Dad? What will *he* say?'

'You leave your father to me, as usual.'

* * *

'Did you ask?' Eddie wanted to know later when he and Jane were comfortably ensconced in his bedroom.

She told him of her mother's compromise, willing him to understand.

'Okay, I suppose it's a start and it's better than nothing,' he said. 'I'll ask Roy and Tim if they'll move in then. It's a brilliant flat. I don't want to lose it, but I can't afford to rent it on my own.'

* * *

Following a few days of begging and borrowing furniture, carpets and anything else their respective mothers and aunts could come up with, Eddie, Roy and Tim moved into the spacious two-bedroomed Wilmslow flat.

'We should have a flat warming party,' Eddie suggested as he and Jane arranged the mismatched sofas and occasional tables in the lounge. Roy and Tim had taken the van to collect more family cast-offs.

'Good idea.' She followed him into the bedroom he'd decided was theirs. 'What about tomorrow after the gig?'

'Good thinking.' He pulled her onto the bed. 'We've just time for a quickie before Roy and Tim come back!'

* * *

Mark stared at the poster on the wall outside The Roulette
Club, proclaiming tonight, The Raiders were happy to
announce the reinstatement of Eddie Mellor on drums. He
watched as Vincento pasted a sold-out sign across the poster
and grinned, his fingers closing around something in his pocket.
The last four tickets for the gig were his.

That morning he'd gone to Vicky's place with the biggest
bunch of red roses he could find and apologised for treating her
badly. The dozy girl had actually believed him when he told her
that Beth's pregnancy was a false alarm and the relationship
was over because he wanted to be with *her*. She'd thrown her
arms around him and said she'd give him another chance if he'd
change his ways.

He'd never be able to tell her the truth about Beth's illegal
termination. A dirty-looking man had answered the door, sweat
oozing from every pore, mingling with the faint smell of Dettol,
three-day stubble on his chin and a mangy dog hanging round
his legs. He'd taken his money, then told Mark to hike around
the block while he dealt with Beth.

He'd protested, told the man he would rather stay, but Beth
said to go – she just wanted it over with. When he knocked on
the door half an hour later, she was seated on a chair in the hallway, her face drained, eyes red from crying. In the taxi home
she wouldn't tell him what the man had done, was writhing in
pain and then puked in her handbag. He had to carry her
upstairs to the flat.

The man assured them that getting rid of the pregnancy at
such an early stage would be no more painful than a heavy
period. How wrong he'd been, Mark thought, as Beth cursed
him to kingdom come, digging her fingernails into his hand. At
one point she was crying and bleeding so heavily, he'd panicked
and called her sister, who took one look at Beth and slapped him
soundly across the face.

They spent the night mopping Beth's brow, holding her

hands while she bit on a rolled-up towel to silence her screams and stop her from waking the rest of the tenants in the house. When the embryo came away, he stared at the transparent, but perfectly formed miniature body and wept openly, ashamed of feeling nothing but revulsion and relief.

He'd left Beth's flat yesterday, after she told him she never wanted to see him again. It was a brief but painful affair he was hoping to put behind him. The one thing keeping him going was the thought of bumping into Jane at tonight's gig.

* * *

The Roulette Club was packed and Jane, sitting at the bar with Sammy and Pat, swallowed the lump in her throat as The Raiders walked on stage dressed identically in smart grey suits and black satin shirts. She took a deep breath as Roy played the opening chords of 'That'll Be the Day' and Eddie did his familiar hair flicking with each drumbeat. The eager audience surged towards the stage, cheering and clapping.

After only a few rehearsals Eddie was really back in the swing of things. Roy's version of 'Jailhouse Rock' had the girls at the front screaming for more. Phil took centre stage and sang Arthur Alexander's 'You Better Move On'. He bent towards a young girl, who was looking up at him with adoring eyes. He blew her a kiss and reached for her hand as the song ended.

'That's tonight's shag lined up!' Sammy nudged Jane, who burst out laughing.

The group finished their first set with Eddie's solo spot and the audience joined in with Sam Cooke's 'You Send Me'.

Amidst cheers and whistling, The Raiders took a bow and walked off stage. Eddie whipped off his jacket and leapt down the side steps. Sweat dripping from his brow and his satin shirt sticking to his back, he made his way over to the bar, beaming from ear to ear. 'What did you think, Jane?' He pulled her into his arms. 'Have I still got it, or what?'

'You were wonderful, of course. What else would I think?' She planted a kiss on his lips.

'I'm gonna change out of this wet shirt. Get me a pint in and I'll see you in a few minutes.'

As Jane ordered the drinks a hand fell on her shoulder, startling her. She whipped round, her eyes opening wide. 'Mark! What on earth are *you* doing here?'

'Come to see Eddie's big comeback.' He drew an almost identical version of Jane towards him. 'Vicky, I'd like you to meet Jane.'

Jane could see the girl was as embarrassed as she was.

Vicky held out her hand. 'Nice to meet you.'

Jane forced a smile and shook her hand as Mark excused himself and left Vicky standing awkwardly by her side.

'Have you been together long?' Jane asked.

'Since you finished with him,' Vicky said. 'Off and on, that is. Eddie's a great drummer and he's got a fabulous voice. The Raiders are much better than Mark's group, but don't let on I said that.'

'I won't.' Jane smiled and held out her hand, showing Vicky her ring. 'I'm engaged to Eddie now, but maybe you shouldn't tell Mark.'

'He knows. Erm, Jane, can we get together for a coffee sometime? I'd like to ask you a few things about Mark. I work fairly near to Flanagan and Grey's. I'm a typist at Robinsons Brewery.'

'That's just up the road from the shop. Pop down in your lunch hour one day next week. Something tells me you don't want Mark to know.'

Vicky nodded. 'He's on his way back,' she whispered. 'See you soon.'

'You go back to Tony and Sarah,' Mark ordered. 'I'll get the drinks in.'

Vicky walked away dutifully and Jane stared after her.

'She's a nice girl, Mark. I'm glad you've found someone else.'

'Don't you dare fucking patronise me!' He grabbed her by the arm, his upper lip curling. 'You and I are a long way from finished. I think you know that.'

He let her go and turned his back. After ordering a round of drinks, he carried away a laden tray without a backward glance.

Sammy, who had just come back from the ladies', said, 'What's he doing here? And why was he holding you like that?'

Jane could see Eddie making his way towards her. 'I think he's had too much to drink. For God's sake, don't tell Ed he was anywhere near me. I don't want them fighting.'

'You okay?' Eddie asked as he picked up his pint and knocked it back. 'God, I needed that.'

'I'm fine. Got a bit of a headache, that's all,' she fibbed.

'Shall I cancel the flat warming?'

'No, but I don't think we should let everyone stay too late. We've got Jonny tomorrow. We need to be up early to tidy the place before Angie brings him over. We should try and create a good impression so she won't stop you having access.'

'Stop worrying, Jane. We'll stick a joint in your hand as soon as we get home. That'll loosen you up a bit.'

'My dad would have a hairy fit if he could hear you,' she said, laughing. 'I doubt he'd let me near you again, let alone live with you.'

15

Jane woke with a throbbing head and a sense of impending doom. She recalled last night's confrontation with Mark and how she'd kept it from Eddie. Also, today, Angie was coming to the flat for the first time. She made a decision to hide in the bedroom so she wouldn't have to face her and slid out of bed, pulled on her nightdress and made her way to the bathroom.

The door to the lounge stood open and she glanced inside. Empty cider bottles and overflowing ashtrays littered the room and the heady smell of cannabis hung in the air. Pat and Tim were sprawled on a makeshift bed, arms entwined, dead to the world. Must be Sammy and Roy's turn for the bedroom. She threw a blanket over the very private pair, who would be horrified to realise they'd been on view in all their naked glory.

The bathroom cabinet yielded no aspirin. In the kitchen she rinsed a glass, filled it with water and drank thirstily. Back in the lounge she opened the windows to let out the sweet smoky smell. Pat stirred and sat up slowly, holding her head.

'Morning,' Jane greeted her.

'What time is it?' Pat groaned and rubbed her eyes.

'Just gone nine. Go back to sleep.'

'Why are you up so early then?'

'I've got a head that feels like someone's playing a drum solo in it.'

'Talking of drummers, how's Ed? He looked a bit worse for wear when you dragged him off to bed.'

'He was, but he survived. I'll let him sleep it off. We've got Jonny today, so he'll need his wits about him.'

'I'll help you clean up. You'll need to pass muster for Angie's inspection.' Pat stood up, wobbling slightly. She picked up Tim's black T-shirt from the floor and pulled it on. 'This'll do, it covers my backside. Don't know where my knickers are! Don't even remember taking my clothes off. Oh dear, my legs are not mine.'

Jane grabbed a carrier bag and began filling it with empty bottles. The noise disturbed Tim, who sat up, pale and dishevelled, blinking like an owl.

'Go and lie on the bed in our room, Tim. Ed's still asleep in there. You can grab another hour while we clean up.' She found Tim's jeans behind the sofa and threw them at him, discreetly turning her back while he put them on.

'I feel terrible,' he mumbled, walking unsteadily across the room.

Pat vacuumed the carpet while Jane wiped down every surface.

'Looks better now,' Pat said and sank down on one of the sofas with a mug of steaming black coffee and a plate of hot buttered toast.

'It does,' Jane agreed, joining her. 'Bet Angie wouldn't notice if we'd left it in a mess. Eddie told me their place was always a pigsty.'

Pat nodded. 'Good night, wasn't it? What I can remember of it, that is!'

'Think so,' Jane agreed. 'Judging by the state we're all in, the number of empty bottles and joint ends, I reckon it must have been.'

The bedroom door flew open and Eddie, clad in skimpy red briefs that left nothing to the imagination, wandered into the lounge, a confused expression on his face.

'Can anyone tell me why I'm in bed with Tim? He flung his arm around me, called me Pat and made lewd suggestions!'

Pat smiled and blushed prettily. 'Hope he didn't give too many secrets away.'

'I sent him in while we tidied up,' Jane said. 'Put some clothes on and I'll make you a coffee.'

'I'll have a wash and shave first.' He stumbled into the bathroom and emerged ten minutes later, groaning. 'What on *earth* did we drink?'

'Gallons of cider,' Jane said. 'You were smoking dope all night. No wonder you feel ill. I'm surprised you can even stand this morning.'

One by one, the others emerged. Sammy sank down on the sofa and drank several mugs of strong black coffee.

'We've got to go home soon,' she said, nibbling delicately at a slice of toast. 'It's Mum and Tom's wedding anniversary. Pat and I promised to cook lunch. Will you give us a lift in the van, please, Roy?'

Roy looked at her pale face and smiled. 'Of course I will, my sweet.' He turned to Eddie. 'Tim and I will make ourselves scarce this afternoon while you and Jane look after Jonny.'

'Thanks, mate.' Eddie smiled gratefully and yawned.

* * *

The doorbell rang at two. Eddie let in Angie's friend Cathy, who was carrying Jonny in her arms, face flushed from the effort of climbing two flights of stairs.

'Why have *you* got him?' he demanded, taking his son from Cathy and looking past her. 'Where's Angie?'

'She's not feeling well, she asked me to drop him off. I'll collect him about seven.' Cathy peered through to the lounge and waved at Jane, who waved back.

'Fine.' Eddie made to close the door.

Cathy nervously cleared her throat. 'My sister was at the gig last night. She said you were brilliant. Is the drumming permanent now?'

'It is. When you go blabbing back to Angie you can also tell her that Jane and I are engaged. I've got back everything she robbed me of. Very soon I'll have custody of my son.'

'There's no need to take that tone with me.' Cathy folded her arms. 'I'm not here to act as a go-between. What happened with you and Angie wasn't my fault. You shouldn't have married her.'

'Huh, tell me something I don't already know.'

'If it's any consolation, I tried my best to talk her out of marrying you, but she wouldn't listen.'

He nodded. 'Sorry for being snappy. Thanks for bringing Jonny round. Once this mess is sorted, I'll have him all weekend until I get custody. I wish Angie would get her finger out and reply to my solicitor's letters, it's been weeks now.' He wanted her to go. Her presence in his flat stirred memories he was trying to put behind him.

She said goodbye. He carried Jonny, and the bag of toys and nappies that Cathy had brought, into the lounge.

'What was all that about?' Jane said, frowning at his tense expression.

'Angie's not well, apparently. Probably hungover, knowing her.'

'Well, look at the state of us two,' she said, laughing at his disapproving face.

He grinned, seeing the funny side. 'I've just had an awful

thought. Can you change nappies? It's the first time I've had Jonny without Mum being around.'

'I've never done one before, but I can probably manage.' Jane held out her arms to Jonny who smiled shyly as she lifted him onto her knee. He snuggled into her and pointed to a book that lay on the coffee table. 'Shall we read a story while Daddy gets us a drink and then we'll go to the park?'

'Yes.' Jonny nodded his head and stuck his thumb in his mouth.

* * *

'I feel better now,' Eddie said as he and Jane strolled home arm in arm from the park, where they'd spent a pleasant hour playing with Jonny. 'The fresh air's blown away a few cobwebs.'

Cathy was late collecting Jonny and by eight, there was still no sign of her. He was tired, so Jane bathed Jonny and dressed him in one of Eddie's T-shirts. She took a blanket from their bed and tucked him up on the sofa. He was asleep within minutes, sucking his thumb.

'Where the hell is she?' Eddie paced up and down the room.

'Calm down, Ed, she'll be here soon.' Jane tried her best to placate him as the minutes ticked by. 'I need to go home. Mum and Dad will be wondering where I am.'

'You can't leave me. What if he wakes up and needs changing again?' he said, suddenly helpless.

'You watched me do it when I bathed him. Look, I'll fold you a nappy, then you just lay him on it and put a pin in each side.' Jane laid Jonny's teddy on the nappy and demonstrated. 'See, it's so simple.'

'But the teddy lies still, Jonny wriggles all over the show! I might stick the pin in him.'

'You're bloody hopeless,' she said. 'What about all these

babies you want with me? Who's gonna help me look after them? I'll call Mum, see if I can stay another night. But try ringing Cathy first, or even Angie. *We* could take Jonny home.'

Eddie tried Angie and Richard's number, but there was no reply. He slammed the phone down. 'She's obviously not ill enough to stay home. Where the bloody hell is she? I can't ring Cathy, I don't have her number.'

Jane called her mother, who agreed it was better if she stayed at the flat until someone came for Jonny. She hung up and turned to Eddie. 'I can stay over again if Cathy doesn't come for him.'

'Oh good,' he said, relieved. 'I half hope she doesn't then. But my solicitor will hear about this on Monday.'

'How come Jonny's still here?' Roy nodded his head towards the sleeping child when he and Tim arrived home.

'Nobody's collected him yet,' Jane said.

'Have you been to the club tonight?' Eddie asked. 'Did you see Cathy or Angie in there?'

'Neither,' Tim said. 'It was very quiet tonight. Just Stu and Mac from our crowd.'

'Right, Ed, I'm off to take a bath,' Jane said. 'I may as well assume I'm gonna be here all night. Jonny won't wake up just yet, so don't panic. Anyway, you're not on your own, Roy and Tim can help you.'

'I don't know the first thing about kids,' Tim said, a look of alarm crossing his face.

'Nor I,' Roy said, frowning. 'That's why women make the best mothers!'

Jane shook her head and went to run a bath.

* * *

As she lay back in the bubbles, relaxing properly for the first time that day and realising just how tired she was, Jane heard the phone ring.

She heard Eddie say, 'Hello,' then, 'Christ, you're joking!' Next thing he was hammering at the door: 'Jane, Jane, let me in, quick.'

'It's unlocked,' she called, sitting up. 'What is it?'

He was white-faced. 'That was Cathy,' he said, closing the door behind him and lowering his voice slightly. 'Angie's been in a car crash. Richard's dead. Angie's being operated on at the moment. Cathy needs me at the hospital. Will you come with me, please?' He threw her a towel. 'Quick, get dry. We'll have to take Jonny to my mum's first. I'll phone her and let her know we're on our way.'

'Bloody hell,' she said, jumping out of the bath. She towelled herself dry and threw on jeans and a sweater.

* * *

Cathy met them in the busy waiting room, where Eddie gripped her shoulders.

'What happened?'

'Oh, it's terrible,' she cried. 'They were on their way back from Wales. A van skidded and hit them head-on. Richard died instantly, Angie went through the windscreen.'

'I thought she was ill. What the fucking hell was she doing in Wales? This afternoon you told me she was ill.' Eddie was shaking Cathy as though everything was her fault. Jane gasped as Roy stepped between them.

'Ed, that's enough. Can't you see the state she's in?' Roy put his arms around Cathy's shoulders and spoke gently, 'Tell *me*, Cathy. Why was Angie in Wales?'

Between sobs, Cathy told Roy that Angie and Richard had been away for the weekend, celebrating their engagement.

Jonny had been left in her care and Angie had concocted the story of being ill so Eddie wouldn't realise she'd left him with her.

Eddie sat down on the nearest chair. 'Why lie? We're getting divorced, she can do what the fuck she likes. But she had no right to leave Jonny with you. He's not your responsibility, he's *my* son.'

Cathy looked away with embarrassment. 'She left him with me because of Jane. She can't bear the thought of her looking after him, that's why.'

'But that's ridiculous,' Jane said. 'I'll be Jonny's stepmother. We need the contact so he gets to know me properly.'

'Where are Angie's parents and sister?' Roy asked.

'Her mum and dad are on holiday. Sally isn't on the phone. The police found my number in Angie's bag. I called Eddie as soon as I could.' Cathy was distraught, choking on her words. 'The police have gone to Sally's house. She'll know where their parents are staying.'

'Jane, see if you can find a cup of tea for us,' Roy suggested, sitting Cathy down next to Eddie.

'I could use something stronger than tea.' Eddie turned to Cathy. 'I know you won't believe this, but I *did* try at first. Perhaps it wasn't enough. She wasn't the easiest person to live with, and I know *I'm* not, but I *did* try. She's the mother of my boy when all's said and done.' His anger spent, his shoulders shook with sobs.

Jane put her arms around him and held him while Roy went off to find the tea. By the time he came back, Angie's sister and her husband, Martin, had arrived.

Between hysterical sobs, Sally told Eddie she'd left a message at the hotel where their parents were staying.

A young nurse walked through the swing doors at the end of the corridor, making her way towards them. 'Mr Mellor?' she looked quizzically at Eddie, Roy and Martin.

'Me, that's me,' Eddie said.

'Follow me, please.' She turned to go.

'I'm Angie's sister, can I come too?' Sally looked down her nose at Eddie. 'He's her ex, they're separated.'

The nurse turned, a look of surprise on her face. 'Then who is Mrs Mellor's next of kin?'

'Me, I suppose,' Eddie replied, stepping forward. 'I'm still her husband.'

'Then please, Mr Mellor, follow me.' She led the way to a small consulting room, leaving Sally staring after them.

The surgeon looked up wearily from his desk and gestured to a chair. 'Mr Mellor, we did everything possible. Your wife suffered severe internal injuries. She haemorrhaged badly. There was nothing we could do to save her or the child. I'm very sorry. We'll require you to make a formal identification as soon as you're ready.'

'What child?' Eddie asked. 'I don't understand. Our child was at home with me.'

The surgeon frowned. 'The child she was carrying. Your wife was five months pregnant. I'm very sorry.'

The nurse, who had shown Eddie into the room, touched his arm. 'You didn't know... about the baby, I mean? I'm so sorry.'

He shook his head. 'I'd no idea. But then, I'd be the last person to be told. It wasn't mine. Her boyfriend was killed in the accident. I can't take this in. I'll identify her then I'll go and tell the others.' He stood up. 'I have a son at home who's not quite three. How on earth do I tell him where his mummy's gone?'

The nurse shook her head. 'There are some questions I have no answers to. Are you ready to do the identification now?'

He nodded and followed her down the corridor into a small side room that felt cold and clinical and smelt strongly of disinfectant. Angie's body, covered with a white sheet, lay on a trolley. The nurse turned back the sheet. Eddie took a deep breath. Tears ran unchecked down his cheeks as he gazed at Angie's cut and bruised face. Dried blood matted her curly hair. Only her cute freckled nose remained unscathed. He nodded at the nurse; there was no need for words.

'Would you like a minute on your own?'

He nodded. He grasped Angie's lifeless hands and sniffed back tears.

'I'm sorry for everything,' he choked. 'For the mess I landed us in. For not loving you as you wanted me to. Jonny was the best thing we did together. I promise I'll always look after him. Goodbye, Angie.' He bent to kiss her bruised forehead and walked out.

Back in the waiting room, everyone's eyes were on him. His legs buckled and Roy helped him onto a chair. He looked at their expectant faces.

'She's gone!' His voice was expressionless.

Cathy collapsed into Roy's arms, crying hysterically. Sally's heart-rending scream echoed around the silent waiting room.

Jane stared at Eddie, shaking her head in disbelief.

* * *

Roy took Cathy to her parents' home and Jane and Eddie back to the flat. Tim poured them a brandy and they sat on the sofa, hugging their glasses.

'Angie was pregnant,' Eddie told them. 'Five months, they said. She lost the baby and bled to death.'

'How awful,' Jane said as Roy and Tim shook their heads.

'You'd better phone your mum, Ed,' Tim said. 'She called twice to see if there was any news. Jane's mum phoned to ask if anyone had picked Jonny up. I explained about the accident. She said she'll see you tomorrow.'

'Thanks, Tim,' Jane said. 'Would you like *me* to call your mum, tell her what's happened?'

Eddie nodded, not trusting himself to speak.

'Don't tell her Angie was pregnant,' Roy advised. 'She obviously had her own reasons for keeping it to herself.'

* * *

Lillian told Jane she'd keep Jonny with her for the next few days until Eddie sorted himself out and she would call them in the morning. Jane persuaded Eddie to go to bed. She cradled him until he fell into a troubled sleep. She'd need to let John Grey know what had happened. They certainly wouldn't be going into work for a few days. And then there was Jonny. How on earth would Eddie hold down two jobs and care for a small child on his own? He would also need to explain to Jonny that Mummy wasn't coming home. She made a snap decision: no matter what barriers her parents might put up, she was moving in with him immediately.

On Monday morning, leaving Eddie sleeping fitfully, Jane hurried downstairs to open the shop, shocking Carl with her hollow-eyed appearance. She briefly explained the situation and rang John Grey at home. He told her to take as much time off as they needed, he had enough staff to cover their absence and he would call and see them later that day.

Richard and Angie's funerals were organised for the Friday.

'I don't think I can do this.' Eddie looked at Jane as she brushed his dark suit. 'The people Angie worked with know I hit her that time. They probably blame me for our marriage breaking down. She'd still be alive now if she hadn't left me.'

'Angie's affair with Richard was her choice,' Jane said. 'She was pregnant with his baby before you left her for good. Stop blaming yourself. It was six of one and half a dozen of the other.'

Roy spoke up. 'Jane's right, mate. You've got to attend the

funeral. Tim and I will be there alongside you and Jonny to show our last respects. And your folks will be there too. We'll all protect you from the wrath of Old Mother Turner.'

'Oh God, the old witch hasn't even spoken to me yet. All the information about the funeral and stuff has come half-heartedly from Sally. That family hates me. I bet they'll give me a hard time over Jonny's custody, too.'

'We'll face that when we come to it,' Jane said. 'Put your suit on while I get Jonny ready to go with you.'

'I wish you were coming with me, Jane. I need you by my side.'

'I'm the last person who should be there but I'll be here waiting for you both when you come home.'

* * *

In Eddie's absence Jane busied herself cleaning the flat, her mind going over the last week when they'd gratefully accepted all the help and support that came their way. Roy had cancelled the group's next few gigs rather than engage a stand-in drummer.

When she went home to collect a change of clothes, her mother had looked at her as though she suddenly realised Jane was now a woman with a life of her own.

'This is it, I'm not coming home, Mum. I'm staying with Eddie at the flat. We have responsibilities to one another and to Jonny.'

Her mum nodded. 'I respect the adult way that you're dealing with the situation, Jane, but I feel like my carefree teenager's disappeared overnight. You know where we are. If you need anything at all, let me know, and I do mean *anything*.'

'I will, Mum. Thanks for being so understanding.' Jane threw her arms around her mum and gave her a big hug.

'It's not the start in life I wanted for you,' her mum continued. 'But sometimes fate has a way of stepping in and you just have to get on with it. As long as you and Eddie feel that you can make it work and be happy for that little lad's sake, you'll have my blessing. Go on now, beat it before I change my mind and beg you not to go. I've a lump in my throat the size of a big cob of coal and it's threatening to choke me.'

After expecting a huge row and not getting one disagreeable word, Jane gave her mum a final hug and left her childhood home, tears tumbling down her cheeks.

* * *

A week after the funeral, Angie's mother paid a brief visit to the Wilmslow flat. The formidable figure of Lydia Turner perched on the edge of the sofa opposite Eddie and Jane, her cold green eyes raking the neat and tidy sitting room.

'Right, whatever you've come to say, get it off your chest,' Eddie prompted, reaching for Jane's hand as Lydia pursed her lips.

'I presume you've given plenty of thought to Jonny's future?' she began, looking down her pert little nose at him.

'Of course I have. I'm his father, he stays with me. Mum's helping out, and Jane and I live together. There's no need to worry about him.'

'You're living with Jane? Why doesn't that surprise me?' Lydia said. 'You've no morals. Your wife's been dead a week and you've got another woman to take her role.'

'Now hang on a bloody minute!' Eddie exclaimed. 'In case you've forgotten, *your* daughter moved in with lover boy. It was *his* kid she was carrying when she died, not mine.'

'You gave her no choice but to leave you,' Lydia said. 'You treated her appallingly.' She looked at Jane, who sat silently, chewing her lip. 'Did you know he was capable of beating up a woman?'

'It was a slap, once, that was all,' Eddie said. 'And *she* was handy with her bloody punches when it suited her.' He jumped up, clenching his fists, furious that this woman could come into his new home and still cause him hassle. 'Angie and I didn't get on, the marriage was a sham. If *you* hadn't been so fucking bothered about your narrow-minded neighbours and listened to what *we* wanted instead of pushing us to marry she'd still be alive. I blame *you* for everything!'

Lydia gasped, hand flying to her mouth. The tears started and she looked in her handbag for a hanky.

'That's right, turn on the crocodile tears! They're your answer to everything. Well, they won't wash with me this time. I've had enough of you interfering in my life. Get out of my home and don't come back.'

'Ed, that's enough,' Jane said as Lydia wept hysterically. 'Would you like a cup of tea, Mrs Turner?'

'Please, dear,' she sobbed.

'Go and get some milk from the dairy.' Jane leapt to her feet, pushing Eddie towards the door.

'Don't let her fool you with those tears,' he began. 'She can turn 'em on like a tap when it suits her.'

'Just go! Leave us for a while. The woman's grieving, give her a break. I've enough milk for tea, that was a ruse to get you out of the way. Don't come back for an hour while I talk to her and reassure her that Jonny will be okay with us.'

She lowered her voice slightly. 'Go and find Mac. Get some dope for later, it'll help you calm down. But for God's sake, don't come back stoned in case she's still here.'

He put his arms around her and held her tightly. 'What would I do without you, Jane?'

'God only knows.' She sighed and pushed him out of the door.

* * *

Jane busied herself in the kitchen, rooting out their one and only china cup and saucer, a Coronation design donated by Eddie's Auntie Minnie. She popped her head round the sitting room door. 'Do you take sugar, Mrs Turner?'

'No, thank you, dear. Just a drop of milk.'

Jane carried the tray through and placed it on the coffee table. 'Help yourself to a biscuit. They're the last of Roy's chocolate digestives.'

'Oh dear, will he mind?'

'Of course not. It's in a good cause anyway.'

'I don't think Roy Cantello would see me eating his last chocolate biscuit as a good cause.' Lydia smiled and Jane thought she saw a twinkle in the red-rimmed eyes.

'Don't worry about it.' She patted Lydia's hand. 'Are you feeling better now? I'm sorry Eddie went off at the deep end. He's tired and on a short fuse. Jonny's been up every night crying for his mummy. Ed's mum and dad have taken him to Belle Vue Zoo today to give us a bit of a break.'

'How on earth will you cope, Jane? You're not used to children.'

'We'll be okay, really. Jonny and I get along fine and Ed's a wonderful father. He thinks the world of Jonny. I know you don't have a very high opinion of him, Mrs Turner, but he's a lovely man. He and Angie weren't compatible.'

'They were compatible enough for him to get my daughter pregnant,' Lydia snorted.

'It was an accident. They were young and careless,' Jane said.

'I had absolutely no idea that Angie was expecting another baby until I spoke to the hospital. She must have been too frightened to tell me.'

'Probably,' Jane agreed.

Lydia finished her tea and placed her cup and saucer back

on the tray. She dabbed her eyes with her hanky and fiddled with the clasp on her handbag.

'I must say, this flat is lovely compared to where Angie and Eddie used to live. You've got it very nice. Who actually lives here besides you two and Jonny?'

'Roy and Tim share the second bedroom to help out with the rent and bills. Jonny is in with Ed and me. It's not ideal, but it will do for now until we can afford to move somewhere bigger.'

'So there are plenty of hands on deck to help out?'

'Oh yes, and Roy and Tim's fiancées are often here too. There are lots of people around to give Jonny a cuddle and read him a bedtime story.'

Lydia opened her handbag. She took out an envelope and handed it to Jane: 'There's a hundred pounds in there. It'll help you out when Jonny needs new shoes and clothes. I'll keep in touch and send something each month until you get on your feet. Now I'd better be making tracks.'

She stood up and smoothed down her skirt.

'Will you tell Eddie that Angie's father and I have plans to retire to the East Sussex coast later this year? I wish him every success in rearing Jonny. I can see by your ring you're engaged. I expect you'll marry Eddie one day soon, now he doesn't have to wait years for his divorce.'

'Maybe,' Jane said, seeing Lydia out. She hugged her and closed the door, then leant against it, her mind reeling. She was in the kitchen washing the cups when Eddie bounced into the flat, a lot more cheerful, but slightly worse for wear.

'Has she gone? Thank Christ for that! I had a few pints with Mac and I've got some supplies for later to share with Roy and Tim. Did you manage to pacify her?'

Jane nodded and told him what Lydia had said, including her assumption that they would marry sooner rather than later.

He smiled, head on one side. 'And do you?' He slipped his

arms around her waist. 'Want to marry me sooner, I mean? Be my little wife and look after mine and Jonny's every need.'

'If I must,' she teased. 'But you know how much I love my job. I don't want to give it up just yet.'

'You don't have to. Anyway, we need both our wages. Mum said she'd look after Jonny while we're working. We can get married later this year.' He looked at her closely and raised an enquiring eyebrow. 'You're having second thoughts about marrying me now, aren't you? Is that because Old Mother Turner called me a wife beater?'

'Of course I'm not having second thoughts. I want to marry you, you know I do, but it would be disrespectful to do it too soon after the funeral. We'll talk about it again.'

'What about just before Christmas, or around your twentieth birthday in November?' he suggested. 'That's a few months away and it gives us time to adjust to being a family.'

She stood on tiptoes in the circle of his arms and kissed him. He pulled her closer, kissed her back and looked at her smiling face. 'I take it that's a yes then?'

16

OCTOBER 1964

Jane felt exhausted as she climbed the stairs to the flat, knowing she looked like a zombie. But then, so did Eddie. He was also worn out, working in the shop, drumming three or four nights a week, then driving miles home in the early hours.

While she was grateful for Roy and Tim's offer to stay on at the flat as lodgers to help with the rent and bills, sharing their bedroom with Jonny gave her and Eddie no privacy. They'd had endless sleepless nights, with Eddie cuddling Jonny, who cried for his mummy, leaving her with a feeling of helplessness. When he eventually dozed off, Jonny was a light sleeper and woke several times at the least little sound.

Eddie had asked Sammy and Roy to babysit tonight while they went out for a meal. It was the last thing she felt like doing. She walked into the flat, kicked off her shoes and just wanted to crawl into bed and sleep for a month.

* * *

'I enjoyed that.' Eddie pushed his empty plate away. They were seated in a candle-lit booth in Rozzillo's, Wilmslow's plush new

Italian restaurant. In the gleaming mirrored walls, that made the dining area look bigger than it actually was, their reflections seemed to go on forever. 'This place is really nice. Bit pricey, but great for a special occasion.' He poured the last of the house wine into their glasses and raised his in a toast.

'What special occasion?' Jane raised her glass to his.

'Well, apart from the fact we're actually out together,' he began, 'it's your birthday next month and we still haven't made any wedding plans. If you're absolutely sure you still want to marry me, then we need to do something about it.'

'Of course I want to marry you. There hasn't been the time to think about it. Shall we arrange the wedding?'

'Yeah!' He took her hand. 'I'll meet you in Stockport at lunchtime tomorrow and we'll book it together. It'll have to be a small affair, we can't afford a big do.'

Jane smiled. 'All I want is to be married to you; the time, place, size of wedding doesn't matter. Anyway, I'm too exhausted to be bothered with anything fancy.'

'Good, 'cos that suits me fine. What about just our parents, Roy, Sammy, Pat, Tim and Phil at the ceremony? Then celebrate later with all our friends at The Roulette Club?'

'Sounds perfect.'

'Let's go, see if we can manage a bit of passion while we've some energy.' He winked at her, looking more like his old self.

'I hope Jonny stays asleep then.' Knocking back the last of her wine, Jane stood up.

'Sorry, Jane. Every time I come anywhere near you he wakes up.'

She raised an eyebrow. 'No need for contraception when you share a room with Jonny Mellor!'

* * *

Sammy and Roy were curled up on the sofa, watching the election results.

'We've set a date for the wedding,' Jane called excitedly, running into the sitting room.

'I'll put the kettle on.' Sammy jumped to her feet and turned off the television. 'Roy's finished the cider, there's nothing left to celebrate with. We'll have a nice cup of tea instead.'

'You sound like my mother. She always has the kettle on, just in case,' Eddie said, pulling his future wife to his side. 'Who won the election, by the way?'

'Harold Wilson,' Roy replied. 'Don't suppose it'll make much difference to us, but a Labour government might make some changes for the better. Now then, are you sure about this wedding business? It's a hell of a big step.'

'Of course we're sure,' Eddie said, frowning at Roy's solemn expression. 'Why are you saying that?'

'Just checking.' Roy threw back his head and laughed. 'We had a bet tonight that you'd come home with some news.'

'So, who won the bet?' Eddie said. 'Who's Doubting Thomas?'

'Neither of us,' Sammy said. 'We both knew you would. What we bet on is the date. I say Jane's birthday, Roy says Christmas.'

'You're right, Sam. Jane's birthday's on a Saturday this year, so we've decided to marry on the twenty-first of November,' Eddie said, laughing as Sammy threw a cushion at Roy. 'Has Jonny been okay?' He nodded towards the bedroom door.

'Not heard a peep from him,' Roy said. 'Sammy looked in earlier and he was flat out.'

'Great, he never sleeps that soundly for us. You wait, Jane, we'll climb into bed, get all fired up and then he'll wake up.'

'No doubt,' Jane groaned.

'Do I get the impression Jonny's cramping your style?' Roy raised an amused eyebrow.

'Every single time lately!' Eddie sighed.

'Have my room tonight then. Sheets are clean. I'm taking Sammy home first. I'll either kip on the sofa or share your room with Jonny. Tim called to say he and Pat are staying at his mum's place, so they won't be back to disturb you.'

'Roy, you're a pal. Was even toying with the idea of asking for the van keys,' Eddie joked.

'Well, you'd be on your own,' Jane said. 'I'm used to comfort these days.'

'Aren't we all?' Sammy yawned loudly. 'God, I'm knackered! Come on, Roy, take me home. Leave these two in peace.'

As the door closed quietly behind their friends, Eddie looked at Jane with longing. It felt like ages since they'd even been alone together, never mind anything else.

'Come here, babe.' She moved into his arms. 'I'm gonna love you till the cows come home and that's a promise.'

* * *

Jane hurried along Stockport High Street and spotted Mark's friend Vicky coming out of Boots the Chemist. 'Vicky, hang on a minute,' she hollered.

Vicky turned and smiled, waiting while she caught up. 'Hi, Jane, how are you? I popped in the shop to see you after we met at The Roulette Club. The young Irish lad told me that Eddie's ex had died. I thought you'd have enough on your plate without me mithering.'

They were outside Redman's café. Jane glanced at her watch. 'Have you time for a coffee? I've some lunch hour left and I could do with a drink.'

Vicky's face lit up. 'That would be lovely.'

Jane led the way. 'Grab the table by the window while I join the queue. Coffee okay for you?' Vicky nodded and Jane shuffled along behind two grey-haired ladies, carrying bulging string bags of groceries, placed her order with a grumpy-faced woman, picked up the tray and made her way over to Vicky. 'That woman wouldn't recognise a smile if it smacked her around the chops! I got us each a chocolate éclair as a treat. So, how are things with you and Mark?'

Vicky made a face as Jane sat down opposite. 'Not great. Don't know where I'm up to. He blows hot and cold. I was glad to see the back of him last night when he went to Chester.'

Jane took a sip of coffee. 'He was very possessive with me, but my mother thought the sun shone out of his backside.'

'Even Tony says he doesn't know what makes him tick these days,' Vicky said. 'And he knows him better than anyone, except maybe you. Do you have any ideas on how to handle him?'

Jane shrugged. 'I'm probably the wrong person to ask. His mother ran his life for him. She always belittled him in front of me. It used to annoy me that he never stood up for himself. Whenever she thought I was out of earshot, she used to go on about my make-up and clothes. He got really angry with her over that, but wouldn't defend himself. I hated going to his house.'

'Maude no longer lives with Mark,' Vicky said, spooning sugar into her coffee. 'She's moved into a flat and Mark shares the house with Tony now.'

'How come?'

'It's a long story. It also sounds so far-fetched that you won't believe it, but Mark has letters that prove it's true.'

When Vicky finished her tale, Jane shook her head. 'Bloody hell! That must have been an awful shock. I can't believe Maude Fisher could live such a lie. So, he hardly sees her at all now?'

'He can't stand the sight of her. I'm beginning to think he feels the same about me.'

'Surely not? You've been seeing him for ages.'

'Makes no difference. He won't commit to anything. I found your engagement ring in his drawer, thought he'd bought it for me. It was the May Bank Holiday weekend. On the Monday he booked a table for lunch. I was getting ready for that when I found the ring and everything went wrong. We had a real bust-up. He had his hands round my throat. I thought he was going to strangle me. Then he told me he'd got a girl in Chester pregnant.'

'What?'

'It's true,' Vicky said. 'Not only that, he told me he's still in love with you. His bedroom's like a shrine. Your engagement photo is on his dressing table and all the gifts and cards you gave him.'

'Oh, that gives me the creeps,' Jane said, shuddering. 'What happened to the pregnant girl?'

'The next week he told me it was a false alarm and he'd packed her in. Turns up on Saturday morning with a bloody big bunch of roses and asked me to give him another chance. More fool me, I took him back. He was very weird that night. First, he introduces me to you, and then he wouldn't come near me, although we slept in the same bed. He tossed and turned, must have had a nightmare. He was shouting stuff in his sleep, things like, "I'm sorry. Please forgive me." When he woke up, he denied saying anything and was very distant. He's been acting odd since he discovered the truth about his parents and it's getting worse.'

'Hmm.' Jane nodded. 'That would be enough to screw anybody's head. Give him time to come to terms with things. I don't think you should tell him we've spoken like this.'

'I won't. He'd go mad. But like I say, he's still got a huge crush on you, so just watch out.'

Jane recalled Mark's words the last time she'd spoken to him at the club, about them being far from over. She checked her watch: 'I'll have five more minutes. I've been to the Registry Office with Eddie to book our wedding.'

'Oh, Jane!' Vicky's face lit up. 'Congratulations. When?'

'November twenty-first, my birthday. I've only got five weeks to plan it. We're not having a big do, just family and close friends. What with looking after Jonny and our jobs, we don't have the time or spare money to organise anything posh.'

'Are you living with Eddie now?'

'I moved in with him the day Angie died. We're bringing up Jonny together.'

'So, you've a nice little family already.'

'I'm very lucky,' Jane said. 'I'm marrying the man I adore and I've got a lovely little boy, too. Anyway, come on; shove that éclair down your neck or we'll be getting fired for bad time-keeping.'

Vicky waved goodbye, after promising to keep in touch and Jane hurried back to work, deep in thought. Mark must be cracking up. He could do a lot worse than Vicky, who clearly thought the world of him. Why couldn't *he* see that?

* * *

Jane put all her problems to the back of her mind and threw herself into the wedding plans. Mario offered to do the evening buffet at The Roulette Club. Her parents said they'd pay for the flowers and a car to transport her and Eddie to and from the Registry Office. She ticked the items off her list and was soon down to her own outfit and something for Jonny to wear.

* * *

Eddie's parents had offered to look after Jonny for the whole of the wedding weekend. Unbeknown to Jane, Eddie had booked a short honeymoon at a hotel in the Cheshire countryside. Everyone had been sworn to secrecy.

'Shall me and Pat pack a case for Jane?' Sammy suggested.

'Please,' Eddie replied. 'She won't need many clothes if it's anything to do with me. But you know how fussy she is about her shampoo and make-up. I'm bound to get it wrong.'

'Leave it with us,' Sammy said, glad that Eddie was taking Jane on honeymoon. It would take her mind off Mark's alleged shrine of a bedroom. When Jane had confided in them, both she and Pat had urged her to tell Eddie of Mark's peculiar obsession.

'No,' Jane said. 'He'll go crazy. It's too close to the wedding to be fighting with Mark. I don't want a groom with two black eyes. And whatever you do, don't tell Roy and Tim.'

But Sammy knew that her friend was very concerned. 'Let's treat Jane to something special to wear on honeymoon,' she suggested to Pat. 'We'll club together with Roy and Tim, and then we can afford to splash out a bit.'

Between them they picked out a pretty baby-doll nightdress and negligee in pale-pink silk, trimmed with the finest cream lace, and a bottle of Jane's favourite perfume.

'Wow, classy as well as sexy,' Roy said, picking up the bottle of Chanel No5. 'This lot'll knock Eddie dead! Wasn't it Marilyn Monroe who wore only perfume in bed? Cor, imagine that!' He grinned at Tim, who grinned back as though imagining exactly that.

'Behave, you two dirty minds,' Sammy said, carefully wrapping the garments in tissue paper. She placed them in the gift box. 'Ed and Jane deserve the best after everything they've been through.'

'Jane's certainly put up with a lot,' Pat said. 'There were

times in the past when I didn't think we'd ever see them together again.'

'The one thing that's got them through all the shit is love,' Sammy said. 'You can see it in every look and touch. I know they'll be very happy. Raise your mugs to Eddie and Jane!'

Four coffee mugs clinked in unison to outbursts of laughter.

17

NOVEMBER 1964

Jane snuggled into the bubbles for one last soak. Sunshine sparkled through the bathroom window, the smell of toast wafted down the hallway and she could hear Pat laughing somewhere. She imagined how smart Ed would look and Jonny in his new sailor suit too. What more could a girl wish for on her wedding day? With a big grin on her face, she pulled the plug with her toes and gazed at the sunshine until the water drained away.

* * *

Sammy and Pat dried Jane's hair, styling it into a French pleat, interwoven with pink silk rosebuds. She did her make-up and slipped into one of Sammy's creations, a cream linen shift that fitted her slim figure perfectly. A cerise pink, edge-to-edge jacket completed the outfit. She stepped into new shoes and picked up her posy of pink roses.

'Do I look all right?' she said, flopping down on the sofa. 'Oooh, I've come over a bit peculiar, like I'm going to faint.'

'You *are* pale,' Sammy said. 'It'll be nerves. But you *do* look lovely. That bright pink really suits you.'

Pat handed Jane a glass of water.

'I feel a bit better now,' Jane said, taking a sip. 'Maybe my bath was too hot? Do you think Eddie will like this outfit? And my hair, what about my hair? He likes me to wear it loose.'

'Stop panicking,' Sammy said. 'If you wore sackcloth, he'd still want to marry you.'

'Should I wear a necklace? I look a bit bare around the neck.'

'No necklace, it's fine,' Pat said as the door flew open and the boys and Phil strolled in.

'Bloody hell, do we know this bunch of smoothies?' Sammy laughed, eyeing up the four young men.

'The Raiders, all present and correct, ma'am.' Roy saluted. 'And that includes one extremely sober but very nervous, second-time-around bridegroom.'

'Well, I must say, you lot have really pushed the boat out.' Pat nodded with admiration. 'You look almost fanciable.'

'So do you, Pat. Tatty old T-shirt and rollers, very classy,' Roy said, laughing.

'Latest Mary Quant, this outfit.' Pat patted her rollers. 'We women have to *do* things with our hair, it's okay for you lot.'

'Don't kid yourself,' Roy said. 'Ed spent hours in the bathroom this morning, messing about with his bloody hair so he could look as ravishing as his bride-to-be.' He winked at Jane. 'Happy birthday, sweetheart. You look drop-dead gorgeous, you really do. If I could, I'd marry you myself.'

Jane giggled. 'I'll take that as a compliment. *You* don't look too bad either. Like Pat said, almost fanciable.' She turned to Eddie, who was sporting a smart navy suit, crisp white shirt and navy and white spotted tie. His long hair, neatly trimmed, was freshly washed and shiny and his gorgeous blue eyes sparkled.

Roy's grey Beatle-style suit and Tim's black pinstripe were equally smart, while Phil, unusually resplendent in beige velvet trousers and a brown leather jacket, wore his freshly washed blond hair cascading freely to his shoulders. Jane smiled her approval as they all stood grinning.

'Will we do?' Phil said.

'You'll pass muster anytime dressed like that, Phil. Though quite what Mum and Molly will make of your flowing locks, I can't imagine.'

'Right, we'll finish getting ready,' Sammy said and she and Pat hurried into the bedroom followed by Roy, Tim and a smiling Phil, who promised to close his eyes and not peep.

Eddie pulled Jane up from the sofa and gazed into her eyes. He squeezed her hands. 'Happy birthday, darling.' He leant in and kissed her lightly on the lips. 'Are you sure you're ready for this? Because it's for life. I promise I'll fight tooth and nail to make this marriage work.'

She nodded. 'I want it more than anything, I always have.'

'Good.' He gave her a big squeeze. 'Because so do I.'

'Do I look okay? I feel a bit bare around my neck. Pat said I looked all right without a necklace. What do you think?'

He dug in his jacket pocket, pulled out a black velvet box and handed it to her.

'You look stunningly beautiful without, but I got this for your birthday.'

She opened the box and gasped. Lying on red satin lining was a gold, heart-shaped locket on a fine chain. Inside the heart were photographs of the two of them and engraved on the back, in old-fashioned lettering, were the initials E and J and the day's date.

'Oh, Ed,' she choked as he fastened it around her neck. 'Do the others know about this? Is that why Pat said "no necklace?"'

'Yes, but they haven't seen it yet,' he said.

The door opened as if on cue and they walked in, smiling.

'It's gorgeous!' Pat exclaimed.

'It's perfect,' Sammy said as Tim peered through the window.

'Wedding car's here,' he announced. 'You two go and we'll follow in the Beetle.'

'Ed, you know that traditionally the bride and groom are supposed to travel separately,' Sammy said as they all hurried down the stairs. 'That you shouldn't even see the bride before the ceremony.'

'Since when have they ever done anything traditional?' Roy laughed. 'Why break the habit of a lifetime? Right, you two, off you go.'

* * *

'Oh, Ed,' Jane said as the car pulled up outside Stockport Registry Office. 'I thought it was only meant to be a handful of people?'

Eddie smiled and squeezed her hand. 'I spoke to your mum and she agreed it would make your day.'

'This is so brilliant. Even my Uncle Jack from Ireland's here. I haven't seen him for years.' Jane climbed out of the car and looked for her parents. She spotted them standing with Tom and Molly and waved. Her brother Peter and his friend Harry from next door swaggered over, dressed in their best, followed by Sammy's sister Susan and her friend, Anna.

Eddie's parents and Jonny arrived with Aunt Celia and Auntie Minnie. Jane smiled as Jonny ran over and she gave him a hug: 'You look lovely,' she said. 'Such a smart boy.' Jonny giggled and ran back to his nana. Jane waved at Eddie's elderly aunts, whose only nephew was their pride and joy. Their flower-bedecked hats nodded back. Everyone crowded into the small Registry Office to watch Eddie and Jane, with Roy and Sammy as their witnesses, tie the knot.

* * *

Blinking back tears, Enid clutched Ben's hand. Never had she seen their daughter looking so radiant and Eddie was positively walking on air.

A low chuckle rippled round the room as Jonny, holding his nana's hand, shouted, 'That's my daddy!' Eddie looked round and pulled a face. Nana stifled a giggle and gave Jonny a jelly baby.

'You may kiss the bride,' the registrar finished.

'This is the bit I've been waiting for, Mrs M.' Eddie swept Jane into his arms, kissing her passionately.

'It's meant to be a token gesture,' she whispered as they moved apart.

'I don't care,' he said, laughing.

Outside the Registry Office a photographer was waiting.

'Where's he come from? I didn't hire him,' Jane said, as the man began ushering guests into groups. 'To be honest, I never gave a thought to photographs.'

'He's a gift from my parents and the aunts,' Eddie said. 'I knew you hadn't mentioned a photographer, so Mum booked him.'

'Any more surprises?' she asked, ducking the confetti as they made their way back to the beribboned car.

'One or two.'

The car was heading in the wrong direction – to her old home.

'Are we going to Rosedean Gardens?' she asked.

'Yeah, we are,' Eddie replied.

'But why? I thought we were going somewhere for a drink. Ed, what's going on?'

'Wait and see.'

The front door stood wide open and Harry's mum, Marge Connell, removed her flowery apron and greeted them. 'Hello, Jane, lovey, congratulations, and you too, Eddie.'

'Thank you,' Jane said, looking round as her parents arrived with the rest of the wedding party. 'What's going on, Mum?'

'Don't stand dithering in the hall. Go through to the dining room,' her mum urged.

Jane did and gasped, for the table was groaning under a sumptuous buffet and a two-tier wedding cake, decorated with pink and white roses and silver bells.

'Your mum and dad wanted to do this for us,' Eddie told her. 'But I asked them to keep it secret.'

'It's wonderful. Thank you, Mum and Dad.'

'It's our pleasure, Jane,' her mum said, smiling. 'We wanted you to have as nice a wedding day as we could afford.'

Her dad coughed loudly to catch everyone's attention. Eddie's dad was pouring glasses of sparkling wine.

'I'd like to say a word or two before you raise your glasses to toast our bride and groom. Now I'm not one for making speeches, so I'll keep it brief. Everyone's aware of the year Eddie and Jane have had. They've come through some very tough times. Hopefully, that's behind them now. So I'm sure you'll all join me in wishing them, and young Jonny here, the very best for the future. Please, raise your glasses to Eddie and Jane.'

As everyone took up the toast, the tears that had threatened all day now tumbled down Jane's cheeks and even Eddie's eyes looked suspiciously moist. He handed her a hanky and smiled. 'Happy, Mrs M?'

'Very. I'm amazed at all this, I never suspected a thing.'

'I'm good at keeping secrets when I need to,' he said. 'You'd best go and sort your mascara out, it's running down your cheeks.'

* * *

'Thanks again, Mum and Dad, for everything,' Jane said, hugging them both as she and Eddie prepared to leave for The Roulette Club. 'And thanks, Mum and Dad Mellor.' She kissed them too and bent to hug Jonny. 'Be a good boy for Nana and Grandad. We'll see you on Monday.'

'I'm so thrilled for you both,' Lillian said, wiping a tear from her eye.

'Thanks, all of you, for being so supportive and understanding all along,' Eddie said, kissing his mum on the cheek. He hugged Jonny. 'Be a good lad.' Jonny smiled and hugged him back.

'Listen, son,' Enid, who'd been knocking back sherry all afternoon, slurred, 'in spite of my initial misgivings about you, I'll admit I had a sneaking suspicion you two were right for one another. Though God knows, you've both gone arse about face in getting there!' She hiccupped, drunkenly slung her arms around Eddie and knocked him off the doorstep.

'Look after our girl, Ed,' Ben said, grabbing his wife and propping her against the door. He shook Eddie's hand and hugged Jane. 'Be happy together, that's all we ask.'

'I can guarantee you we will be,' Eddie said. He led his giggling bride outside to the waiting Beetle, where Pat and Sammy were festooning it with ribbons, balloons and tin cans. 'Hope you two won't do this to my Ferrari when I get it,' he quipped, helping Jane into the car.

* * *

Jane looked around the function room, smiling with delight. Mario's family had done them proud. The cream walls were decorated with balloons, streamers and *Just Married* banners. Another sumptuous buffet was laid out on tastefully decorated trestle tables and Rosa and Vincento were handing out glasses of champagne to the guests as they arrived.

Jane sipped her champagne, reflecting on what an amazing day she'd had so far. She was so happy, she thought she might burst and her smile felt a mile wide.

Stuart was DJ-ing and he called for the Bride and Groom to take to the floor for their first dance. Eddie grabbed Jane, removed the glass from her hand and gave it to Sammy. He pulled her close as they danced to Sam Cooke's 'You Send Me'. He sang along, looking deep into her eyes. They were joined on the floor by several couples all swaying together.

Halfway through the evening, Mario declared the buffet was being served and a queue formed by the tables, headed by Roy.

Jane laughed as he waved at her. 'Always first where food's concerned,' she said.

'Do you want anything to eat?' Eddie asked, stroking her cheek. 'You look a bit pale. Are you feeling okay?'

'I'm fine. Bit tired. It's been a long day, I'm not really hungry.'

'Tell you what,' he whispered. 'Let's go home. I want you all to myself while we've got the flat to ourselves.'

She nodded. 'I'll nip to the loo and then we'll say our goodbyes.'

Rosa waved to Jane as she made her way to the cloakroom. 'You got a minute, Jane?'

She followed Rosa into her father's office.

Rosa rummaged in a desk drawer and handed her an envelope. 'Vicky asked me to pass this on. I didn't want to give it to you out there in case it caused a problem with Ed.'

Jane opened the envelope and pulled out a congratulations card. There was a short letter tucked inside.

Dear Jane, just a note to wish you all the best for today. I've kept quiet about your wedding plans. I'd hate Mark to ruin the day for you in any way. I don't think Tony or Sarah knows either, nothing's been said. But just to put your mind at ease, Mark is staying in Chester this weekend. I hope it all goes well. Love Vicky. x x x

'Thanks, Rosa.' Jane's hands shook as she pushed the card and letter back into the envelope. 'I'm sure Vicky means well, but can I leave this with you? I don't want Eddie to see it.'

'I can get rid of it for you,' Rosa offered. 'I'll chuck it in the bin out the back.'

'Please. Don't say anything out there, I don't want Eddie going nuts.'

'I shouldn't have given it to you,' Rosa said, looking worried.

'It's okay, really,' Jane assured her. 'I just don't want Mark mentioned tonight.'

* * *

Back in the function room, Jane spotted Eddie in a huddle with Sammy, Roy, Pat, Tim and Phil. 'What's going on?' she asked as they jumped guiltily apart.

'Nothing!' a chorus of innocent voices replied.

'That means something is.'

'I was just telling them we're going home now,' Eddie said. 'Let's say goodbye to everyone.'

They did the rounds and thanked Mario and his family for the reception. Outside the club, they were joined by their friends and Phil.

'We'll bring your pressies to the flat on Monday,' Sammy said. 'We'll take them home for now.'

'Have fun, see you soon,' they called as Eddie and Jane drove away.

* * *

Eddie pulled up at the traffic lights in the town centre and took Jane's hand.

'Now for my final surprise.'

'What? Aren't we going home?'

'You just be patient and wait and see.' He smiled mysteriously as the lights changed.

They drove into the countryside and after an hour, he pulled in through the gates of a Victorian country house bearing the name Blackfriars Hotel. Jane frowned and got out of the car. Eddie lifted two small cases from the boot.

'What's in the cases? I never packed one.'

'Sammy and Pat did it,' he said, ushering her through the open front door. 'You'll have everything you need, I'm sure.'

'This is very posh,' she whispered, looking round the grand entrance hall with its tasteful burgundy and cream décor, carved oak staircase and polished wooden floor.

Eddie led the way to the reception desk. 'Mr and Mrs Mellor,' he announced proudly.

'Ah yes,' the receptionist greeted them. 'The Honeymoon Couple. Would you sign the register, sir?' Eddie took the pen, signing with a flourish.

'If you'd like to wait a moment, I'll get someone to take your cases up,' she said, handing him a key. She rang a bell and a smartly uniformed porter hurried into the hall.

'Honeymoon Suite please, Charlie.'

They followed Charlie up the wide sweeping staircase. Eddie thanked him and gave him a tip as he left the room.

Jane gazed in wonder at the beautifully proportioned room, with its butter-yellow walls and ornate corniced ceiling. A log fire crackled in the grate and a willow basket, piled high with freshly cut logs, stood by the side of the cast-iron fireplace.

'Oh boy, we'll have some fun in that!' Eddie pointed to the

bed that took pride of place. Hung with blue and cream floral drapes that complemented the curtains and satin bedspread, the four-poster dominated the room. A small table at the foot of the bed held an ice bucket, where a bottle of champagne was chilling. Vases of fresh red roses had been placed on every available surface.

'Red roses, and at this time of year, too!' Jane said. 'They must have cost a fortune. How did you manage to organise all this without me finding out? More to the point, Ed, how the hell are we going to pay for it?'

'John Grey helped me organise it,' he said, smiling. 'And it's all paid for. Our wedding present from my parents and the aunts.'

'As well as the photographer? How kind of them.'

'They wanted us to have the best start possible, one we'll always remember. Do you want to eat downstairs, or shall we have room service?'

'I'm not really hungry. I ate some of the buffet at Mum's and the club. Let's just relax and open the champagne. Are you going to order any food?'

'I'm not bothered,' he replied.

Jane nodded. 'I'm going to freshen up. Which case is mine?'

'The green one, it belongs to Pat.'

Jane smiled at all this secret packing and intrigue that she'd been oblivious to. She undid the small case. Inside, nestling on top, was a shiny pink box tied with an elaborate arrangement of cream ribbons. 'What's this?'

'Now that's something I know nothing about. Open it and see.'

She untied the bows, lifted off the lid and removed several layers of white tissue paper. 'Oh, look!' She held up delicate silk and lace garments for his inspection. 'Aren't they gorgeous?' A small white and gold embossed card fell out of the wrappings.

Eddie picked it up and read out the message, *'For You Both.*

Enjoy! All Our Love, Roy, Sammy, Tim and Pat xxxx'. Ah, they're wonderful friends. This lot must have cost a small fortune,' he said, eyes sparkling as he picked up a large bottle of Chanel No5, which nestled in the tissue paper. 'Go and put them on while I open the champagne.'

* * *

In the en suite, Jane undressed and let her hair down, carefully picking out the rosebuds and brushing her locks until they shone. Pushing the thoughts of Vicky's card and Mark out of her mind, she stepped into the silk and lace and felt like a film star. She splashed on the perfume and took a deep breath as she prepared to join Eddie in that magnificent four-poster.

* * *

Eddie hung his clothes in the mahogany wardrobe that graced one full wall of the room and opened the champagne with a bang and filled two crystal goblets. He lay back on the bed and couldn't believe they'd done it; they were actually married. He loved Jane with all his heart and vowed he'd never let her down again, whatever challenges the future held, and he was quite sure that if past experience were anything to go by, there would be plenty. The bathroom door opened and he gasped: 'You look beautiful!' He patted the space beside him.

She clambered up, reaching for the goblet of champagne he was holding out, and took a sip: 'This is crazy.'

'What's that, sweetheart?'

'I feel as nervous as I did that first time, back at your mum's place. All butterflies and things.'

'Believe it or not, so do I. You wouldn't think we'd been lovers for months.'

Jane put her goblet down and moved into his arms, her

nerves disappearing as he kissed her and untied the ribbons on her negligee.

'I love you so much,' he whispered. 'I've waited so long for this.'

'I love you too, Ed,' she breathed. 'Love you too.'

18

Roy and Sammy were holding court at the flat when the honeymooners arrived home. Sammy had prepared a welcome home spag bol and the place was sparkling. The small dining table was covered with a crisp white cloth and decorated with a red candle in a Chianti bottle.

'This is very romantic,' Eddie said, taking a seat at the table as Sammy placed a laden plate in front of him. 'We must go away more often.'

Roy poured four glasses of red wine. 'To Mr and Mrs Mellor, may all your problems *not* be little ones!'

'You'd prefer them all to be big ones then, Roy?' Jane teased.

'Well no, but you know what I mean.' Roy took a swig of wine and smiled.

'We'll do our best not to have any little ones for a while,' Eddie said, tucking into his meal. 'Compliments to the chef, Sam, this is really good.'

'Thanks, Ed. It's genuine Italian – Roy's dad's own recipe.'

'Frank James called this morning and asked us to a meeting,' Roy told Eddie. 'I went along with Tim and Phil and made your apologies.'

Eddie almost choked. 'Blimey, what does *he* want?'

'The Raiders – at last!' Roy was unable to suppress the excitement in his voice. 'He's offering us a place on tour with leading groups. He's knocked out with our new show, wants to sign us. How do you feel about that? We need to be managed properly or we're never gonna make it big. I'm getting pissed off just playing pubs and clubs, it's time we earned more for all our hard work.'

'I suppose it'll mean being away from home a lot.' Eddie glanced at Jane, who was staring into her empty glass.

'I'm afraid so, Ed. I explained your situation to Frank. He's very understanding, got a couple of kids of his own. The tour he's offering is going out mid-December with The Dave Clark Five, The Hollies and a couple of American singers, no names released yet, but he hinted at Chris Montez and Brian Hyland. We'll be bottom of the bill, of course, but it's a great start.'

Eddie could see the excitement in Roy's eyes as he saved the best news until last. 'There's also the chance of a record deal *if* we play our cards right.'

'What? Bloody hell! Well, let's go for it then. It's the chance we've been waiting for, we can't turn it down.'

'So, you're up for it?' Roy grinned. 'Great! Without you, Frank's not interested. He says for a white man, you've got the nearest voice to Sam Cooke he's ever heard. If that's not a compliment, I don't know what is. He's away on business for the next few days, I need to give him an answer early next week.'

* * *

Jane remained silent during the conversation between Roy and Eddie. She followed Sammy into the kitchen to help make coffee, leaving them to talk music and tours.

'You don't look too pleased, Jane,' Sammy said, spooning coffee powder into four mugs.

She shrugged. 'I'm pleased for them, of course I am. It's what they've always wanted. I just wonder how the hell *I'm* supposed to cope with Jonny *and* my job on my own.'

'*I'll* help you. When the boys are away, I'll move in and keep you company. Don't worry, we'll manage. How was the honeymoon, by the way? You've hardly said a word, but you look absolutely glowing and so does Ed.'

'It was wonderful. The room was out of this world – four-poster, log fire, champagne *and* red roses.'

'Bloody hell, he's a romantic bugger! Was the hotel nice?'

'Couldn't tell you,' Jane said, feeling her cheeks warming. 'I only saw reception. We never left the room for the whole two days, just had room service. Thanks for the lovely gift, by the way. Ed loved it.'

'I'm sure he did.' Sammy raised an amused eyebrow as Jane giggled. 'Is Jonny coming home tonight?'

'I hope not – I want one more night on our own. Ed hasn't mentioned it, so I'm keeping my mouth shut.'

'I don't blame you. He's a sweet little boy, but being a stepmum at your age is a lot to take on.'

'I know, but I love them both. I'll cope somehow.'

* * *

Eddie talked long into the night about the group touring for The Frank James Organisation. 'I know we have loads of work and play regularly, but it's clubs and dance halls. This is different. Frank's very well respected. Every group in Manchester would give its right arm to be on his books. We'll be right up there with the big names. Do you remember years ago when I promised you a posh house in Wilmslow? Well, I may manage it yet, who knows?'

'Ed, I'm happy with this flat and what we've got. Stop

talking now please and kiss me for goodness' sake, we've only got tonight on our own.'

* * *

Sunday afternoon Jane was curled up on the sitting room sofa, reading a magazine, when the doorbell rang. She frowned, for she wasn't expecting anyone and the others had their own keys. She opened the door a crack, peered out and was shocked to find Angie's friend, Cathy, standing on the landing: 'Cathy! What brings you here?'

'I hope you don't mind me calling round,' Cathy began. 'I wondered if it would be okay to see Jonny. I've brought him a little present. Maybe Eddie hasn't told you that he's my godson?'

Jane shook her head. 'He hasn't, but come in anyway. Sit down and I'll make you a coffee.'

'Where *is* Jonny?'

'Ed's taken him to feed the ducks and to visit his mum and dad. I wasn't feeling well so I thought I'd have a rest. Make the most of the peace and quiet.'

'I'm sorry if I disturbed you. I hope you weren't sleeping?'

'No, I was reading, actually. We had a late night, as usual. The boys played the Oasis Club and then everyone came back here.' Jane yawned loudly. 'Oh, excuse me. That's the trouble with Manchester gigs, they always turn into all-night parties. Sit down, Cathy, please.'

'Who babysat for you?' Cathy asked. She slipped off her jacket, sat down opposite Jane and put her handbag and the parcel for Jonny on the coffee table.

'Carl and Tina – they work with Ed in the shop.'

'If ever you're stuck for a sitter, you can always call on me. I'd love to spend some time with Jonny again. I miss him – Angie too, of course...' Cathy tailed off, tears running down her cheeks. She took the tissue Jane handed her. 'I'm sorry, didn't mean to get upset.'

'Hey, it's okay; don't worry. If I put myself in your place and lost Sammy or Pat, I'd be devastated. I'll make the coffee... and would you like a cheese and tomato sandwich? Ed and Jonny shouldn't be too long now... stay until they come home.'

Cathy smiled. 'Thanks, that would be lovely.'

As they sat chatting over their coffee and sandwiches, to Jane's surprise she found she liked the girl who'd been her rival's best friend. Without Angie by her side, Cathy was a different person, quiet, caring and nothing at all like Jane had imagined she'd be.

Mid-conversation, the front door burst open and Eddie dashed in, carrying Jonny.

'Quick, Jane! His nose is snotty. It's dripping on my suede jacket, *and* he's wet his pants again. Mum's only just changed him, too.' He stopped, catching sight of Cathy.

'Hello, Ed,' she said shyly.

'Hi, how are you?' His tone unsure, he put Jonny down.

'Fine, thank you,' she replied. 'I just wondered how Jonny was and how you're coping with him.'

'Has *she* sent you to spy on us?' he asked, bristling.

'Who's she?' Cathy and Jane chorused.

'Old Mother Turner!'

Cathy gasped. 'No, of course she hasn't. I haven't seen her since Angie's funeral. I came because I wanted to see Jonny – I miss him.' Cathy was on the verge of tears again. 'I used to see him every day.'

'There's nothing sinister about Cathy's visit,' Jane said, willing Eddie to relax. 'She's brought him a present. Come here, Jonny. Come and see Auntie Cathy.'

Jonny ran across the room. Jane wiped his nose, took off his quilted jacket and bobble hat and ran her fingers through his flattened curls. He leant against her legs, sucking his thumb.

'He's wet through!' Jane grimaced. 'I'll change him.'

'Mum said we need to try harder with the potty training. He should be dry by now,' Eddie said helpfully. 'She said it's the shock of losing his mum and getting used to living with us that's holding him back.'

'Well, until he *is* trained, it's time you learnt to change him. He's *your* son,' Jane reminded Eddie as a horrified expression crossed his face. Shaking her head, she disappeared into the bathroom with a giggling Jonny tucked under her arm.

* * *

'Perish the thought,' Eddie muttered. 'Listen, Cathy, I'm sorry about before. So, how are you doing?' He sprawled on the opposite sofa, swinging his legs over the arm, and offered her a cigarette.

'No thanks, Ed. I'm okay, I suppose. I have up and down days. I'm thinking of going to live in London with my cousin. She's got a flat and she's asked me to share. There's not much left for me around here at the moment.'

'Well, good luck. I hope it works out.'

Jane reappeared with Jonny, now clean and dry and his curls freshly brushed. He ran over to Cathy. She gave him a hug and his present. He pulled the toy car from its colourful wrappings and ran to Eddie, chuckling.

'Look, Daddy, car!'

Eddie took the car and crawling on his knees, pushed it up and down the room as Jonny crawled after him. 'C'mon, Jonny. Vroom, vroom!'

'Boys will be boys,' Jane said, laughing. 'Who did you say you bought it for?' She looked at Cathy, who was studying Jonny closely, a frown playing on her face as her colour drained. 'You okay, Cathy? You've gone very pale.'

'Oh, yes, of course I am,' she replied quickly. 'I was just

thinking how tall Jonny's grown. Look, I must go. I've a bit of a headache starting, it might be a migraine. I really shouldn't have eaten the cheese. But thanks for your hospitality, Jane. I'll see you again maybe.'

'Anytime. Just pop round. If we're in, we're in. You should come and see The Raiders play again, before they get too big for their boots.' Jane accompanied Cathy to the door.

'Maybe I will. Goodbye.'

Cathy dashed away quickly.

'That was a bit weird,' Jane observed as she rejoined Eddie. 'The way she was staring at Jonny as though she'd seen a ghost and then rushing off like that.'

'She was always a bit of an oddball.' Eddie shrugged. 'Anyway, how are you feeling, sweetheart, any better? *You* look pale, never mind Cathy.'

'Still feel a bit grim. Think I'm just overtired.'

'I'm meeting the lads at the pub later. We're having a final discussion about the tour before we sign any binding contracts. Why don't you ask Pat and Sammy over for a girlie night?'

'I will, but I'll give Jonny his tea and bath him first.'

'I'll do that. You go and lie down for an hour and I'll call Sammy for you. I need to ask Roy something and he's over at their house anyway.'

* * *

Jane lay on the bed, thinking. She wanted Eddie to have his chance of playing on a theatre tour, but at the same time she was also dreading it. There wasn't going to be much of a home life for her and Jonny with Ed away all week. She wouldn't even be able to go out with her friends. For the first time since Angie's death, Jane felt resentful and was almost envious of Pat and Sammy, who were able to go out and enjoy their freedom.

She'd wanted to be with Eddie more than anything in the

world. What she hadn't bargained on was being married just yet, *and* a stepmum to boot. His divorce would have taken another couple of years, during which time they'd have been having fun together, as they had until the accident. Perhaps her mum had been right all along and they'd rushed into things. Well, it was too late now: what's done is done.

* * *

Jane said goodbye to Eddie at the door as Pat and Sammy clambered up the stairs, carrying a bottle of wine.

'Hi, you two,' she greeted them. 'Those stairs are a killer.'

'You can say that again,' Sammy said as Eddie pecked her and Pat on the cheek.

'I won't be late home, Jane.' He kissed her and turned to Sammy: 'She's a bit down at the moment, see if you can cheer her up.'

'What's wrong, Jane?' Pat asked, closing the door.

Jane shook her head. 'Everything!' Her lips trembled and she burst into tears.

'Have you two had a row?' Sammy put her arm around Jane's shoulders.

'No, nothing like that,' she sobbed. 'I'm so tired and I don't feel very well. Everything's getting on top of me and now Ed will probably be away all week, *every* week. I have to look after Jonny and go to work, and, oh God, Sam, I wish I was single again.'

'You don't mean that,' Sammy said. 'You love Ed to bits, you know you do. Come on, sit down.' She led Jane to the sofa and sat beside her.

'It's not Ed, it's Jonny,' Jane said. 'He's such hard work. We hardly ever have any time to ourselves. He's always climbing into bed with us. I know he's had an awful upheaval for a little lad, but he's coming between us in more ways than one.'

'Can't Ed's mum have him to stay occasionally?' Sammy said.

'She has him all day, so it's not really fair to ask her. She's getting on a bit and he wears her out.'

'Well, what about Carl and Tina? They enjoy babysitting and it gives them somewhere to do their courting.'

Jane sighed. 'It's not just the babysitting, I want Ed to myself. I know it's selfish of me. Poor little Jonny's not even three until next month. It'll be years before he leaves home. Listen to me. I'm a rotten stepmother, aren't I?'

'No, you're not,' Sammy said. 'You've taken on a hell of a responsibility for your age. Everyone thinks you're wonderful for doing that. Especially after the way Eddie two-timed you with Angie in the first place. I certainly couldn't have done it.'

'He's more than made up for that, Sammy,' Pat reminded her.

'Yes, I know he has. But while *he's* out achieving his dreams, Jane's the one tied to the flat and left holding the baby, so to speak, and he isn't even hers.'

Jane looked at them both and muttered quietly, 'Babies, Sammy! I'll be left holding the babies.'

'What babies?'

'Our baby – mine and Ed's. I think I'm pregnant. That's why I feel so sick and grotty all the time.'

'Wow, that's fantastic,' Pat said, giving her a hug. 'A honeymoon baby!'

'Christ, *you* don't waste time,' Sammy said, joining the hug. 'Does Ed know?'

'No, and it's not a honeymoon baby. I've been so busy lately that I didn't realise I haven't had a period since the second week of September. I thought I must be due soon and that's why I feel off colour. Checked my diary earlier and it's there in black and white. I can't believe it. Must have happened the night we decided to get married, when we slept in Roy's room. It's one of the only nights of peace we had before the wedding, and since for that matter.'

'I remember you feeling faint on your wedding day,' Sammy said. 'No wonder, you must have been a couple of months gone by then.'

'I know,' Jane nodded. 'I felt a bit grim at times while we were on honeymoon, but I put that down to too much champagne.'

'So why haven't you said anything to Ed?' Sammy asked.

'I'll wait until I've seen the doctor. When I know for sure, I'll tell him. I don't want to ruin his chance of fame. He might not want to go on the tour if he knows. I want him to get the contract signed and then he can't back out. I know in the long run he'd find it hard to forgive me if he missed out, and I won't be responsible for that. He never forgave Angie for his lost dreams. It's not that I don't want kids,' she continued, 'I do, and Ed definitely wants more. But I wasn't planning on getting pregnant so soon. I wanted to wait until Jonny started school. It's bad timing all round.'

'Pat and I will help you all we can,' Sammy said. 'I told you I'd stay when the lads are away, and if you *are* pregnant, then Roy and Tim should move out when the baby's born. The kids can have their room and you and Ed can have some privacy.'

Jane smiled, feeling much more cheerful for sharing her worries. 'We'll end up with a football team at this rate. One good thing about sharing a room with Jonny, he's an effective contraceptive!'

Sammy laughed as she uncorked the bottle of wine and poured them a glass each.

'That's one way of looking at it.'

Jane took a sip and told them of Cathy's earlier visit and how she'd suddenly dashed away.

'She's always been strange,' Sammy said.

'She told Ed she's thinking of going to London,' Jane continued.

'Good luck to her,' Pat said. 'It'll do her good to get away and start a new life. She was always in Angie's shadow.'

The boys arrived home later that night, a little the worse for drink.

'Be quiet, you lot,' Pat chided as they rolled in singing. 'Wake Jonny and Jane'll have your guts for garters.'

'We're really going to do it,' Roy slurred, bending to plant a beery kiss on Sammy's lips. 'We're going straight to the top!'

'I'll tell John tomorrow that I'm leaving my job,' Eddie said to Jane. 'We'll manage on the money I get from the tour. There'll be others, this is just the beginning. *You're* working, Jane. We'll be okay for money for the time being.'

Jane tried her best to look pleased.

* * *

Eddie lay on his side, gently stroking Jane's face. 'You're okay about me going away, aren't you? Only I thought you were a bit quiet earlier. You would tell me if something were wrong?'

'I'm just tired, that's all.' She smiled reassuringly. 'Of course I want you to go, it's the chance of a lifetime. Go to sleep, Ed. We've got to get up early for work.' She kissed him goodnight and turned on to her side. He put his arms around her and snuggled in behind.

Eddie fell asleep, snoring softly while Jane lay awake all night, her mind working overtime. The following morning, he brought her a cup of tea, took one look and said, 'Stay in bed, you look awful. I'll see to Jonny. Can you do his nappy for me though?'

Jonny ran into the bedroom and leapt up beside her. She stripped off his pyjamas and wet nappy. 'Carry him into the bathroom and I'll give him a wash,' she said, climbing out of bed. 'Get him some clean clothes and pass me a nappy.'

Jonny squirmed away from the wet flannel as Jane tried to wash him. 'Stand still,' she ordered and he burst into tears.

'Why are you shouting at him?' Eddie asked as he came back, his hands full. 'Come here, son.' He scooped Jonny up and frowned at Jane.

'I wasn't,' she said, sitting down on the side of the bath. 'I feel faint. You're going to have to do it yourself.'

'Just do the nappy then, please. Come on, Jane. I've got to drop him off and I'm gonna be late for work. I need to finish dressing.' He put Jonny down and dashed out of the bathroom.

'Lie down, Jonny,' Jane said. He wriggled as she fastened the right-side pin and she stuck it in her finger. 'Ouch! Now keep still while I do the other or...' Too late, the pin jagged him and he screamed.

'For God's sake! What the hell's happened?' Eddie yelled, running into the bathroom. Jane leapt up, pushed past him, flew into the bedroom and slammed the door. She could hear him comforting Jonny and then they appeared in the doorway, Jonny still sobbing.

'What's wrong, Jane?' Eddie demanded as he sat down on the bed and pulled Jonny's sweater over his head.

She burst into tears. 'Nothing,' she said, turning her head into the pillow. 'I feel lousy. Maybe I've got the flu.'

'That's no reason to cry. I'm sorry for shouting, but he was screaming as though he was being murdered.' He finished dressing a tearful Jonny then turned to look at her. 'Will you be okay if I go now? Call the shop if you need me. I'll pop up at lunchtime and make you a sandwich. Sorry I've got to dash. Bye, love.' He bent to kiss her and left.

She sat up and sipped her tea, wiping her eyes with the back of her hand. Their first argument and it could have been avoided if she'd shared her problem. But no – it would have to wait.

* * *

A visit to the doctor on Tuesday confirmed Jane's suspicions: the baby was due on Eddie's twenty-second birthday in June. Jane walked back to work, a half-smile playing on her lips, her mind in a whirl. She tried to picture the look on his face when she told him the news. She hoped he'd be pleased, remembering his horrified expression the last time he'd been informed of impending fatherhood. Back at the shop, she sent her assistant Sean to make coffee while she called Sammy at work.

'Well, are you?' Sammy asked.

'Yes, and it's due on Ed's birthday,' Jane said, grinning into the receiver.

'Congratulations! I'll come into Stockport at lunchtime and we can go out for a sandwich to celebrate.'

'Don't tell a soul, unless Pat phones you. I need to tell Ed first, but not until the contracts are safely signed. I don't mind you two knowing, of course.'

'Discretion's my middle name. See you in an hour.'

'How do you feel about it now?' Sammy asked later, over coffee and sandwiches in Redman's.

'Excited, nervous. I'm dying to tell Ed. I hope he won't go mad because of the timing with the tour.'

'He won't, believe me,' Sammy assured her. 'He'll be thrilled to bits.'

* * *

The following week, The Raiders signed their contract. On the Saturday night Eddie took Jane to a restaurant in Wilmslow. It was the last full weekend they would spend together before

Christmas and Jonny was staying with Eddie's parents for the night. The tour was due to start the following week and Eddie was currently working his last days in the shop – John Grey had told him that he was welcome to work for them in-between tours if he wanted to.

Jane was secretly relieved; she was constantly worrying about them not having enough money to live on, while Eddie kept reassuring her they would. She'd have to give up working in March the following year, but of course he didn't know that yet. They enjoyed their meal, relaxing in one another's company, and halfway through the evening, Eddie asked the waiter to bring them a bottle of champagne.

'What's that for, and can we afford it?' Jane frowned.

'To celebrate, of course, and yes, we can,' he said as the waiter opened the bottle with a loud bang.

'Celebrate? Oh, the tour, you mean?' She took a sip and grinned as the bubbles fizzed up her nose.

'Yes, and our one-month anniversary.' He held his glass up to hers. 'Here's to us, Jane, and the success of The Raiders.'

Jane drew a deep breath; it was an ideal moment. 'There's something else to celebrate, too. It's to do with your birthday.'

'Well, that's not till next June. I think we can probably run to another bottle of champagne then, don't you? What is it? You look all secretive. Are you planning something special for my birthday? A trip to Hawaii or somewhere equally exotic?'

'Well, if I am,' she said, 'you'll be going on your own. 'Cos I'll be too busy giving birth to our new son, or maybe even our first daughter.'

She watched as his mouth fell open. He put down his glass and took her hand.

'You're pregnant? Honestly? Oh, Jane, that's fantastic!'

'You're not upset or anything? I thought you'd go mad, what with everything that's happening at the moment.'

'Why on earth would I go mad? I'm over the moon. If I'm

honest, I had a feeling you would be after the honeymoon. It *was* pretty wild, wasn't it?' He refilled their glasses, grinning broadly.

'It's not a honeymoon baby,' she whispered, conscious of the stares they were getting from the middle-aged couple at the next table. 'Work it out, your birthday's in June. I'm three months gone.'

'Ah, I see.' He smiled as the penny dropped. 'Well, it doesn't matter, does it? We're married now anyway. At least I don't have to go cap in hand and tell your parents that I've got you into trouble, like I had to with Angie's.'

Choking sounds came from the next table.

'Let's go,' Jane said, feeling suddenly on top of the world. What did it matter what anyone else thought? They were in love; they were happy and were expecting their first baby.

They bought bottles of cider on the way home and let themselves into the flat. Their friends were sitting in the lounge watching a film on TV. Eddie marched over to the set and turned it off.

'Get the glasses out, we've something to celebrate,' he announced as Sammy winked at Jane.

'Oi! We were watching that,' Tim said.

'I've an announcement to make.' Eddie pulled Jane to his side. 'We're pregnant – well, at least Jane is. But without my small contribution it wouldn't have been possible.' He patted her still-flat tummy proudly.

Cheers rang out and they were smothered in hugs and kisses.

'When's the happy event?' Roy asked.

'My next birthday,' Eddie said.

'Oh boy, what a wonderful present!' Tim exclaimed.

Roy looked thoughtful. 'So, it's not a...'

'Honeymoon baby?' Jane and Eddie chorused helpfully.

'No,' Jane laughed, 'it's *pre*-honeymoon!'

'You've done it again, Mellor,' Roy teased. 'But at least this time you won't deny it's yours *and* she's got a ring on her finger.'

'I wish you'd told me before I signed up for this tour, Jane,' Eddie said, on a more serious note. 'I don't like the thought of leaving you on your own now. Will you be okay?'

'Eddie, she'll be fine. We'll be here for her, and we'll look after Jonny too, don't you worry. Just as long as you phone every day and we know where to get in touch if we need you,' Sammy reassured him.

'You lot are the best friends anyone could ever have. What on earth Jane and I would have done over the last few years without your loyalty and support, I just can't imagine,' Eddie said, smiling round at them all.

19

DECEMBER 1964

Mark dumped the large pine tree in the middle of the lounge floor. Tony followed him in, arms laden with boughs of holly.

'Know something, Tony? This is going to be the best Christmas ever. No Maude getting in the way, barking orders and hauling us off to bloody church.'

'Too right,' Tony said, 'and I've got tickets for The Roulette Club's Christmas Eve bash.' He dropped the holly onto the rug in front of the fire and retrieved a sprig of mistletoe from his jacket. 'My mum wants you at our place for Christmas dinner. Sarah and Vicky are having dinner with their families and they'll join us here later.'

'Are The Raiders playing on Christmas Eve?' Mark asked, taking the mistletoe from Tony and fixing it up on the door frame.

'No. Rosa said Stuart Green's doing his DJ bit and Mario's laying on a buffet, so it should be a good night. Anyway, The Raiders won't be playing local clubs any more now they've hit the big time. It was in the *Advertiser* a couple of weeks ago that they're on a winter tour with Chris Montez and The Hollies.'

'Fucking hell! So Mellor's gonna be lording it that he's a

star. I bet Jane's been put on a back-burner now that he'll have his pick of women. No doubt he'll be dumping her soon.'

Mark gave Tony a cigarette, lit one for himself and flopped down on the sofa. He stared into the flames, smiling. This was good news. With Mellor preoccupied, Jane would be alone for Christmas. 'So, is the group away at the moment?' he asked, flicking ash into the fire.

'I don't know,' Tony said. 'They were, but they'll probably have Christmas off.'

Mark nodded. 'Do you happen to know the current score between Mellor and Jane?'

'Err, I'm not sure,' Tony replied, turning away from his friend's piercing stare. 'I haven't seen them since that night in The Roulette Club.'

Mark nodded and changed the subject. 'Are Vicky and Sarah looking forward to Christmas Eve?'

'They certainly are. Big night of the year for the girls. They've been talking about it all week. They've bought new dresses, fancy shoes, and Sarah showed me her sexy new under-wear last night. Prancing around in front of me, then had a go at me when I chucked her on the bed.'

'Bloody women,' Mark snarled. 'They're all prick teasers! Flaunting themselves then saying no at the last minute. They deserve all they get.'

'Hey, mate!' Tony frowned. 'What's got into *you*? Sarah was just larking around, that's all. Lighten up. Has somebody in Chester been giving you a hard time?'

'What do you mean?'

'Well, you've been acting weird since Jane dumped you, but even weirder since you stopped seeing that Beth bird.'

Mark went cold at the mention of Beth. He went to the drinks cabinet, poured a large whisky and knocked it back in one. 'Want one?'

Tony nodded and took a seat by the blazing fire.

'Sorry, Tony.' Mark joined him on the sofa and handed him a glass. 'I think I'm fucked. I really need this Christmas break.'

'Yeah, you look tired,' Tony agreed. 'Anyway, you never told me what happened to Beth. When I mentioned her then you went really pale. What's the story there, mate?'

Mark sighed and took another slug of whisky. 'I ballsed it up with her and we split.'

Tony stared silently at him.

'What?'

'Vicky told Sarah that Beth was pregnant.'

'Bitch! She had no right to say anything.'

'Then she said you told her it was a false alarm.'

'Yeah, that's right it was. It's over. I don't wanna talk about it.'

'I don't believe you,' Tony said. 'That it was a false alarm, I mean. Why would you even bother telling Vicky there was a problem unless you were sure? Mark, talk to me, mate, it may help. *Was* Beth pregnant?'

Mark nodded, staring into the fire. 'She was, but being a good Catholic lad you won't like what I'm gonna say.'

Tony got up to refill their glasses.

'I asked her to marry me. She turned me down, didn't want the kid either.' Mark sniffed loudly. The whisky was making him maudlin. It always did, but it helped blot out the nightmare of the faceless baby who invaded his dreams.

'She got rid of it?' Tony frowned.

'Yeah.' He took a slug of whisky as Tony's jaw tightened. 'Backstreet affair. I won't go into details, but it was pretty grim. She really suffered and I wish we hadn't done it. I just went along with the idea because Beth didn't want a baby and it seemed the easiest way out at the time.'

Tony topped up their glasses again while Mark stared into the fire.

'All I could think about while she was going through hell

PAM HOWES

was what if I'd married her and Jane changed her mind. But I should have insisted Beth kept the baby. I should have married her. Because of my feelings for Jane I allowed my kid to be destroyed. Never gave the poor little soul a chance.'

Tony stared at Mark, shaking his head. 'Beth didn't want it anyway,' he said gently. 'And she refused to marry you. So don't blame yourself. I'm sorry you felt you had to cope alone. Bottling things up like that can't be good for you.'

'I was ashamed of putting Beth through all that. I couldn't bring myself to talk to anyone, not even you. As soon as I knew she was gonna be okay I walked and I haven't been in touch since. I'm not sleeping well since it happened and when I do, I have these bloody awful dreams.'

'You should see your doctor while you're on leave,' Tony said. 'You've had a lot of stuff happen this year. You might need a bit of help coping with things.'

'I'm not going fucking loopy, Tony, if that's what you're implying.'

'I wasn't, but you're hitting the bottle more than you used to. Since you split with Jane, you've become a bit of a piss artist.'

Mark sighed. 'You're right. I'll go and see my doctor after Christmas. Maybe he can sort me out.'

'You do that,' Tony agreed. 'Right, let's get some grub before the girls come round to help us decorate that tree.'

'Fish and chips?' Mark suggested.

'Fish and chips it is. I'll nip out and get them.'

Left alone, Mark lit another cigarette. He dug in his pocket and pulled out Jane's ring. He'd have it back on her finger by New Year if it killed him.

* * *

'Bloody hell, it's crowded in here,' Eddie said. The Christmas Eve bash at The Roulette Club was in full swing as he and Jane made their way to where the others were seated.

'Thought you two weren't coming,' Roy yelled above the thumping music. 'You're late. They're about to serve the buffet.'

'Jane needed a rest,' Eddie said. He handed Roy a five-pound note. 'Get a round in while we have a quick dance.' He took Jane's hand and led her onto the dance floor. 'Baby Love' by The Supremes was playing. 'Appropriate song.' He patted her tummy proudly.

She smiled and put her arms around him and they swayed together. As the song ended, DJ Stuart announced the buffet was up and running.

'Let's grab something to eat before it all goes,' Eddie said. 'Roy's piling his plate up like there's a ration due to start! He was the same at school, winning the dinner ladies round with that sexy smile. They always gave him more than anyone else.'

'You eat as much as Roy; you're as greedy as each other,' Jane said as they joined the queue by the buffet tables.

'Don't forget you're feeding two, Jane,' Roy said. 'Pile it up. What Junior doesn't want, Uncle Roy will have.'

'If Daddy doesn't get to it first,' she quipped. 'What time does your mum want us for dinner tomorrow?' she asked Eddie as they sat down with laden plates.

'About one, but if we manage to get up early I'd like to go and see Jonny open his presents. He was really excited when I nipped round to see him earlier. He understands about Father Christmas this year, so he'll have Mum and Dad up at the crack of dawn. Mum said she'd let him open a couple of parcels and then keep the rest until we arrive.' He sank his teeth into a sausage roll, the crisp pastry flakes spilling down the front of his satin shirt.

'Let's not stay too late here then,' Jane said, brushing his crumbs away. 'Sammy, Pat and Tim are sleeping at Roy's place.

Then they're all going to Tom and Molly's for dinner, so we've got the flat to ourselves tonight and most of tomorrow.'

'Great! It'll be good to have you all to myself after being away. These sausage rolls are good,' he said, eyeing her plate.

'S'pose you want mine?' Jane laughed, handing it over. She stood up, putting her hands on her back. 'I'm just popping to the ladies'.'

'Okay, take your time. I'll have a fag while you're gone.'

* * *

Jane fought her way through the revellers, thinking how she was never off the loo lately.

Rosa, at the coat check, called out: 'Hi, Jane! Haven't seen you for ages.' She patted the little bump and kissed her on both cheeks. 'Congratulations. Bet you're over the moon.'

'Thanks, Rosa, we are,' Jane said. 'Bit of a shock at first, but we're really excited now.'

'What did your mum say?'

Jane rolled her eyes. 'Oh, she's dead chuffed. There were a few little digs and she said it's as well we're married. But she's knitting for England, so I know she's looking forward to being a granny, and Ed's mum and dad are made up, too.'

She said goodbye, turned to walk down the short corridor and bumped headlong into Mark Fisher.

'I'm terribly sorry,' he began, putting out his hands to steady her. 'Jane!' he gasped, looking down at her shocked face. 'How are you?'

'Fine, thanks,' she said as he stared at her, head cocked to one side.

'What have you been up to?' he asked. 'I heard Eddie Mellor's wife was killed.'

Jane nodded. 'Yes, she was.' Reluctant to discuss Angie, she changed the subject: 'How are you doing? You still dating Vicky?'

'I'm here with her tonight,' he replied. 'Been for a drink with Tony and Sarah first.' Jane nodded as he rambled on. 'I'm surprised The Raiders aren't playing tonight.' He slurred his words and was swaying slightly.

'The Raiders are on tour with The Hollies and Chris Montez but they've got Christmas off.'

'So, what's the score with you and Mellor? Still seeing him, or is it over now he's away touring?'

As he looked down at her, eyes glazed, she realised he probably hadn't a clue about her marriage. Maybe Vicky, very wisely, still hadn't mentioned it.

She cleared her throat. 'Actually, Mark, Ed and I are married now.' She clasped her hands over her bump as his jaw dropped. 'I'm expecting a baby.'

'No, you're not!' he said, his colour draining. 'You *can't* be married to him?'

'Well, I am,' she said, frowning. 'We've lived together since Angie's death. Ed needed help with Jonny.' She took a deep breath to stop any further babbling. Why the hell was she explaining herself? It had nothing to do with him and the way he was looking at her was very unnerving.

She jumped as he grabbed her upper arms, scowling. '*He* fell bloody lucky, didn't he? You'll never learn, Jane, he's a fucking user.' He shook her and brought his face up close to hers.

'I suppose you're stuck at home minding his bloody brat while *he's* swanning up and down the country, screwing for England!'

She beat her fists on his chest. 'Let me go, you creep! And how dare you say that about Eddie. You don't know anything about him or what we've been through this past year.'

* * *

Eddie was about to ask Sammy to check if Jane was all right, as she'd been gone ages, when he caught sight of Rosa frantically signalling to him. He leapt up and made his way across the room.

'What is it?'

'You'd better go and rescue Jane from Mark Fisher. He's giving her the third degree, down near the ladies'.'

'What?' he exploded. 'Get your fucking hands off my wife, Fisher!' Eyes blazing, he pushed Mark backwards. Mark stumbled and released his grip on Jane. He glared at Eddie, who squared up to him.

'Need some help, Ed?' Roy said from behind.

'I'm okay thanks, Roy. Just sorting this twat out.' He put his arm around Jane's shaking shoulders and summoned Rosa, who brought a chair out for her to sit on. 'What's going on, Jane?' he asked.

'There's nothing going on. Mark didn't know we're married. I was telling him how happy we are about our baby.'

Eddie relaxed slightly, kneeling down beside her.

'I see.' He laid his hand on her stomach, looking up at Mark, a challenge in his eyes. For two bits he could punch the living daylights out of the bastard, but not in front of Jane. 'I warned you to stay away from Jane, Fisher. Now I'm telling you again. If I see you anywhere near either of us, I'll kill you.' He helped Jane to her feet. 'Come on, sweetheart, I'm taking you home. You look fit to drop. See you, Mark... oh, and by the way, Merry fucking Christmas.'

'Fuck you!' Mark growled.

* * *

Rage swept through Mark as Eddie and Jane walked away with their arms around one another. He sat down on Jane's chair, putting his head in his hands. He'd been so certain he would find her alone. All he'd thought about on his lonely nights in Chester was him begging her to take him back and her saying yes. He'd brought the ring out with him, stupidly imagining the romantic scenario of going down on one knee and proposing all over again.

He'd never dared allow the thought that Jane may be married to Mellor, let alone expecting his baby, to cross his mind, But what was hurting him most was that while *his* kid had been carelessly conceived and disposed of, Jane and Mellor's had been created in a loving relationship and it marked the end of his dreams of any future with her. Oblivious to his surroundings, he dropped to his knees, howling, and beat his fists on the floor.

* * *

Jane was shaking as Eddie helped her into the car and drove back to the flat.

'I'll swing for Fisher, upsetting you like that.'

'Calm down, Ed. I'm fine, really. He's still very bitter and he's jealous of you. You've got everything he badly wants – a successful group, me, this baby. I suppose it's too much for him to take in one go.'

'Well, he had you for three years, which is more than I've had. He never made you as happy as I do, *and* he had his bloody chance. I suppose you think I should feel sorry for him.'

'No, I don't. But let there be an end to all the rivalry now,' she said wearily. 'Let's go inside and relax.'

As she searched in her handbag for the key, Eddie spotted a large, gaily-wrapped parcel propped by the door. He looked at the label tied to the ribbons.

'It's for Jonny, from Cathy.'

'That's kind of her,' Jane said. An envelope addressed to them both was lying on the mat and she bent to pick it up. As she pulled out the enclosed Christmas card, a sheet of paper fell out.

Eddie caught the paper and flopping down on the sofa, he scanned through it.

'She says congratulations on the baby and sorry she hasn't been to visit for a while. She hopes we're all okay. She's off to London in the New Year but she'll come and see us before she goes. She'd like to take Jonny out for the day.'

'I'm pleased she's made a decision about her future,' Jane said.

'Yeah, she's proved to be not such a bad sort really – she's very fond of Jonny.'

'Can I get you a drink, Ed?'

'I'm okay.' He pulled her onto the sofa. 'I love you.'

'And I love you,' she said. 'More than anything in the world.'

He slid to the floor and knelt in front of her, laying his head on her knees. 'What have I done to deserve all this love?'

She stroked his hair, glad that they'd left the club early. They had so little time together these days. Now the group was making a name for itself, she would see even less of him.

'You're just you, Ed. That's why I love you.'

He spoke softly, stroking her tummy. 'Hello, baby, this is Daddy. I'm dying to meet you. I wonder what you are.'

'She's a girl,' Jane said, with the conviction of one who knows.

'How can you be so sure?' He looked up, shaking his fringe from his eyes.

'I have this feeling, it's a woman thing.'

'Have you thought of any names for our daughter then?'

'I like Jessica.'

'Jessica,' he repeated. 'Yeah, I like that too. Jessie for short?'

'It matches Jonny,' she said. 'Jessie and Jonny, they sort of go together. It's a lovely name.'

'She'll be a lovely baby, just like her mum.'

'And her dad. Hope she's got your blue eyes.'

'Supposing it's a boy, will you be very disappointed?'

'No, but I feel sure it's a girl for some reason. If it's a boy, I like the name Justin.'

'Justin time!' Eddie grinned. 'Well, he would be.'

Jane stood up, stretching. 'I'm going to make a cuppa. Would you like one? Then we should go to bed because we've got to get up early.'

'I'm going to sample my Christmas present from Roy and Sammy first.' He pulled a small package from his jeans pocket.

'He's gone a bit overboard with the fancy paper and ribbons.' Jane laughed.

'I suspect Sammy had a hand in the wrapping. It's more her style than Roy's. Do you want to share some?'

'No thanks, Ed, it makes me feel a bit sick. And we don't want a stoned baby, do we?'

'Heaven forbid! You don't mind if I do?'

'Of course not, it helps you unwind. I'll make some tea and get out of this dress.'

'Jane, are you sure you're okay? I mean, after that business with Fisher.'

'I'm fine, really. Put it out of your mind, please.'

'It's not easy. The thought of him anywhere near you does my head in.'

'He'd had too much to drink, that's all. It won't happen again.'

'It'd better not, or I mean it, I'll kill him!'

* * *

Jane slipped out of her clothes and pulled on her nightdress. She sat down on the bed to brush her hair. She didn't want Ed to know that she was still feeling shaken by Mark's outburst and terrified by the cold look in his eyes as he'd pushed his face close to hers. Hopefully, now he knew she was pregnant *and* married to Eddie, he would get on with his own life.

She thought she might contact Vicky in the New Year, just to make sure Mark was all right. Though why she was bothering, when he seemed to have no concerns for her other than wanting to upset her, she didn't know. But there was something very strange about him tonight and it scared her: she wanted to be certain he was going back to Chester as soon as possible.

20

FEBRUARY 1965

Mark swallowed his pills and gulped down a mouthful of whisky. He threw the Isle of Wight letters into his briefcase, slipped the whisky bottle into his holdall and propped his luggage by the front door while he looked for his car keys.

As he rummaged on the hall table he knocked a large plant off. The pot smashed against the wall, spilling soil all over the carpet. 'Fuck it,' he muttered, grabbing his keys.

He chucked his bags into the boot of his new Austin-Healey Sprite, shot off the drive and began the journey to Portsmouth. In spite of Tony, Sarah and Vicky's protestations about the trip, he'd decided it was time to find his roots. He had four older half-siblings and someone on the island must know their whereabouts. The last-known address for their late father was in Freshwater, which is where he planned to make a start.

He fiddled with the car radio, trying to tune in to Caroline, but settled for *Housewives Choice*. As Jim Reeves warbled 'I Won't Forget You', he thought of Jane and turned the radio off. His mind wandered over the events of the last few weeks and the visit to his doctor, who told him he'd suffered a nervous breakdown. He was glad the doc had suggested a holiday, a

complete break from Stockport. It would get him away from
Vicky and her bloody clingy ways.

He thought about Mellor, threatening him in the club. 'I'll
kill the fucker one of these days,' he mumbled, swerving onto
the A34 in front of a laden lorry. The driver tooted and Mark
stuck two fingers up and pulled away. He put his foot down and
his thoughts turned to Jane again and he tried to imagine a
scenario where she might leave Mellor and come back to him.
He blinked rapidly; his eyes were getting misty again. The pills
did that for the first hour or so, especially when he downed
them with whisky.

He turned the radio back on and this time joined in the
chorus of 'Yeh Yeh', singing along with Georgie Fame. The
traffic was fairly light for mid-morning as he blasted along in his
racing-green, frog-eyed car. He'd stop somewhere in an hour or
two for coffee.

Mark flicked his collar up against the chilly afternoon and
strode purposefully down the main street. He'd made good time
on the roads yesterday and the 1:00 p.m. ferry had left
promptly. He'd booked into the hotel, collapsed on the bed and
slept all night and most of this morning. He felt relaxed but was
out of fags and whisky. He'd intended to buy more at the ferry
terminal yesterday but his head had been fucked and he'd
forgotten. He crossed the road and popped into the
newsagent's. He paid for his fags and asked the middle-aged
assistant for directions to the doctor's surgery.

'There are two hereabouts,' the woman said. 'Doctor Mainwaring and Doctor Lovell. Which one do you want?'

'I thought Doctor Mainwaring was dead?' Mark said,
frowning.

'Lord no! He's very much alive and kicking. In fact, only

yesterday I took my bunions along to see him. Doctor Jack passed some years ago, but his son, Doctor Charles, well, he took over the practice when his father died.'

Mark nodded. Of course, it made sense that one of Jack Mainwaring's sons should follow in his father's footsteps.

'And where's Doctor Mainwaring's surgery, please?'

'Where it's always been, my dear. Two streets down on this side and take a left turn. You can't miss it. There's a sign outside the door. It's best to ring for an appointment. Do you have the number to hand?'

'No, I don't,' he replied. 'Could you write it down for me, please? And thanks for your help.' He pocketed the piece of paper. Saying goodbye, he spotted an off-licence two doors down, nipped in and bought two bottles of whisky.

He lit a fag and made his way back to the hotel. It seemed as though it was going to be pretty easy to trace his family. One brother was called Charles. Mark wondered about the other Mainwaring offspring – their names, where they lived, what they were doing. Amelia had referred to Jack's sons and daughters in some of her letters to Maude, but not by name. No doubt if he'd spoken to Maude he could have gleaned a bit more information but asking her anything about his late father's family was something he couldn't bring himself to do.

Back in his room he picked up the engagement photo of him and Jane and ran a finger over her face: 'One day, girl, you'll be mine again. You'll be begging me to take you back.' He remembered saying that to her last year. Did she ever think about him at all? It was a year this week since they'd split up.

A whole year and his life had been turned upside down. He put the photo back on the bedside table and poured a large whisky. He took a slug with a handful of pills and reached for his briefcase. He looked through the letters from Amelia and the firm of Portsmouth solicitors. There were also details of the five thousand pound legacy he'd got for his twenty-first. His old man had been generous in seeing him financially provided for. He didn't know where this visit was going to lead, but it was something he felt compelled to do.

He glanced at the piece of paper with the scribbled phone number. He wasn't going to make an appointment though. He'd turn up tomorrow, maybe after morning surgery, tell them he was ill and it was an emergency. Surely they'd agree to see him? He checked his watch, not quite six. He drained his glass and lay back on the bed, hands folded behind his head. Dinner was at seven. He should call Tony and Vicky, let them know he was okay. But he couldn't be bothered. The booze and pills were having that feel-good effect where he could imagine he was not one, but two, very different people.

In his head he was living his imaginary life with Jane. He closed his eyes and groaned, hands reaching to his crotch. If he called home now, it would take him out of his reverie and he couldn't wank when he was thinking of Vicky. His thoughts of Jane also helped block the faceless-baby nightmares he still had and the reality that she was married to Mellor.

'Doctor Mainwaring will see you now, Mr Collins.' The receptionist's pleasant voice jolted Mark from his daydream. He'd been deep in thought, thinking that the slim, dark-haired woman, who'd greeted him when he arrived at the surgery, was doing the same job his late mother had done. She'd agreed to squeeze him in if he was prepared to wait.

'Thanks,' Mark replied. He picked up his briefcase and walked down the corridor. He knocked on a door bearing a brass plaque inscribed *Doctor Mainwaring*. The plaque was old but well-polished. He wondered if it was originally his father's.

'Come in!' a disembodied voice called.

Mark entered as Charles Mainwaring looked up from behind an old mahogany desk. Had that been his dad's, too?

'Good morning, Mr Collins. My wife tells me you're on holiday and feeling unwell?'

'Your wife?' Mark frowned. 'Oh, your wife's the receptionist.'

'She certainly is. Take a seat, please.'

Mark sat down and placed his briefcase between his feet. He stared at Charles and took a deep breath. It was like looking in a mirror. His half-brother was his spitting image: same brown hair and soft grey eyes. Mark wondered if Charles was also aware of the likeness. But how could he be? He'd probably no idea to this day that his dad had fathered a bastard.

'What are your symptoms?' Charles began.

'Actually, I'm not ill,' Mark confessed. 'My name's not Collins and I really don't know where to begin.' Charles looked up with surprise as he continued: 'My name's Mark. I believe we may be brothers. Well actually, we *are* definitely brothers.'

He fell silent as Charles frowned and shook his head, a look of bewilderment in his eyes.

'I'm sorry. Did you say, brothers?'

Mark lifted his briefcase onto the desk and opened it. He handed Charles the snapshot of Jack and Amelia. Charles's eyes widened as he stared at the photograph.

'That's my late father, Jack!' he exclaimed. 'That lady used to be the receptionist here when I was a boy, Amelia Saunders.'

'That's right,' Mark said. 'Amelia was my mum and Jack was *my* dad too.'

'But I don't understand,' Charles faltered. 'How on earth…? I mean… Amelia died years ago. How do you know she was your mother? Where have you been all this time? I'm sorry, Mark, I'm afraid I'm at a loss.'

'I felt exactly the same when *I* discovered the truth,' Mark said. 'But believe me, it *is* the truth. I have enough letters and documentation to prove it.'

Charles looked totally bewildered. 'Listen, Mark, don't think me really rude, but I have to go on my rounds shortly. I'm a one-man band and there's nobody who can stand in for me. Where are you staying?'

'The Springfield Hotel,' he replied.

'Come back tonight about seven. Have something to eat with us and we'll discuss this then.' He indicated Mark's papers with his hand. 'My elder sister Dorothy lives up the road in Yarmouth. I'll call her and invite her to dinner and then we can all sit down and talk properly.'

Mark rose and extended his hand. 'Thanks... err, Charles. I'm sorry to keep you from your work. I'll see you tonight.'

Charles grasp was firm and his smile friendly. 'I'm truly intrigued. But looking at *you* is like looking in a mirror a few years back. I'd better go and grab a quick snack and let my wife know that we've two extra for dinner tonight.'

* * *

Mark towelled himself dry and pulled on black trousers and a clean shirt. He brushed his hair and sat down on the bed. He popped three pills in his mouth and swallowed them down with whisky again. That'd keep him going for a while, he thought, yawning. He was knackered; it was tiring having nothing to do all day. He'd taken a walk after leaving Charles, then spent the afternoon in his room, dozing and thinking about Jane. The short walk to the surgery would wake him up – he'd call in the off-licence and get a bottle of wine to take with him.

* * *

'So, you're my sister,' Mark said, shaking the hand of the plump woman Charles had introduced as Dorothy. 'Nice to meet you.' She was tall with the same grey eyes as he and Charles, but her hair was darker and she wore it long. She was dressed in a short, over-tight dress and the buttons strained over her huge breasts. She looked a bit what Maude might call a floozy, he thought, and stifled a grin.

'It's nice to meet you, too,' she said, her smile not quite reaching her eyes.

'And this is my wife, Penny,' Charles said and Mark reached out to shake her hand. 'But of course you met her this morning. Come through to the dining room, Mark.'

Mark took a seat at the table and Penny placed a heaped plate in front of him. 'Hope you like chicken casserole,' she said. 'Help yourself to veg.'

'Lovely. Thank you.' Mark stared at Dorothy, who kept her gaze on her meal and he wondered why. Mind you, he thought, when some geezer turns up out of the blue claiming to be your long-lost brother, what more could he expect?

There was an awkward silence as they tucked in. Mark knocked back a glass of wine.

'A refill, Mark?' Charles stood up and reached for the bottle. 'Dot?'

'Just a drop, Charles,' Dorothy said. 'I'm driving and I've had two glasses already. We were at the bottle before you arrived,' she told Mark.

'I see. Well, I'm walking so I'll have another, thanks.'

'That was one of Dad's traits,' Dorothy said. 'He had rather a passion for the old vino.'

'Did he?' Mark sighed. 'I wish I could remember him *and* my mum.'

She nodded. 'You must excuse me if I seem a little distant, Mark. I'm just getting over the shock of you turning up out of the blue.'

'I guess you are,' he said. 'When we've finished the meal, I'll show you my papers, prove to you that I'm really your brother.'

'I have no doubt that you are,' Dorothy said. 'The resemblance to Charles is uncanny. And *I* also have something to show *you*.'

Mark nodded as Penny jumped up to clear their plates. 'Sherry trifle for dessert, everybody?'

'Oh, yes, please.' Charles grinned. 'You've never tasted anything like Pen's trifles,' he said to Mark. 'They're out of this world.'

* * *

Mark excused himself as Penny and Dorothy cleared the table and he and Charles retired to the sitting room.

'Take a seat.' Charles gestured to the sofa. Mark flopped down in front of a blazing log fire. Charles parked himself on a chair opposite. 'Right then, let's have a look at the letters and stuff.'

Mark handed over his briefcase. Charles sifted through the letters from Amelia and the documents from the solicitors, nodding from time to time.

Mark glanced around the large room, with its tall ceilings and elegant furniture. He was sure it hadn't changed that much since his father lived here. Seeing a photograph on the mantelpiece, he got up to look.

'May I?'

'Certainly,' Charles replied. 'It's Mum and Dad, taken a couple of years before Mum died and about a year after Amelia's death. Poor old bugger, eh? Lost both his women.'

Mark smiled and studied the photo. Charles's mother was a large, formidable-looking woman. No wonder his dad had been tempted into a fling with the lovely Amelia.

Penny carried in a tray and placed it on the coffee table.

Dorothy followed, carrying a bottle of brandy and three glasses. Under her arm was tucked a large brown envelope.

Dorothy took a seat on the sofa and patted the space beside her.

'I want you to have a look at the contents of this envelope, Mark. You see, I've known of your existence for a number of years, since just before Dad's death. What I didn't know was if *you* knew anything about *us*. I put Charles and Pen in the picture before you arrived.'

Mark tipped out the letters and photographs from the envelope. There were several of Jack, Amelia and him, and more with just him and Amelia. He swallowed the lump in his throat as he read his father's death-bed confession. How he'd loved Amelia, but to avoid scandal, had stayed with his wife and family. He'd never forgotten Mark and hoped that should he ever contact his brothers and sisters in the future, they'd welcome him into the family. He also asked for forgiveness as he'd tried to do his best in protecting and providing for all his children.

Mark folded the letter and put it away with the photos. He held the envelope out to Dorothy, but she shook her head. 'Keep it, Mark. I don't expect you have many photos of your mum.'

'Just one or two that were in the letters she sent to Maude. Those that Charles has on his knee. Feel free to read the letters,' he said to Dorothy. 'Take them home with you and I'll collect them before I leave the island.'

'It must have been quite shocking to discover the truth, after believing Maude to be your mother,' Penny said, pouring coffee.

'It was. My wife, Jane, was very supportive though. She helped me get through it.'

'You're married?' Dorothy exclaimed. 'How lovely, you should have brought Jane with you.'

'How long have you been married?' Charles took a swig of wine and smiled.

'Since last September. Our first baby's due in June. We're thrilled about it and now that I've found my family, well, you're the icing on the cake.'

'So, I'm to be an auntie?' Dorothy exclaimed with delight. 'How wonderful! I thought it would never happen. You're the only Mainwaring offspring to breed. Well done, Mark.'

'It would have been nice for Jane to meet you all but she's not been too well and she's been told to rest. The journey would have been too much for her. Next time I visit, after the baby's born, we'll all come together.'

'Oh, you must,' Penny said. 'That would be lovely, Mark.'

'Right!' Dorothy downed the last of her wine and rose to her feet. 'I'm off. I'll have a read through of your letters tomorrow, Mark. They may throw a bit of light on how very difficult it must have been for all concerned. Come and visit me before you go home and pick them up. Get the directions off Charles. It's very straightforward. You can't possibly get lost on this island. If you end up in the harbour, you know you've gone too far!'

Mark and Charles saw Dorothy to the door.

'It's really lovely to suddenly be an expectant auntie. I'll have to get out my knitting needles,' she said.

'You'll be in your element,' Charles teased.

'I tell you what, Mark, come and live here,' Dorothy said. 'We'll get to enjoy our nephew or niece growing up.'

'Mark's got a home, friends and roots in Stockport,' Charles said as Mark smiled. 'Why on earth would he want to move here?'

'Because we're his only family.'

'True. But Jane's probably got family in Stockport. Anyway, we'll see. We don't want to frighten you off, Mark, by being over-possessive as soon as you meet us.'

Mark grinned and waved as Dorothy got in her car and pulled off the drive.

Back indoors, Charles poured more wine and topped Mark's up. They downed that and then Charles opened the brandy.

'Would you two alcoholics mind if I go up to bed?' Penny said, yawning loudly.

'Not at all,' Mark said. 'I'd better be hitting the road, I promised to call Jane before eleven and it's not far off that now.' He stood up, swaying slightly. His head felt fuzzy again and his eyes were misty – he just needed to lie down.

'Ring her from here,' Charles said.

'Oh no, it's okay. I'd rather call her in private.'

'So you can whisper sweet nothings?' Penny teased.

'Something like that,' he replied. 'Besides, the fresh air will sober me up a bit so I don't slur my words. Jane doesn't like me drinking too much.'

'Come and visit us again tomorrow.' Charles stood up to shake Mark's hand. Penny reached up and planted a kiss on his cheek.

'Thank you, I will. And thanks very much for your hospitality,' he said as he left.

Mark reflected on the success of the evening as he strolled back to the hotel. His family was extremely nice and had totally accepted him. Jane would love them, of that he was certain.

* * *

Back in his room, Mark swallowed more pills with a slug of whisky and dialled a number. Vicky answered after a couple of rings and he told her of his visit to his brother's home. He felt excited, rambling on, not letting her get a word in. He ended the call by slurring, 'I love you, Jane. Take care of that baby till I get home!' He fell back on the bed in a drunken stupor.

* * *

Jane rolled over as the bedroom door opened and Eddie came in. 'Hi, I wasn't expecting you till tomorrow,' she said, sitting up.

'We decided to come back tonight instead of another night in a hotel,' he whispered.

'It's okay. Jonny's at your mum's to give me a break.'

'Oh, great!' He threw off his clothes and climbed in beside her.

'How did it go?' she asked, snuggling up to him. The Raiders had been recording their first lot of songs at Abbey Road Studios and she'd really missed him. She'd hardly seen him at all apart from the odd day for the last couple of months. First, the Winter Tour, then the recording sessions and he was off on tour again soon, this time with Roy Orbison.

'It was brilliant. We've enough in the can now for three singles and an LP. "My Special Girl" will be released as the first single in a couple of weeks. We're on *Scene at* 6:30 beginning of next month and *Top of the Pops* the following week.'

'Wow!' Jane stared at him open-mouthed. 'Oh my God, my famous husband!'

He laughed and hugged her. 'Anything exciting happen while I've been away?'

'Not compared to *your* news. Tina's dumped Carl. She's dating Sean now, and Sammy's got a new design job.'

'Great news, not for Carl, of course, but Sean and Tina are well suited. That's brilliant for Sammy – Roy will be chuffed to bits for her. Right, now that's all out of the way, let's get down to business while Jonny's not around. I've really missed you, woman!'

21

MARCH 1965

'There it is!' Eddie pointed to the imposing, modern building that housed the Granada Studios. 'Turn right here.'

Roy turned into Quay Street and pulled up at the barrier.

'Who are you?' asked the peak-capped attendant.

'The Raiders, mate,' Roy said.

The man ran his finger down the list then raised the barrier. 'Studio two loading bay, straight ahead,' he said.

'Thanks,' Eddie called. 'Bloody hell, I can't believe this is happening!' He jumped out of the van, leaping around on the pavement. 'We're gonna be on the telly,' he called to a passing woman, who smiled at him as he waved his arms in the air.

Laughing at Eddie's excitement, Roy, Tim and Phil clambered out.

The loading bay doors were open and Roy popped his head inside. A long-haired man in jeans and an open-necked shirt hurried forward.

'You The Raiders?' he asked, scanning the clipboard he was carrying.

'We are,' Roy replied.

'One minute while I grab a trolley. I'm Jim, by the way, your production assistant.' He vanished for a couple of seconds then reappeared, pushing a trolley. 'Load your gear onto this and follow me.'

* * *

Roy and Eddie manoeuvred the loaded trolley into the building, followed by Tim and Phil, carrying their guitars and bags containing The Raiders stage outfits. Phil winked at two dark-haired girls, who giggled at each other.

'Okay for later,' he mouthed. The elder of the pair shook her head, stuck her hand in the air and waggled her ring finger. The other girl nodded, waving her ring-less hand at him. Phil stuck up a thumb. 'That's me sorted!'

'Christ, Jackson, I don't know how you do it.' Eddie laughed. 'Everywhere we go, you manage to line one up.'

'It's my charm and sincerity they go for,' Phil smirked.

Eddie's face lit up as they walked down a long, well-lit corridor and passed a man in police uniform. 'Bloody hell,' he muttered to Roy. 'That was Fancy Smith!'

'Brian Blessed,' the production assistant corrected and burst out laughing as the actor turned and smiled, then carried on his way. 'We're filming Z Cars today, so you'll probably bump into more of the cast.'

Eddie glanced into open doorways, spotting props and scenery. 'This is brilliant,' he said. 'There's stuff lying around in those rooms that I recognise from programmes we watch.'

Jim stopped outside a door bearing the sign STUDIO TWO. 'This is where we'll be recording your spot and the interview with Bill Grundy,' he said. 'Set up, do sound checks, then we'll take it from there.'

Eddie unloaded his drums and chatted to Jim while he put the kit together. Roy was busy tuning his guitar and Tim replaced a string on his bass.

'Where's Phil sloped off to?' Roy looked around. 'We're ready.'

'Gone for a pee,' Eddie said and twirled his sticks in the air. 'He'll probably be chatting up that bird. I'll go hurry him up.'

He made his way to reception and spotted Phil leaning against the wall, talking to the girl. 'Jackson, get your arse into gear!' he called. 'We're waiting to do a sound check.'

Phil turned and waved. 'On my way. See you later, babe,' he said to the blushing girl, who gave him a simpering smile.

'Bit of all right, her.' Eddie nodded as he and Phil walked back to Studio Two.

'Tell me about it. She's a Raiders fan *and* she's got her own flat in town. I'm staying there tonight.'

Eddie rolled his eyes and grinned as they took up their positions.

'Ready when you are, Jim,' Roy said after a quick run-through of 'Sweet Little Sixteen'.

Jim made his way to a glass booth beside the mixing desk. He put on headphones and nodded to the band. Eddie counted to four and Roy began to sing 'My Special Girl'.

Jim's face broke into a wide smile as the song came to a melodious end. He stuck up both thumbs. 'The sound's spot on, lads,' he said, strolling out of the booth. 'Bloody good song, too, should do well after tonight.'

'Thanks, mate.' Eddie put down his sticks and Roy, Tim and Phil placed their guitars on stands. 'So, what happens now?' Eddie asked.

'Make your way to Wardrobe and the girls will sort out your make-up and give your suits a quick press.'

'Make-up?' Eddie looked at Roy.

'Just a touch to get rid of the shine on your faces,' Jim said, laughing. 'Don't worry, you won't look like tarts! When you come back, Lighting will run through the set up with you, make sure you look okay on camera. We'll record the session, check through it and then it'll be ready to air tonight. Bill Grundy will have a chat with you when he arrives and we'll record the interview, too.'

'Great!' Eddie said. 'Anywhere we can grab a sandwich?'

'The girls on reception will point you in the direction of hospitality. I'll see you later.'

* * *

'Everybody got enough to eat?' Jane asked, flopping down beside Sammy on the sofa. The Wilmslow flat was crowded as everyone waited in anticipation to see The Raiders TV debut.

'It's like a Flanagan and Grey's staff outing in here,' John Grey said. Alongside the girls and Jonny, his employees were sprawled on the sofas and floor, tucking into plates of sandwiches and sausage rolls. Stuart arrived with bottles of cider and wine and a party atmosphere developed.

Jonny was mesmerised at seeing Eddie on TV. 'There's Daddy!' he exclaimed, pointing a chubby finger at the screen and making them all laugh. He clapped his hands and cheered when the song came to an end.

'That was great,' Sammy said.

'Superb,' John added, 'but then, I wouldn't have expected anything less.'

The phone rang and Sammy dashed to answer it. 'It's Ed's mum, Jane. She's all weepy. Come and talk to her.'

'I can't believe it,' Lillian said. 'My lad's on the telly. I'm a very proud mum, Jane. Will you tell him that when he gets home? I've never told him I'm proud of him.'

'I will,' she said. 'It'll mean the world to him. I'll get him to call you as soon as he can.'

Eddie eventually rang. 'Did you see us?'

'Of course we did,' Jane said. 'Thought you'd be back by now, seeing as it was a recording. Hurry up, and bring some more booze. We've a party going on here and we're almost dry.'

'Will do. Be with you in the hour.'

* * *

Mark sat transfixed, eyes glued to the screen, watching Mellor banging his fucking drums and warbling as though he hadn't a care in the world. Bastard!

Beside him, Tony pointed his glass at the screen. 'Smashing song, they wrote it themselves.'

Vicky, leaning against Mark's legs on the floor, inclined her head and smiled.

'It's so romantic. Rosa told me Roy and Eddie wrote it for Sammy and Jane...' She fell silent as Tony shot her a warning glance.

'Erm, you okay, Mark?' she asked, hesitantly.

Glassy-eyed, he stood up, took the heavy ashtray from Tony's side and hurled it at the television. Vicky screamed as the screen exploded and sparks flew everywhere. Tony jumped to his feet – but Mark was off, grabbing his car keys and slamming the door behind him. They heard the Sprite's engine scream into life and the tyres squeal.

* * *

Tony ran across the room and yanked the plug from the socket. 'For fuck's sake!' He turned to Vicky in bewilderment. 'What the hell was that all about?'

'Jane, of course,' she said, blinking back tears. 'I told you he's getting worse. He'll end up killing himself, driving like that.'

'He won't go back to the doctor,' Tony said. 'He's due a check-up and needs another sick note. He'll lose his job if he doesn't send one in soon.'

'Well, if *you* can't make him go, nobody else can,' she said. 'This is the last straw for me. In bed last night he called me Jane, again.'

'I'm sorry, love,' Tony said, running his hands through his hair. 'I don't even know where to go and look for him. This is getting too much for us to cope with, we need professional help.'

'Yes, we do,' she agreed. 'And tomorrow, I'm going to do something about getting it. I think I know where he'll have gone. He'll be parked at the back of the shops in Wilmslow, where Jane and Eddie live.'

'How do you know that?'

'An educated guess. Where else would he go?'

'The Isle of Wight?'

'That needs planning. This is spur-of-the-moment.'

'Well, it's a long shot, but I suppose it's worth a try. Give it an hour, see if he comes back first.'

They sat in silence as the minutes ticked by and then jumping up, Tony grabbed his keys. 'Let's go!' He drove at speed to Wilmslow and turned towards the shopping precinct.

'There he is.' Vicky pointed to the very back of the car park.

'You've got good eyesight,' Tony said, squinting at the dark shape of a low-slung vehicle.

'I caught the glow of a cigarette. Let's try and talk to him.'

They made their way to the car and Mark looked out of the open window as they approached.

He glared at them. 'What the fuck do you want?' he slurred. 'Where's Jane?'

'She's not here,' Vicky said. 'We should go back to the house, she might be home by now. Come on, we'll go in Tony's car and collect yours tomorrow.'

Tony stared at her as she helped a bewildered Mark from the Sprite, shoved him into the passenger seat of Tony's car and slammed the door. 'Why did you tell him Jane might be home?'

'If you can't beat 'em, join 'em!' she said. 'Let's get back and call the doctor. He needs sectioning for his own safety. What if he does something really bad to Eddie or Jane?'

'Why would he? He's just confused. He's not going in a fucking nut-house, Vicky.'

'I'm not arguing with you,' she said. 'You said we need professional help. Well, that's what we're gonna get.'

* * *

Following The Raiders' television appearance, 'My Special Girl' hit the singles chart and shot to number three. The Roy Orbison tour began and the girls saw the group perform in Manchester. Sitting in the front circle at the ABC Theatre, Jane was overwhelmed as the screaming audience demanded MORE.

'How on earth can these girls hear anything?' she shouted at Sammy and Pat, who were whistling through their fingers and stamping their feet.

'Don't know,' Sammy shouted back. 'Brilliant though, isn't it? *And* we get to meet Roy Orbison after the show.'

In the hospitality room the excited girls were introduced to the tall, dark-haired Texan.

'Would you mind if we have a photograph with you?' Jane asked.

'Go right ahead,' he drawled.

'Ed!' She shouted across the room to where he was chatting to members of the press. 'Bring the camera over.'

The girls grouped together, Jane and Pat either side of Sammy, Roy Orbison standing behind, his big hands resting on Sammy's shoulders.

Jane could feel her own hands shaking with excitement as Eddie snapped away.

'Thank you so much,' she said.

Roy Orbison smiled shyly. 'One for your family album,' he

said. He signed their programmes before being whisked away by his manager.

'Wow!' Sammy exclaimed. 'Can you believe that? Roy Orbison had *his* hands on *my* shoulders. Oh my God!'

Jane and Pat laughed as the boys' agent Frank James strolled towards them.

'Word in your shell-like, Jane,' he said, taking her to one side. 'Don't get upset, love, but we've told the press the lads are all single. Better for the group's image if the fans think they're available, you see.'

'Okay.' She nodded. 'As long as Eddie doesn't forget he's married. How do I explain this away if we're seen out together?' She pointed to her bump.

'No problem,' he said. 'We'll say you're his married sister.'

* * *

'Sorry, Jane,' Eddie said, after taking a call from a local paper who wanted to interview and photograph The Raiders. 'I know I promised to take you and Jonny shopping later, but it looks like we'll be out for most of the afternoon. I'll be home tonight and we've got the morning together. Let's go for a walk with Jonny, do something normal for a change.'

Frank's secretary rang at lunchtime: the boys were needed first thing the following day for a promotional photo shoot. Jane shook her head; it seemed everyone wanted a piece of her husband's precious time.

'I'll just have to get used to it,' she said as he kissed her.

'I promise we'll go dancing at the club tonight with Roy and Sammy. Or waddling, as in your case!' he teased. 'Get Sean and Tina to babysit, will you?'

* * *

Jane smiled as Vincento pounced on her and Eddie as they entered The Roulette Club.

'Blimey, Vinnie! You pleased to see us, or something?' she said, as he grabbed her and kissed both cheeks.

'I'm always pleased to see you, Jane,' Vinnie said. 'I need to ask Ed something, so I'll get you both a drink on the house while you find a seat. Cider?'

'Pint of draught for me and half for Jane. Thanks, Vinnie.' Eddie led the way to a table at the back of the room.

Vinnie carried a tray of drinks across and plonked himself down. 'Right, cheers to you both, and the new bambino, when it arrives.' He took a slug of cider and wiped his mouth with the back of his hand.

'Thanks, Vin.' Eddie looked at him. 'So, what's on your mind?'

'We get bombarded with questions about the group,' Vinnie began. 'I reckon you need a fan club. Me and Rosa, well, we think we could run a club here for you from Dad's office.'

Eddie nodded. 'Well look, here's Roy with Sammy. Why don't we get his opinion, too?' He told them about Vinnie's suggestion.

'Why not?' Roy said. 'Can we leave it to you and Rosa though? We're a bit bogged down with promotional stuff at the moment.'

'That's the idea,' Vinnie said. 'Rosa said we need a monthly news-sheet, official autographed photos and membership badges. We'll get onto it this week.'

As Jane chatted to Sammy she heard her name being called. She looked round. 'Won't be a minute,' she said, hauling herself off the chair. 'Rosa wants me.'

On her return she flopped back down next to Eddie, letting out a lengthy sigh.

'What's wrong?' he asked, lighting a cigarette. 'You look like you've seen a ghost.'

She bit her lip to stop it trembling and took a deep breath. 'Rosa said she saw Mark's girlfriend yesterday,' she began, watching Eddie's face tighten. 'Vicky told her he's flipped his lid. He's been sectioned.'

'Fucking hell!' Eddie drew on his cigarette. 'I knew there was a screw loose.'

'Ed, don't. He's had a bad time of it lately. He found out Maude's not his real mum. He got a girl pregnant. *She* had an abortion. That's probably why he was so weird with me on Christmas Eve. But what's really scary is he thinks Vicky's me and we're married. I hope they don't let him out.' Jane swallowed before continuing. 'I need to tell you something, Ed, but please, don't go mad.'

'What?' He stubbed out his cigarette and stared at her.

'He was at the first gig when you started drumming again. He said me and him were far from finished. I didn't tell you because I didn't want to spoil the night. Then Angie died the following day and I pushed it to the back of my mind.'

'For fuck's sake, Jane! You should have told me. I'd have laid him out good and proper.'

'That's precisely why I *didn't* tell you,' she said. 'Anyway, he's locked away now, so it's all over. You told him at Christmas to stay away and he has done. All that other stuff is just in his head. Perhaps I should talk to Vicky and Tony.'

'I don't want you anywhere near them. Come on, I'm taking you home, you look worn out.'

'I don't want to go yet. Roy and Sammy have only just arrived and we might disturb Sean and Tina. Give them a bit longer, at least.'

'An hour and then that's it,' he said.

* * *

The Raiders' second single, released in May, shot up the charts to number one. TV appearances and radio interviews helped promote 'You Give Me That Feeling', which was a favourite with the Radio Caroline disc jockeys.

By the time Jane gave birth to seven-pound four-ounce Jessica on June fifth, the day before Eddie's twenty-second birthday, his marriage was no longer a secret. Local fans were privy to the fact and it hadn't taken much sniffing around by the press to seek out Jane and Jonny.

The *News of the World* had run an inaccurate story, claiming that Raider Eddie had cheated on his late wife with his schoolgirl sweetheart, who was expecting his child.

Jane was furious when she read the report. 'How dare they print lies? I left school three years before we got back together and Angie was already dead before I got pregnant. This story makes you sound like a right bastard, Ed.'

Frank thought it in everyone's best interests for Eddie to give a press interview and put the facts right. Far from losing fans, he gained further popularity.

* * *

When Eddie collected Jane and one-week-old Jessica from hospital, it suddenly dawned on him that their lives had changed forever. There were groups of reporters and photographers outside the hospital, jostling for news and shots.

Eddie put his arm around Jane's waist as they stood posing beside the car. 'Smile,' he said through gritted teeth. 'Then we can get home.'

Hoards of young girls were milling around outside the flat and more were camping out on the landing by the front door. They screamed, pulling at Eddie' clothes and hair as he tried to shield Jane and the baby.

'I don't believe that,' Jane said when they eventually got inside.

'If I'm honest,' Eddie said, 'the novelty of fan adoration's wearing a bit bloody thin. We've got to move from here, we need more space anyway. If we're to get any peace at all to enjoy this baby, we need a secret address.'

'I just want to rest and enjoy the first precious moments alone with you and Jessica,' Jane said wearily. In the bedroom she flopped down on the bed and Eddie laid Jessica beside her.

'She's so beautiful, so perfect,' he said, as the baby's tiny fingers curled around his thumb. He touched her cute button nose and her face wrinkled in an almost smile. Her mop of thick dark hair and heart-shaped face were like Jane's, but she had the bluest eyes with long dark lashes that fanned her cheeks, just like his.

'Put her in the cradle and come and hold me, Ed.'

Eddie picked Jessica up, kissed her forehead tenderly and placed her in the cradle. He lay down beside Jane and took her in his arms. 'That feels better,' he said, wriggling closer. 'Not that I didn't like you pregnant. You were all ripe and, erm, womanly. But I love being able to fit right up to you again.'

'It's wonderful,' she said. 'The baby felt like a mountain between us. Anyway, what you just said about moving. Where would we go? I realise we can't stay here, not just because of the fans, but because we're bursting at the seams.'

'Ah well,' Eddie said. 'When we went to wet Jessie's head and have a drink for my birthday, Roy was having a moan about the flat being too small and all the fans and stuff. Vinnie told us that his dad bought Hanover's Lodge at auction. You remember it, Jane, that derelict old farmhouse near Ashlea Village. Well, it's been totally renovated and Mario's looking for tenants.'

Her face lit up as he continued: 'Vinnie's gonna ask his dad if we can rent it for a while. I'd like to buy a house of our own, but I can't do that until I get some royalties. The LP's being released next month. We should be laughing if it does as well as the singles.'

Jane nodded. 'Will the house have enough room for all of us?'

'Plenty,' he said. 'Vinnie says there are four bedrooms, two bathrooms and loads of rooms downstairs. It's on a private lane, there's a big garden for Jonny to play in and it's surrounded by woodland so it's quite isolated. What do you think about that?'

'It sounds like a dream come true. Can we talk about it tonight with Roy and Sammy?'

'Of course. Roy's definitely interested and I'm sure Sam won't need much persuading. Right, I'll call my folks, ask them to bring Jonny home later. I don't fancy venturing out again just yet and I'm not leaving you two alone.'

The phone rang out in the lounge. Jane went to answer it.

'We won't come over today, Jane,' her mother began. 'We'll let you get settled in first.'

'Don't come at all, Mum, it's chaotic,' she said. 'There's fans outside the flats and all over the stairs. We'll come and see *you* later in the week when things quieten down a bit. I'd better go now, I can hear Jessica crying.' She hurried back into the bedroom. 'Pick her up, Ed, while I mix a feed.'

Jane's eyes filled with tears when she took the bottle into the bedroom. Eddie was on the bed, cuddling his daughter, singing 'My Special Girl'. This precious child meant so much to them, making up for some of the heartache of the last three years. She hoped Jonny would like the new arrival and not feel pushed out.

When Eddie's parents brought Jonny home, Jane's fears seemed unfounded as he gazed at his new sister with adoring eyes. He carefully stroked her hair and kissed her forehead, announcing, 'I like that baby.'

'Perhaps as well, son,' Eddie said, hugging him. 'Because

she's here to stay so you've got to be a good big brother and *always* look after her.'

Jonny nodded solemnly. 'Sweeties now, Nana.'

'There are girls twenty-deep on those stairs,' Lillian grumbled, handing Jonny his bag of jelly babies. 'What on earth do they want?'

'Me, of course,' Eddie teased from the kitchen as he poured her a cup of tea.

'Well, I hope you're not encouraging them,' she said. 'You've quite enough responsibilities on *your* plate, my lad!'

Jane laughed at his mum's disapproval. 'It's all part and parcel of being a pop star. Now relax and enjoy your tea before you brave the stairs again.'

'We're going to move somewhere more private for the sake of our sanity,' Eddie said. 'Mario's bought and renovated Hanover's Lodge, so we're hoping to rent it for a while.'

'It's a big house, that,' his dad said, scratching his chin thoughtfully. 'Can you afford it, Ed?'

'I think so, Dad. Roy and Sammy will pay half towards the rent and bills. We'll manage fine between us.'

'Well, if you come unstuck, you can always ask us for help. I won't see you struggle now you've these two nippers and Jane to look after.'

'Thanks, Dad. I really appreciate that.'

* * *

When Sammy and Roy arrived home, Roy's black satin shirt was ripped from his back, shreds dangling.

'This is fucking ridiculous! We've gotta get out of this mad house. Get on the blower to Vinnie, Ed. See if he's asked Mario about us moving into Hanover's Lodge.'

'Why on earth those mad girls all want souvenir bits of

Roy's tatty old shirt, God only knows,' Sammy said. 'It's seen better days!'

Vinnie told Eddie that his father would be proud for them to live at Hanover's Lodge. They agreed on ten pounds a week rent, and, as a favour to Mario, Eddie promised The Raiders would perform at the club on Christmas Eve for old time's sake.

'I'm game for that,' Roy said. 'We owe Mario big time for believing in us.'

22

JULY 1965

'Oh wow, it's wonderful,' Jane said, gazing at Hanover's Lodge for the first time. Confined to barracks while she got over the birth of Jessica, she'd been itching to see her new home, and as she and Eddie bumped down the private lane in their laden car, she felt the mellow stone farmhouse, with its lofty chimneys and Gothic-style windows, reaching out to welcome them.

'You like it, then?' Eddie said, helping her from the car. He took Jessica from her and she snuggled into him, sucking hungrily on her fingers. He unlocked the front door and carried her through to the kitchen, Jane following.

Jane spun around, gasping. 'Like it? Ed, it's fabulous. This kitchen's bigger than the whole of the Wilmslow flat put together. And I love the dining table,' she added, running her hands over the waxed pine surface.

She plonked herself down on one of the chairs and he handed the baby over.

'Sammy chose the table and chairs to match the kitchen units,' he said. 'Actually, she's chosen everything. Roy and me just dipped our hands in our pockets when she asked.'

Jane nodded. Decisions like those were always best left to

Sammy. She had the knack of knowing just what looked right. 'There's more cupboards in here than you can shake a stick at and I love the beams.'

'It'll be cosy in the winter with that Aga thing blasting away,' Eddie said. 'Right, I'll leave you to sort out madam. Roy and Sammy are here, I can hear the van pulling up. I'll go and help Roy unload.'

Sammy carried a box in and joined Jane in the kitchen. 'First things first,' she said, rooting in the box. 'I'm sure I thought to put in a jar of coffee. Ah, here we are.' She filled the kettle and placed it on the Aga hob as Eddie struggled into the kitchen, arms laden.

'I'll put Jess down when Eddie brings her pram in, then I'll help you get sorted, Sammy,' Jane said, sitting her daughter forward to wind her. Jessica obliged with a loud burp. She closed her eyes with a contented sigh as Eddie pushed the pram indoors.

'That's her settled for a few hours.' Jane tucked the baby under the knitted blanket. 'I'm going for a wander round, see what you've all been up to behind my back.'

'I'll come with you while we wait for the kettle to boil,' Sammy said. 'We need to measure the lounge windows. I haven't had time and I've seen some lovely curtain fabric in Habitat.'

Sammy sized the windows while Jane jotted down the measurements. Overwhelmed with the spacious house after the overcrowded flat, Jane couldn't wait to make the place a home.

The beams and floors had been stripped and polished throughout and in the airy lounge, two red leather Chesterfields were positioned either side of an inglenook fireplace. Rolling out a large cream rug, Sammy arranged it between the sofas and tossed several cream and red cushions at Jane.

'Sam, this looks fabulous,' Jane said, tweaking the cushions into place. 'I love the sofas.'

'Thought you would,' Sammy said, grinning at Jane's delight. She unpacked new chrome lamps and placed them on the side tables. 'The fabric I've seen has a cream background with huge jazzy flowers in purple and red; should look great in here. The windows are so big, they'll take a bold pattern. Put the plants in place, Jane, then we'll go and have that coffee.'

Jane gathered up several lush plants in fancy pots that were standing in the corner and placed them at strategic points. Sammy had already hung colourful framed prints on the ivory painted walls. Jane put the last plant in place and stepped back to admire the room. Sammy called out to Eddie and Roy to come and view the finishing touches.

'Wow, this looks superb!' Eddie's jaw dropped as they strolled into the lounge.

'Very trendy,' Roy said. 'Are we allowed to walk on that rug, or what?'

'Probably *what*.' Eddie laughed bawdily. 'Sammy called it shag pile.'

'Oh well, in that case, it's definitely *what*!' Roy said. 'We'll try it out later, Sam.'

'For God's sake, Roy, do you *ever* think about anything else?' she said, rolling her eyes.

'Eddie started it,' Roy said, grinning like a schoolboy. 'It's fabulous, girls. You've done us proud. It's the sort of place that really befits a couple of rising young pop stars.'

Jane laughed at his modesty and looked around with pride. 'We've Sammy to thank for her good taste, you two for paying, and Habitat for the rest.'

'I'm picturing how fantastic we can make this house look for Christmas,' Sammy said, eyes dreamy, already planning months ahead. 'I noticed loads of holly bushes on the lane as we drove up. I'll decorate the wooden banisters with holly and red ribbon garlands and we can have a tree in the hall as well as the lounge.'

'Are we tossing a coin for who has the en suite bedroom?' Roy asked, taking a half-crown from his pocket. 'Otherwise we'll be dithering all day. I want to get the beds upstairs before we go back for our other stuff. And we need to load up the old sofas and take them to the tip. Then we'll pick Jonny up from your folks' place, Ed.'

'Heads,' Jane called as the coin landed tail side up.

'Not to worry,' Eddie said, slinging his arm around her shoulders as she pulled a disappointed face. 'The front bedroom will be better for us. It's next to the bathroom and it's opposite the room I chose for the kids' nursery.'

* * *

'Wow, look at this.' Eddie stared at a cheque that had arrived in the morning post. 'Ten grand!'

'What's that for?' Jane grabbed the cheque and looked at it, wide-eyed.

'It's our share of the bank job we did last week,' he teased as she smacked his hand. 'It's songwriting royalties for me and Roy. Fantastic! Told you we'd be rich one day, Jane. This is only the start.'

He waved the cheque in Roy's direction as he and Sammy strolled into the kitchen. 'It's arrived,' he announced gleefully.

'Brilliant,' Roy exclaimed. 'You can set up your own design business now, Sam.'

'Oh, fantastic! Can I pinch a corner of your music room for my studio?'

'Course you can,' Eddie said. 'It'll be nice for Jane to have you working from home while we're away touring.' He stared again at the cheque and smiled. No more struggling to get by. Now he could give Jane and his kids everything they deserved.

* * *

Busy writing new songs, Eddie and Roy were thrilled by the release of the group's first LP. Simply called *The Raiders*, it went straight to number one on the album charts.

'I can't believe it!' Roy held up a copy of *Melody Maker*. 'Listen to this review:

> *The Raiders' long-awaited debut album has stormed the charts in a manner only previously achieved by The Beatles and Rolling Stones. With a mix of rock 'n' roll favourites and self-penned ballads, including the hit single, 'My Special Girl', this masterpiece proves the group is a serious contender for the title of Princes of Pop.'*

'Hmmm, not too sure about Pop Princes, I'd rather be King!'

'Not a chance, Roy,' Sammy said. 'Elvis is King. Always has been, always will be, so there.' Then seeing his frown, she added, 'But you're not doing *too* badly for a lad from Stockport.'

* * *

'We'll be away on tour for ten days before we get a day off,' Eddie told Jane as they curled up together on the sofa. It was a cool evening for August, he'd lit a log fire in the lounge and the room was bathed in a cosy glow from the lamps. 'We've got to promote the album.'

'I know.' She looked at him, pushing his floppy fringe from his eyes. 'I hate you being away, Ed, and Jonny misses you, too.'

'It's my job, love. We wouldn't be living in this nice place if I was still managing the store.' He kissed her and lowered her down onto the rug. 'Anyway, you'll have Sam for company. You should think about coming on the European tour. I'm sure my folks will look after Jonny and we could take Jess with us.'

'I don't need to think,' she said, stroking his cheek. 'I'm coming with you.'

'Great,' he murmured, unbuttoning the front of her top. 'It's so nice to have the place to ourselves.'

He kissed her again as a loud wail reached their ears. 'I don't believe it!' He sighed, rolling onto his back. 'Right on bloody cue.'

Jane sat up, smiling. 'It's time for her ten o'clock feed. *She* doesn't know Daddy's feeling randy.'

He jumped up, laughing. 'I'll bring her down while you warm her bottle. So much for romance!'

* * *

Jane handed Sammy a mug of coffee and took an admiring glance at the pastel sketch of a jacket she was working on.

'I'm so glad you're here, Sam. I hate it when the lads are away. We never see a soul because nobody passes by.'

'It's what we need though, a bit of privacy after that mad flat,' Sammy said, looking through the music room window at the rolling Cheshire countryside behind the house. 'It's a beautiful day. I'll take a break in a few minutes. Fancy a walk down the lane with the kids?'

'Okay.' Jane nodded. 'I'll sit in the garden and wait for you while Jonny runs some energy off.'

Jane took her coffee and *Honey* magazine outside and sat in a deckchair on the patio. Jessica was asleep in her pram under the old apple tree in the middle of the lawn and Jonny was zooming up and down on his pedal car, making engine and beep-beep noises.

She took a sip of coffee, glancing around and thinking what a lucky girl she was to have such a lovely home and a safe garden for the children to play in. She thought briefly of Angie for some reason and although there'd been no love lost between them, she felt sad for a moment, thinking of what she'd missed.

Seeing her little son growing up; the joys of holding her new baby and the loving she would have shared with Richard. She wiped a sudden tear from her eye. Why on earth had she thought of Angie at all, she wondered and then remembered. It was almost the first anniversary of her death. She must remind Eddie to take flowers to the grave with Jonny.

Sammy strolled outside and sat down on the steps leading to the lawn. 'This is the life,' she said. 'Being my own boss and knocking off whenever I feel like it. You need to learn to drive, Jane. Ed's Beetle's stuck out here for days on end. I'll give you a few lessons up and down the lane if you like, to get the feel of the car. Then you can book in with a driving school.'

'I fancy that,' Jane said. '*You* learnt easily enough, so it can't be that difficult.'

'I was okay once I got a proper instructor. Roy was hopeless. He kept grabbing the wheel and frightening me to death. I'm surprised we didn't end up in a ditch. So whatever you do, don't let Ed teach you.'

'I'll get a provisional licence then and I'll get cracking,' Jane said. 'I'll book the lessons after Jess's christening.'

The promotional concerts behind them, the boys were struggling to finish a batch of songs they couldn't agree on. Frank was hoping time at home would give Eddie and Roy some inspiration.

'The invites have gone out for Jess's christening,' Eddie told Pat, Sammy and Tim over breakfast. 'Will you lot be godparents? I'll let Roy sleep off his hangover and then I'll ask him, too.'

'According to this leaflet of christening etiquette, it's supposed to be two godmothers and one godfather for a girl,' Sammy said.

'It is, normally,' Jane said. 'But the vicar said there was no reason we couldn't have two of each. We didn't like to leave one of the boys out.'

'Seeing as you and Ed never do anything by the book, that's just about right,' Pat said, jumping to her feet. 'Thanks for the bed and breakfast. C'mon, Tim, you can drive me to work. See you all later.'

'Have you sorted out the catering arrangements, Jane?' Sammy asked, buttering a slice of toast. She yawned loudly as Pat and Tim made their escape. 'Oh, excuse me. I didn't sleep too well last night. Roy was talking in his sleep.'

'I've ordered the cake from the bakery in Wilmslow,' Jane replied. 'Mario's given me the number of a caterer he uses for functions so I'll give them a call.'

'Tell you what, babe,' Eddie said, pulling Jane onto his knee. 'Why don't I take you out tonight? Would you and Roy babysit for us, Sam?'

'Yeah, why not? I can give Jessie a bottle. Jonny's no trouble. It'll do you good to go out and it'll give me some practice, just in case.'

'Just in case what?' Eddie raised an enquiring eyebrow. 'Is there something you're not telling us?'

'Not yet. But Jessie brings out a maternal need in me that I didn't realise I had.'

'Are you serious?' Jane said. 'Have you told Roy how you feel?'

'No, but I'm going to.'

'Talk to him tonight while we're out,' Eddie suggested. 'Make him a nice meal, pour some wine down his throat then drop it on his toes.'

'We'll make sure the kids are settled before we go out,' Jane said. 'Jessie will wolf her milk down when she wakes, but she'll go straight back to sleep.'

'Thanks for the encouragement. I never expected to want

kids for ages. I hope Roy feels the same. He goes all gooey when he holds Jessie, but he might not want one of his own.'

'You can but try,' Eddie said.

Sammy nodded. 'By the way, Jane, I saw Cathy the other day. I forgot to tell you. She's back in Stockport, the London thing didn't work out. Why don't you invite her to the christening? I bet she'd be pleased to see Jonny again. She said she'd been to the Wilmslow flat but the new people don't have our forwarding address.'

'Is she back with her parents?'

'She is.'

'I'll call her later then. It'll be really nice to see her again. Jonny will be thrilled to bits. He loves his Auntie Cathy.'

'Would you like to visit your mum, Jane?' Eddie asked.

'Yeah, that would be nice. Might as well go out while you're home to chauffeur me around.'

* * *

'What a lovely surprise!' Enid exclaimed, letting in her daughter and Eddie. 'Go and sit in the lounge while I pour a drink.'

Jonny dragged out a basket of toys that Grandma kept for him under the stairs. He chose a ball and took it into the garden.

'That's him sorted,' Enid said. 'How are you doing with the christening plans?' She handed them mugs of tea and took Jessica in her arms.

'Okay, thanks, Mum. I need to buy Jess a robe and that's it. Trouble is, when we go shopping, Ed gets recognised and people always want to talk to him about the group.'

'The price of fame, eh?' he said, grinning. 'It won't last forever. We're flavour of the month. Next year, it'll be someone else's turn.'

'You both look very nice. Trendy, do they call it?' Enid said, looking at them with pride. Jane, was, as always, stunningly attired. Her houndstooth-check dress and long white boots were the height of fashion and her glossy hair cascaded down her back like a dark velvet cloak.

Eddie's black leather trousers and white shirt, with a ruffle down the front, made him look every inch the rising young star. No wonder the pair were the centre of attention wherever they went, she thought.

'Thanks, Mum.' Jane smiled. 'This is one of Sammy's creations. It's the first time I've worn it.'

'It's lovely. Bit short, but you can carry it off with your nice figure and long legs. This baby's making me feel very broody.' She tickled her tiny granddaughter under the chin and Jessica chuckled. 'I'll give Molly a call, let her know you're here.' She handed Jessica to Eddie and left the room.

* * *

Eddie leant across to kiss Jane. 'It's so nice to visit my in-laws as a normal family, instead of being treated like an outcast.'

Jane nodded. 'I'm sure it is.'

Enid finished her call and brought in another mug of tea as the doorbell rang. 'That'll be Molly, she must have run here.' She went to open the door and let in her excited and breathless friend.

Eddie smiled as Molly cooed over his daughter. 'Oh, she's such a darling. Let me have a cuddle, sweetheart.'

'Come on then, Molly,' he teased. 'I'm sure Jane can spare me for five minutes!'

'I meant the baby, you silly devil!' Molly laughed, giving him a playful push. 'You're as bad as Roy for leg-pulling. How's Sammy? I haven't heard from her for a few days.'

'Feeling broody,' Eddie quipped, handing Jessica over.

'Eddie! That's top secret,' Jane said. 'She's fine, Molly, and busy working on her new collection.'

'She's always been streets ahead when it comes to fashion,' Molly said, beaming proudly. 'She'll be the next Mary Quant. But why did Eddie say she was feeling broody? Sammy told me she doesn't want kids for years.'

'Everyone feels broody when they see Jessie,' Jane said, glaring at Eddie, who was grinning innocently. 'Go and call Jonny in ready to go,' she ordered.

'I love it when you're angry with me, Mrs Mellor,' he teased. 'It drives me wild!' He dashed out of the room, leaving Jane blushing furiously.

* * *

'What's he like?' Jane rolled her eyes heavenward. 'Sorry, Mum.'

'Don't worry, love; he's a man,' Enid said, laughing. 'They've all got this notion they're God's gift! Oh, while I think on, I saw Mark in Stockport the other day.'

Jane looked up from fastening Jessica's matinee jacket. 'And?'

'He asked how you were. I told him you'd had a little girl and moved house. We talked a bit about The Raiders and how well they're doing.'

'I see.' Jane nodded. 'Don't mention this to Ed.'

'Why not?'

'Because mentioning Mark would be like waving a red rag at a bull.'

'Surely Eddie's not jealous of Mark? Because if he is, he's being very...' Enid stopped mid-flow. 'Don't look so anxious, Jane, I won't say a word. But Mark wished you all the best, and then he was joined by a young woman who'd been in one of the shops.'

'Vicky?'

'That's right. He introduced her as his girlfriend. Funnily

enough, she had a look of you about her, but with blue eyes. She seemed very nice. Mark doesn't look too well. He's lost a lot of weight.'

'He's been ill,' Jane said. 'Mum, you didn't tell him where we're living, did you?'

'Err, you know, I can't remember. I might have done,' Enid said, faltering as Eddie walked into the room with Jonny riding on his shoulders.

'Ready when you are,' he said.

'We'll see you soon, Mum.' Jane smiled reassuringly. 'I'll call you later, okay?'

'Okay, love. Drive carefully, Ed.'

The aromatic scent of garlic and red wine mingled with the homely smell of wood-smoke as Eddie and Jane walked into the kitchen.

'Smells good,' Jane said and glanced at the cookery book propped up on the table. It was open at the recipe for beef bourguignon, Roy's favourite.

Sammy looked up and pushed her hair off her flushed face.

'I'm knackered. This housewife malarkey's not as simple as designing clothes. Do you want to eat with us? I've made plenty.'

'No thanks, we'll eat out and leave you two in peace,' Jane replied. 'Ed's blabbed to your mum that you're feeling broody.'

'Big gob!' Sammy said. 'I've got to convince Roy first.'

'The way to a man's heart is through his stomach,' Eddie said. 'If *this* man's opinion counts for anything, I reckon you're halfway there.' He helped himself to an apple from the dish on the table. 'Wasn't it Eve seduced Adam with an apple?'

'So they say,' Sammy replied. 'And look at the bloody legacy she left us with! If you ask me, Eve's got a lot to answer for.

Right, I'm going to jump in the bath and make myself irresistible. *I* won't need Cox's Pippins tonight.'

Jane turned to Eddie as Sammy left the room. 'Don't you dare say anything to Roy when he comes in, or I'll not be responsible for my actions.'

'Come here, woman. You drive me crazy when you shout at me.' He pulled her onto his knee and kissed her. 'Come to bed,' he whispered, running his hand up her legs.

'What about the kids?'

'Jessie's still asleep and Jonny's playing in the lounge. Come on, Jane, I need you.'

'We can't leave Jonny unattended down here. The oven's on, he might burn himself. You'll have to wait till later. You've been horny all afternoon. Take a cold shower when Sammy's finished running her bath.'

'You're a hard woman,' he said, tickling her ribs.

'And *you're* a bloody sex maniac.' She squirmed away from him as Roy strolled into the kitchen.

'*Who's* a sex maniac?'

'*He* is,' Jane said, jumping up from Eddie's knee.

'He always was!'

'Ah, pot and kettle,' Eddie quipped. 'Where've you been?'

'To see a man about a dog,' Roy replied, picking up the kettle. 'Anyone for coffee?'

'No, thanks,' Jane said. 'Where's Tim, I thought he went out with you?'

'He did. He's gone to collect Pat from work. They're going for something to eat and then to The Roulette Club. Me and Sam are meeting up with them. Why don't you get a sitter and come with us?'

'Actually, mate, *you're* going nowhere,' Eddie said. 'You're babysitting for us. Sammy cooked you something special. She's pampering herself in the bath at the moment. She wants you to stay home and have a nice evening.'

'Right!' Roy gave a lewd chuckle. 'Sounds like I'm on to a promise! You two can make our apologies to Tim and Pat then.'

'Did you get anything for *me* today?' Eddie asked.

'Certainly did.' Roy patted his jacket pocket. 'Found a new dealer, very reasonable.'

'So, what's happened to Mac?' Eddie asked. 'Why has he disappeared off the surface of the earth?'

'Banged up in Strangeways,' Roy replied. 'Two years for dealing and possession.'

'Fucking hell!' Eddie exclaimed.

'I like Mac, but he's always been trouble,' Jane said. 'Make sure no one sees *you* buying gear, Roy. We don't want the police or press here.'

Roy laughed, swaying slightly, his eyes glazed. He ruffled Jane's hair. 'Don't worry. Come upstairs to the music room, Ed. I'll show you what I bought and work out what you owe me.'

Jane stared after them, shaking her head. Roy was getting more into drugs and it worried her. He'd driven the group's van home from Manchester after drinking God knows how much and had no doubt smoked at least one joint. And for all Eddie insisted cannabis was harmless, she wasn't totally convinced.

Eddie had told her Roy was taking speed before a show followed by pills to slow him down. One day he would have an accident and kill himself, or someone else, then the bubble would burst. She sighed, mixing a feed for Jessica while going over the conversation she'd had earlier with her mother about Mark – there was always something to worry about.

Before feeding the baby, she quickly phoned Cathy and invited her to the christening. Cathy was pleased to hear from Jane and congratulated her on Jessica's birth and said how thrilled she was about the group's chart successes.

'People in London wouldn't believe I know The Raiders personally,' she said. 'Even when I told them I was Eddie's son's godmother.'

Jane smiled into the receiver. 'Come over and eat with us tomorrow night, then you can see Jonny and Jessie.'

'Jane, I'd love to.'

'Ignore the fans at the gate. I'll send Eddie down at seven thirty to open up. If you get out of the car to do it yourself, you might get jostled. He can sign an autograph or two while he's waiting.'

'Sounds exciting.'

'It's not really, it's a bit of a pain. Still, it won't go on forever. See you tomorrow, then. By the way, we live at Hanover's Lodge. It's a short drive up from Norman's Woods and it's sign-posted. You can't miss it.'

'I know the place. See you tomorrow then. Bye.'

* * *

'Evening, you two.' Jane tapped Pat on the shoulder.

'Hi.' Pat moved her chair to make room. 'Where's Roy and Sammy?'

'Having a night in, babysitting for us. They send their apologies,' Jane said.

'Is Sammy okay?' Pat asked as Jane sat down beside her. 'When I phoned her this afternoon, she seemed a bit preoccupied.'

'She is. Come to the cloakroom and I'll tell you,' Jane whispered. 'Get the drinks in, Ed. Won't be a minute.'

'Don't you hate the way they stare at you?' Pat said, as they made their way through a crowd of gyrating girls.

'I'm getting sick of it,' Jane agreed. 'There were loads of girls chasing after our taxi tonight.'

'How's Jessie?' Pat took her lipstick from her handbag, pouting to touch up.

'Lovely. She's growing so fast, I just hope she behaves herself tonight.'

'So, tell me what's going on with Sammy?'

'She wants a baby. She's asking Roy how *he* feels about the idea.'

Pat's jaw dropped. 'Sammy wants a baby? But she doesn't even like kids that much, does she?'

'Since I had Jessie she's gone all broody.'

'What about her business? She's only just getting off the ground with it. Has she really thought this through, or is it a whim?'

'She's given it a fair bit of thought,' Jane said. 'She's been really quiet lately. I assumed she was tired, what with working on her collection and us moving house.'

'I'm gobsmacked! But if it's what she wants, let's hope Roy does, too. Actually, I'm quite concerned about Roy.'

'Why?' Jane pulled a brush through her hair.

'Tim said he bought loads of dope and pills today. Being hooked on drugs isn't an ideal start to raising a family.'

'I didn't see what he bought and some of it was for Eddie,' Jane said. 'But I have to admit, having drugs in the house bothers me. The boys are so well known now, I can imagine the police hammering on the door and raiding the place. Then we'll *all* be in the shit, like Mac.'

Pat nodded. 'Heaven forbid!'

'Oh well, you make your bed, as my mother's so fond of saying,' Jane said. 'By the way, talking of Mum, she saw Mark and Vicky in Stockport the other day. Mum said he was asking questions. What bothers me though, she can't remember if she told him our new address.'

'What did Eddie say?'

'He didn't. He was outside with Jonny. I asked her not to tell him.'

'Why, for God's sake?'

'Oh, you know, just to keep the peace. We'd better go back to Tim and Eddie or they'll think we've left them. Come over tomorrow night for dinner. Cathy's coming, she's home from London.'

'Thanks, we will. Can we stay over? I'm off work for a few days and I want to spend them with Tim.'

'Course you can,' Jane said as they walked back into the club.

Tim and Eddie had disappeared from the table. Nudging Pat, Jane pointed. 'They're on the dance floor.'

The pair were surrounded by a crowd of mini-skirted girls, dancing for all they were worth.

'Show-offs! Shall we leave them to it or join them?'

'Join them, of course.' Pat arched an amused eyebrow. 'Why should *they* have all the fun?'

Eddie spotted Jane. He reached out and pulled her close.

'I was accosted by these women the minute your back was turned,' he said. 'Sorry, ladies, I'm spoken for. Meet the wife!'

'I can't leave you on your own for five minutes,' she said.

'It was Tim's fault, he wanted to dance.'

'Oh yeah?' She looked across at Tim, who was holding Pat, his cheek resting on top of her head, as they swayed in time to the music. 'Pull the other one.'

'Got you a drink, it's on the table. I could do with a ciggie.' He waved to his admirers, leading Jane off the dance floor.

She sat down and picked up her glass. 'Me and Pat have just been talking about Roy and Sammy,' she began.

'The baby thing, you mean?' Eddie lit a cigarette and took a long drag.

'And the drugs. Roy has a problem.'

He narrowed his eyes. 'What makes you say that?'

'He's always stoned. He even smokes dope for breakfast. It can't be doing him any good. It worries me with the kids around. I feel light-headed when he's been smoking near me, so God knows what it's doing to Jessie. Will you ask him to smoke outside or up in the music room, please?'

Eddie looked away and was silent for a moment before nodding. 'Of course. I never gave it a thought about the baby. I'll talk to him tomorrow, I promise.'

'Thanks, Ed. I don't want to be a misery and I'd hate for you and Roy to fall out, but at the end of the day we all have to live together.'

'You were right to bring it up. Roy's problem is boredom. Everything he's ever wanted for the group's happened almost overnight. He's okay when we're touring or recording, it's sitting at home all day that's doing his head in. Unless he's drunk or stoned, he says he can't find the inspiration to write songs. Maybe having a kid would give him a focus.' He drew on his cigarette again. 'I'll finish this and then we'll go.'

Mark stifled a yawn and sat up, alert now that the headlights were coming towards him. He nodded as the taxi swung round and entered the private lane. In the dim light he could just make out that the two people seated in the back were definitely Mellor and Jane.

He waited until the taxi returned and shot off down Ashlea Road. He inched his Sprite forward, dimming the headlights. He read the sign that clearly stated *Private Road to Hanover's Lodge Only. No Vehicular Access.* He'd found her, thanks partly to her mother. Rosa calling Vicky tonight had been a stroke of luck, too, and him overhearing the conversation that Jane and Eddie were at the club.

As soon as Vicky had gone to bed, he'd left the house. He'd parked close to the club and waited for the couple to leave. He watched Eddie hail a taxi and had overtaken the vehicle. Earlier in the week, Jane's mother told him they'd moved from the Wilmslow flat to a new home, but she'd only given away that it was a refurbished farm house in Ashlea Village.

Taking a lucky guess it was Hanover's Lodge, his hunch had paid off. Now he could check on Jane and the baby every day until they returned to him. The house was bordered by fields and woodland he'd often played in as a boy. He knew the layout like the back of his hand and there were plenty of bushes and trees to disguise his presence.

* * *

Eddie unlocked the front door and Jane followed him in. The house was in darkness, except for the kitchen light. A note, propped against the teapot, declared, *Jessie fed and changed, Jonny asleep. Gone to bed to make babies! Love, Roy and Sammy.*

Jane grinned. 'The beef bourguignon obviously did the trick.'

'Obviously!' Eddie laughed. 'You know what they say, if you can't beat 'em...'

'Minus the baby bit, I think,' Jane said.

'Oh, most definitely, Mrs Mellor!'

23

Jane dithered between two christening robes laid out on the counter of Jumping Jack's store. The young assistant asked Eddie for his autograph and fussed over Jessica, who wailed miserably in his arms.

'Which one, Ed?' Jane fingered the delicate satin and lace. 'Long or short?'

'You choose,' he said, shifting Jessica onto his shoulder.

'I'll have the long one then and I'll take one of those, please.' She pointed to a delicate white cobweb of a shawl that was draped over a stand.

'Is that it?' Eddie asked as the assistant wrapped the purchases in tissue paper and placed them in a box. 'Do we need anything for Jonny?'

'Not today,' Jane replied. 'I got his outfit from Lewis's last time we were in Manchester.'

'Right then, what's the damage?'

The assistant gave him a handwritten bill. He gave Jessica to Jane and pulled a roll of notes from his pocket, peeling off two fivers.

The girl popped the box in a carrier bag and gave him his

change. He signed a page in her diary and she thanked him, grinning with delight.

'I think Jess is hungry,' he said. 'We'll call on Sean and Carl next and you can feed her in the shop.'

* * *

Carl was working alone and was pleased to see them.

'Where's Sean?' Jane asked, taking a pew behind the counter. She took a bottle of baby milk from her bag and Jessica from Eddie.

'He's taken Tina to Blackpool,' Carl said.

'Come over tonight, Carl,' Eddie invited. 'We're having a bit of a dinner party and you'd be more than welcome.'

'Brilliant, I'd love to. I'm dying to see your new place.'

'Roy bought a Vox Continental last week. We'll have a jam session and you can play with us,' Eddie continued. 'Come about seven thirty. We'll eat early then make some music. I'll nip and get some fags, Jane, while you finish feeding Jess.'

'Okay,' she called as he shot off up the stairs.

Jane looked at Carl's gentle, smiling face as he watched Jessica polishing off her milk. He'd make a great dad someday, she thought. Pity it hadn't worked out with him and Tina. She knew he was lonely and wished she could fix him up with a new girl, but there wasn't a single unattached female amongst their friends at the present time.

'You okay, Carl?'

He nodded. 'Yeah, I s'pose so. I get a bit fed up spending every night stuck in with Mum. I got used to hanging around with Tina and her mates and I miss all that, so it'll be nice to come to your place.'

Eddie reappeared and tossed a Mars bar in Carl's direction.

'Keep you going till lunchtime. If Jess has finished, we'd better make tracks, Jane. Go and prise Roy out of his bed.' He smiled as Jane sat Jessica forwards to wind her. The contented baby obliged with a loud belch. 'Just like Daddy, eh, Jess? Come on, sunshine. Let's get you home.'

'We'll see you later, Carl,' Jane said and handed Jessica to Eddie.

'Thanks for the chocolate and I'll look forward to tonight,' Carl replied.

* * *

Sammy and Roy were sitting at the kitchen table, eating toast and gazing into one another's eyes.

Eddie sang the opening lyrics to 'Hello Young Lovers' as he moved through from the hall. He placed a sleepy Jessica in her pram as Roy grinned at him.

'You have to stop listening to *The King and I*, Ed,' Roy quipped. 'Feel like an old lover this morning, Sammy's worn me out!'

'So, what's new about that?' Jane said, pouring coffee for her and Eddie.

'Ah, but she's a woman with a mission now. Aren't you, my love?' Roy looked at Sammy, who was beaming.

'I hope you've got the energy to write some songs,' Eddie said. 'Frank's baying for blood. We need to finish the next batch by the end of the week.'

'Yeah, I'm fine. I may be tired, but I feel loved and inspired. There's a melody buzzing round my head. Let's go and make a start.'

'Ed, take Jess upstairs with you and put her in the cot,' Jane said. 'And don't forget, you've got to pick Jonny up from your mum's no later than four.'

'I'll take Jess,' Roy offered. Sammy raised her eyebrows behind his back and smiled as he bent to lift the baby from her pram and followed Eddie.

'So, come on, tell me all,' Jane said. 'I presume from the note it was yes.'

Sammy nodded, eyes shining. 'Yep, no objections whatso-ever. He said he'd always wanted kids but thought I didn't because of my career. He wants to get married. He said if we're starting a family then we'll marry straight after the European tour. I'm so happy, Jane, I could burst.'

Jane leapt up and flung her arms around Sammy. 'I can't believe it. I just can't imagine you and Roy married *and* parents as well. I'm so thrilled for you.'

'I'm sure it's the right thing to do. Roy needs a focus other than the group. I've been so worried about him recently, he's not sleeping *or* eating properly and he's always stoned. He's promised to cut down, so fingers crossed. It's a start and all I can do is support him.'

Jane nodded. 'We all will, Sam.'

'You can help me to organise the wedding, Jane, seeing as you know what to do. I want a no-fuss, quick five minutes at the Registry Office, type of do. I'm gonna phone Mum in a minute. She'll have such a surprise.'

'She'll be thrilled to bits for you,' Jane said. 'We'll cook a special meal tonight to celebrate. Pat, Tim and Cathy are coming over and Eddie just invited Carl.'

'Great, we'll make a party of it then. I'll take a quick shower, throw on some clothes, and we'll nip out and buy some nice food and drinks. The boys can look after Jess for a while – Roy can put in some practice.'

* * *

Eddie cracked open a bottle of champagne as Roy announced to the happy gang around the dining table that he and Sammy were planning to marry as soon as the European tour finished.

'A toast to the future Mr and Mrs Cantello,' Eddie said. 'Raise your glasses, please.'

Everyone took up the toast and Eddie winked at Jane. He'd told her earlier that he'd spoken to Roy about smoking dope in front of the kids. Roy said it was his intention to cut down anyway, because Sammy was worried about him. They'd finished their songwriting session on a happy note, with two of the new songs completed.

'Would you girls mind if we go upstairs, so Carl can have a go on the new Vox organ?' Eddie asked as they finished their meal.

'No, go on. We'll wash up and bring you coffee later,' Jane said, gathering up the dishes. 'Make sure the kids' bedroom door is closed before you start.'

* * *

'Come and sit in the lounge, Cathy,' Jane invited as melodies old and new drifted downstairs.

'It's a good job the children are sound sleepers,' Cathy said, following Jane down the hall.

'They're not really, especially Jonny. But he's getting better. What do you think of him? Hasn't he grown tall?'

'He certainly has. He's lovely, such a polite little boy. Jessie's gorgeous too. You're very lucky, Jane. You've got this beautiful home, a nice lifestyle, and I have to say this to you, I've never seen Ed looking as happy as he does now. He's like a different man.'

'Thank you,' Jane said, knowing how difficult that compliment must have been for Cathy.

Sammy brought a tray of coffee through to the lounge and Pat took a laden tray up to the music room. She came downstairs, chuckling.

'You've got an admirer, Cath,' she said.

Cathy choked on her coffee. 'An admirer! Who?'

'Young Carl. He's asking Ed all about you. You know what that lot are like for teasing. The poor lad's beetroot red.'

'They're an insensitive bunch.' Jane tutted.

'Where do you know Carl from?' Cathy asked.

'Me and Ed used to work with him at Flanagan and Grey's,' Jane replied. 'He's lovely. You wouldn't go far wrong with Carl, he's a really decent lad.'

'I've never had a boyfriend,' Cathy confessed.

'What, never in your life?' Sammy exclaimed. 'Bloody hell, Cath, you've never had sex? You don't know what you're missing, girl!'

'I've always been shy,' Cathy said, blushing at Sammy's directness. 'Angie was the one who pulled the lads. She was very pretty and I was always the plain one. Still am, in fact,' she finished, eyes downcast.

'No, you're not,' Sammy said. 'You've got lovely hair and eyes and you've lost a lot of weight lately.'

'I've no confidence. That's why I wouldn't stay in London. My cousin wanted me to go to wild parties and clubs and I couldn't stand it. In the end we fell out and I came home. I'm hopeless with make-up and can't do my hair nicely. I never know what to wear, or which clothes suit me.' Cathy's lips trembled and Jane could see she was on the verge of tears.

But Sammy's observations were right, she thought. Cathy's hair was a warm caramel shade, although her unflattering topknot was an old-fashioned style. She had big blue eyes, clear skin and was tall and slender. Her outfit of a knee-length, black skirt and baggy grey sweater did nothing for her figure at all, and her shapely legs were crying out for a mini.

Jumping up, Sammy said, 'Come with me. I'll sort you out, come on,' she cajoled, pulling Cathy to her feet.

Cathy looked hesitantly at Jane, who nodded her head. 'Go on, Cathy.'

'What do you think of that?' Pat said as the pair left the room. 'Carl would be ideal for her. Launch her gently into the world of men.'

'Yeah!' Jane agreed. 'They'd be perfect for one another. Carl's a few years younger, but I don't suppose it matters that much.'

'Imagine trying to fix her up with Phil Jackson?' Pat said, laughing. 'It would put her off men for life.'

'Half an hour with Phil and she'd definitely lose her virginity,' Jane said, rolling her eyes.

* * *

'Where are Sammy and Cathy?' Roy said, as the boys strolled into the lounge. He sank onto one of the Chesterfields, plonking his feet on the coffee table.

'Upstairs, they won't be long now,' Pat replied, smacking his feet down.

Eddie sat down next to Jane and slung his arm around her shoulders as Sammy and Cathy walked in. He stared at Cathy, open-mouthed.

'Wow! You look stunning,' he said.

'Bloody hell, for a minute there I thought Sandie Shaw had walked into the room!' Roy exclaimed as Eddie started to whistle 'Long Live Love'.

Dressed in a purple and white, swirly patterned mini dress and white tights, hair and make-up immaculate, Cathy had been transformed.

Tim, Pat and Carl stared in amazement. Carl jumped up. He took Cathy by the hand.

'Come and sit beside me,' he said as she blushed prettily. 'You look fabulous. And Roy's right, you *do* have a look of Sandie Shaw.'

'Thanks for the compliments, all of you,' Cathy said,

accepting a glass of cider from Jane.

* * *

'More drinks, anyone?' Jane asked as the clock struck midnight.

Carl shook his head and sighed. 'I'd better get off home. I'll never get up for work tomorrow. Can you call me a taxi, Ed, please?'

'I'll give you a lift home, Carl,' Cathy offered.

'Are you sure?' he asked as Jane caught his eye and smiled.

Cathy nodded and went off upstairs to change back into her own clothes.

'You're well in there, mate.' Eddie nudged him. 'I bet you were hoping she'd offer you a lift. Tell her to park up at Norman's Woods and get your leg over.'

'Eddie, not everybody's like you,' Jane said, tutting.

'What have I said wrong now?' He turned to her, raising an innocent eyebrow.

She pushed him away, annoyed with him for embarrassing Carl. 'Well, if *you* don't know, *I'm* not going to tell you.'

After waving Carl and Cathy off, Sammy said, 'Now wasn't that nice? I feel like Cupid.'

'I think they make a lovely couple,' Pat said.

'So do I,' Jane agreed, pleased that she'd asked Cathy to join them tonight. 'I bet he'll send her flowers and buy her chocolates. Carl's romantic like that, he used to buy them for Tina.'

'Are you two staying over?' Eddie looked at Tim and Pat.

'Yeah. Pat's got a few days off,' Tim said. 'We thought we'd camp out here for a while. I'll nip out and get our bags from the car.'

'Come on, Jane,' Eddie said. 'We'll sort out the bed settee for these two then hit the sack, seeing as the kids will have us up early.'

The music room window was wide open and Jane shut it, shivering. 'It's chilly in here, why was the window open?'

'Roy's very conscious of what we discussed earlier. We shared a couple of joints and he made us stand by the window. He was horrified when he thought he might be affecting Jess.'

'I'm glad he wasn't upset,' she replied. 'But you shouldn't leave the window open when you're not in the room. One of the fans from down the lane might get in. I'll put extra blankets on for Pat and Tim. No doubt they'll soon warm one another up. I hope something comes of Carl and Cathy, they're perfect for one another. I don't know why we never thought of it before.'

Eddie smiled and pulled her into his arms. 'You little matchmaker!' He helped her make up the bed and then scooped her up and carried her into their bedroom. He dropped her onto the bed and knelt beside her. 'Don't you dare tell me you're too tired now.'

'I'm not,' she said, unzipping him. 'But you'd better be quick before Jess wakes for her next feed.'

24

SEPTEMBER 1965

'Jonny, take your cars into the lounge before Mummy breaks her neck falling over them,' Jane said, fastening a bib around Jessica's neck. It was the weekend of the christening. She was up early, rushing round, trying to feed the baby, see to Jonny, and cursing Eddie for spending too long in the shower, when someone knocked loudly at the front door.

Expecting it to be fans, Jane opened the door a crack and peered out. She was shocked to find a tall man in green overalls, clutching the largest bunch of red roses she'd ever seen.

'Mrs Mellor?'

She nodded, eyes wide. 'For me?'

'Someone loves you a lot.' He handed her the bouquet.

'Thank you.' She waved goodbye. There was an envelope stapled to the wrapping. She took out a card, which read, *Will these do? I love you, Mrs Mellor.*

She bit her lip, eyes filling with tears. Hearing a noise, she turned. Eddie was leaning against the doorframe, looking at her. He was bare-chested, wet hair glistening from the recent shower, blue eyes shining with love.

'Well, will they?' he asked.

Jane nodded, not trusting herself to speak. She wiped her eyes with the back of her hand. 'But why?'

'Come here,' he said. 'I never gave flowers a thought until you said Carl used to send them to Tina. I wondered if that was a hint.' He put his arms around her, holding her close.

'They're beautiful, Ed, thank you.' She smiled through her tears. 'You're so romantic.'

'Well, I do try,' he said. 'Flowers are a nice way of saying I love you.'

'They are,' she sniffed. 'But you don't need to go overboard. We had all those red roses in our honeymoon suite, too. Twice in a year is pretty good going.'

Jessica behaved impeccably at the christening. The local church was packed with family and friends and outside a gathering of fans waited eagerly to catch a glimpse of their idols. Having done her best to keep the christening as secret as possible, Jane was dismayed to see photographers jostling for the best shots.

Everything they did was under public scrutiny. No wonder Sammy said she wanted to keep her wedding day quiet, she thought, hurrying towards the waiting cars.

Back at Hanover's Lodge the caterers were finishing laying out the buffet and their respective fathers were officiating over the drinks, pouring glasses of champagne to toast Jessica's special day.

'Ed's really pushed the boat out for our Jess,' Fred said proudly as he handed out champagne.

'Aye,' Ben agreed. 'Nothing's too much trouble for him where Jessica's concerned.'

Sean and Tina arrived, closely followed by Cathy and Carl, and Jane was thrilled to see the pair holding hands. She'd been a little concerned that there might still be a touch of rivalry between Carl and Sean over Tina, but she needn't have worried. Cathy was positively glowing and Carl was looking extremely pleased with himself.

'Thank you for introducing us, Jane.' Carl kissed her lightly on the cheek.

'It was my pleasure. You were both under one another's noses, almost. You just needed to be in the right place at the right time. You look happy.'

'We are,' Cathy said, smiling at Carl. 'Very.'

Carl went off to get drinks as Sammy joined Jane and Cathy.

'Well?' Sammy raised a knowing eyebrow. 'Any luck with him?'

'Sammy!' Jane said as Cathy smiled.

'It's okay, I don't mind. Yes, actually, and you were right, Sam. I didn't know what I was missing, he makes me feel very special.'

'Really?' Sammy said, grinning in Carl's direction. 'Well, well, well... What was that you once said about the quiet ones, Jane?'

Carl walked back to the group of young women and blushed as Sammy dug him in the ribs and said, 'Keep it up, Casanova!'

Cathy quickly changed the subject. 'I can't believe all these people, Jane. There were only a handful of guests at Jonny's christening.'

'Well, there's the family from both sides. That's my brother Pete and his mate Harry over there. We've a lot of friends, and then there are people who've got something to do with the group. That tall, dark-haired guy over there is Frank James, their agent, and the woman hanging from his arm is Helen, his secretary. The sexy blond guy chatting up my mother is Phil Jackson from the group.'

'Yes, I recognise him and there's John and Stuart from

Flanagan and Grey's. Would you mind if I take some photos, Jane? I want to use up the film. There's some of Jonny on it from ages ago that I'll let you have when I get them developed.'

'Thanks, that would be lovely,' Jane replied. 'Eddie has hardly any early photos of Jonny.'

'Eddie's trying to catch your attention.' Cathy pointed across the room. 'He looks ready to make a speech.'

'I'd better go, make sure he keeps it clean in front of my mother. I'll catch up with you later.'

Eddie called for silence and asked everyone to raise their glasses to toast Jessica, and to Jane for giving him such a lovely daughter. He then called on Roy to make an announcement. Sammy took Roy's hand and together, they announced that they would be getting married straight after the European tour. A cheer went up and congratulations echoed around the room.

* * *

Jane saw the last of the guests out while the caterers cleared away. Her mum had packed Peter and Harry off home in a taxi and stayed behind to help tidy up and her dad had followed Roy and Eddie upstairs.

'Thanks, Mum,' Jane said as Enid put the last clean plate on the pine dresser and hung the apron she'd borrowed on the back of the kitchen door.

'That went off very well, Jane,' Enid said.

'It was great. Jessie and Jonny were as good as gold,' Jane said. 'I noticed you and Phil Jackson getting on like a house on fire while Dad's back was turned.'

'Well, I never really got a chance to talk to him at your wedding. He's *very* nice. Flattered me something shocking. Told me I don't look old enough to be your mother.' Enid patted her curls in place, blue eyes twinkling. 'If I was twenty years younger, *I* could give him a run for his money!'

'Mother!'

'Don't tell your father, but it did my ego good. Phil's the nicest-looking lad I've ever been chatted up by.'

'Phil's a randy romeo, Mum. He used to chat *me* up all the time. He's had more women than the rest of the group put together and than *you've* had hot dinners. Isn't that right, Sammy?'

Sammy nodded. 'It certainly is. You've had a lucky escape there, Enid.'

'Oh well, the flattery was nice while it lasted.'

'Anyone for coffee?' Sammy put the kettle on and reached in the cupboard for mugs.

'Not for me, love,' Enid replied. 'The next party here will be your wedding. Your mum and Tom are over the moon.'

'I know they are.' Sammy smiled. 'We'll get this tour out of the way and then we can plan the day properly.'

'Are *you* going to Europe with Roy then?' Enid asked. 'Your mum told me Pat's going with Tim.'

'I am. I've never been to Europe, I'm really excited,' Sammy replied.

'What about you, Jane, are you going, too?'

'Yes, Mum. We're taking Jessie with us and Jonny's staying with Eddie's mum and dad for a couple of weeks.'

'Would you like to leave Jessie with your dad and me? Then you and Eddie can relax and enjoy yourselves properly.'

'That's a good idea. I'll ask Ed, see what he thinks. Would you be able to cope, Mum?'

'Jane, I brought you and Peter up and you lived to tell the tale! It'll be nice to push a pram again. Molly and Susan are on hand, I'm sure they'd love to help.'

'All right, you've convinced me. But I'll check with Ed first.'

'Right, we'd better be going,' Enid said, gathering up her handbag and jacket. 'The taxi will be here in a minute. Where's your father got to? He always seems to disappear when there are things to do.'

'They all do. This kitchen's a man-free zone.' Sammy laughed. 'They're upstairs in the music room. Can't you hear them?'

'I thought that was a record. Who's singing?'

'Eddie and Roy, of course. It's definitely not Dad,' Jane said.

'Your father likes to think he sounds like Dean Martin!' Enid grinned. 'Will you tell him I'm ready to go, Sammy?'

Enid followed Jane into the lounge, where Jonny was playing with his train set.

'You've got this house lovely, Jane; it's like something from *Ideal Home* magazine.'

'You always said I would never have anything if I got involved with that Mellor lad,' Jane teased. 'Come and say bye to Grandma Enid, Jonny.'

'Well, it just goes to show how wrong I was,' Enid admitted. She held her arms out to Jonny and kissed him. 'I shall never again judge a book by its leather jacket.' She was laughing at her own joke when Ben strolled into the lounge with Sammy.

Jane stared at her dad, who was grinning broadly, his eyes slightly glazed. *Too much to drink*, she thought. He grabbed hold of her mum and waltzed her round the room.

'Wish I were twenty years younger, Enid,' he said, slapping her playfully on the backside. 'I feel like joining the group and having some fun with the lads.'

'You're a daft sod, Ben Wilson,' Enid said, pushing him away.

'You okay, Dad?' Jane asked.

'Me? Couldn't be better, Janey, lass,' he replied. 'I've just shared a roll-up with Roy. Big fat bugger it was. Best baccy I've had in a long time, much nicer than Woodbines.'

He turned to Sammy and smiled. 'One thing puzzles me, Sam. When Roy has all that money coming in, why does he still roll his own fags? Mind you, with baccy like that, I don't blame him. I meant to ask him what brand he buys. I'll treat myself someday, start rolling *my* own.'

Jane caught Sammy's eye behind her parents' backs. Her hand flew to her mouth as the penny dropped. 'Oh – my – God!' she mouthed as Sammy's shoulders began to shake. Jane tried to control the laughter that bubbled up and said goodnight to her mum and dad as the taxi arrived.

'Thanks for a lovely day, Jane.' Enid kissed her on the cheek.

'Aye, thanks, love,' Ben added. 'Could have done with a bit more grub though. All that dainty stuff's not for me. Me belly thinks me throat's been cut. I'm gonna get that taxi to drop us off at the chippy. Come on, Enid, get a move on.'

Jane shook her head as she closed the door. 'No wonder Dad was skittish when he came downstairs,' she giggled. 'He'd have a holy fit if he knew what he'd really been smoking.'

Sammy was doubled up, tears running freely down her face. 'Trust Roy to roll up in front of your dad. I can't believe he'd do that.'

Roy and Eddie strolled into the kitchen, finding the girls helpless with laughter.

'Jane, I'm really sorry about your dad,' Roy began. 'I skinned up out of habit and he said, "Give us a drag, it smells really good." I couldn't refuse, could I? He would have wondered why I wouldn't share with him. Trouble is, once he'd had some, he wouldn't stop.'

'Was he all right, Jane?' Eddie asked.

'He was pretty much stoned and very frisky with Mum. Said he wanted to join the group and have some fun. But there's no real harm done, don't worry.'

'Thank God for that,' Eddie said, grinning. 'He'll end up chasing your mother round the bedroom when he gets her home!'

'Oh, don't,' Jane howled, clutching her sides.

* * *

Jane told Eddie about her mother's suggestion of leaving Jessica with them while they went to Europe.

'I think that's a really good idea,' he agreed. 'Having her with us might be a problem at times. It would be a bit difficult to sterilise bottles and wash nappies in a hotel room. It's fine by me if *you* don't mind. It'll be a second honeymoon, all that time in bed with no interruptions.'

'Now there's a thought,' she said, snuggling closer. 'I'm so tired. It's been quite a day, but a nice one all the same.'

* * *

Vicky buttered toast and cut it into fingers. She popped them on a plate next to a boiled egg. 'There you go, a nice boiled egg and soldiers,' she cooed. She placed the plate in front of Mark and sat down opposite.

He pushed the plate away. 'I'm not a fucking baby! You have it.'

'I'm not really hungry, I'll just have a cup of tea. You need to eat, Mark. You lost a lot of weight in hospital.'

He rolled his eyes, grunted and pulled the plate back to his side of the table. He chipped the top off the egg and dunked a toast soldier into the soft yolk, staring as it spilled over, leaving golden trails down the speckled brown shell. 'Are you going to work today?'

'Later. I'm only working part-time at the moment so I can take care of you, remember?'

He looked momentarily puzzled and then nodded. 'Yeah, of course. But I'm not ill any more, I can look after myself.'

'That's all very well, Mark, but I promised Tony I'd do my share while he's at work.'

'Suit yourself.' Mark dunked another soldier in his egg.

Vicky sighed and poured herself a cup of tea. This was hard work and she truly wished she'd listened to people who'd advised her that looking after Mark was not going to be easy. Especially after learning the truth from Tony about Beth's abortion.

Mark's stay in hospital and the correct medication had stabilised his mental state, but keeping certain facts from him that she felt could tip him back over the edge was proving very difficult. There were Raiders' songs being played constantly on the radio. Numerous TV appearances and this week, photos of Eddie and Jane at their daughter's christening featured in countless newspapers.

'Right, I'm going to have a bath and make the bed. Will you be okay down here on your own?'

'For Christ's sake,' Mark snapped. 'I'm fine when I'm alone and you're at work. It's your constant fucking prattling that gets me down.'

Tears stung the back of her eyes. 'You ungrateful bastard!' She turned her back and stormed out of the room, slamming the door behind her.

* * *

Mark carried on eating his breakfast as though he hadn't a care in the world. He smiled as he thought about his regular afternoon trips, when he'd watched Jane most days, wheeling the pram up and down the private lane, with Mellor's brat riding a tricycle beside her. He was familiar with her afternoon routine and quite often she walked with Cantello's tart. He'd eaves-dropped on their conversations as he knelt behind the dense hawthorn hedges and holly bushes that bordered the lane.

He'd watched curiously as Cantello and Mellor hoisted a cot and pram into The Raiders' old van. He heard Cantello telling the brat that Jessica was going to stay with Grandma Enid and he was going to stay with Nana Lillian while Mummy and Daddy were away with the group.

Mark smiled. Perfect, now he could do his observations in comfort. Jane and Mellor would be away, but he could still see the baby and keep an eye on her. He recalled that Jane's mother spent most of her day in the back rooms of the house and knew she would struggle to get a pram so large through the narrow side gate. It would need to go in and out the front door, which meant the baby would very likely be parked on the front lawn at some point.

He'd have a stroll round to Rosedean Gardens later and see how the land lay. If Jane's mum spotted him, he'd say he was taking a walk and just happened to be passing.

He finished his breakfast and washed the dishes, thinking that he really must phone Charles to confirm his next visit. The hospital had been good in that they'd allowed him contact with his family by telephone. Embarrassed to admit he was receiving psychiatric care, Mark told Charles he was working away and would be in touch as and when he could and Charles hadn't questioned it.

* * *

The Raiders' entourage flew from Manchester to Munich for the start of their European shows. Slightly worried by the thought of flying, Jane had been living on her nerves all week. Leaving the children was a wrench. She'd never left Jessica for longer than a few hours and felt sick as they'd unloaded the cot and pram at her parents' house, convinced she'd never see her little daughter again.

'The weather's good today, Jane. Flying conditions should

be great and it's only a short flight. We'll be there in no time.' She knew Eddie was trying his best to take her mind off things as they'd taken Jonny to Nana's on their way to the airport.

'Yes, but Munich! Of all the airports we have to go to for my first flight, it has to be there.' She shook her head, remembering the tragic Manchester United Team crash in 1958.

As she took charge of Jonny, Eddie's mum showed concern when she saw her pale-faced daughter-in-law. 'Are you okay, Jane? You're white as a sheet, love.'

'She's all right, Mum,' Eddie said, seeing Jane's eyes filling with tears. 'She's feeling nervous about flying and we've never left the kids for so long before.'

'They'll be fine. This is Jonny's second home and I know your mum's really looking forward to having Jessie stay. They're both in safe hands, so go and enjoy yourselves.'

The late-afternoon flight wasn't half as bad as Jane had feared. The take-off was smooth and Eddie held her hand. By the time she'd had a couple of brandies she was relaxed enough to turn round and talk to Sammy and Roy, who were sitting behind.

25

Enid manoeuvred the large Silver Cross pram down the garden path and pushed it onto the lawn beneath the bay window. Jessica was still sleeping so she pulled the cat net up. She looked over her shoulder to see if the ginger tom from next door was lurking under the bushes – the blasted cat was a beggar for jumping on the pram.

Satisfied the tom was nowhere in sight, she knocked lightly on the front door and placed a warning finger to her lips as Molly exclaimed with delight when she answered.

'I thought you weren't coming today, you're a lot later than usual.'

'We've had a bad night. I think she's teething,' Enid said. 'I had a lie-in this morning while she was sleeping. I'll bring her indoors when she wakes. There's a bottle in the pram, so you can feed her if you like.'

'That would be lovely.' Molly led the way through to the kitchen. 'Sit yourself down while I brew the tea. I've made a nice Victoria sandwich, so we'll have a slice of that as well.'

'Have you heard from Sammy today?' Enid asked, removing her coat and sitting at the table.

'She called first thing. Said she wasn't feeling too well.'

'Oh dear! I hope she's not caught that flu bug Eddie's had. Jane said he was really off colour. Anyway, he's a lot better by all accounts and they're in Paris for the next few days.'

'The tour's going well, according to Sammy,' Molly said as she poured two mugs of tea and handed one to Enid. She cut two slices of cake. 'Help yourself, it's not often we have a whole cake to ourselves. Tom usually demolishes them before they've even cooled.'

Enid bit into the feather-light sponge and rolled her eyes. 'Beautiful! Mine never taste this good, you must give me the recipe.'

They sat in companionable silence for a few minutes, enjoying their tea and cake.

Enid licked her fingers and stood up. 'I'll see if Jess is awake.'

'I'll get her. You sit yourself down in the lounge and have a rest while I bring her in,' Molly said, jumping up.

'I'll rinse the mugs and plates for you, then. Put the cat net back up or that tom will be peeing in the pram. The bottle's wrapped in a nappy under the storm cover and there's a bib there, too,' she called over her shoulder as Molly disappeared down the hall.

Enid ran water into the sink and then turned off the tap as she heard Molly calling her name. 'I'm coming.' She wiped her hands on a tea towel and hurried to the front door. 'I'll swing for that bloody cat if it's on the pram.' She stopped short as a white-faced Molly pointed to the empty space where the pram had been parked.

Enid looked around, ran to the gate and stared up and down Primrose Avenue. 'Oh my God! Someone's taken Jessica.' She ran out onto the avenue followed by Molly. 'You go that way and I'll go this,' she gesticulated wildly and ran towards the main road. She stopped a passing woman: 'Have you seen anyone pushing a navy-blue Silver Cross pram?'

The woman nodded slowly. 'Coach built, chrome wheels?'

'Yes,' Enid said. 'That's it.'

'Posh prams them! You must have plenty of money if you can afford one like that.'

'Have you seen it?' Enid cried.

'Why, have you lost one?' The woman screwed up her face as though thinking.

'Someone's taken my granddaughter,' Enid screamed at the infuriating woman. 'HAVE YOU SEEN A PRAM LIKE THAT?'

The woman backed away from Enid, fear registering on her face at being confronted by a mad woman. 'No, love, sorry, I haven't.'

'You time-wasting cretin!' Enid shrieked as she ran on and rounded the corner, Molly hot on her heels.

'Enid, slow down! A woman on the avenue said she saw a young man pushing a navy-blue pram about ten to fifteen minutes ago. He was going in the direction of the town centre.'

'A man? Oh Lord, why on earth would a man take a baby? We'd better go back to your house and phone the police.'

They made their way back to Molly's, where she helped a shaking Enid to the sofa and quickly dialled 999.

'They're sending someone right away,' she told Enid, who was now crying hysterically.

'What if this man hurts her? She's only a tiny baby. Jane and Eddie will never forgive me for this, they'll not allow me to look after her again. We need to phone them, tell them what's happened.'

'Wait until the police arrive. They'll get word to Jane and Eddie quicker than we can,' Molly said, patting her shoulder.

* * *

'Now just take your time, Mrs Wilson,' the officer, who introduced himself as PC Jones, said. 'How long was Jessica outside before you realised she and the pram were missing?'

'Well,' Enid's voice wobbled, 'no more than fifteen minutes. Wouldn't you say, Molly?'

Molly nodded. 'About that, ten to fifteen, no longer.'

'And neither of you saw or heard a thing?'

'Nothing,' Enid replied as Molly left the room saying she would make some tea. 'We were in the kitchen at the back of the house.'

'Was there anyone hanging around the avenue when you arrived? Anyone you thought looked suspicious?'

'Not a soul, it was deserted,' Enid sobbed. 'And I certainly wouldn't have left her alone if I *had* seen anyone lurking around.'

'And you say Jessica is three months old, weighs around twelve pounds and has dark hair and blue eyes? What is she wearing?'

'Erm, a pink cotton dress, white knitted jacket with matching bonnet and booties,' Enid replied, wiping her eyes.

'And the pram is a navy-blue Silver Cross model?'

'Yes. High coach built with chrome wheels. The bedding's white and the cover is a pink and white knitted blanket. There was a small, pink knitted teddy pinned to the hood of the pram,' she said, a sob catching her throat.

'Okay, you're doing very well. This can't be easy for you.' PC Jones smiled encouragingly. 'Ah, here's your friend with the tea.'

Molly placed the tray of mugs on the coffee table and handed one to Enid.

'I've put extra sugar in and a drop of brandy. It'll steady your nerves.'

'Thanks, Molly.' Enid sniffed. She turned to the police officer. 'Is your colleague with the lady who saw the young man with a pram?'

'Yes, he shouldn't be too long. Ah, speak of the devil, here's PC Swindells now.' He nodded as a second officer entered the room.

'The front door was open...' PC Swindells began.

'That's okay,' Molly said, 'I left it ajar for you. Sit down and have some tea. Any news from my neighbour?'

PC Swindells reached for a mug and helped himself to a ginger snap.

'Mrs Franklin, from number twenty-six, said she was out walking her dog when a young man careered into her with a large navy pram as she rounded the corner of the avenue. She gave the time as eleven thirty, or thereabouts.'

'Well, that was only a couple of minutes after I arrived here.' Enid put down her mug. 'So he would have had a good ten-minute advantage over us when we went outside to bring Jess indoors. Oh God, he could be anywhere by now.'

'Mrs Franklin shouted after him that he needed L-plates, but he ignored her and carried on in the direction of the town centre. She described him as being in his early twenties. He was wearing a long, brown leather coat, with untidy brown hair, and she said his eyes could have been blue or grey, she wasn't that sure. But she said they seemed to stare right through her.'

'We need to let my daughter and son-in-law know what's happening,' Enid said. 'They'll be devastated by this.'

'*We* can do that,' PC Swindells offered. 'Where *are* Jessica's parents?'

'They're in Paris. My son-in-law is Eddie Mellor. He's the drummer with The Raiders. The group are on tour and my daughter Jane has gone with them.'

'Ah yes, The Raiders – "My Special Girl".' PC Swindells nodded. 'If you let us have the hotel address where the band is staying, we'll get word to them immediately. I don't wish to alarm you, Mrs Wilson, but in view of Jessica being Eddie Mellor's daughter, it could throw a whole new light on the abduction.'

'What do you mean?' Enid's hand flew to her mouth. Molly put a comforting arm around her shoulders and offered to furnish them with the hotel address and phone number.

'You think Jessica's been taken by someone who knows she's Eddie's child and they may demand a ransom?' Molly's tone was incredulous.

'It wouldn't be the first time something like this has happened,' PC Swindells replied. 'We'll get back to the station and make sure a news bulletin is issued within the next hour. We'll run you home, Mrs Wilson, and maybe you could let us have a photograph of Jessica so that we can circulate her details nationwide.'

Enid nodded and jumped to her feet. 'I've a framed photo that was taken last month. It's a very good likeness and she hasn't changed that much. I just hope to God whoever has her knows how to look after babies. She'll be ready for feeding and changing now *and* she's teething. Oh Lord, this is the worst thing that's ever happened to me.'

Molly handed PC Swindells a piece of paper with the name and address of the Paris hotel. He rushed outside to his patrol car, telling Molly and Enid he would relay the information to headquarters immediately. Molly followed Enid and PC Jones to the door as PC Swindells came back down the garden path.

'A message is being sent to Mr and Mrs Mellor as we speak and we'll fly them home as soon as we can. Please try not to worry, Mrs Wilson. Whoever has taken your grand-daughter has probably done it for money and won't harm her. I'm sure we'll have her back safe and sound within the next few hours.'

'Well, I hope whoever *has* taken her rots in hell,' Enid cried. 'That little baby is the heart and soul of my family and the apple of her daddy's eye. Eddie will kill whoever has done this, you mark my words!'

* * *

Vicky checked her watch and placed the cover over her typewriter. She collected the stack of letters from her out tray, deposited them on her supervisor's desk, took her jacket and handbag from her locker and hurried out of the office. She kept her head down on the walk to the bus station so that she didn't catch anyone's eye. She wasn't in the mood for friendly chitchat. Her mind wandered back to the conversation she'd had with Mark that morning.

He'd told her out of the blue that he was changing his car today, trading in his Sprite for a larger vehicle. She'd bitten her tongue to avoid the inevitable argument that would follow if she reminded him that he wasn't supposed to be driving while taking his medication. He wouldn't listen to her advice anyway, so what was the point? Especially as he seemed to be in a reasonably good mood for a change.

'Why do you want a bigger car?' she'd asked.

'I can't get much in the Sprite's boot. It's too small and I can only take one passenger. It's not a very substantial car for a family.'

'You don't have a family,' she said.

'Yet!'

'But you don't want to commit to me, Mark. We can't start a family without commitment, it wouldn't be right.'

He shot her a cold look and his good mood disappeared instantly. 'Who said anything about starting a family with *you?*'

She jumped up, scraping her chair back on the kitchen lino. 'Well, who else do you have in mind? I'm the one looking after you and sharing your bed. It was me who picked up the pieces after Jane dumped you and again when the Beth affair blew up in your face. And who else in their right mind would put up with your awful mood swings?'

'You know what to do if you don't like it, Vicky. Fuck off! I don't need you. Tony looks after me, too, don't forget. Anyway, I thought you were working all day again now. Isn't it time you went?' He turned his back and lit a cigarette.

She clenched her fists and left the kitchen before she landed him one. Upstairs in the bedroom they shared, framed photographs of him and Jane that he still insisted on keeping by the bed seemed to mock her. *I must want my bloody head examining, staying with him,* she thought. She dressed hurriedly and left for work, slamming the door behind her as hard as she could, knowing the action would really piss Mark off. But serve him right, she'd just about had enough.

Eight hours later, she was still fuming inwardly and had a banging headache to boot. The bus was crowded and she found a seat upstairs for the short journey. Her footsteps dragged as she walked down Maple Avenue, wondering what sort of mood would greet her tonight. The house was in darkness and there was no vehicle on the drive. He wasn't in and she felt her spirits lifting slightly. At least she could have a cup of tea, two aspirins and unwind in peace. Unless, of course, he was sitting in the dark as he was wont to do on occasion. Maybe the new car was in the garage, which, thinking about it, she recalled he'd spent time last week clearing out.

Vicky squinted through the grimy garage window, no car in sight. She could just about make out the shape of something with chrome wheels in the gloom at the bottom of the garage. Probably an old pram that Maude had hung on to, buried for years beneath the junk Mark had recently disposed of.

She let herself into the house and called his name. No reply. In the lounge she switched on the lights and drew the curtains. Tony wasn't home from work yet and the house felt chilly and unwelcoming. She kicked off her shoes, switched on the new gas fire and strolled into the kitchen to make a pot of tea.

Propped beside the kettle was a scribbled note addressed to her and Tony.

Gone away to sort out my future.

His future? Bastard! What about hers? Vicky let the note slip from her fingers, where it fell silently to the floor. Tears that had threatened all day scalded her cheeks and she sat down heavily on a chair, head in hands, as the front door flew open and Tony called out a cheery greeting.

'Vicky? You home, love?' He sauntered into the kitchen and stopped. 'What's up? Where's Mark? His car isn't on the drive.'

Vicky looked up through her tears. 'He left a note to say he's gone away to sort out his future.'

'He's taken the car? For fuck's sake, he shouldn't be driving!' Tony removed his coat and threw it over the back of a chair.

'He told me this morning that he was trading his Sprite in today for a family car,' she told him tearfully. 'It was all arranged, apparently.'

'You what? He never said a dicky bird to me. What the hell is he playing at? Why does he want a family car?'

'I pointed out the obvious, that he hasn't got a family and his reply was "Yet!"' Vicky sniffed. 'I've had enough, Tony. Mark doesn't love me, he never has. He's never stopped loving Jane and I'm sick and tired of playing second fiddle to an obsession and being used for sex. I want my life back and I've done nothing but think about it all day. I'm going back to Mum, I want to be out of this house before he returns.'

Tony sighed and ran his hands through his hair. 'I'm really sorry, love. I don't blame you one little bit. Although you might not realise it, you've held Mark together these last few months. Without your care and support I think he'd have topped himself. Look, don't go just yet. Give it another couple of days, see how things are when he gets home. I don't know about you, but I'm starving. Let's not bother cooking tonight. I'll nip to the chippy, my treat. You butter some bread and get the kettle on. One of us should stay here in case he calls to let us know where he's staying.'

'To be honest, I couldn't care less, but I fancy fish and chips,' she said wearily.

'That's my girl. Back in two ticks.'

Tony poured a glass of cider and settled on the sofa, feet on the coffee table, to watch the ten o'clock news. He belched loudly, lifted his left buttock and farted. 'Bloody mushy peas,' he chuckled. Grabbing a cushion, he wafted away the noxious smell. Good job Vicky was upstairs finishing her bath, or she'd have had a go at him for being uncouth. He stared at the television screen for a few seconds, then shot off the sofa and turned up the sound.

Vicky slipped her dressing gown on and sat in front of the mirror to dry her hair. She dragged a brush through her long locks and switched on the hairdryer.

'Vicky! Vicky, come down here, quick!' Tony was yelling above the noise of the dryer.

She switched it off and hurried out onto the landing. 'What is it?'

'The news on the TV – Jane and Eddie Mellor's baby has gone missing.'

'Oh my God!' Vicky flew downstairs and stared at the image of the pretty baby girl on the screen. 'Has someone taken her?'

'Yeah,' Tony replied. 'Listen, they're going over the details again. The Raiders are in Paris and the police reckon it's a kidnapping for money because of the group's fame.'

'But who'd do such a wicked thing?'

'Somebody out to make a fast buck,' Tony replied, lighting a cigarette. 'See, there's Ed and Jane at Le Bourget Airport. They're being flown home tonight.'

'Jane's crying and Eddie looks very strained,' Vicky said quietly. 'What a terrible thing to happen, I can't believe it.' She fell silent and listened as the details of the abduction of baby Jessica Mellor were relayed to the nation.

26

Mark drove off the ferry at Fishbourne, sped a few hundred yards down the road and stopped the car. He leant towards the back seat and adjusted the pink and white blanket. Thank God the girl in Jumping Jack's had suggested buying the carrycot. The baby had travelled well and he'd only had to stop twice to feed her.

A bottle of baby milk had been in the pram and he'd given her that first, then one mixed by him. There'd been no objections on the baby's part when she'd sucked eagerly at the teat and happily burped her wind up over his shoulder, so he'd obviously got it right. He'd traced around her heart-shaped face and she smiled and held onto his finger.

He'd even managed a nappy change without too much difficulty. Jane would be proud of him. The baby was fed, dry and fast asleep. Satisfied, he continued on his journey. His brother was expecting him and it was getting late. An earlier ferry would have been preferable, but Enid had taken her outing much later today, which had thrown his plans awry by several hours. Such a shame that Jane was too ill to accompany him but at least he could show off their daughter, Elinore.

* * *

Jane, her face a mask of misery, clung tightly to Eddie's hand as the plane touched down at Ringway Airport. 'Perhaps they'll have found her by now.' She choked on her sobs.

'Let's hope so, sweetheart.' Eddie, ashen-faced, patted her hand as the plane taxied down the runway. 'I can't believe anyone could do this to us. What the hell have we done to make them steal our child?'

'Maybe this is a nightmare and we'll wake up soon.' Jane grasped hopefully at a straw.

Eddie pulled her close and sighed. 'I only wish it were, but unfortunately, we're having the same dream.'

'Mum must be going crazy. I imagine she's blaming herself for this. But it's my fault, I shouldn't have left Jess with her. I should never have agreed to come on tour with you,' she cried.

'Jane, stop it. If anything, I shouldn't have persuaded you to come away with me. But we can't go on blaming ourselves. The person to blame is the bastard who's taken her. Wait until I get my hands on him, I'll make him wish he'd never been born.'

'Mr and Mrs Mellor, there's a police escort for you as you leave the plane. If you follow me, we'll get you off before the other passengers.' The stewardess smiled as she helped Jane to her feet. 'I really hope your baby is found safe and well.'

'Thank you.' Tears blinded Jane as she stumbled towards the exit door. Eddie caught her arm as she swayed at the top of the steps and led her safely down to the waiting police car.

* * *

Mark pulled onto his brother's drive and stopped the engine. The front door flew open and he waved as Charles and Penny hurried out. He hugged Penny and shook Charles's hand. He reached into the back of the car and lifted out the carrycot.

'Here she is. Meet Elinore,' he said proudly as they peered into the cot.

'She's beautiful, and what a mop of hair,' Penny gushed. 'Come on inside, Mark, you must be tired. Did you miss the afternoon ferry?'

'I got delayed,' he replied, following Charles and Penny indoors and through to the kitchen. 'I had to pick up my new car this morning and by the time I left the house I was way behind. Jane's still not well enough to travel and I needed to make arrangements for her before I could leave. A friend of ours is staying with her until she's well enough to join us.'

'Do you want to call Jane?' Charles asked. 'Let her know you've arrived safely.'

Mark placed the carrycot on the table. 'I'll call in the morning, no need to disturb her at this time of night.'

'Okay, you know best. Well, we've saved you some dinner. Chicken casserole followed by sherry trifle. Penny remembered you enjoyed that on your last visit.' Charles looked at Jessica again. 'Did you ever see such a lovely child? She obviously takes after our side of the family for her looks.'

'Actually, she's the image of Jane,' Mark said, gazing at the sleeping baby.

Jessica stirred and her eyes flew open. She looked from one face to the other until her gaze rested on Mark and she smiled with recognition.

'Bless her, she knows her daddy right enough,' Penny said and gently stroked the soft baby cheek. 'Can I pick her up?'

'Go ahead,' Mark replied. 'She'll need feeding and changing soon. You can do that, too, if you like.'

'You sit down and eat your dinner then and I'll see to this little bundle of love.' Penny reached for Jessica. She sat down on a rocking chair beside the fire and undid the ribbons on her matinee jacket. 'Let's change your nappy and get you into your nightdress, Ellie,' she cooed as Jessica gurgled contentedly.

'All the baby stuff's in the black suitcase,' Mark said. 'There's Cow & Gate and bottles, clothes and nappies, too.'

The girl who'd served him in Jumping Jack's had been more than helpful when he told her he needed a complete wardrobe of clothes for a three-month-old baby girl. He'd come away laden with bags and the carrycot, complete with a set of wheels.

'I'll get her clothes and take her up to the room I've given you,' Penny said. 'Then I'll top 'n' tail her.'

'Top 'n' tail?' Mark frowned.

Penny laughed. 'Wash her face and bottom, silly,' she said. 'It's what we used to say when I was nursing and we washed the babies. Don't they use that saying in Stockport?'

'Oh! Oh, yes, of course,' he stammered. 'I don't really do much of that. Jane looks after her while I'm at work.' He lowered his eyes and concentrated on the casserole.

'I thought Jane was too ill to look after the baby?' Charles sat down opposite. He poured two glasses of red wine and pushed one towards Mark.

'She is,' he replied, knocking back the wine. 'But like I say, she's got a friend over.'

'Come on, little lady, let's get you clean and comfortable and then I'll make you a nice bottle.' Penny left the room with the baby while Charles stared at Mark.

'Apart from Jane being unwell, is everything else okay? It's a while since we heard from you. Are you all right for money?'

'Err, yes, fine, thanks. I earn a good salary at the bank and they've been very understanding when I've taken time off to look after Jane. How's Dorothy?' Mark changed the subject. Things were beginning to get muddled in his head. He would need to take his pills soon. He'd refrained from taking any at all so far today as they caused that misty vision for an hour or so and he hadn't wanted to risk an accident.

Fortunately, the pills were in his jacket pocket and before Charles had a chance to reply, he excused himself and slipped away from the table. In the tiny cloakroom under the stairs he popped two pills in his mouth, crunched them up and washed them down with a slug of whisky from the small bottle in his pocket.

He stared at his reflection for several seconds and took a deep breath. He must be careful not to drink too much tonight. It wouldn't do to sleep through if the kid woke up crying. He strolled back into the kitchen, where Charles was topping up their glasses.

'You were asking about Dot before you dashed off. Is everything all right, Mark? You look quite pale.'

'I'm fine, really. Just a bit tired with the long journey and I can feel a headache coming on. I won't join you in a second glass of wine, Charles, sorry.'

'Oh, no problem. All the more for me. Anyway, Dot's just fine. She'll be over tomorrow morning. She's been knitting clothes for Elinore and she's dying to see her. Being a doting auntie is a dream come true for our Dot.'

Mark forced a smile. This was where he and his kid truly belonged, with family. He and Jane could make such a happy life together on the island with Elinore.

Tomorrow, after a good night's sleep, he might call Tony and instruct him to get the house valued. He'd no intention of going home to Stockport. Most of what he wanted was right here, his real family and, more importantly, his daughter. When Jane joined them, their lives would be complete. The time was right.

* * *

Jane lay on the big brass bed, staring up at the crack on the ceiling, willing her eyes to stay open. She'd refused a sedative from the doctor, telling him she wanted to stay awake and in control until her daughter was found safe and well. Only then did she feel she would ever sleep soundly again.

She pressed Jessica's cot quilt to her nose, breathing in the baby scent, her eyes welling once more with uncontrollable tears. She could hear Eddie talking downstairs to both sets of their distraught parents, who were keeping a vigil with him. Jonny had been put to bed in the nursery and was sleeping soundly after running all over the house, looking for his sister.

The phone had rung continually since they'd arrived back from Paris, each call bringing fresh hope that it might be the police with good news. But it was now after midnight and they were still waiting. Her mother had been beside herself with grief and Ben had insisted that she, too, be sedated, but, like Jane, Enid had refused.

Eddie popped his head around the bedroom door and Jane struggled to sit up.

'Any news?'

'Not yet, sweetheart. But Sean, Carl, John, Stuart *and* Mario have called and they send their love. They've all seen the news. Everyone's very shocked.'

Jane nodded. 'Are the police still here?'

'Just PC Swindells, he's been assigned to us all night. They think the abductor may try and contact us with a demand for money. They're keeping a low profile in case he's watching the house. They've searched the woodlands and fields and found nothing of any significance. There was flattened grass and bushes bordering the garden, but the fans probably caused that.

'What *I* don't understand,' he continued as Jane stared at him, 'is how on earth the kidnapper knew that the baby in the pram outside Sammy's mum's was *my* daughter? I'm wondering if they're not barking up the wrong tree with the kidnapping theory. Maybe it was someone who stole her to give to somebody else.'

Jane clutched the cot quilt even tighter, her eyes wide with fear.

'You mean a person who really wanted a child and couldn't have one? You think the man took her to pass on? Oh, Eddie, we might never get her back if that's the case! She could be miles away by now, maybe even in a foreign country.'

They held each other and sobbed, then drew apart at a knock on the door.

Eddie's mum came in, her face grey, eyes red-rimmed. She carried two mugs of tea.

'Oh, my loves, look at you both.' She placed the mugs on the bedside table and sat on the bed beside them. 'Now come on. They'll find her, I just know they will. You need to be strong for each other. Drink this tea and then try and get a few winks. We're all downstairs and we'll let you know the minute we hear any news.'

'Thanks, Mum,' Eddie replied. 'We just can't believe this has happened. After everything we've been through, too.'

'I know, Ed. You don't deserve it. I thought your luck had turned a corner at last.'

'So did we,' Jane sniffed. 'I know we've got to have faith, but it's so hard.'

'Well, you've got each other and that helps. Now come on, sup up and try and get an hour or two's sleep. I'll leave you in peace.' She left, closing the door quietly behind her.

Eddie finished his tea and took Jane's empty cup. She lay down and he smiled and brushed the hair from her face. 'Let's do as Mum says. We'll need all our strength to get through the next twenty-four hours.'

* * *

Vicky woke with a jolt at six thirty, surprised she'd even slept at all. She'd tossed and turned for hours, worrying about Mark and concerned for Jane and Eddie Mellor and their missing baby.

She crept quietly downstairs and into the kitchen. She made toast and coffee and carried her breakfast into the dining room, where she pulled back the curtains on the still-dark autumn morning. At least it wasn't raining and today was payday. No work tomorrow and shopping with Sarah in the afternoon to look forward to while Tony went to watch Stockport County play a home game. Life wasn't all bad.

It would be a long weekend without Mark. Moody sod that he was, she'd still missed his warmth next to her in bed last night. She finished her breakfast and rinsed her mug and plate in the kitchen as a bleary-eyed Tony, dressed for work, sauntered downstairs.

'Kettle's only just boiled,' she said. 'Would you like a coffee?'

'No time, thanks, Vicky. I'll skip breakfast and have a fag on the bus. I can't afford petrol until I get paid later, so I'll leave the car. Are you okay?'

'I think so. I didn't sleep too well, but I've decided to stay until Mark comes home.'

'That's the spirit,' Tony said. 'Right, I'll have to fly or I'll miss the bus. I'm meeting Sarah for a drink straight from work and then we'll come back here and eat with you.'

'That sounds great, Tony.' She gave him a hug. 'Thank you for being there for me, both you and Sarah.'

'Hey, that's what mates are for. I'll see you later. If you hear any more about the kidnapped baby, give me a call at work.' He kissed her cheek and left. Vicky ran upstairs to get dressed.

As she hurriedly made the bed, she spotted a sheet of paper sticking out from beneath the divan base. She grabbed it and caught her breath as she realised she was clutching a scribbled timetable for the previous day's Isle of Wight ferries. So, she nodded thoughtfully, Mark had gone to visit his family. Well, that was no bad thing, apart from the risk of driving a new and unfamiliar vehicle while under the influence of his pills, which, she hoped, he'd taken with him.

At least the Mainwaring clan would take care of him, although as she understood it, they were unaware of his mental instability. Vicky pulled open the top drawer of his dressing table and glanced inside: no pill bottle. That was a good sign. He could pass for almost normal so long as he kept up his dosage. A receipt, lying on top of the muddle of things in the drawer, caught her eye. It was dated yesterday, for a lengthy number of items, and the store was a local baby-wear retailer, Jumping Jack's.

Vicky quickly scanned the list of goods. Nightdresses, vests, bibs, dresses, terry napkins, woollen blankets, a carry cot and a set of wheels. What business did Mark have buying all these baby items?

She sat down heavily on the bed as a terrible thought hit her: could he have made up his differences with Beth? Maybe he was seeing her again and they'd had a child. That was it; the reason why he was so horrible all the time was because he'd hooked up again with bloody Beth. He was forever disappearing for hours at a time, probably taking the train to Chester to meet up with her. The bastard had got her pregnant again and this time they'd decided to keep the baby.

She sucked in her breath and her stomach rolled. Mark didn't know how to tell her it was over as she'd stood by him through thick and thin. Being horrible to her was his defence mechanism, a way of driving a further wedge between them to make *her* leave *him*.

She'd bet her life that he'd taken Beth and their baby to meet his family and would probably be bringing them home with him. So that's what he'd meant when she taunted him about not having a family. 'Yet!' he'd replied, when all the time he knew full well that he and Beth had a bloody kid.

She retched and shot to the bathroom, where she was violently sick in the toilet. Wiping her sweaty face with a damp flannel, she sank to the floor and hugged her legs to her chest. Head resting on her knees, she cried heartbrokenly. Well, that was that; it was over. Mark wouldn't want her now that he had Beth and their baby. When Tony had told her about Beth's abortion and how the trauma had helped push Mark to the limit, she'd been appalled. It had, however, given her some insight as to why he was so upset on discovering that Jane was pregnant.

She'd been hoping that since his discharge from hospital, Mark would suggest they start a family of their own. She believed that a child would bring them close enough to want to spend the rest of their lives together but all the time he'd been secretly seeing Beth.

'You lousy bastard!' she muttered, pulling herself up from the floor.

She made her way shakily downstairs to call in sick. She couldn't face the pitying looks of her colleagues, who were all aware of the rough time she was having with Mark.

She stared at the telephone and chastised herself: 'Come on, Vicky! Shape your bloody self or Miss Gillings won't send your wages home. Tomorrow's shopping trip with Sarah will be off and Lord knows, you need *some* cheering up.'

* * *

'I've run you a bath and put some fancy oil in it,' Eddie said to Jane after another sleepless night. 'Why don't you hop in and then come downstairs for some tea and toast?'

She sat up and rubbed her eyes. 'Is there any news?'

'Not yet, but PC Swindells has been replaced by PC

Stanley in plain-clothes. He's doing something to our phone in case the kidnapper tries to make contact. The police will be able to listen in to the call. The new officer said they've been making house-to-house enquiries on your parents' estate and they've had several reported sightings of a guy around my age, wearing a full-length, brown leather coat, pushing a pram. Each time the description of him is the same and the pram is definitely ours, because everyone remembers the knitted teddy dangling from the hood. They've asked if the guy's description means anything to me, but without seeing a picture, it could be anybody.'

Jane sighed. 'I suppose they're doing everything they can, but I wish there was more we could do ourselves. I feel so useless waiting around here.'

'Well, let's see what today brings. If there's no news in the next few hours I'm going to suggest we offer a reward. See if that brings the bastard out of the woodwork. Jump in your bath and then come downstairs. Mum's calling, I'll see what she wants. The phone was ringing, too. I'll come straight back up if it's anything to do with Jess.'

Eddie ran downstairs into the warm kitchen, where his mother stood clutching the telephone receiver. 'It's Roy, he's anxious to know if there's any news.'

'Okay. Thanks, Mum.' Eddie grabbed the phone. 'Roy. Hi, mate. No, no news yet. Not a fucking thing. They've a description of the guy who's taken her, but beyond that, they've drawn a blank. How did the gig go? Did Frank manage to find a stand-in for me in time?' Eddie listened as Roy confirmed that Frank did. 'We'll see you back here on Monday, then,' he continued. 'Yeah, it *is* a nightmare, Roy. We can't believe it's happened. Jane's in a right state. Okay, mate, I'll be in touch if we hear anything. Thanks for calling.'

He hung up and sighed. The last couple of shows could still go ahead and he could now quit worrying about the group and concentrate fully on his family. He heard Jonny shouting and turned to his mother.

'I'll get him up and pop him in the bath as soon as Jane's finished,' she said. 'You see to her breakfast. We'll take Jonny home with us again and then you can wait quietly here with Jane for news.'

'Thanks, Mum. It's not that I don't want him here, but he keeps asking for Jessie and Jane's upset enough as it is.' As his mother went upstairs, Eddie glanced through the kitchen window. The sound of crunching gravel heralded the arrival of a vehicle.

He opened the door to Tom and Molly. 'Come on in, there's tea in the pot. Sit yourselves down. I'm just going upstairs to see Jane.'

'We couldn't sleep for worrying,' Molly said, 'so we thought we'd come here first thing to see if there's anything we can do to help. How's Jane?' She rubbed Eddie's arm gently.

'Weary, upset and angry,' he replied, his eyes filling with tears.

'Who can blame her?' Tom shook his head. 'What a terrible business, and that it could happen outside our own front door. What's the bloody world coming to when you can't leave a child sleeping in her pram in your own garden?'

Eddie dashed his tears away with the back of his hand. 'I won't be a minute.' He excused himself and ran upstairs. Jane was sitting on the edge of the bed wrapped in a large towel, her lips trembling as she listened to Jonny shrieking with laughter in the bathroom down the landing.

'I might never hear Jessie laugh in the bath again,' she began, the tears sliding down her cheeks.

Eddie took her in his arms. 'Jane, stop it! You will, of course you will. We'll get her back. The police reckon the kidnapper will make demands soon and will probably be in contact today.'

'And what if they're wrong and it's like you said? That

they're barking up the wrong tree and she's been stolen to order?'

'I shouldn't have said that, I'm sorry. It was just my imagination running away with me. Come on, let me help you get dry and then you can come down for a cup of tea.' He rubbed her back gently as she slumped against him, sobbing.

* * *

Vicky slunk along Stockport High Street, hoping that no one from work would see her. It was only just after eight thirty, far too early for people taking a break, but you never knew who might be nipping out for five minutes to do a spot of shopping, especially as it was payday.

In her coat pocket, her hand closed around the receipt from Jumping Jack's. While getting dressed, she'd recalled that an old friend, Elaine, had started working there after leaving school. Vicky hadn't seen or heard from her for a couple of years, but was hoping she was still working at the store.

'Elaine's on holiday this week,' the pleasant-faced assistant said to her enquiry.

'Well, maybe *you* could help me then? I want some baby nightdresses. I'd like two, for a gift. They're for my niece,' Vicky fibbed. 'A friend of mine purchased some from you yesterday. Can I have the same design, please?' She showed the girl the receipt with the stock number.

The girl smiled. 'Ah yes, Mr Fisher. He was so excited about his baby. Said he was taking her to visit relatives on the Isle of Wight and wanted to kit her out. He told me that he and his wife had been waiting quite some time for a family.'

Vicky stared at the girl, who was taking two nightdresses from a drawer behind the counter. 'Excuse me, did you say, his wife?'

The girl's brow wrinkled as she wrapped the garments in

tissue paper and she nodded. 'Yes, that's right, his wife, Jane. I remember because it's my name, too, you see. Now, can I get you anything else, madam?'

Vicky's head was reeling with dreadful realisation as she replied, 'Err, not at the moment, thank you. I don't suppose you can remember what Mr Fisher was wearing yesterday morning? I know it's a long shot, but it's quite important.'

'Yes, actually, I can. He had on a brand-new, full-length brown leather coat. I know it was new, because he asked me to dispose of the bag he'd been given in Jerome's. He said he'd bought it for his trip but he was cold and decided to wear the coat over his jacket.' The girl's friendly smile began to disappear as Vicky nodded her head, things suddenly clear as daylight.

'Look, what is this? Why are you asking me about Mr Fisher? Has he done something wrong?'

'I'm not sure. I must go.' Vicky grabbed the receipt for Mark's purchases and ran out of the shop, feeling as though she'd been punched in the stomach. She made her way to Lloyds Bank and asked to speak to Tony urgently on a private matter. She was ushered into a small office. Tony appeared within seconds and Vicky burst into tears.

'Vicky, what's wrong? Have you heard from Mark? Has something happened to him?' He helped her onto a chair and knelt beside her.

'Oh, Tony, I think, well no, I'm certain that Mark has taken Jane and Eddie's baby.'

'What?' Tony stared at her as though she'd gone mad. 'Don't be daft. Why the bloody hell would he do that?'

'Look at the receipt I found in his drawer earlier.' She flung it on the desk. 'I've been to the shop and the assistant told me that when Mark bought the goods he said he and his wife Jane had a baby girl. A man wearing a long brown leather coat took Jessica yesterday afternoon.'

'Mark doesn't possess a long brown leather coat, or a short one for that matter, so that rules *him* out,' Tony said, frowning.

'He does now. He bought it yesterday and wore it when he made his purchases in Jumping Jack's.' Vicky's hand flew to her mouth. 'Oh my God, I've just remembered something else, too. When I looked through the garage window last night to see if Mark had put the new car in there, I thought I saw something down at the bottom. It was too dark to see properly, but you know he's been clearing the garage out this last week and I thought maybe he'd unearthed a pram that Maude had held on to. Jessica's pram is a navy Silver Cross.'

Tony looked at her for a long moment. 'Right, wait there. I need to see my manager, tell him I've got a family emergency. Won't be a minute.' He shot out of the room.

Vicky took a long, shuddering breath. This was a nightmare. What if she was right and Mark had really taken Jessica? Vicky was sure he wouldn't hurt the child, because she was part of his beloved Jane. On the other hand, she was also Eddie's daughter and Mark hated Eddie Mellor with a vengeance.

Tony was back within seconds. 'I've got the rest of the day off and I've called a taxi. We'll go and wait by the staff entrance. Christ almighty, if your theory *is* right, Mark's in really deep shit! Kidnapping a child, for whatever reason, is a terrible offence. They'll throw the book at him and I wouldn't like to be in *his* shoes when Eddie Mellor catches up with him.'

* * *

Tony rummaged in the kitchen drawer for the garage keys and held them aloft.

'Right, come on, Vicky, the moment of truth awaits.'

Vicky followed him outside and held her breath. He unlocked the door and it creaked back on its rusty hinges. She walked slowly to the bottom of the musty smelling garage and stood silently beside the navy-blue pram, its chrome wheels glinting in the faint light filtering through the grimy windows. The pink knitted teddy bear was still pinned to the hood, exactly as described by last night's TV newsreader.

She turned to Tony, who was shaking his head in disbelief.

'I told you he'd taken her,' she said simply, tears running down her cheeks.

'You did, and you were right,' Tony said, putting his arm around her shoulders. 'But where's he gone? Come on, Vicky, we need to call the police.'

'He's taken her to the Isle of Wight,' she choked. 'The ferry details were on the bedroom floor. The girl in Jumping Jack's said so, too. Oh God, Mark, what *have* you done?'

27

Eddie answered the phone and passed it to PC Stanley, who was seated at the kitchen table, dunking a ginger snap into his mug of tea. 'It's the station – for you.'

Jane, sitting opposite PC Stanley, clutched Eddie's hand. 'Maybe they've got some news.'

'Hope so,' he said, squeezing her hand gently.

PC Stanley replaced the receiver and turned to the expectant faces.

'The pram's been found in the garage of a private house in Stockport,' he said.

'And Jessica, any sign of her?' Eddie hardly dared to ask.

PC Stanley shook his head. 'Not yet, but at least it's a breakthrough. The couple that reported finding the pram are being interviewed as we speak. We'll be informed of any further details shortly.'

Jane jumped up. 'Which couple? What house? Is Jessica there? Is Jessie all right? Is she? *Is* she?' She broke down, sobbing.

Eddie pulled her close and stroked her hair, crying with her. 'She isn't there,' he sniffed, 'just the pram. But it's something.

Come on, let's walk down the lane. We won't go as far as the gate because of the reporters, but I need to stretch my legs a bit. I'm getting cabin fever stuck in here. There might be more news when we come back.'

* * *

'And you say Mr Fisher had a complete mental breakdown and was sectioned for his own safety?'

'Yes, that's right,' Vicky sobbed as the police officer addressing her made notes, while two further officers examined the pram in the garage.

'Mark had many personal problems that led to his breakdown,' Tony chipped in, flopping down beside Vicky on the sofa.

'Perhaps you'd like to enlighten me while our officers carry out further investigations to establish that the pram is indeed the same one that baby Jessica Mellor was abducted in.'

'Put it this way,' Tony said, speaking slowly, as though to a child, 'it appeared out of the blue the day Jessica disappeared, only we didn't realise that until today. Vicky assumed it was an old pram that had been stored in the garage and had been hidden under loads of old junk that Mark recently got shut of. The baby's mum, Jane, is Mark's ex and he never got over her leaving him for Eddie Mellor. It really doesn't take Einstein to work it out.'

'There's no need for sarcasm, Mr Collins. My officers have to follow procedure. I don't doubt it's Jessica's pram for one moment but we need to examine it for fingerprints and any further clues. Now perhaps you can give me the story to Mark's background.'

The officer listened intently as Vicky and Tony told the tale between them. He radioed back to the local station that he believed he knew the identity of Jessica's kidnapper and possibly his and the child's whereabouts.

'We don't actually have Mark's brother's address or phone number,' Vicky said. 'But his name is Doctor Charles Mainwaring and he has a practice in Freshwater, so it shouldn't be too difficult to find him.'

The officer collected his notes together and stood up. 'Many thanks for your co- operation. I can see how shaken the pair of you are. Our main concern now is to find and return the baby safely to her parents and to help Mr Fisher get the medical help he's obviously in need of.'

'Mark will have taken good care of the baby,' Vicky said, wiping a tear from her eye. 'He adores Jane and I'm quite sure he wouldn't harm her daughter in any way. He's a very confused man, but he's harmless enough.'

'Well, let's hope you're right, miss. I'll bid you good morning and we'll keep you informed as to the outcome of our enquiries. Could you stay near the phone, just in case we need you?'

Tony saw the officer out and closed the door behind him. 'Get on the phone to the operator and ask for Charles Mainwaring's number, Vicky. I think we should warn him that Mark's on his way and he's got Jessica with him.'

'He'll already be there. His family must have realised something wasn't right when he turned up out of the blue with a baby. They'll probably have seen last night's news about the kidnapping and put two and two together. That's if Mark's ever mentioned Jane to them.'

Tony shrugged. 'God only knows what sort of line he's been spinning them. Remember when he was there before and he phoned you, called you Jane and said take care of the baby?'

'I'd forgotten about that. He's probably already told them he has a baby daughter, so they won't realise she's not his.'

'We have to warn Charles about Mark right away and then he can at least keep his eye on Jessica until the police arrive. We owe that much to Jane and Eddie,' Tony said as Vicky snatched up the receiver and asked for directory enquiries.

'I don't believe I'm hearing this!' Eddie roared, slamming his fist down on the kitchen table. '*Mark Fisher*! Mark-fucking-Fisher has taken our daughter? I'll kill the bastard when I get my hands on him! If he's hurt so much as a hair on her head, I'll fucking swing for him!'

'Ed, calm down. You're not doing yourself or Jane any good, shouting and swearing like this.' Lillian forced him onto a kitchen chair next to Jane, who was crying hysterically.

'But he's taken Jess, Mum. He's taken our baby.' He rounded on Enid, whose face was a mask of horror at this latest news. 'You used to think the sun shone out of his fucking arse and that I was no good! Well, so much for Mr Perfect now, eh, Enid?'

'Eddie, that's enough,' his father shouted. 'Enid doesn't need it, none of us do. Pull yourself together, for God's sake. You and Jane are being flown to the Isle of Wight immediately, so stop wasting time and get ready to go.'

Eddie took a deep shuddering breath and looked at Enid. 'I'm sorry. I'm so wound up, I don't know what the fuck I'm saying.'

Enid patted his shoulder. 'I know that, Ed. Go on, get off and bring our Jessie back, safe and sound.'

* * *

Charles Mainwaring dropped the telephone receiver back onto the cradle and turned to Penny, who was standing behind him, an enquiring expression on her face.

'What is it, Charles? You look worried to death.'

'That was Mark's friend, Vicky. You'd better sit down, Pen. I have something very serious to tell you.'

'No!' Penny's hand flew to her mouth as Charles related the tale of kidnapping and deception. 'That can't be right, surely? Elinore adores her daddy, you can tell she does. She beams at him when he goes anywhere near her and he handles her so well, as though he's been doing it all her life. Are you sure that Vicky isn't some jealous ex trying to cause problems for Mark?'

'No, Penny, and the police will be here at any moment. According to Vicky, Mark's mentally unstable. I'm afraid he's had us all fooled about his wife and child.'

A loud knocking that almost took the stout front door off its hinges interrupted them and Charles crossed the room to answer.

'Doctor Mainwaring?' The tallest of the four policemen standing on the doorstep took command.

'Come in,' Charles said, ushering the officers inside. 'I know why you're here. I just received an urgent call from my brother's friend. I believe Mark is responsible for the abduction of the Mellor baby.'

'That's right, sir,' the officer in charge replied. 'We have reason to believe Mr Fisher is staying with you?'

'He is, but at the moment he and the baby are visiting my sister. I can ring her if you like. She can make sure he stays put.'

'That won't be necessary, sir. Just give me your sister's address and we'll radio ahead for members of the constabulary to meet us near the house. We don't want to alarm Mr Fisher in any way at this stage, or jeopardise the baby's well-being.'

'Oh, Mark wouldn't hurt the child, he dotes on her like she's his own,' Penny assured the officer as she wrote Dorothy's address on a sheet of paper.

'Yes, well, she's not and we won't be taking any chances on that score. Excuse me while I go to the car to radio this address to HQ.'

'The baby's parents are being flown to Southampton as we speak and then a naval helicopter has been commissioned to bring them to the island,' a second officer told Charles and Penny.

'They must be absolutely frantic.' Charles shook his head. 'We saw the news about the abduction on TV before Mark arrived last night but we never dreamt for one moment... Well, you wouldn't, would you?' he tailed off.

'No, sir, you certainly wouldn't,' the officer agreed. 'Terrible business, for the parents, and for your family, too.'

'My sister will be devastated. She was so proud of Mark for making her an auntie. I find it incredible that for months he's been lying to us about his life in Stockport. We believed that he was happily married to Jane in spite of her so-called fragile health and all the time she was married to someone else. Vicky told me that Mark and Jane were engaged,' Charles continued, 'but she left him for that musician fellow, the baby's father. Mark was unable to accept she wasn't coming back to him and he'd built up a fantasy life in his mind that he thinks is very real. He firmly believes the baby is his.'

The officer nodded. 'I know, it's a very sad story and your brother is obviously an extremely sick young man, all the more reason for us to tread carefully at this stage.'

'Right, Doctor Mainwaring.' The first police officer walked back indoors. 'We're going to drive to your sister's house to join our colleagues and try and gain custody of the child.'

'We'll follow you in our own car,' Charles replied. 'Mark may need us and I don't want him to think we don't care or understand what he's going through or why he took the action he did. While I don't in any way condone what he's done, it's too dreadful for words. I think I understand what drove him to it and he's my flesh and blood at the end of the day.'

'You being a medical man will understand the workings of a disturbed mind far better than I do, sir,' the first officer said.

'Just follow us, but keep a discreet distance until I give you a signal that it's safe to come closer.'

'Fair enough,' Charles replied. 'Lead the way.'

* * *

'She's certainly settled well,' Mark said, tucking the blanket around Jessica, who was wedged between two pillows on his sister's double bed.

'Bless her, she's sleeping like a baby,' Dorothy said.

Mark smiled at her excitement and hugged her affectionately. 'That's because she *is* a baby, Dot – you daft so-and-so.'

'I know. I'm so thrilled to bits to have her here that I've gone all soppy. Let's go and have a cuppa and you can tell me what you've been up to recently.'

Mark followed Dorothy out of the bedroom and excused himself. He nipped into the bathroom and popped a handful of pills in his mouth, crunched them up and washed them down with a swig of whisky. Things were going well, his family adored Elinore, as he knew they would. There'd been one tricky moment last night when Charles had asked why he hadn't sent them any photos of the baby following her birth. He frowned now as he tried to recall what his answer had been, but he couldn't remember. It must have been satisfactory though. Charles didn't pursue the subject. He joined Dorothy in the kitchen and picked up the mug of tea she pushed across the table.

'So!' She leant across and swept his fringe out of his eyes in a motherly gesture that brought a lump to his throat. 'What are your future plans? Any more thoughts on making a home on the island with us?'

'Yes,' he replied. 'I'm going to call Tony tomorrow and ask him to put my house up for sale.'

'And who's Tony, when he's at home?'

'He's my best friend. You remember, he lives with me and Vicky.' Mark reached for a custard cream from the selection Dorothy had laid out on a china plate.

She frowned, mug halfway to her mouth. 'Who on earth is Vicky?'

'My girlfr— erm,' Mark faltered. He racked his brains to remember which life he was currently living. It was so confusing sometimes, but, he thought, it would be so much simpler when Jane arrived, she would be able to explain things to his family properly. 'Vicky is err, Tony's girl. They live with me and Jane.' That was it, he was back on track. 'They help me look after Jane when she's too ill to do things for herself.'

'I see. Well, it must be very crowded since Ellie arrived.'

'That's why I want to sell up and look for a place here for me, Jane and the baby. I've discussed it with her and she agrees with me. When she feels up to it she'll join me here. Meantime, I'll try and find us somewhere to live.'

'Why don't you all move in with me? I've two spare bedrooms, we can make one of them into a nursery for Ellie. In fact, we could make a start today. It will be a lovely surprise for Jane when she arrives.'

'That would be brilliant, Dot, thank you.' Mark gave her a hug. 'I think I can hear Ellie stirring.'

'I'll go and check on her. You stay there and finish your tea.'

'Go on then, Auntie Dot. You have a way with her. She seems to like you very much.'

* * *

Dorothy crept into the bedroom, where Jessica was turning her head from side to side, rooting for her dummy. She settled down immediately, sucking noisily as Dorothy replaced the errant dummy and walked across the room to close the window.

'Dratted seagulls, they're noisy enough to awaken the

bloody dead, never mind a baby!' She frowned and leant forward, peering across the road to where a group of police officers were congregating. One appeared to be pointing in the direction of her bungalow, gesticulating wildly, as though giving orders to the others.

'Something must be going on,' she muttered. 'What have you been up to now, Dorothy Mainwaring?' She crept out of the bedroom and made her way back to the kitchen. Mark was standing by the open back door, smoking.

'Good lad. You remembered that I don't like the smell in my bungalow. Can you see anything out on the lane at the back there?'

He frowned and flicked his ash on to the patio. 'What sort of anything? I can see my car by the back gate, but that's all.'

'Hmm, I wonder what's going on. Come into the lounge with me and peep through the nets. See if you can fathom out what they're up to.'

'What who's up to?' Mark stubbed out his cigarette and followed her. 'You're talking in riddles, Dot.'

'There, look.' She pointed across the road, where the gesticulating policeman was now standing by a patrol car, talking into a radiophone. He was looking directly across at the bungalow and pointing.

Mark paled and pulled back from the window. Oblivious to his discomfort, Dorothy prattled on. He silently left the room while she was still squinting through the nets.

* * *

Mark snatched up Jessica, wrapped her in a blanket and headed for the kitchen door. He ran to the car, placed her in the carrycot on the back seat, thanking God that he'd not taken it indoors, and leapt into the driving seat.

He threw the vehicle into gear and it shot forward, causing

him to bang his head against the windscreen. The car bounced down the narrow lane that ran along the back of the seafront properties. He swung onto the main road and put his foot to the floor, ignoring the honking of the angry driver he'd swerved in front of.

He took a deep, steadying breath and slowed down slightly, checking his rear-view mirror. The police were not following. Why should they be? He was guilty of no wrongdoing. He shook his head from side to side to clear the fuzzy feeling that his recently consumed pills had created. The knock on the head hadn't helped either. He blinked frantically to clear the mist from his eyes. The baby had woken up and she was crying.

He should turn back. If Jane arrived on the island, she wouldn't know where to look for him. She might decide to return to Stockport alone. The car hurtled towards the cross-roads. He slammed on the brakes and looked up at the road sign. If he took the left-hand turn, he would be heading towards the local beauty spot, The Needles. That would do. He would take Elinore for a short walk along the cliff path to clear his head and stop her crying. He drove on, still puzzling over the police presence outside his sister's front door.

Maybe a prisoner had escaped from nearby Parkhurst Prison and there'd been a sighting in Yarmouth. That would be it. He nodded at the obvious answer and continued towards The Needles, gripping the wheel as Jessica screamed.

* * *

Still talking to herself, Dorothy frowned as another car pulled up further down the seafront. 'Now what on earth does *he* want?' she muttered. 'Charles is here.' She turned to address Mark and was surprised to find herself alone. 'Mark,' she called, 'has Ellie woken up? Our Charles has just arrived. God knows what he wants. Probably to make sure I'm not spoiling her by picking her up too often.'

She made her way to the bedroom, where she assumed Mark would be. Seeing the empty bed, she hurried to the kitchen and stared at the open back door.

'Mark, where are you?' She looked out to the garden, where the gate was swinging in the breeze, and saw that Mark's car had gone from the back lane. 'How very odd.' She scratched her head in bewilderment.

'What the blazes!' she exclaimed as someone hammered loudly on her front door. 'Bloody hell, Charles, are you trying to break down my door?' She flung it open and stepped back in shock as four burly police officers pushed their way inside, closely followed by Charles and Penny.

'Would somebody mind telling me what the hell is going on?' she yelled as the officers rushed from room to room, their large frames filling her home.

'Where's Mark?' Charles demanded, clutching her arm.

'You might well ask,' Dorothy said, dumfounded by the invasion.

'What do you mean?' Charles asked frantically. 'He was supposed to be visiting you.'

'He was; then he disappeared while we were looking out through the front window at this lot.' She pointed to the red-faced officers who were standing around like spare parts. 'One minute he was here, the next, he and Ellie had vanished into thin air. His car's gone too. It was parked out in the back lane.'

'Oh, great.' The officer in charge sighed despondently. Then, as though remembering his position, he pulled himself together and took command once more. 'Have you any idea where Mark may have gone, Miss Mainwaring?'

'None at all; I didn't even *know* he'd gone until just now when you all barged in. We were having tea in the kitchen. I went to check on Ellie, looked out of the bedroom window and saw all the activity. I called Mark to come and twitch the nets with me, which he did, and then he vanished, just like I said. For God's sake, will someone *please* tell me what's going on? Why do you want Mark? What on earth has he done?'

'Sit down, Dot, I'll explain.' Charles led her to the sofa. Her jaw dropped as she listened to him.

'That can't be right,' she butted in. 'This Vicky you spoke to, well, she's Tony's girlfriend. Mark was just telling me that the couple live with him and help him take care of Jane and Ellie. You've got it all wrong, Charles.'

'Mark's been lying, Dot. He's very ill,' Penny said, sitting beside her. 'The baby's parents are on their way here, they shouldn't be long now.'

There was a further flurry of activity and hammering at the front door. The officer in charge ushered in a young couple and two further police officers.

'Mr and Mrs Mellor, Jessica's parents,' he announced to the assembled crowd.

Eddie looked at Mark's family and nodded warily. He turned to one of the officers who had accompanied him and Jane on their journey. 'This island's not that big to search. What are you doing now to find our child?'

'We've officers and dogs drafted in from the Hampshire force who are searching every inch of the island and manning the ferry terminals to make sure Mr Fisher can't leave that way, Mr Mellor.'

'Sir,' the second officer called from the open front door. 'HQ on the radio for you.'

'Back in two ticks,' the first officer told Eddie and left the room.

'My dear Jane, I'm so very sorry,' Dorothy began, her voice wavering. 'I had absolutely no idea. I thought Mark was married to you and that Jessica was my niece.'

'Huh, he wishes!' Eddie said. 'Mark Fisher has put my wife

and me through hell. He needs locking up. He's dangerous and if he's harmed my daughter, I'll kill him!'

Penny, who was still in shock, spoke up quietly: 'Mark wouldn't harm your daughter, Eddie. He's in such a confused state of mind that he really thinks she's his own child. He dotes on her and he's looked after her very well. I washed and changed her last night and I bathed her this morning. She was absolutely fine and there wasn't a mark on her, I can assure you.'

Jane nodded and wiped her eyes. 'Thank you for that. Did she feed okay? She can be a bit cranky if the bottle isn't warm enough.'

'She fed very well. In fact, I commented how much she loves her food. She's a bonny little girl and very beautiful, and now I can see where she gets her pretty looks *and* her big blue eyes from.' Penny smiled in Eddie's direction as the first police officer rushed back into the room.

'We've a sighting of him. He's parked out on the cliffs' car park, near The Needles. He's pushing a small pram up and down the path. He has no idea we're observing him. Mr and Mrs Mellor, you come with me. The rest of you stay here for now.'

Eddie sighed with relief and pulled Jane to her feet. 'Come on, girl, let's go get our baby back.'

28

Mark strolled along the cliff path, talking to Jessica, who was propped up in the carrycot. She was smiling and cooing now after her screaming fit. He stopped and gazed at the chalky white needle-like points in the bay, watching the clouds roll in and the waves break against the beach far below. He lifted the baby out and sat down on the grass, wrapping her in the knitted blanket. He pulled it up around her ears. The damp sea breeze blew through her tufts of dark hair.

'Looks like it's going to rain, Ellie. Let's hope Mummy gets here before it starts. We're all going to be together and maybe soon you'll have a brother or sister to play with. Won't that be fun?' He tickled Jessica under her chin. She grasped his finger and pulled it to her mouth.

'We're going to live with Auntie Dot. Daddy will build you sandcastles on the beach. Mummy will make picnics for us. I'll teach you to swim in the sea and Uncle Charles will take you out in his boat. We'll be a proper family. I never knew my real mummy and daddy, Ellie, but I'll make sure you grow up knowing yours.'

Jessica blinked as a drop of rain landed on her button nose.

'Oh dear, here it comes. Let's go back to the car. We can have something to eat at Auntie Dot's. Dopey Daddy left your bottle behind.' Mark got to his feet and placed Jessica back in the pram. He tucked her in as a loud voice hailed him.

'Mr Fisher, stay right where you are, please!'

Mark spun round. A police officer, carrying a loudhailer, strode out from behind a nearby rock.

'Stay away from me,' Mark yelled back. 'I've done nothing wrong, I'm going to wait in the car for my wife.' He snatched Jessica from the pram, holding her to his chest. She squirmed and started to cry. 'See what you've done,' he called. 'She was fine until *you* showed up, shouting all over the place.'

'Mr Fisher, I want you to walk slowly towards me and hand me the baby, please.'

'No! This is my daughter, Elinore. Ask my wife, she'll tell you.' Mark began to back towards the cliff edge.

'Mr Fisher, please try and stay calm. Walk forwards and hand me the baby.'

'No, go away! Find Jane, she'll tell you.'

Jessica squealed in Mark's arms.

'Please, Mr Fisher, bring the baby to me. We can help you, but first of all you have to hand her over.'

Ignoring this last command, Mark stood transfixed, his eyes on the slender figure standing beside the police officer: 'Here's Mummy, Ellie. I told you she'd come.'

* * *

Jane, heart pounding, dragged her jelly-like legs across the springy turf, eyes fixed on one thing: her precious daughter in Mark Fisher's arms, so precariously close to the edge of the cliffs. She took a deep breath and concentrated on putting one foot in front of the other.

She'd been briefed that Mark, in his confused state, was

probably waiting for her to join him. Eddie had been all for charging at Mark like a madman to gain custody of Jessica, but had been warned to stay out of sight as the situation was deemed too dangerous.

Jane knew that the short walk had to be the performance of her life. She had it in her power to convince Mark that she wanted and loved him. Sick at heart though it would make her feel to say it, it was a small price to pay.

'Mark,' she called, her voice wavering as he continued to stare at her. 'Pull the blanket tightly around her. She's feeling insecure and it's very cold up here.'

Mark nodded and tried to wrap the wriggling baby. The rain was falling heavy now and her hair was flattened to her tiny head. Almost there, Jane held out her arms. Mark took a step forward then paused.

'No, I'll hold on to her,' he said and stepped backwards, closer than ever to the cliff edge. 'She's heavy and you're too weak from being ill.'

'Mark, for God's sake be careful. You're very near the edge and the grass is slippery.' Conscious that her voice held an edge of hysteria, Jane swallowed hard, remembering the instructions to stay as calm as possible. She breathed in deeply but the air didn't seem to be getting through and her heart hammered in her ears. She prayed she wasn't going to pass out and touched Mark's arm. He looked at her, smiling.

'I knew you'd come. I kept telling Ellie you wouldn't be long.'

'Ellie?'

'Our daughter,' he replied, frowning.

As she stared at Mark, Jane was shocked to see the change in him. His face was gaunt and unshaven and his clothes hung off him. She looked into his eyes and could see the madness. Even more terrified now for Jessica's safety, she swallowed and nodded, remembering that Elinore was the name she'd chosen when she and Mark had talked about starting a family.

'I'm sorry, Mark. I'm confused and upset that you and Ellie came away without me. Everything seems so hazy. I can't remember why you left me behind. Can you tell me what happened?' Did she sound convincing enough, or would he see straight through her? Turn the tables, she thought, pretend *she* was the mad one. Let him think he was helping *her*.

'You were too ill to travel. I told you I would like to live here, but *you...*' His eyes stared straight through her, his expression one of confusion. Spittle formed at the corners of his mouth. 'You weren't ill, you were lying.' He threw back his head and laughed manically. 'You didn't want *me*, or our baby. You left us because you were shagging Eddie Mellor.'

'No, Mark, you're wrong. I wasn't. I love you and Ellie. I want us to be together, always. We'll make a home here with your family. I met your sister Dot and your brother Charles. They're nice people. I could be very happy here. *Please*, Mark, I'm begging you, take me back. I won't ever leave you again.' Jane cringed inwardly, remembering back to the time in Flanagan and Grey's stockroom last year when Mark had prophesied that she would beg him to take her back one day. How right he'd been, but never in her wildest dreams had she envisaged this nightmare.

'And you won't ever leave me again for Mellor?' Mark put his arm around her shoulders.

'Never.' Jane looked at him and gave what she hoped looked like a please-forgive-me smile. 'You're the only man for me, you always have been.' She stroked his cheek and her stomach rolled, threatening to throw up its contents at any moment. The rain battered down on them. She was soaked through and her long hair whipped in wet strands around her face. Her short dress was sticking to her, revealing her every contour, while Mark seemed oblivious to the rain.

Jessica was still now in his arms, almost as though the fight had left her. Mark hitched her up onto his shoulder. She nuzzled against his neck, sucking hungrily on her fingers.

'Will you kiss me, Jane? Then we'll go back to Dot's place to get dry. Ellie is ready for a feed now.'

Jane nodded and lifted her face, almost gagging as his hungry lips met hers and she tasted the whisky on his searching tongue. His hand slid down her back, gripping her backside.

She pulled away, forcing a smile. 'Mark, stop it, people are watching! Give Ellie to me now and we'll walk back to your car.'

As Mark turned the baby to face her, the look of recognition in her daughter's eyes was a joy to behold and the accusing *where have you been?* pout tore at Jane's heart.

'Come here, Jess, come to Mummy.' Jane snatched her daughter as Mark's face contorted with rage.

'Her name's Ellie. What sort of a fucking mother doesn't even know her child's name?'

'I'm sorry, Mark,' Jane faltered, holding tightly onto her baby. 'I feel confused and ill. Please, let's go to the car.'

'Give her to me.' Mark tried to wrestle Jessica out of her arms but Jane held on for dear life as he pulled them closer to the cliff edge.

'No, Mark! Let go,' she pleaded. 'I'll carry her. She's terrified, let go, you bastard!' She kicked out, connecting with his shins but he didn't seem to notice.

'Give her to me,' he yelled, pulling at the blanket. Jessica's cries became hysterical.

As the baby slipped from her grasp and fell to the ground, Jane dropped to her knees and at the top of her voice screamed, 'For God's sake, Eddie, help me!'

* * *

Behind a nearby rock and flanked by two burly police officers, Eddie watched the emotional scene unfolding before him with mounting anger and frustration. As Fisher put his arm around Jane and kissed her, Eddie gritted his teeth and when he squeezed Jane's arse, his anger knew no bounds.

'Get your filthy hands off my wife, you moron!' he muttered. 'I'll fucking kill him when I get my hands on him!'

'Mr Mellor, please stay calm.' One of the officers tried to placate him.

'How the fuck do you expect me to do that?' he retorted. 'He's got my wife and kid out there. He's feeling Jane's arse and you want me to stay calm?' He watched as a tug of war over the baby seemed to be taking place. When he saw Jessica fall and Jane sinking to her knees, screaming for help, Eddie had had enough.

Before the officers could stop him, he bounded forward with an angry roar and sprinted over the grass, pushing Mark away from Jane. He scooped up Jessica, who was screaming again, and held her close. Jane scrambled to her feet and moved to Eddie's side. Mark's shocked expression quickly changed to one of fury.

'Give me back my child, Mellor! This is between my wife and me.'

'She's *my* wife, you fucking cretin!' Eddie roared back. 'And this is *my* daughter.'

'How can she be your wife? Jane's married to me.' Mark darted towards Eddie, who dodged to one side, shielding Jane with his body as several officers rushed forward.

'About fucking time too!' Eddie yelled as Mark stepped towards the cliff edge.

'Mark, no!' Jane screamed, as, looking back over his shoulder in her direction, he shouted 'I love you, Jane,' and jumped. The long, ear-splitting scream faded out and was followed by total silence.

'Oh, my God!' Jane cried hysterically.

Speechless, Eddie wrapped his arms around his wife and child and drew them away from the scene.

More officers rushed forward with blankets and threw them around the young couple and Jessica, leading them towards a waiting car.

'We'll get you straight to hospital, have Jane and the baby checked over,' one officer told Eddie. 'We'll take statements and then fly you all home.'

'Jess is hungry and cold,' Jane said. 'She's very pale and quiet.'

'I'm not bloody surprised,' Eddie said. 'Poor little mite, she's used to a peaceful life. I don't think she's injured from the fall. She seemed to bounce on the grass.'

'God, Ed, she could have gone over the cliff with him,' Jane sobbed. 'Do you think he's dead?'

'Shush, sweetheart. Don't think about it, we'll find out soon enough.'

* * *

Dorothy and Charles identified Mark's body, Dorothy breaking down at the sight of her younger brother's bruised and battered face.

'Poor Mark. We failed him badly, Charles, all of us, and that includes our father,' Dorothy sobbed.

'Well, if anyone's to blame, Dot, it should be me. When I think back now I should have spotted the signs. He was very clever at hiding things. I look at the facts and a lot of what he told us didn't add up, yet I still didn't question it.'

'I want him buried on the island with Father,' Dorothy said.

'Is that wise?' Charles frowned.

'Yes, and I don't give a hoot about the gossips. Most of them

are dead from around that time anyhow and those that aren't –
well, tough!'

'Okay, Dot,' Charles said. 'We'll make the funeral arrangements and let his friends, Tony and Vicky, know. Do you think
we should allow Maude Fisher to come?'

'I'd rather we didn't. Oh, I know she brought Mark up, but
she also caused a lot of his problems. No wonder his head was
screwed up. No, we'll have a close family and friends' affair.'

* * *

Jane stroked her baby's cheek and smiled as Jessica snuffled
contentedly and blew bubbles in her sleep. Loathe to let her
daughter out of her arms for any longer than was necessary, she
looked up as Sammy entered the bedroom and plonked herself
down on the big brass bed.

'How is she?' Sammy lounged back on the pillows beside
Jane.

'She's absolutely fine, Sam. Thank God!'

'And you? You still look very pale to me. Eddie told Roy that
you're not sleeping too well.'

Jane sighed. 'I'm terrified to close my eyes. I keep thinking
that unless I watch her like a hawk, someone will take her again.
Not only that, on the odd occasion I *do* nod off, I hear Mark's
scream as he jumped. It was horrendous and the very last word
he said was "Jane". He put us through hell, but I didn't want
that to happen – I just wanted Jessica back safe and sound.
When I was with Mark on the cliff tops, I could see the
madness in his eyes and I was terrified. He really, really
believed that Jess was Elinore, *our* child. He needed help so
badly. I'm sure he would never knowingly hurt Jess, but I
couldn't take any chances, that's why I screamed for Ed when
she fell. Mark might not have jumped if I hadn't panicked. I
killed him.'

'No, you didn't.' Sammy put her arms around Jane and hugged her. 'It was his choice to jump. There were enough eyewitnesses to back that up. They say he didn't suffer, his neck was broken and he died instantly.'

'I know, but I feel so bad about the whole thing. I'm responsible for sending him round the twist.'

'No, Jane! You finishing with him was only one of many things that led to his breakdown. You mustn't let Ed hear you say anything like this. He thinks Mark's done more than enough damage. Roy said he's struggling to get his head around seeing Mark kissing you. He told Roy he would have willingly pushed him over the cliffs there and then.'

'He keeps going on about it.' Jane sighed. 'He's almost obsessed by it. But I would have promised Mark anything to get Jess back, even though it sickened me to kiss him. At the end of the day I expected the police to come to my rescue, but to Ed, stuck behind that rock, it must have looked as though I was selling my soul to the devil by kissing Mark.'

'Ed will come to terms with it eventually,' Sammy said. 'It's been an awful time for both of you. You have to try and put it behind you and move on. Roy and Ed have agreed to Frank's suggestion of a minder staying with us when they're away on tour in the future. To be honest, I'd feel happier about it, especially now that Cantello junior is on his way.' Sammy patted her tummy.

'You're not supposed to be counting your chickens until after tomorrow when you've seen the doctor.' Jane smiled through her tears, cheered by Sammy's excitement.

'Well, it's bound to be yes! I'm three weeks late, throwing up for England and we've been trying like crazy to get pregnant so I must be.'

'I'm inclined to agree,' Jane said.

'Go and take a soak and I'll cuddle Jess here on the bed for you,' Sammy suggested as Jane hesitated. 'Go on. What can possibly happen? *I'm* here, Eddie and Roy are in the music room with Tim and Phil, Pat's across the way reading Jonny a bedtime story. Go on, Jane, a warm bath will do you good.'

'Thanks, Sam. I know I've got to learn to relax again. A bath would be such a treat. I've only taken quick showers lately because I don't like being away from her.' She kissed Jessica's downy head and handed her to Sammy. 'I'll nip to the music room and put in an order for drinks all round. I can sip mine while I'm soaking.'

'That's the idea. But make mine an orange juice, please. Alcohol knocks me sick at the moment.'

* * *

Eddie looked up as Jane entered the music room. 'You okay, darling? Where's Jess?' He put his arm around her and squeezed her affectionately.

'On our bed with Sammy. She's looking after her while I take a bath.'

'That's good. You need a little break and Sammy needs to put some practice in.'

Roy puffed up with pride at Eddie's comment and winked at Jane. 'You okay, sweetheart?'

'Fine thanks, Roy. How about *you* getting a bit of practice in? Jess needs changing.'

He screwed up his face. 'I'll leave that sort of thing to Sammy. Anyway, I've done my bit.'

'So it would appear.' Jane raised an amused eyebrow. 'Sammy's even refused a drink tonight. So, Ed, cider for me and Pat and orange juice for Sammy, please.'

'We'll finish what we're doing and then your wish is my command. Be with you in five minutes.' He dropped a kiss on her lips.

* * *

'She'll get there, mate.' Roy patted Eddie's shoulder. Tim and Phil voiced their agreement.

'I know she will, I just hate seeing her so uptight. She was so happy and contented before Fisher took Jess.'

'Well, it's done with now, Ed. The worst is over and behind you. Life can only get better for you both,' Phil said, putting down his guitar.

Roy nodded and handed round cigarettes. He held his lighter out to Eddie and said, 'It's strange though, both yours and Jane's exes are dead and they were so young, too.'

'Yeah!' Eddie nodded. 'It just goes to show that it's a good job you don't know what's round the corner. Like you say, Phil, the worst is over – neither of them are a threat to Jane and me any more.'

29

Sammy strolled into the kitchen, threw down her keys and burst into tears.

Roy sprang immediately to her side. 'What is it, Sam? Oh, sweetheart, I'm sorry. Don't cry, there's all the time in the world.' He drew her into his arms and planted a kiss on her lips. 'We'll try a bit harder. We've got our wedding to look forward to. That'll take your mind off babies for a while.'

Sammy smiled at him through her tears. 'We don't need to try harder, Super Stud! We did it. You're gonna be a daddy, Roy. I'm crying because I'm so bloody happy.'

'Women!' Tim muttered to Eddie, raising an amused eyebrow.

'Yes!' Roy yelled, punching the air. 'Oh, yes! I love you, woman. When?'

'Middle of May,' Sammy said, laughing at his excitement.

'The month before Jessie's first birthday,' Eddie said. 'They'll grow up together, like we did. Well done, mate, and you too of course, Sam.'

'Sammy, I'm so pleased for you,' Jane said, sniffing back tears of joy.

Pat threw her arms around her stepsister. 'Well done, Sam, and you too, Roy. I feel quite left out, but I'm not ready for a baby yet. Maybe I'll go for a career change instead.'

'You could give up work and baby me,' Tim suggested, slinging his arm around her waist. 'I'd like us to spend more time together. If you changed your career, we'd probably see less of one another.'

'We'll see. Who knows what's in store? This last year has been like nothing I could ever imagine, not in my wildest dreams,' Pat said. 'It's been a bit of a bumpy ride at times, especially this last month.'

'You can say that again,' Eddie said as the others nodded their agreement. 'It's not a month I'd like to repeat in a hurry.'

'Coffee, everybody?' Jane got up to fill the kettle as the phone rang.

Tim strolled across the kitchen to answer. 'Oh hi, Frank! Yes, we're all here except Phil. Fucking hell! That's fantastic, brilliant. Yes, I'll tell them. See you soon.'

He turned to face the others, who were staring at him with shocked expressions.

'What?' Eddie and Roy chorused curiously. Unlike the rest of The Raiders, Tim hardly ever swore. It must be something serious.

'"You Give Me That Feeling" is number one in the States,' he announced, grinning broadly.

'Fucking hell!' Roy echoed Tim's expletive. 'Forget the bloody coffee, Jane! Get the champers out. We've two things to celebrate now.'

'Christ, I don't believe it!' Eddie exclaimed. 'Are you sure you heard right, Tim?'

'Course I did. Right, that's it; I'm going to order my dream car. E-Type Jag Convertible, here I come.'

* * *

The Raiders released their third single, 'The Girl's in Love with Me', the second week of December 1965. They were beaten by The Beatles' 'Day Tripper' in the race for the Christmas number one.

'This year, lads,' Frank announced in January, following the New Year break. 'You'll do it Christmas '66 or I'll eat my best hat!' He took a gold cigarette lighter from the top drawer of his desk and lit a cigar, contentedly puffing circles of smoke into the air. His secretary Helen waltzed in with a tray of coffee and flashed him her secret lover's smile. He winked at her as she closed the door and left him to his meeting with Roy and Eddie.

'I've been having a good think over Christmas,' Frank said. 'Those tapes you brought me a few months ago from that jam session you had with young Carl... Have you ever considered having him on board as a permanent band member?' He lounged back on his swivel chair in his plush Manchester office, looking proudly round. The ivory-painted walls were adorned with silver-framed photographs of his stable of artistes, past and present. He drew on his cigar, waiting for their reaction.

Roy spoke first. 'That's bloody amazing, because as a group we've been thinking exactly that. It gave us a whole new sound and we loved it! Carl and his girl are coming for dinner tonight, so we'll drop it on his toes, see what he thinks. He's not a very confident lad, but he's a bloody good piano player with a real boogie style. With him on board, we could really let rip with our rock 'n' roll numbers.'

'Well, in that case, let's haul him in for a meeting. You lot will soon boost his confidence. Run the suggestion by him tonight, let me know tomorrow.'

* * *

'We've a bit of a favour to ask you, Carl,' Roy began, rolling an after-dinner joint. 'How would you like to be our keyboard player? Our agent, Frank, was knocked out with the jam session tapes we gave him.'

'You didn't let your agent hear them, surely?' Carl stuttered, his face flushing a deep crimson.

'Oh, we did,' Eddie said, grinning, 'and he loved 'em. So, how about it, Carl, wanna be a Raider? You'll have to give up your job with F and G's, of course.'

'I can't believe I'm hearing right.' Carl looked stunned as he gazed at Roy and Eddie's smiling faces. 'Me, a Raider? What about my hair? It's always such a mess.'

'I'll sort it out for you, Carl,' Cathy said. 'Just tell them yes, for God's sake!'

'Can you cope with a musician for a boyfriend, Cath?' Roy asked. 'Angie couldn't.'

'I'm not Angie,' she said firmly. 'And if it's what Carl wants, I'm right behind him.'

'Good on you, girl!' Eddie hugged her affectionately.

* * *

An ecstatic Carl joined The Raiders during the last week of January. A short tour was organised, along with TV appearances and newspaper interviews, to help launch him gently into the world of stardom.

Cathy, proudly looking after the boy she adored, taught Carl how to blow-dry his hair. She also dyed it a rich auburn and encouraged him to grow it longer.

Jane thought the style and colour suited Carl so much better and told him so.

'You look lovely, Carl, quite the good-looking young man.'

'Thank you, Jane.' He blushed as Roy and Eddie whistled when he strolled into the kitchen. He was proving to be a superb pianist and took his role with the group seriously. The

Raiders were proud to have him onboard and Carl, likewise, was equally proud to be a Raider.

Life at Hanover's Lodge was good. Sammy and Roy were now happily married and looking forward to their new baby. Jessica was fast growing and trying to crawl. Jonny was chatty and happy, and Jane and Eddie were working hard to put Jessica's kidnapping behind them.

Pat and Tim moved into a new house in the smart suburb of Wilmslow and Tim proudly took delivery of his dream car. After much persuasion on Tim's part, Pat gave up her job to spend more time with him. It was a move she had no regrets about doing and it meant she was now free to accompany him on tour.

Jane took her driving test and passed first time.

'Well done, babe.' Eddie handed her the keys to his beloved Beetle. He'd treated himself to a Mercedes Roadster, but couldn't bear to part with his first car. 'When I'm mega rich, I'll buy you a Porsche and myself a red Ferrari.'

* * *

During the month of March, the group toured America accompanied by Cathy and Pat. Jane, the kids and a heavily pregnant Sammy waved them off at a fan-besieged Ringway Airport, before making their getaway back to a peaceful, but very empty, Hanover's Lodge.

'Fancy having to have a bloody police escort back to our car,' Jane grumbled, helping Sammy out of the passenger seat. 'We can't do anything normal any more.'

'Well, it won't be forever,' Sammy said, struggling to her feet. 'The fame will be short-lived, so they might as well make the most of it while they can and earn some decent money. What time's Harry Bennett due? Roy said he'd be here when we got back from the airport, but there's no strange car on the drive.'

Harry Bennett, Frank James's appointed minder, was due to arrive that day to look after them during Roy and Eddie's absence and they'd made up the bed settee for him in the music room.

'Here he is now.' Jane squinted down the lane as a vehicle came into view and the driver parked discreetly beneath the trees.

'Thank God for that,' Sammy muttered, hitching her bump into a more comfortable position. 'I can relax now. Though I suppose, taking all things into account, nothing like Jess's kidnapping is likely to happen again. That was Mark's illness, not because he was a deranged fan out for money.'

'Well, I'd rather not take any chances,' Jane said. 'And Harry looks the part if any fans wander up the lane. One look at the size of him, with his boxer's nose and cauliflower ear, and they'd run a mile.'

'Morning, ladies,' Harry called as he lumbered towards them, holdall in hand. 'Did the lads get off all right?'

'Morning, Harry,' Jane said as Jonny squealed with delight, ran towards the big man and wrapped himself around his legs. 'They did, thanks, but it was chaos at the airport, total chaos.'

'Ah well, make the most of it. I've seen stars come and go like you'd never believe. You have to take the rough with the smooth while they're at the top. Now then, young man.' Harry placed his bag down on the ground and swung a giggling Jonny into the air. 'I'll put my stuff inside and then we'll have a game of football, give Mummy and Auntie Sammy a bit of peace.'

'Have a coffee first, Harry,' Jane said, leading the way indoors. 'Show Harry to his room, Jonny, while I brew up.'

'Oh no, excuse me, please!' Sammy's hand flew to her mouth and she pushed past them, shutting herself in the down-stairs cloakroom.

'Still chucking up?' Harry frowned. 'Poor kid, my missus was only sick for the first few weeks with our two. Right, young Jonny, lead the way to my room.' He smiled down at the little boy, who was pulling on his hand. 'He's eager for his game of footy, aren't you?'

'Thought this morning sickness was supposed to last for three months,' Sammy complained, strolling back into the kitchen. 'I'm okay after midday, but I dread waking up some mornings.'

'You're just unlucky,' Jane said, handing Sammy a mug of tea and a plate of dry toast, her second breakfast that morning. 'Here, see if you can keep this lot down. I hope Pat and Cathy keep their eyes on Eddie and Roy while they're in the States.'

'They will and they'll phone us as soon as they can,' Sammy said. 'My main worry's drugs, I hope the lads don't get caught with anything on them. I told Roy not to take anything with him because of going through Customs. He's trying so hard to give up. Do you know, I could throttle Mac for getting him started in the first place.'

'Roy's doing his best, Sam. At least he's not doing heroin like Mac was. Eddie told me he's stopped taking speed now before a gig. All you can do is support him through it and thank your lucky stars that he didn't get on to the hard stuff. That would have been a disaster, both for *you* and the group, not to mention your new baby.'

'Roy and I are going to have to think seriously about leaving here when this baby arrives,' Sammy said, changing the subject. 'There won't be enough room.'

'We'll be okay for a few months. It can sleep in your room while it's tiny but you won't want it in with you when it's older. It'll cramp your style and you know what you and Roy are like,' Jane teased.

'*Were* like, you mean.' Sammy sighed. 'Couldn't manage it if I tried. I look and feel like a beached whale! Roy said he's enjoying the rest, but I think he's saying that to be nice to me. Hope he doesn't go astray out there.'

'He won't, not Roy. He's devoted to you, always has been. Come on, let's visit our mums and then go shopping. Can we leave Jonny with you, Harry?' Jane said as Harry, with Jonny on his shoulders, appeared in the kitchen. 'He hates shopping.'

'Of course,' Harry replied as Jonny screwed up his face. 'Shopping's not a man's thing, is it, lad? We'll play footy for a while. I'll take him fishing for tiddlers in that little pond out in the woods later.'

'That's very kind of you,' Jane said. 'His fishing net's in the laundry room and you'll find a couple of jam jars for the catch in there, too. But no frogs, please, or we'll have Sammy giving birth tonight!'

'Understood,' Harry said as Jane pulled a shuddering Sammy to her feet. 'Get any bigger, Sammy,' he added, 'and we'll need a crane to hoist you up.'

* * *

'Christ, I'm pissed off with this!' Roy gazed out of the top-floor window of the Plaza Hotel in the centre of New York, at the mob of screaming girls below. 'We'll get ripped to shreds if we go out there.'

'Yeah, it's not exactly how we dreamt our first trip to America would be all those years ago,' Eddie said. 'I wanted a wander round some of the more obscure record stores. And there's no way we can come to New York and not visit The Brill Building. But short of wearing a disguise, we haven't a chance of moving from here.'

Tim looked up from his *Playboy* magazine and smiled. 'Good job the suite's nice,' he said from the confines of a plush leather sofa, one of three grouped around a low glass-topped table. The tastefully furnished Penthouse Suite, with its striking colour scheme of rich brown, cream and turquoise, was airy and spacious with a well-equipped bar for their personal use.

'There's the press conference this afternoon,' Tim continued. 'We'll ask Frank to help us get out after that, or we'll end up seeing bugger all at this rate.'

'If I don't get a shag soon, I'm gonna go mad!' Phil groaned. 'Hundreds of crazy women out there and not one of 'em looks over sixteen. All bloody jailbait!'

'In some states in America, it's legal at fourteen and under,' Carl chipped in. 'Jerry Lee's wife Myra was only thirteen when he married her.'

'But not in New York,' Eddie pointed out. 'Don't even think about it, Phil.'

'I'm gonna have to pay for it then,' Phil grumbled. 'I've never had to pay for sex in my life, it's always been handed to me on a plate.'

'Here.' Tim threw the *Playboy* magazine at him. 'Stop being so bloody tetchy. Sod off into the bog with that if you're desperate but don't stick the pages together!'

'Oh, it's okay for you and Carl,' Phil said. '*You're* not going short, you've got Pat and Cathy with you. Not only that, they're the only ones who can go outside without being recognised.'

'Christ Almighty, Phil, you knew it wasn't going to be all fun and games,' Eddie said. 'You shouldn't begrudge Cathy and Pat a trip to the hairdresser's. They're as sick of being cooped up as we are.'

'If this is how you're going to be all tour, I'll bloody make sure Frank gets a regular woman lined up for you after each show!' Roy said. 'Me and Ed are in the same boat but do you here *us* complaining?'

'Sorry.' Phil grinned sheepishly. 'I'm beginning to see sense in what you lot are always telling me: "Get yourself a proper girlfriend, Phil." If I had one, she could come on tour with me and relieve the tension a bit. Maybe I'll look into it when I get back.'

'Anyone in mind?' Eddie asked curiously.

'Yeah, I have,' he replied. 'I've been keeping in touch with that little redhead in Nottingham, Laura Kennedy. You remember her, has a look of Jane Asher. She's always waiting for me backstage when we play the area. Reckons she loves me – and she's very obliging. Best blow jobs I've had in my life!'

Roy grinned. 'What you waiting for? Get on the phone and ask her to fly out, give us all a bit of peace. Frank will arrange it for you.'

'She's not on the bloody phone.' Phil sighed. 'I have to call her at her grandma's. Don't suppose for one minute that her folks will allow her to come out here and join me – she's still at school.'

'School?' Eddie frowned. 'How old is she?'

'Sixteen,' Phil replied.

'Well, how long have you been giving her one?' Roy asked. 'We haven't played Nottingham for a few months and she was around long before that.'

'Since before Ed rejoined,' Phil admitted sheepishly. 'But I didn't know she was only fourteen then. She told me she was seventeen *and* she looked it.'

'Jesus Christ, Phil!' Roy shook his head in despair. 'You'll get yourself hung, drawn and quartered if that makes the headlines.'

'Pot and kettle, Roy,' Eddie reminded him.

'Yeah, but Sammy was almost sixteen,' Roy said.

'Well anyway,' Phil continued, 'whatever happens over here will be my last fling. When I get back, I'll be asking Laura to be my girl. I'm gonna do right by her and stick a ring on her finger. An engagement ring, that is. One step at a time.'

* * *

Sammy answered the phone as Jane was putting Jessica to bed and Harry was reading a bedtime story to a very tired Jonny.

'Hi, Roy! Oh, it's great to hear from you. I miss you, too. I feel so fat and fed up. How's it going? When do you do *The Ed Sullivan Show*? Oh, of course, Sunday, when else? It's like the Palladium here, the big show of the weekend. We see the daily newspaper and TV coverage of the tour, but it's not as good as being with you.' Sammy listened intently as Roy told her the group's itinerary for the next couple of weeks.

They were travelling by train to Washington DC on Monday, following *The Ed Sullivan Show*, to perform two concerts at the Washington Coliseum and to guest on a radio show. Then the entourage would be flying to Miami for a further five shows and another two TV appearances.

Roy promised to call again the following day and asked Sammy to get Jane for Eddie. Jane flew downstairs, snatched the receiver from Sammy's outstretched hand and burst into tears as she heard Eddie's voice.

'No, I'm fine, Ed, honestly. Yes, the kids are great and Harry is here looking after us. Don't worry. I'm just missing you so much, that's all. I love you too.'

Sammy put the kettle on while Jane nodded and oohed and aahed.

'Have a wonderful tour. Be safe, look after one another,' Jane finished and hung up. She turned to Sammy. 'Well, there's a turn up for the books.'

'What?' Sammy said, spooning coffee into three mugs. 'I presume Harry will want one?'

'I expect so. Phil's getting engaged when he gets back.'

'Engaged? Phil?' Sammy's mouth fell open. 'Who the hell to?'

'Some girl called Laura from Nottingham.'

'Bloody hell! Is she pregnant?'

'Ed didn't say, but what he did say was she's still at school,' Jane replied.

'The dark horse! Wait until he comes home. But I'll believe it when I see it.'

'Me too. Maybe he's turning over a new leaf.'

30

APRIL 1966

Eddie replaced the receiver and looked up as Jane walked into the room.

'That's those two monkeys settled for the night.' She kicked off her shoes and flopped down on one of the Chesterfields. 'Who was on the phone?'

'Carl. He's coming over with Cathy. Wants to talk privately about something. Sounded a bit mysterious.' He poured two glasses of red wine, handed one to Jane and sat down beside her. 'I hope he doesn't want out of the group.'

'I doubt it; Carl loves being a Raider,' Jane said. 'He really enjoyed the American tour. Cathy said he's not stopped talking about it.'

'Well, whatever it is, he sounded very agitated.'

* * *

Carl and Cathy arrived at seven thirty. Eddie invited them into the lounge and offered drinks.

'Sit down.' Jane patted the space beside her. 'So, what's up with you two? You look really worried.'

Cathy looked as though she hadn't slept a wink for days and Carl stared at Jane with such a haunted expression that her stomach turned over.

'Carl, you look awful. Has something happened?'

He cleared his throat. 'Cathy has something to tell you. You're not going to like it, but please, let her finish before you say anything.'

Cathy took a deep breath. 'I don't know where to start,' she mumbled nervously and took a sip of wine.

Jane looked at Eddie, who shrugged.

'Try the beginning,' he suggested.

Cathy opened her handbag and took out a packet of photographs. 'This is the film I finished at Jessica's christening,' she began. 'I only got round to having it developed this week, along with the ones I took on the American tour.' Her hands shook as she handed Jane several colour photos of Jonny. Jane glanced at them and then passed them to Eddie.

'Pictures of Jonny, and they're very good,' Eddie said, frowning. 'So, what's the problem?'

'Angie took those photos, using my camera, before she went off to Wales,' Cathy explained. 'She also took these.' She handed two more photos to Jane, one showing a smiling Angie with Richard Price and one of Richard with Jonny on his shoulders.

Jane studied the photographs, colour draining from her face as realisation dawned. Richard and Jonny were living images: dark curly hair, green eyes, even matching dimples. Jane looked from Eddie to Cathy in horror. Cathy was sobbing now, her head in her hands. Eddie snatched the photographs from Jane. He stared at them, a look of disbelief on his face.

'Cathy, are you telling us what I think you're telling us?' Jane's voice came out in a squeak.

Carl placed an arm around Cathy's shaking shoulders and nodded slowly.

'Tell them what you told me. You can't keep it to yourself any longer, they've a right to know the truth.'

Her voice barely audible, Cathy turned to face Eddie and began her tale.

'When you and Angie split up over you seeing Jane, Richard took her out for a meal to cheer her up and they slept together. Then the following week, she slept with you. She asked me never to tell you that she'd been with Richard.'

Cathy paused to wipe her eyes. 'A few weeks later, Angie told me she might be pregnant but wasn't sure who the father was. I said she had to tell you and Richard, but she was too scared.'

Eddie shook his head, lost for words as Cathy continued.

'By that time Richard was finalising his wedding plans. Angie said she couldn't destroy his future.'

'Oh, that's fucking rich!' Eddie retorted. 'So instead she destroyed mine and Jane's.'

'That wasn't her original intention, Ed, but when she tracked you down and found you in bed with Jane she was so angry and jealous that she decided you *would* be the father, whether you were or not. As soon as Jonny was born she said she thought he looked more like Richard than you, but she still wouldn't tell you.

'It was only after she went back to work at the salon that she realised Richard was alone, his marriage hadn't worked out. When they got together, Angie eventually told Richard that Jonny was his. He already had his suspicions, because of the likeness to himself as a child, but he was waiting for her to say something.

'When she did, he insisted she tell you the truth. For all her faults Angie just couldn't bring herself to do it; you doted on Jonny. As you know, the weekend the two of them went to Wales, they were celebrating getting engaged and the fact that they were expecting another baby.' Cathy took a deep shuddering breath and blew her nose before continuing.

'The weekend Angie left Jonny with me, she told me they were going to tell you, her parents and Richard's family about the baby and Jonny when they got back, but of course they never arrived home. You and Jane took on the responsibility of raising Jonny and I kept my mouth shut because I didn't know what else to do.

'I pushed it to the back of my mind. I swore I'd take the secret to the grave. I told myself it would do no good to upset everyone. Jonny was happy and settled with you two. Then I had the photographs developed. Carl was looking through them and he passed comment on Richard being the image of Jonny. He thought he was Angie's brother, Jonny's uncle. But of course Angie had no brothers. I was sure it was only a matter of time before Carl would innocently mention the likeness to you, so I told him the truth there and then.'

* * *

Cathy broke down completely at this point, relieved to get the terrible secret off her chest once and for all. She told Eddie and Jane that the afternoon she'd seen Jonny at the flat in Wilmslow, she'd realised then how much like Richard he'd become and she felt she'd given the game away by dashing off so suddenly.

Eddie and Jane, sitting side by side, tried to come to terms with what they'd just been told. Silent tears ran unchecked down Jane's cheeks and she turned to look at Eddie. All his anger gone, she could see he was equally shocked.

'Ed.' She shook his shoulder gently. 'Darling, please say something.'

He turned to look at her and Jane was devastated to see such utter despair in his blue eyes for the second time in less than six months. He shook his head silently, as though words would choke him.

Cathy stood up. 'We'd better go home, I can't stay here. I've wrecked your lives – I should have kept my big mouth shut.'

Carl looked at the three of them and shook his head. 'Jane, I persuaded Cathy to tell you the truth. I felt you had a right to know. It would have been wrong to keep it to ourselves forever. Being denied the truth about his parents helped destroy Mark Fisher. God forbid the same should happen to Jonny.'

Jane nodded slowly. 'Carl, you're right, but please, just go home now. Eddie and I need to be alone. I'll call you tomorrow sometime. Don't discuss this with anyone else for the time being.'

'We won't,' Carl assured her as she showed them out and shut the door. She walked back into the lounge to Eddie and put her arms around him. He leant against her shoulder and cried heartbrokenly. She led him upstairs to their room. They lay locked in one another's arms all night.

* * *

Jane rose early to attend to Jessica, leaving Eddie dozing fitfully. Jonny was still sleeping peacefully. She plucked the baby from her cot and carried her downstairs.

Sammy, cool blue eyes in a face whiter than the cotton bathrobe she was wearing, was sitting at the kitchen table, drinking tea. She poured Jane a cup and handed it to her.

'I'm sorry, did my puking wake you?'

Jane shook her head. 'I've hardly slept a wink all night.' She fastened Jessica into her high chair and gave her a rusk to chew on.

'You were in bed early, before we came home anyway. Why on earth didn't you sleep?'

Jane's eyes filled with tears. She wiped them away on her dressing-gown sleeve.

'Jane, what is it?'

'Something terrible's happened, I can't quite believe it.' She told Sammy the events of the previous night.

Cathy's packet of photographs lay on the kitchen table where she'd left them. Jane picked out the one of Jonny and Richard and handed it to Sammy.

'Oh God, yes. Peas in a pod! You couldn't deny *that*, could you? It doesn't really surprise me, Jane. Right from the beginning, I said it might not be Ed's baby.'

'Yes, you did,' Jane nodded, remembering. 'But what could we do? Angie convinced Ed he was responsible. Dear God, here I am bringing up a child that's neither of our own flesh and blood. What a cow to do that, just because she didn't want to lose Ed to me! And poor little Jonny, he doesn't deserve this.'

Roy padded barefoot into the kitchen, put his hands on Sammy's shoulders and kissed the top of her head. 'You all right, sweetheart? Been sick again?'

'Yeah, but it'll pass by lunchtime.'

'Morning, Jane. Why the tears? Had a barney with Ed?'

She shook her head. Without saying a word, Sammy handed him the photo of Angie and Richard. He stared at it for a long moment and looked up at Jane with a puzzled expression.

'No!' His eyes opened wide as the penny dropped. 'You have to be joking?'

Jane shook her head. 'Carl and Cathy came over last night and told us.'

'Fucking hell! How's Ed taken it?'

'He's devastated. Hardly slept a wink. He's dozing now but I don't suppose he'll sleep for long. God, as if we haven't had enough to cope with these last few months.'

'What do you think he'll do?' Sammy frowned. 'I mean, this

is a little boy's life and future we're talking about; Jonny doesn't know anything else. As far as he's concerned, you're his mummy and Ed's his daddy. You really can't do anything other than carry on as normal, can you?'

'Well, that's all we can do. When Eddie's got himself together we'll have to sit down and talk about it properly. It was such a horrendous shock last night, we both went to pieces. Can you two do me a big favour? Will you take Jonny out for a few hours so we can have some time to talk? You could drop him off at Ed's mum's place later. Tell her we've had a bad night with Jessie teething or something, we're having a lie-in and we'll pick him up at tea time.'

'Of course we will.' Sammy nodded. 'I'll go and get ready. Shall I see if Jonny's awake and send him down for breakfast?'

'Please,' Jane said.

*   *   *

By the time Eddie surfaced, Roy and Sammy had taken Jonny out. Jane had dressed him in one of his trendy outfits and brushed his curls. He looked lovely, she thought, and her heart went out to him. No matter how painful the whole thing was, the little boy's well-being was the main thing that counted now. She made Eddie a mug of coffee and handed it to him.

'Sit down, Ed. Could you manage some toast?'

'I think it would choke me. I can't begin to describe how I feel. This is almost as bad as what I went through when Jess was missing. I never thought I'd feel such pain again.' He gazed around the kitchen. 'Where is he?'

'Out with Sammy and Roy. They'll drop him off at your mum's later and I said we'd pick him up. I thought it best while we get our heads together. Ed, one thing we have to remember, none of this is Jonny's fault.'

'I know that, Jane, and I don't love him any less, believe me.

Should I arrange to have blood tests done? Do you think there's any point?'

'No, he's so like Richard. I don't think there's any doubt, do you? It wouldn't be fair to subject him to needles and tests when your own eyes and Cathy's word can tell you the truth. What we need to decide is what we intend doing in the future. Do we tell him, or do we keep it to ourselves?'

'God knows. What did Sammy and Roy have to say?'

'They were absolutely stunned,' she replied.

Eddie nodded and scratched his chin thoughtfully. 'I think we'll sit down with them tonight and ask what they would do. We could go over it again and again ourselves. Two extra heads might help us think things through more clearly.'

Jane nodded. 'Good idea. Right, I'm going to bath smelly Jessie. Do you want to come and help me?'

'I'll carry her upstairs for you. Smelly or not, Jess, at least I know you're all mine.' He tickled his daughter, who gave him a delightful toothy grin through the sticky rusk plastering her face.

Eddie put his arms round Jane and held her close. 'If only we could turn back the clock and the Angie thing had never happened. It just seems to go on and on, almost like she's haunting me.'

'Don't be silly, Ed. We'll get through this like we got through everything else,' Jane said reassuringly.

* * *

Later that night Roy handed out drinks as he, Sammy, Jane and Eddie sat down in the lounge.

'How are you feeling now, mate?' He patted Eddie on the shoulder.

'Shell-shocked,' Eddie replied and took a sip of whisky. 'I keep thinking I must have dreamt it – and wishing I had.'

'I don't know how any woman can do what Angie did,' Sammy said. 'Trapping you into marrying her because she was jealous of Jane. Did she never once stop to think about the long-term consequences for poor Jonny?'

'That was typical of Angie, I'm afraid,' Eddie replied. 'Right now, I feel so angry inside that if she wasn't already dead, I would fucking well strangle her myself! When I think back, I should have realised the baby wasn't mine. I'd hardly seen her the month she got caught.

'We weren't even getting on very well, never mind anything else. And Jonny... Well, he looks nothing at all like me, or *her* for that matter. All right, she had curly hair and bluey-green eyes, but he's got thick dark curls and vivid green eyes.' He shook his head in despair. 'Why didn't I see it? Am I stupid or blind or something?'

'You trusted her when she told you the baby was yours. Don't blame yourself for this.' Jane touched his arm comfortingly. 'None of us really saw Richard close enough to take much notice of his features. He was usually sitting in his car and nearly always wore dark glasses. I couldn't have told you the colour of his eyes if my life depended on it.'

Eddie shrugged helplessly. 'I feel such a fool. She really took me for a ride. And Cathy, why the hell didn't she say something sooner? All this time and she never said a word, never even gave me a fucking clue!'

'You can't blame Cathy,' Jane said. 'It must have been awful for her, keeping something like this to herself. And remember, she did tell you last year that she tried to persuade Angie not to marry you.'

'I've just thought of something else,' Eddie said. 'Richard had parents, a family. Cathy said that Angie was going to tell them about Jonny. Somewhere out there he has grandparents and probably aunts and uncles. If this gets out, we could lose him. They might fight for custody, and there's also Angie's parents and sister. They didn't particularly want him after she died, but they might now if they find out I'm not his real father. Jesus, what a fucking mess! As long as I live, I'll never be able to forgive Angie for this.'

'We need to be calm, keep our wits about us,' Roy advised. 'No one knows except us, Carl and Cathy, and *she's* kept it to herself all this time. I doubt she'll say a word to anyone.'

'I asked her not to,' Jane said.

Roy nodded. 'Right, well in that case I think we need a proper meeting. Pat and Tim should be told. We're all so close, they'll know something's wrong immediately we see them. I'll phone them now, and call Carl and Cathy as well, get them to drive over. If we sort this out tonight, we can put it behind us and learn to live with it. You two are absolutely sure you want to continue bringing up Jonny as your own?'

'I couldn't do anything else, I think the world of him,' Eddie replied. 'What about you, Jane?'

'Yes, of course I do. He's our little boy, I couldn't be without him now.'

Roy strode into the kitchen to make his calls. Eddie topped up their drinks and sat down on the Chesterfield beside Jane.

'Will someone help me up, please,' Sammy groaned. 'I'll go to the loo before the others arrive. The little bugger's playing football with my bladder again!'

Eddie heaved her to her feet. 'Don't knock it. At least you and Roy know whose baby it is.'

'Very true,' Sammy said, waddling out of the lounge.

Eddie took Jane's hand. 'I don't half lumber you with some bloody problems, Jane.'

'I know.' She smiled and stroked his cheek. 'But I wouldn't have it any other way.'

'You could have had such a normal, peaceful life with Mark Fisher,' he continued, holding her close. 'He might not have lost the plot if you'd stayed with him.'

'Eddie, don't say that. I hate being reminded of him and I wouldn't ever swap what we've got for normal.'

Sammy laughed as she lumbered back into the lounge. 'Normal, huh! From the moment Jane clapped eyes on you, she wanted *you* and only you and that's why she's here now. A normal lifestyle would never have suited her.'

Roy strolled back into the lounge. 'They're coming over and picking up Carl and Cathy on the way.' He topped up their glasses as they waited for the others to arrive.

Jane jumped up as the doorbell rang. She let in a worried-looking Pat and Tim, accompanied by Carl and Cathy, who was in tears.

'What's happened?' Tim blurted. 'Cathy keeps saying it's all her fault. What's she done, for God's sake?'

'Go and sit in the lounge and I'll get you all a drink,' Jane said and busied herself in the kitchen pouring glasses of red wine. She handed round the drinks as everyone found a seat.

Eddie explained to Tim and Pat what had happened the night before. They were as shocked as everyone else had been.

'I don't believe it!' Tim exclaimed as he looked at the photos Jane handed him.

'He's a dead ringer.' Pat shook her head in disbelief. 'Oh, Ed, why didn't any of us see it?'

'Right!' Roy took charge of the situation and addressed Cathy. 'We gather Richard had a family?'

She nodded. 'Yes, parents and two younger sisters. But I'm absolutely certain they had no inkling that Jonny was his son. The family was at the funerals and not a word was said.'

'Okay. But that means Jonny has family on both his mother and father's side. Now if this ever leaks out, Eddie and Jane could lose him. You're all aware of that fact, aren't you?' He looked at the group of solemn faces.

They nodded silently.

'We have to keep this to ourselves. If the press ever gets to hear a word, it will be all over the papers and TV. It won't matter a jot that Ed's name's on the birth certificate or that he and Jane have brought Jonny up so far. The families would have rights and they could be forced to hand him over to strangers. In the best interests of young Jonny, I vote that we make a pact not to reveal his true parentage to another living soul for the time being. Not even to your parents or Phil,' he advised Eddie and Jane.

They nodded in agreement, Jane squeezing Eddie's hand reassuringly.

'It must never go beyond these four walls,' Roy continued. 'If even *one* of you has any doubts that you can't keep this secret for as long as is necessary, speak up now.'

The room remained silent.

Roy nodded. 'Right, we're all agreed. It will be up to you and Jane what you tell Jonny later, Ed. Will you tell him the truth then, or will you still keep it to yourselves?'

Eddie shrugged. 'I honestly don't know, Roy. It's too far into the future to think about now. We'll see how things go. His birth certificate, should he ever need it, shows Angie and me as his parents. Jane and I had already decided to tell him about his mother when he's old enough to understand. Maybe we'll leave it at that.'

He stood up and walked across to the fireplace. He leant against it, stared into the dying embers for a long moment, then turned and smiled. 'Thanks, all of you, for being so understanding. I don't know why these awful things keep happening to me and Jane, but without your support we'd be lost.'

'I'm so sorry, Eddie.' Cathy wriggled uncomfortably. 'I wish I'd thrown that damn film away, I could have kept it to myself forever then. You've had enough on your plate recently.'

Jane touched her arm. 'It's okay, Cathy. There's bound to be a time in the future when it would all come out. Eddie and I love Jonny; we'll always love him. As far as we're concerned, he's as much our son as Jessie is our daughter.'

Eddie smiled round at his loyal and trusted friends. The secret would go no further than these four walls for the foreseeable future. He held up his glass to propose a toast. 'Here's to our son and daughter – and all future Raiders' offspring, however many there may be!'

A LETTER FROM PAM

Dear reader,

I want to say a huge thank you for choosing to read *The Mothers of Mersey Square*. If you did enjoy it, and want to keep up to date with all my latest releases, just sign up at the following link. Your email address will never be shared and you can unsubscribe at any time.

www.bookouture.com/pam-howes

To my loyal band of regular readers who bought and reviewed all my previous stories, thank you for waiting patiently for another book. Your support is most welcome and very much appreciated.

As always a big thank you to Beverley Ann Hopper and Sandra Blower and the members of their Facebook group, Book Lovers. Thanks for all the support you show me. Also, thank you to Deryl Easton and the supportive members of her Facebook group, Gangland Governors/NotRights.

A huge thank you to team Bookouture, especially my lovely editor, Maisie Lawrence – as always, it's been such a pleasure to work with you again – and thanks also to copyeditor/line editor, Jane Eastgate, and proofreader, Jane Donovan, for the copy edits and proofreading side of life.

And last, but definitely not least, thank you to our amazing media team, Kim Nash, Sarah Hardy, Jess Readett and Noelle

Holton, for everything you do for us. You're 'Simply the Best' as Tina would say! And thanks also to the gang in the Bookouture Authors' Lounge for always being there. As always, I'm so proud to be one of you.

I hope you loved *The Mothers of Mersey Square* and if you did, I would be very grateful if you could write a review. I'd love to hear what you think and it makes such a difference helping new readers to discover one of my books for the first time.

I love hearing from my readers – you can get in touch with me on social media.

Thanks,

Pam Howes

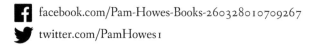

facebook.com/Pam-Howes-Books-260328010709267

twitter.com/PamHowes1

ACKNOWLEDGEMENTS

As always, for my partner, my daughters, grandchildren, great granddaughters and all their partners/spouses. Thanks for being a supportive and lovely family.